THROWN FOR
A CURVE

Greenliner Series
Book 1

FAITH O'SHEA

Cover Design by Jaycee DeLorenzo at Sweet 'N Spicy Designs
Formatted by Woven Red Author Services, www.wovenRed.ca

Cold Sweat/Faith O'Shea—1st Edition, version 2
ISBN eBook: 978-0-9987229-2-4
ISBN print book: 978-0-9987229-3-1
www.faithoshea.com

Printed in U.S.A.

ACKNOWLEDGMENTS

No book is ever written alone. There are many details an author pulls from memory or observation. *Thrown for a Curve* is no exception. At times, it's the experiences that contribute rather than people.

I grew up watching baseball. Every Sunday the family would gather at the beach and watch the home team, through good years and bad. I've had my favorite players over time, and still do.

Here's a shout out to my family, my Dad specifically, who introduced me to the sport and the home team. Without the highs and lows, the pitching duels, the rivalries, I wouldn't have grown to know and understand the hero. My brother often reminds me that my father took me to one of the series playoff games before he took him. Being the oldest was a coup at times.

My son pitched in high school and I did attempt to "catch" him from time to time. Melinda's experiences with bruising from the high-speed curve balls, was a direct personal experience. I thank him for his input on the pitches I describe in the book. No one knows, like a pitcher knows.

My reader, Bunny, is not only a good friend, but a wonderful resource. If she likes the book, I believe others will as well. She told me I have a homerun with this one.

I want to thank Jaycee from Sweet N Spicy Designs for her cover and Joan from Woven Red for her formatting skills.

I'd also like to thank my husband, Jeff Shea, for doing an amazing amount of marketing. He's not much into romance novels but is willing to ask everyone he bumps into, to buy a copy.

CHAPTER ONE

Izabella dos Santos was late.

Hurrying along the curving road, she scanned the intersection coming up and slid through the stop sign, hoping one of the very efficient policeman who usually hid in the speed trap ahead found himself in a very long donut line. Melina had been contrary all morning, Hoover too rambunctious, and the priest had droned on and on, reminding her again why she skipped Sunday morning church services more than she attended. The slightly bent leg of the advertising sign had ripped her nylons as she was stuffing the awkward thing into her trunk before Mass, necessitating a stop at the drugstore for a replacement pair. Her brother had run late from his newspaper and coffee run, which meant she was going to be almost fifteen minutes late for the open house, and the blasted pantyhose crotch was riding way too low for comfort. If the rest of the day went like this, she'd be sorry she didn't stay in bed like she'd wanted to.

Of course, if she looked back on her recent past, she could lay the blame for the sleepless nights and the bungling mess her life had become on one man's doorstep.

Her world had changed course the minute that "Crackerjacks" was traded to Boston.

In just three days, her whole world had turned upside down.

She'd just poured herself a cup of coffee, her morning news show on in the background. As she made her way to the sofa to wait for the weather report, the sports announcer hit her with such a smack she spilled scalding coffee all over her legs. Ignoring the pain, she dropped down to listen, her mouth ajar. It was when her breath had hitched that she knew she was in trouble.

"As of midnight, the Greenliners have acquired left-hand pitcher Reid "Crackerjacks" Jackson from Oakland. Home grown in the town of Andover Massachusetts, Jacks will be a huge addition to the current roster. The six-foot-two-inch lefthanded pitcher has had some bad luck over the past year, but in his first ten seasons he netted over 150 wins, and we're all hoping he can find his groove again. Going to Oakland in return are two minor league pitchers and Consentino, the veteran right fielder who's done a lot of bench warming as of late. Stay tuned for our interview with Jacks later this morning."

Racing out of the house right after she heard the news, her stomach a riot act in progress, she'd stopped in at her favorite coffee shop for her usual medium iced coffee, one sugar, extra cream, please, but it had been like walking into a nightmare.

Two telephone workers, with nice, tight buns, had caught her initial interest, but their conversation on the very public newsworthy event had taken her mind off their anatomy.

"I can't believe Perry did it."

"Yeah, it's got to be the trade of the year. I wonder what the hell made the team get rid of him."

"Maybe his arm's ready to fall off. He's over thirty, isn't he?"

"The guy's stats are incredible. And he should just be coming into his prime."

She hadn't stuck around to hear the rest.

But then again, she hadn't needed to.

She'd followed his career in Oakland like a bloodhound on a hot trail.

Pushing her way into Starbucks, shorter line, all women, she'd waited her turn. Okay, she'd pay more, but it was well worth the cost if she could evade any kind of Greenliner dialogue.

Then, in came a suit, opening up the *Globe* to that section she wanted no part of. Glaring headlines told the story she'd already heard at least a dozen times in the last few hours.

BOSTON GETS THE PRIZE: CRACKERJACKS COMES HOME.

He was a prize, all right.

Every hitter's nemesis.

Every sports fan's idol.

Every girl's dream.

Her worst nightmare.

Smug. Arrogant. Shallow.

Slanting her head, she'd caught herself trying for a closer look at the picture and cursed under her breath.

Over the past few days she'd seen him on every local talk show, heard him dissected on every sports radio show, praised, maligned, interviewed. Each segment she followed had been inundated with clips of his past successes, his Cy Young win, his All Star starts, his lifetime achievements. His trade was being hailed as the highlight of the year.

As she listened to the interviews, his voice was just as she remembered. A low, baritone growl that swaggered.

So sure, of himself it made her sick.

Better get used to it, girl. He's here for more than a few days at a time.

The Greenliners were picking up the last six years of his eight-year, 160-million-dollar contract, an obscene amount of money.

What was he going to say? No, no, please don't pay me twenty-million a year.

What did a person do with that kind of money?

Okay, a baseball player couldn't ply his trade until the normal retirement age, meaning he had to rake it in while he could.

"Big friggin rake, don't you think?

Don't think about him. Think about the open house and the time.

She initiated the burst of speed by pressing down on her accelerator.

What accounted for the burst of speed of her heart rate, she didn't want to contemplate.

Then his voice came out of nowhere, her radio fixed to the sports talk dial out of habit.

"I'm really looking forward to being back home. I'll be joining the team tonight for the start of the season but a couple of the guys have called and I already feel the welcome mat is out. I'm looking forward to playing with Harrington again. He caught a couple of my games in high school. I've been listening to the games since the trade, and last night's run by Reyes, in the eighth, was just what the team needed. I can't wait to put on the Greenliner uniform."

The interview had been recorded earlier this morning and would probably play throughout the day. Her finger poked the FM channel, not wanting the play-by-play on Reid's current life.

Adele filled the car with a rumor that had it.

After pulling to the side of the road, she placed the first open house sign at an intersection near the residence that saw a lot of traffic. Maneuvering back into the flow of oncoming cars, she poked the radio dial again and Jammin', the rap station, gave her something more tangible to complain about.

It was better than the incessant thoughts of one particular ballplayer.

Taking a deep breath, letting the jibber-jabber rhyme punctuate her mood, she pulled up to the front of the house and tugged out the other sign for placement. Hoping against hope that no one had beaten her to the house, she rolled along the curling driveway before braking to a stop.

Filha da puta!

She should have known, considering…

There was a brand-spanking-new Lincoln Town Car taking up a good portion of blacktop, the REMAX license plate giving it away.

Peggy Gill.

Peggy must have taken the opportunity to show off the back yard and the incredible pool area while waiting for her arrival, because she was nowhere in sight. Even though spring hadn't sprung and the landscaping hadn't begun in earnest, the back of the house was beautifully detailed.

Izabella knew for a fact that Peggy was the only agent in town who would make the clients she brought along know how very unprofessional it was to show up late to your own Open House, so she hurried her pace. Scrambling out of her fairly new Honda, she leaned into the passenger side of her car, scooping up the brochures, her business card holder, her briefcase, and her newspaper. Hitting the door with her hip, in an attempt to close it, she lost her balance, and all her materials fell tumbling to the ground.

With a heavy sigh, she knelt and started picking up the pieces of her scattered life.

She glanced around to see if there was an audience, and relieved that there wasn't, she struggled to pick everything back up. After making a mad dash to the front door, she jostled what was in her arms, opened the door with her key, and ran inside, her short, three-inch-heeled boots clicking on the tile.

When Izabella heard the door open not a few minutes later, she knew she would soon have company and waited with bated breath for Peggy's scathing critique on her unprofessionalism. A deep, male voice echoed in the foyer, stunning her into silence and she seriously thought for a second of hiding in the pantry closet. Heat immediately suffused her face, the quaking turned her legs to jelly, and she cringed, wondering how she was going to face the person on the other side of the doorway.

Peggy's voice grated as she described the entry way to her client, a man Izabella had no desire to see or hear. Maybe she could just slip out the back door, pretend she hadn't arrived yet. Let Peggy run the showing, which she'd probably do anyway.

Her heart thudded in her chest as the voice came closer, and she closed her eyes, willing herself to stop this foolishness.

Of all the luck...

But not much of a surprise if she really thought about it.

He'd be looking for a house in his hometown. He had said as much during one of those interviews she'd been trying to avoid.

Management must have given him a day to shop around so he'd be settled before the first game of the season. He'd been traded at the tail end of spring training so the final game in Florida was just a day away. It made sense that the front office offered the transitional time for him to make the move.

What did surprise her was that he had come to one of her listings.

This house was impressive but well below his price range if you considered what his yearly salary was. He could afford to spend millions on a showcase, which seemed more his style.

Taking a deep breath, she tried to regain her composure but the quivering had reached her fingers and the listing sheets fell out of her hands, splaying out across the kitchen floor.

Why hadn't she gotten here earlier?

Making things worse, long, tanned fingers entered her frame of vision and that voice said, "Here, let me help you."

A female whined from behind. "We've been here for almost a half an hour. Mr. Jackson's time is valuable. We're just going to take a peek. This shouldn't take long."

Without looking up, Izabella took the flyers from manicured fingers, keeping her face hidden from view, her hair partially covering it so she could hide her identity for a few minutes longer. She needed to prepare herself for the revelation, get the thundering of her heartbeat down to at least a canter. Quickly turning her back on him, she began setting up on the opposite counter, while agreeing with her new nemesis. "Of course, Peggy. I'll be just a minute. I apologize for my tardiness. I would have regretted being late for anyone. Mr. Jackson isn't the only one whose time is valuable."

He was close on her heels now and she knew her refusal to look at him, had heightened his curiosity. He didn't like to be ignored.

Taking a deep breath, she turned to face him. His cobalt-blue were eyes penetrating, just as she remembered.

CHAPTER TWO

Reid's perusal had followed the slim frame from the tips of her black boots, up her shapely legs, to the slight flare of her hips, thinking she might be too thin although he couldn't be sure until he got her undressed. Her upper assets were hidden, and long ebony hair curled around the point where her breasts lay beneath the fitted jacket. His gaze continued to her round chin, a nose perhaps too big for her face but with her full, sensuous lips, the high forehead and the huge doe-like eyes, he had too much to appreciate, to notice.

He'd gotten a glimpse of her when he was coming around the corner of the house and all but stopped in his tracks. She was making a bee-line for the front door, the black gabardine suit showcasing a graceful, lithe body, the short-flared skirt giving him ample evidence of lean legs. Midnight-black hair flowed down her back and he wondered if her face would match the rest of her.

The hairs on the back of his neck had stood up, and he'd felt something disturbingly familiar but couldn't pinpoint what it was. Intrigued, wondering if she might like a night with a famous ballplayer, he'd asked his agent what her name was.

Peggy had looked at him, her expression relaying that she didn't know and didn't care, stating it would be on the listing sheet if it ever got set up.

After helping her with the sheets of paper scattered over the floor, he began to follow close on her heels, irritated that she was evading him.

Then she spoke and he was instantly aroused. There was a memory, a fleeting vision, something vague that invaded his mind, jarred his brain, and incited his body.

He couldn't know her already.

This was a woman a man didn't forget.

Long, lean, and leggy.

And then she'd turned around to face him and his mouth went dry.

He barely scratched out her name.

"Izzie?"

He took a few paces forward, his heart beating rapidly, his chest humming in response.

"Hello, Reid."

Her voice was thick with annoyance.

It stopped him dead in his tracks. He blundered, thinking she'd welcome the bear hug he was about to offer, and stumbled back a step to take her in again, contrasting the dark beauty to the woman he remembered.

His friend Keith had told him she'd lost some weight, but he had not told him the half of it. There was no mention of a complete transformation.

The change was phenomenal and he couldn't quite keep his mouth from watering.

But this wasn't the Izabella he knew.

This woman was too different.

His Izzie was overweight and happy with it.

She loved all kinds of food, ice cream sundaes, the Italian cookies they'd buy at the bakery on Common Street, those mini coconut flans her mom used to make.

A man could sit down and enjoy a meal with her. She didn't pick at it as if it were distasteful, but ate right alongside him.

This Izzie looked like she didn't eat anything anymore.

And it bothered him.

His jaw tightened and his lips thinned.

"What have you done to yourself?"

Shaking her hair back, her chin raised in defiance, she said, "You make it seem as if I've gained thirty pounds instead of lost it."

"You're just not you anymore."

"Sure I am. Same me, different package. That's all."

"No. You look so…so grown up."

She scoffed at him.

"Reid, I was mid-twenties the last time you saw me, not twelve."

That he remembered.

It had been close to three, no maybe four years back. Her mother, Juliana, had just died. Izzie was distraught, exhausted from the job of taking care of not only the Jackson household but her mother as well, and it had shown on her face. Without makeup to give her color, with clothes lacking style, and with the additional weight, she had looked completely different.

He had been in Oakland for years by then but came home that winter for the wake and funeral.

He had loved her mother.

Juliana had worked for the Jacksons for almost half of Reid's life. For years, she'd clean and cook a couple of days a week. After his mother's accident, Juliana had taken on the chores of nursemaid as well. She'd baked the best desserts he'd ever tasted. Izzie had helped with some of the domestic chores after school and during summers and had taken over all of it once her mother got sick. When Juliana passed away, Izzie had to find a replacement for her mother's other customers but had stayed on at the Jacksons' for a few months longer.

His mother, Melinda Jackson, was not good with change.

As if looking through him, Izzie said, "Peggy, why don't you take Reid through the house. I'll be happy to answer any questions you might have when you're done."

Before Peggy could urge Reid to comply, he asked, "Can you have dinner with me tonight?"

A slight frown curled her lips downward.

"That wasn't exactly the type of question I had in mind. But I'll answer it anyway. No."

He looked even more stunned now than before.

"What do you mean no? We have a lot of years to catch up on."

He caught the sneer in her response.

"I disagree. There is nothing about your life I want to *catch up on*."

He interrupted her plan to sabotage his request with an honest statement.

"Well there's lots I want to know about yours. Why won't you have dinner with me? Don't you eat anymore?"

He could hear the sting in his words and saw her frown dip further.

Spinning away from him, she dug into her purse, pulled out her business card case and replenished the bracket with listing sheets. She busied herself with other things, ignoring him completely.

Peggy walked ahead of him, calling begrudgingly from the distance, "Come on, Mr. Jackson, we have some other houses to see and we're running late."

Without taking his eyes off the tall, stately beauty, he said, "Cancel the appointments. I found the house I want."

Izabella spun around to face him, her eyes flicking up to meet his.

"You haven't even seen the rest of it."

"I don't have to. I knew what I wanted when I started looking. This is it."

She let her guard down to agree with him.

"It is beautiful, isn't it? If I could have, I would have bought it myself. The family was one of my mother's customers that I took over for a while. I loved coming here."

He could understand why.

The exquisite entry, the multiple fireplaces, the high ceilings, the magnificent windows all blended together to make the space sunny, airy, and open. It had over four thousand square feet of living space which was less than he'd intended but the overall beauty of the house made up for it.

Peggy tried to steer Reid out of the house, brushing the dried, bleached-blonde hair away from her eyes. "Don't say too much more, Reid. We can go back to my office and put the offer on paper."

Without looking in her direction, Reid fired back, "No. I want Izzie to handle it."

He noticed an almost panicked look take over Izzie's beautiful face.

"No, Reid. Peggy found you the house. She's entitled to write the offer."

Moving closer, his voice barely a whisper, he explained, "No. She didn't find it for me. I found it myself and she was reluctant at best to show it to me. The price is far less than the other houses we've seen so far, so I'm sure her commission was driving her agenda."

He turned back to Peggy and asked pointedly, "Don't I get to choose who represents me?"

The fact that he didn't like the broker he'd hired was one small reason for the transfer of service. The more important one was the desire to steal more time with the stunning beauty who was back in his life.

Peggy answered, her tone insistent and filled with animosity. "Of course, you do, Mr. Jackson, but I still get the commission because I procured the sale."

He spun on his heel, his tone menacing.

"You didn't *procure* anything. I'll call the board or whoever is in charge of handling disputes and explain exactly why I don't want you working for me. Pursue this and it will get extremely unpleasant."

He heard Izzie mumble under her breath, "Oh, Meu Deus. What are you doing? Don't cause problems."

Izabella shifted her attention to the other broker. "You will get your fee. I wouldn't have it any other way. As soon as the transaction is closed, I'll have the company draw you up a check."

Peggy issued a further command.

"For the full amount."

"Of course."

Reid didn't like the way Izzie was giving in but he kept his mouth shut for once in his life. He couldn't afford to piss her off if he wanted that night out.

Without a good-bye to either of them, Peggy stomped out the front door.

Reid's tone was caustic.

"She is one royal bitch. She doesn't even look professional. She's got bags under her bags. Why didn't you fight her for it?"

"I'm not a Crackerjack. I'm more of a Milk Dud. Besides she could make my life miserable and I'd rather avoid that if possible." She paused before adding, "Peggy can be...difficult at times. She's just driven. Correct me if I'm wrong but she spent most of the morning with you?"

"Yeah, showing me..."

"I know. Houses you didn't want, but she still put all that time into it. She should be compensated for that. It was, in essence, her sale."

"Bull. I drove by here very early this morning and called her on it. And if I hadn't been adamant she wouldn't have shown it to me. If I'd noticed it was your listing I would have called you. She wasted *my* time, I didn't waste hers."

He watched as slender fingers rubbed a flawless forehead, heard the long, heavy sigh.

Izzie glanced up at him before retrieving an offer form from her briefcase and placing it on the island counter. Her hand was poised over the paperwork ready to begin. She raised her eyes to meet his.

She cleared her throat, and informed him, "You really should use another agent. I work for the seller and I won't accept anything less than asking price. It's fair and I will not negotiate it for you."

"That's fine with me. It's well within my range. Or so Peggy said. Do you believe she made me get a letter from the bank stating I was approved for the mortgage she thought would work for me?"

Giving a fake gasp, she said, with the hint of the Portuguese accent she hadn't lost completely,

"You mean someone, somewhere didn't know who you were, Mr. Baseball?"

Playing along, he stuck out his lip in a pout and said, "Yes. And it bruised my ego."

They were getting very close to the give-and-take that made being together fun, memories creating sparks. She put them out when she let the remark go and got down to business. Fiddling with the pen she still held in her shaking hand, she suggested, "Before we do this, why don't we go through the rest of the house. I really would feel more comfortable writing the offer after you've seen it."

They paused a moment gazing into each other's eyes.

The spell was broken when the doorbell rang.

Izabella shakily excused herself, and headed for the vestibule.

He appreciated the sway of her hips as she walked away from him, gentle yet alluring. He shook his head, still not believing it was the girl he once knew.

She used to watch him play baseball from the kitchen window while waiting for her mother to finish up the housework. He'd catch her on occasion, her nose almost pressed against the pane. For some reason, it would motivate him to put everything he had into the pitch.

He remembered the way his high school friend Josh would throw the glove on the ground, shake the sting off, and yell at him for throwing all out.

He grimaced as he thought of one day in particular, although it wasn't the first or last time it happened.

Josh was jumping up and down, complaining, "This was supposed to be catch. You know, you throw normal, it lands in the glove."

He'd nodded his head in Izzie's direction.

"We have a fan."

The laugh as offensive as the comment, Josh had said, "You couldn't get a bigger one."

Izzie had heard the insult through the open window and had scrambled away like a timid rabbit. He'd beaned Josh with a throw after she fled into the interior of the house.

His friends could be merciless when someone had a visible flaw. He should know. He had fine- tuned the art of the wisecrack and he hadn't been afraid to showcase it.

He'd scalded Izzie with his stinging tongue through the years, and the remorse was still there in his conscience's back pocket.

Hearing voices, he focused on the lilting rhythm of Izabella's as she welcomed the house hunters into the cool foyer. Only when she began her sales pitch did he amble out of the kitchen to where they stood.

He halted them in their tracks when he informed them, "Sorry, the house is already taken."

Looking ready to jump in with a retort, Izabella stifled it when the gentleman stepped forward with enthusiasm, looking back at his wife as if he couldn't believe his eyes. "Oh, my God. It's Reid Jackson."

Extending his hand, he introduced himself. "I'm Bruce Seiford and this is my wife, Carla. I can't tell you how excited I am you'll be playing for us this year. I had all but given up hope that we'd have a chance. Sorry."

He reddened a bit…paused the babbling before he went on.

"This is just such an unexpected pleasure. Once I heard about the trade, I knew the year wouldn't be a lost cause. We lost so many great pitchers that I thought …Well, you'll make the difference."

Reid turned on the charm and he had it in spades. "Great to meet you, Bruce. Carla. I'm so glad to be home again. I hope I don't let anyone down. There are such high expectations."

"I caught every game when you were in town. Now I won't have to wait so long between outings."

Reid put his hands into his pockets. Making sure he sounded like a team player, not totally convinced his words were true, he said, "The pitchers we have are really good ones and Bullard will be a great anchor."

"If his back doesn't go out. My wife keeps saying he should put on some weight. I think she might have a point."

Carla seemed as knowledgeable about the game as her husband. "It's a shame the team can't get the runs to win. Even when the ERAs are good, they lose."

Turning to Izabella, whose eyes looked a bit glazed, he instructed her to remove the signs so they didn't waste anyone's time.

Coming out of her stupor now that the baseball talk had subsided, she said, "I'm sorry I can't do that. There may be someone willing to top your offer."

"I'll top any offer that's on the table."

"Yes, I'm sure you would, but we won't know what that would be if I take the signs down."

He was getting riled. He was used to getting what he wanted.

"Izzie, I want this house. If I have to give you more to cover any eventuality, then I'll do it. Now remove the signs."

"I may not be able to sit on you anymore to get you to cave, but you can't bully me. The signs stay until four p.m. when the open house is over."

The dig carved out a little piece of his heart.

Josh again.

He had hoped that she'd forgotten that slimy remark.

He had certainly tried over the years but wasn't any more successful than she had been.

Juliana had been heading out of the house, her thirteen-year-old daughter slightly ahead of her. Reid and Josh were wrestling in the front yard, just goofing around, when Josh had called out for Izabella to help.

"All you have to do is sit on him with all that weight and he'll cave."

Reid had elbowed Josh in the gut, but the damage had been done.

Those doe eyes had filled with sadness, a sadness that was still palpable in the part of his memory that was flooding him.

He also remembered Juliana's stinging reprimand. It was in Portuguese but the pointing finger and the menacing tone had told him exactly what she thought of him.

It had taken him another year and plenty of ragging by Keith but he'd stopped hanging around with Josh. The day Josh had said something about Reid's mother's wheelchair was the last day he talked to him.

Examining the tall brunette, Reid looked for a sign of the old, self-conscious Izzie. He couldn't find it. She had nothing to be self-conscious about anymore because she was stunning.

There was a spark that had been missing when she was younger, but today a fire danced in her eyes and he had a feeling she wasn't the Milk Dud she purported to be. He almost said something to get her going to see if there was a sizzle, some indication of the Brazilian temperament lurking just beneath the surface.

A sudden awareness that he liked the remarkable change swept over him.

"Hey, Bruce, are you working with an agent? Izabella's about the best there is."

Her look was quizzical.

He had no idea whether she was good at her job or not, hadn't been around in a very long time and it didn't seem like she wanted his help acquiring new clients.

But before she could argue, Bruce said, "My wife and I just started looking, so, no, we aren't. We figured we'd find a house we liked and then think about the agent."

"I think you should hook up now. I'm sure she could save you some time and effort."

Glancing at his wife, who gave him a nodding go-ahead, Bruce turned back and asked, "Do you have a card...Izabella?"

"Yes, Mr. Seiford, but please don't feel compelled to take Reid's advice. I know he'd disagree with me on this, but there are times he really doesn't know what he's talking about."

Narrowing her eyes at Reid, she stopped any retort in its tracks.

He couldn't help grinning as Bruce asked good naturedly, "Are you good at what you do?"

Modestly, she admitted, "Yes, I am. I'd be better equipped to do the best job for you if you'd allow me to work as a buyer's agent. Then I can tell you everything you want to know so you can make a sound decision. Otherwise, I can only tell you what's on the listing sheet because I am technically working for the seller."

Reid's pride swelled. He liked her style. She wasn't pushy but came across as someone who truly cared about her customers best interests.

His curiosity was piqued, so he asked, "What's a buyer's agent?"

"Someone you should have working for you."

He gave her the best smile in his arsenal.

"Don't want anyone else. I'm all yours."

Turning her back on him, she directed the conversation to the Seifords.

"If you want, we can set up an appointment to discuss it. It will take some time to do it right and I promised I'd take Mr. Jackson on a tour of the house he wants to buy sight unseen. Are there any other houses you intended to look at today?"

"Yes, there are a couple."

Moving to where her materials littered the counter, she plucked out some of her business cards.

"Why don't you take these with you. If you want, tell the agents you are working with me. That way they won't try to push you into a decision today and they'll pretty much leave you on your own. If you don't, that's fine, too. We can touch base later in the week. I'd love the opportunity to work with you."

"Okay, Izabella. Thank you. We'll be in touch."

Taking his hand, she pumped it firmly before seeing them off. "Have a nice day."

As soon as he heard the door click closed, his smile still settled on his face, Reid said, "Well done, Izzie. But I hate that saying. What if I'm in a pissy mood, and don't want to have a nice day?"

She faced him, her hand on her hip, and he got a glimpse of the fiery nature that seemed so naturally a part of who she was now.

"Well, then I guess you'd let everyone know and make damn sure no one else had one either."

He pretended to be offended.

"Watch the mouth. What happened to you, Izzie? You used to be so nice."

Simmering heat flowed through his veins. He liked seeing the lightning flash when her back went up.

"The name is Izabella. I haven't been called by that nickname in years."

He had to admit Izabella suited this new, altered version, but she would always be Izzie to him.

He felt a sting as she continued, "And I was too nice, *nao achas*? I don't let people hurt me anymore."

His eyes followed every line of her body.

"There's nothing to insult anymore."

The splash of cold memory revived her.

"I thought I looked terrible."

Reid's brow arched as if rethinking his opinion.

"I liked the extra layer. It was you."

"I was the target for too many tongues and you ranked with the best of them."

He blew out a breath, backed away as his eyes traveled the length of her.

"You're just skin and bones."

A small frown slipped across her face.

"Still unable to let a thought go through your head without speaking it out loud."

"Pretty much."

"Well, let's get this over with so we can write the offer and you can go away."

"I thought maybe I'd stick around to protect my interests."

"Don't you have to go play catch or something?"

He was beginning to enjoy her spurts of bratty-ness and even though she was much too thin now, he had to admit he'd been enjoying the scenery since he'd walked in, too.

"Nope. Got the whole afternoon. Besides, I came with Peggy. I'm going to need a ride home."

Rolling her eyes, she mumbled under her breath, "*Meu Deus.* Will this day never end?"

CHAPTER THREE

He was sitting and watching her.

There had been a flurry of activity in the first hour, couples coming through for a tour, but they were more intrigued by the celebrity among them than the features of the unique colonial.

Since then, quiet had descended.

And she was becoming more uncomfortable by the minute, wishing he'd just evaporate into thin air, but she had no choice but to grin and bear it. Keeping her eye on the end goal, that big commission check she'd get from this sale, she waited him out. The offer was already on the table and the Costello's were thrilled that they had gotten more than the asking price and impressed at who was buying it. If by four o'clock they hadn't gotten another offer that exceeded that amount, it would be accepted. They had already agreed to every condition. For all intents and purposes, she could call it a day and just put a sale pending sign out for anyone who might stop by later.

But she was not going to let him have his way that easily.

She busied herself on her iPad, researching comps, checking Facebook, emails, anything to make his proximity bearable, until she couldn't stand it any longer and said, "You must have friends. Can't one of them come and pick you up?"

She was severely disappointed when he just shrugged his shoulders and shook his head.

With still over an hour to go she mentally pushed the hands of the large wall clock along, but his voice intruded on her meditation.

"Are you still with Patrick?"

Her eyes flew up to meet his serious gaze.

She couldn't believe he remembered.

Hoping he couldn't hear the wariness in her voice, she answered, "No. That ended about four years ago."

"Are you seeing someone else?"

His eyes had turned on her and she was mesmerized by the intensity of his gaze. She answered automatically as if hypnotized to do his bidding.

"Not at the moment."

The eye contact was making her shift in her seat, his seriousness such a rare commodity it was making her uneasy. Their time together had been brief but it had been filled with laughter. It had also been followed by a period of bereavement. Reid had a great sense of humor but no sticking power.

"Then why won't you have dinner with me?"

She should have known where this was going, but she honestly hadn't seen it coming so absorbed by the blueness of his eyes, the rugged good looks, the scruffy stubble that must have sprung up overnight.

Unsettled, she didn't put the zing she intended into her response. Instead she heard trepidation.

"Because I don't want to."

Taking her hand in his, he kissed her palm and began nibbling the underside like he had once.

"We had some good times, Izzie."

Forcing herself to break the spell he had her under, she slipped out of her place at the kitchen table, taking the still-tingling hand he had munched on and busying herself with re-arranging things that didn't need re-arranging, casting over her shoulder a line he didn't appreciate.

"Speak for yourself."

Leaning forward, looking deflated, he scoffed, "You're going to tell me you didn't enjoy those secluded dinners, or the walks along the beach?"

Cocking her head at him, her hands on her hips, she almost laughed at his audacity.

"Let's see. The moonlight dinners were in out-of-the-way places and the beaches were in other states. The fact is you didn't want anyone seeing you with me. That tends to put a different kind of spotlight on it for me."

He cleared his throat. The look he gave her bordered on sheepish.

"What, did you think I didn't know what you were doing? You kept me away from every one of your friends."

"I loved being with you."

He had never admitted that to her before, and she felt a sizzle of satisfaction before the sting of reality.

"As long as no one knew."

His arm was slung around the chair post, his body slouched.

"That's not entirely true."

Her voice rose an octave.

"Oh, so why didn't you ever invite me to one of your friends' parties, or let me go to watch your scrimmages or take me to the movies or hang out with me at Luaogo's?"

It still hurt. Almost as much as it had back then. The ache had never dissipated nor had the longing.

But that was something he would never find out.

After scraping back the chair, he got up and closed the distance between them. Taking her hand in his, he entwined their fingers.

"Look, I'm sorry. I should never have done that."

His closeness was disconcerting, so she kept her eyes downcast as she attempted to regain her balance. This wasn't real. She was only a diversion. He was only out to charm himself back into her good graces, and she had to keep that thought crystal clear. It was the thrill of the hunt for him and she had once again become the prey.

"Too late for that now."

"It's too late to offer an apology and to hope you accept it? Can't we at least be friends?"

He looked so hopeful she let the idea float around while she thought about it.

Friends was fine.

Maybe.

Possibly.

Probably out of the question.

She was glaring now, the streak of nervous energy hitting her below the belt. Prying her hand loose, she stepped away.

His mouth was open as if he had something to say but she got there first.

"What about Rachel?"

From what she heard from her friend Sofia, he had been with her for just over a month. It had caused a moment of panic but she'd diligently worked through it. Wishing that Sofia wouldn't give her periodic updates, she didn't know how to ask her to stop without telling her why.

He threaded his hand through his hair, his deep-set eyes showing his discontent with the subject.

"Rachel's no longer part of the equation."

"What happened?"

"She...wasn't..."

"What you were looking for?"

He nodded, his eyes now looking heavenward.

"What was the problem? Her hair too red? Eyes too wide apart? Didn't like baseball?"

He smiled that smile that could melt butter on a sub-zero-degree day.

"What can I say? She didn't like Cocker."

Izabella couldn't stop the laughter from bubbling out. Such a ridiculous reason to break up with someone but so Reid.

"Hey, a man's music is important to him. Besides, she stopped appreciating my jokes. Now, you, you always loved my jokes."

It was never the jokes as much as the cute way he had of telling them.

He paused, looking serious, and added, "And there was no way I was inviting her to move home with me."

When he looked back up and into her eyes, there was an intensity that unnerved her and she came crashing back down to earth, the smile on her face dying a quick death.

He had a way about him of making a woman seem special just like in a fairy tale, but she knew the ending and it was not a happily ever after. He didn't have it in him.

She'd made the mistake, for a sweet second, believing that he did, becoming one of his jokes in the process and it still hurt.

He had never wanted what she so longed to give him.

"I was a game that summer. And I have to admit you played it perfectly."

He looked up stunned.

"You were no game, Izzie."

Almost to himself, he muttered, "You were an exclusive that whole summer. It broke all records."

"Did anyone else know?"

His head dropped.

"No."

"You were such a jock. You could never have handled the razzing that came with it."

He looked up, meeting the accusation in her eyes, but remained mute.

There was click from the front door, signaling another visitor and Reid was up and half way across the kitchen when Keith Zamoutto, his friend, attorney and agent walked through the archway, his pretty wife on his arm.

Two pint-size kids were running headlong into who ran headlong into the room behind them.

"Izabella, are you coming with us this afternoon?"

Four small arms wrapped around Izabella's neck and she bestowed them with a smile.

"No, Junie bug I can't. I have to work longer than I thought."

Now that she had the offer, she had to get the necessary signatures to make it valid. She should be walking on air. This was one of the easiest sales she'd ever been involved in and the commission would be a sizeable one. But it meant having to spend too many hours with a man who was her idea of perfect and yet one she knew could never be hers.

Too arrogant by half.

Here today, gone tomorrow.

Standing back up now that she'd gotten her hugs, she watched the muscles under Reid's grey

V-neck shirt ripple as he shook Keith's hand and she felt the saliva in her mouth start to collect. Swallowing hard, she knew from experience that it was much safer to watch his form on TV. That way she could drool over him to her heart's content without any consequences.

Reid's voice, another one of his very irritating traits, washed over her when he suggested, "Izzie, why don't you take Sofia and show her the house while I go over the offer with Keith."

June and Holly Zamoutto scrambled around the women, chirping, "Can we come, too, please?"

She couldn't help overhearing Reid's thank you.

"You were right. It is perfect."

Izabella's eyes shot up to Keith. With an arched brow, he admitted, "I knew this was what he was looking for. I hope you're not too mad at me."

She split her attention between the two men, seeing the past: the pitcher and his catcher, the inscrutable duo who had taken Andover High to states in both junior and senior year, part of a small clique that ruled the field and the classrooms. They had kept in touch during their college years and the friendship was still solid. Where Reid had gone on to become a first-rate pitcher, Keith had become a lawyer and sports rep and had guided and directed the trade that had brought Reid back home.

"You could have warned me."

"I guess I could have but where would the fun be in that? I didn't tell Mr. Baseball either. Thought it would be twice the enjoyment."

Taking a small hand into her own, Izabella said, "You're impossible. The two of you. Come on Hollyberry. Let's go see the living room. I want to show Sofia the fireplace."

Looking at her friend, she said, "It's gorgeous."

Keith was already scanning the standard offer contract while Reid took a moment to watch Izzie walk away. He could watch that a hundred times and never lose interest or appreciation.

Getting right to business, having plans for later in the afternoon, Keith asked, "Is this the asking price?"

"No. I put in a higher offer to get her to take the open house signs down. It didn't work, but I won't renege now."

"It's probably worth it anyway. The price was fair. Izabella seems to have a keen sense for market value but paying a little extra won't hurt the appraisal."

Going back to the document, he went point by point.

"You want to close next month. Will you be around on this date?"

"Yeah, I checked my schedule. We'll be home for over a week. If it's a problem I'll give you power of attorney and you can finalize it."

"Does she think it's doable on the other end?"

Most sellers wanted a buffer of at least six weeks to pack up and move.

"She already talked to the Costello's. The additional sum motivated them to accept the condition."

"Home inspection has to be done within the week. You're flying to Philly tonight, aren't you?"

"Yeah, but if we make the arrangements the inspector can send me the report and verbally give me the details. Izzie will be there, right?"

"She's working for the seller, Reid. You can't expect her to be looking out for your interests."

"She would never screw me over."

"That wouldn't be her intent. She's highly ethical but she owes her loyalty to the Costello's'."

"Look, if there's something wrong with the house, I'll fix it. I don't care, Keith. This is the one I want."

Looking up, wanting to make certain the women weren't within hearing, he asked, "Why didn't you tell me?"

His eyes still on the fine print, Keith continued to read as he asked, "Tell you about what?"

"About Izzie."

"I think I did."

"No. You said she lost some weight. You didn't tell me she looked like...that."

The tone of voice grabbed Keith's attention and his eyes bored into his old friend.

"You sound as if you don't like the change."

"It's too much. She looks terrible."

Keith's eyes went wide.

"You think Izabella looks terrible? Most men can't take their eyes off her when she enters a room."

Reid's answer enlightened him.

"Yeah, she used to be so real. Now...now she's...like...like..."

Keith finished the sentence that Reid was having trouble with.

"Like all those women you've gone out with most of your life?"

Affronted, Reid looked hurt. "Size never had anything to do with anything."

"Right. That's why you wouldn't be caught dead with her out in public or anyone else who weighed more than a toothpick."

"What do you mean?"

"You were dating her one summer, weren't you?"

Reid put his hands on his hips, vigorously shaking his head.

"No. We weren't dating. We just hung out. Spent some time together. Did Izzie tell you that?"

Reid was discomfited. It was as if Izabella had given away state secrets.

"Izabella has never uttered a word about you, at least to me. You really don't think I would've figured out what you were doing? I made it a point to see where you went when you snuck away."

Incredulous, he asked louder than he meant to, "You followed me?"

"Of course, I did. I needed to satisfy my curiosity. Don't worry. I played I spy alone. No one else knew."

"You never said anything."

"No need to."

"It wasn't as if it were serious."

"Nothing ever is with you. I just hoped she understood that. Because she knew you better than most, I had to assume she did. Looking back, I'm not so sure."

Izabella did know the real him and that was an under-lying problem. When he was with her, he wasn't trying to impress. It felt good being himself but it also felt extremely limiting.

"She knew where I stood about...things."

"Probably made her feel like Cinderella at the beginning, like the belle of the ball, before crushing the glass slipper. You never want it to fit."

"What is it with all the kid metaphors? And what do you mean I never want it to fit?"

"I guess I read too many Disney princess stories. Holly and Junie love them. And you haven't spent more than a month with a woman since I met you. As soon as she does the forward press you're out the back door."

Somewhat reluctantly, he agreed.

"Didn't Izzie start dating someone else that fall. She couldn't have been that traumatized after the summer was over."

He had been somewhat miffed. Okay, downright angry that she had replaced him so easily but he had talked himself into being happy for her, and if memory served him, he'd started going out with a local model before college was back in session.

"Did you ever hear the term rebound?"

"It didn't seem like rebound to me. She was with him for over a year, wasn't she?"

"From what Sofia told me, it was closer to two. Where did you hear about Carlo anyway?

You don't usually keep tabs on the hearts you break."

"I didn't break her heart, number one. And number two, my brother told me."

"And he just volunteered the information?"

"Actually, he did. He got the information from my mother. She always loved Izabella. I think she often wished I would have fallen madly in love with her and had lots of children. I was glad to hear Izzie was fine, though."

"Izabella was always fine. It's you who has the problem."

"What problem?"

"Not seeing the forest for the trees."

"What are you talking about?"

Keith paused and shook his head.

"You can lead a horse to water, but you can't make him smarter than he is."

Before he could ask what the hell that meant, he heard the women returning from the grand tour.

Sofia was holding Junie's hand but she had a sweet smile on her face. Much curvier than Keith's first wife, Mariah had been, she had deep-set brown eyes and an aquiline nose, was no more than five-feet-three-inches tall. He'd given Keith all kinds of shit about dating the nanny during the divorce proceedings, but he had to admit she suited Keith better than Mariah had. And she seemed to be better mother material. Mariah had fought for custody until Keith offered her a sizeable check. Then she'd signed them over to him without a backward glance.

Sofia's soft, accented voice pulled him away from his musings.

"Reid, it is a beautiful house."

"Thanks, Sofia. I think so, too."

Keith was flipping the last page back and he placed it on the counter.

"The contract looks good. Sign away, my friend."

Handing him a pen, Keith watched as Reid scrawled his signature and initialed in all the appropriate spaces.

Stepping away from the island, Keith rubbed his hands in anticipation and said, "Okay, my lovelies, it's time to go."

"Can Leeni come?"

Sofia crouched down and whispered, "No, honey. I'm sorry she can't. But we'll have a play date soon. I promise."

Putting her head down, lip out in the kind of pout only this age could affect, she said, "Okay."

Her father, unable to miss the disappointment, scooped her up and kissed her cheek. "What kind of animals do you think we'd see at the zoo?"

"I don't know."

"Maybe a lion." And he roared in her neck, causing her to drop the pout and squeal in delight.

Reid watched with amusement. There was nothing like the sound of a child laughing. Even he couldn't help but be captivated. In a weak moment, he thought that maybe someday, if he ever found the right woman, he'd be able to envision this for himself.

He watched as Sofia stuffed little bodies into heavy jackets. The horrible winter might be coming to an end, but it was still downright cold outside.

Izabella asked hopefully, "Can you take Reid with you?"

Keith laughed, still holding his daughter.

"To Chucky Cheese? I don't think so."

"But he's such a kid at heart."

Keith glanced in his direction.

"Nope. It appears he's all grown up from what I can tell."

"Come on. He plays catch for a living."

Reid's voice carried across the room. "Hey, it's a good living."

Before exiting, Keith asked Izzie, "Who's the seller's attorney?"

Holding the open door ajar, Izabella said, "Tim Mahoney. We'll have to nudge him."

"Then nudge away. We need to get the inspection ASAP."

"I will."

Keith corralled the kids, tucked his wife's hand inside the crook of his arm and led them out.

Reid couldn't help but feel the easiness that had ensued upon the Zamouttos arrival seep away as soon as they left the house. Izzie had gotten downright quiet, drawing into herself like a mummy in a tomb. Her expression was just as closed and he wondered what she was thinking.

When she'd finished packing the offer in her briefcase, she looked up to where Reid was standing and said, "Okay, it's close enough to four. Let me get the house locked up. As soon as I drop you off, I'll come back and have the Costello's sign the paperwork. I'll email the signed copy over to Keith's office when I get home."

"Do you still live in Lowell?"

She didn't give him a lot of information, simply said, "No. I have a house not very far from here."

He was pleasantly surprised. She had to be doing quite well for herself.

"In Andover?"

"On the very edge."

"Which edge?"

"Lawrence"

Gathering her things, she headed for the door, let him go out ahead of her, then locked it up.

"Isn't my mother on that edge?"

"Yes, she is. Come on. Let's get this over with."

Unlocking the car doors, she dumped her materials in the back seat, before climbing behind the wheel. Looking over to Reid, who was now ensconced in the passenger seat she asked, "Where are you staying?"

"My mother's condo."

Her eyes widened in mild shock. "How did that happen?"

"She's still in Florida. Won't be back until next month. She offered, I accepted."

Izabella knew where Melinda was and when she was coming home but she didn't tell Reid that. "Wasn't that big of you."

"Yeah, well it works out well for us. She did her motherly duty and I did my good son routine."

His chiseled features had hardened, which meant the topic was closed, so she eased out of the driveway and made the right towards Beacon Street and the west part of town. Not far at all from where she lived.

Starting to relax, the conversation nonexistent, she bristled when Reid asked, "Why did Keith marry Sofia so soon after the divorce? What was it, a couple of weeks?"

She should have known that he'd say something like this and her Brazilian blood started to boil. "The divorce would have been final years ago if Mariah hadn't fought so hard for custody. That raged on even though everyone knew Mariah didn't want those kids. But you know all that, I'm sure. And in the real world, people get married if they fall in love."

"Yeah, right. It doesn't last forever, something I think Keith would have already found out through Mariah."

She couldn't quite veil the impatience with his viewpoint. It was a topic they had visited more than once.

"Your parents' marriage shouldn't be your ruler."

"Right. They spent the last decade not speaking."

Her fingers clutched the steering wheel, her tone became chilly.

"You know it was more complicated than that."

His eyes hardened.

"All I know is that my father did everything he could to make it up to her and she never forgave him. She finally pushed him out of his own house. It's the guilt that killed him."

Stephen Jackson had sold the house Reid had grown up in to move Reid's mother into town but over the years with the icy distance his mother had kept between them, he'd begun to work more and be at home less, until he'd finally moved out completely. She had been witness to all of it.

Reid was way off base.

"It was a heart attack that killed him. And whatever went on between them had nothing to do with the contempt you've held your mother in since the accident."

He stiffened.

"She did nothing but sit there. Out on the porch watching the world go by."

"She was in a wheelchair. What did you want her to do?"

"Anything but give up. She was pathetic."

She glanced over at him, her eyes shooting daggers.

"Please, save me from the 'I'm a victim of a love-deprived childhood.' I know the family history too well."

His lips twisted when she eased out of the topic and into his mother's driveway.

"Here you are. Don't let the door hit your ass on the way out."

Shifting to sit against the door for a better view, he asked again, "So when can I pick you up for a celebratory dinner? I'll order champagne and we can toast to my new house."

She wondered if it would ever become a home.

Tapping the steering wheel with her fingers she said simply, "Never."

He seemed to study her, before digging in.

"I'll up the ante. Tickets to a game and dinner after."

"You must have me confused with someone who likes baseball."

"Come on, you used to watch me practice."

"From the window of your living room. Why do you suddenly want to see me out in the light of day? I thought I looked like a plucked chicken."

He offered her an irresistible devastating grin.

"I might have been a little hasty in that assessment."

"So, it *is* because I look different! So now you won't be ashamed of being seen with me?"

He paused, becoming more serious before looking up into her eyes and telling her the truth.

"No. I've missed you."

She gave a throaty chuckle and waved her hand at him.

"Whatever. I need to go, so please get out of the car."

Bringing his fingers up, he threaded a strand of her hair behind her ear, caressing the beauty mark that adorned her cheek.

"You used to think I was charming. I haven't changed. Did you see the last couple of interviews?"

Not wanting to meet his gaze, the tingling from his touch streaming through her, she lied easily. "I don't have time for such nonsense."

She couldn't deny he'd been droll and self-deprecating or that the audience had loved him. Charm was one of his biggest assets but arrogance one of the offshoots.

"If you won't go out with me for my charm, then maybe you'll accept if I take you to a very exclusive restaurant. I don't know whether you heard or not, but I'm fairly well-off."

She laughed to cover up her annoyance.

"I don't care about your millions. I'd rather go out with someone who has a kind heart."

Resting her chin on her hand as if in thought, she added, "Nope, that's not you."

Flicking his fingers through his razor-cut blond-streaked hair, he sighed.

"How about my looks? You told me once that I looked good enough to eat."

She noticed his forehead creased as if he didn't know where that came from, as her eyes flew up to meet his, her mouth slightly ajar.

He did look good enough to eat, a five-star four-course meal with a dessert that left her longing for another taste. His new haircut only emphasized his features, brought out the high cheekbones, the strong jaw, the thick, muscled neck. Staring far too long, she felt a pull, sensing he was in for the kill, and one of his kisses could easily have set her on fire. Breaking the spell, she responded sharply, "Must be having dreams about me, Crackerjack. Because I never said that."

Throwing in a dose of honesty, she added, "It would have made it far too easy for you to hurt me."

"You're telling me that being seen out with an incredibly sexy stud wouldn't motivate you?"

She found his chest with her index finger and poked.

"You're the one who needs to project that image, muchacho, not me. I have different taste in men now. I like them tall, dark and handsome, with a bit of humility thrown in for good measure."

This lie almost choked her on the way out.

Most women thought he was gorgeous, for very good reason.

"Well, okay then."

He slanted his head at her and said, "You know Izabella, a person shouldn't judge someone by looks alone."

Izabella's dark eyes glared at him and he swallowed hard.

"I'm...I never…"

"Stop trying to extricate your foot from your mouth. Although by now I'd have thought you had that down to a science."

With a jolt, resignation in his tone, he countered, "What you're saying is that I have no redeeming quality that could convince you to accept an invitation to dinner."

Her eyes pierced into him.

What could she say? The qualities he admired all had to do with externals. Like the car he drove, the women he dated, the clothes he wore. They didn't mean much to her.

Quirking a smile, she finally answered, "You have good taste in houses. Now get out so I can close the deal."

When her fingers began their tapping motion on the steering wheel, he finally gave up trying to convince her, got out, and slammed the car door closed.

CHAPTER FOUR

As she drove off, he stood watching her.

What could he have said or done to change her mind?

She certainly hadn't fed his confidence, not that he usually needed that, but he was more than a little disappointed in her answer. Glancing in the direction she drove in, his lips compressed in a tight line.

How could she have rejected his invitation with such ease?

He didn't like how it felt. The smooth operator was gone but then again, he'd never played the operator with her. He didn't have to. He was always comfortable with her company and she touched a part of him that he had never let anyone else see.

After inserting the key, he opened the door to his mother's condo. His footsteps on the tile floor echoed the emptiness. He moved into the kitchen, and poured himself a glass of wine, sat on a bar-stool and took a long swallow. Looking around he noticed how sterile the room was, nothing familiar, no pieces of history, nothing to remind him that he might belong to the owner. But he couldn't exactly blame her for that. When his mother was struggling in the aftermath of her injuries, her self-pity became too much for him to accept. The withdrawal from her children and her outright refusal to learn to walk with braces had disappointed him so much that he had severed her from his life. There was no way he could watch her slow, demoralizing slide into oblivion, so he'd stepped away and abandoned her as she had abandoned him.

He hadn't been around when she moved into the condo, but if he was honest, he could understand why she had sold the house on Main Street once his father had passed on. She could never have kept it up even with live-in help. The thing that had bugged him was that he hadn't even know about the move until it was a fait accompli. Just like years before when he'd arrived home from school to find a moving van in the driveway. Throwing a fit hadn't changed anything, and at fifteen, he didn't have the influence to change the outcome. With no recourse, he'd had to accept the fact that his father had altered their living arrangements to fit the new dynamics. The move had created a shift, and it had shredded the family ties that had tethered him to a world filled with love and laughter. The breach had changed him and created a hole that he still hadn't been able to fill.

Restless, he moved from room to room, trying to find something familiar, something that would ease the loneliness that hung over him like a dark cloud since...when. He couldn't even remember the last time he'd felt part of something bigger than himself. And that was almost laughable. He was part of a team, a team that had done well over the course of his tenure there. His teammates had been great and he had formed tight friendships.

Maybe it was just that it had been a long time since he'd felt a challenge, felt the quick spurt of adrenaline. It was coming more rarely each year. A big game. A collision with a rival team. But he wasn't pitted against the best anymore. He had fallen to third in the rotation in Oakland, the same spot he found himself in with the Greenies.

It was something he just couldn't get used to, and the attitude had created conflict, primarily within himself. It was something that spilled out onto the field when he couldn't control it. After the public argument he had with his manager when he'd pulled him out of a game early got press coverage, he'd been on the hot seat for a few days. The public apology hadn't helped his reputation. It's probably what got him traded.

Maybe if everything hadn't come so easily it would be less unsettling. His talent for pitching had come naturally, something his father had helped him refine, but there had been no work involved. It was a game that he played well. In high school, he had made states three years in a row. He could have gone on the signing block right after but his mother had insisted he attend college.

Just in case.

Even though they weren't speaking, she'd still held some clout with him back then. He'd enrolled in some of the premier baseball programs and ended up at USC, one of the highest- ranked in the country. His number one priority had been distance, and he couldn't get much further away from Andover than Southern California. Majoring in business had been a well- thought-out decision as well. He figured he'd need to know what to do with all the money he'd earn when he made the big leagues.

He was signed in his junior year by the Oakland Athletes with the stipulation that he finished out his senior year in the off-season, which meant staying in sunny California.

He couldn't have been happier.

He had barely been twenty-one.

It had been a party but he was finally getting tired of the cake and ice cream.

He was beginning to want something more substantial, and he hoped the leap to his home team would shake his world a bit. He needed to feel alive again and he had hoped this would be the remedy.

The Beantown barrier, a twenty-foot wall in right field, had become his nemesis and he wondered how he'd pitch against its backdrop.

He wanted to be a winner. Wanted it as badly as he ever wanted anything. It was that simple, but he couldn't seem to get out of his own head at times, and without control and discipline he wouldn't go far in that pursuit.

This was where he'd always wanted to be and it was his last stop.

If he couldn't find what he wanted here in Boston, he'd have to give it up.

He wouldn't settle for being mediocre. It wasn't in him.

He paused in front of the hall mirror for a closer scrutiny.

His mother had replaced it, although it was similar to the one that hung in the foyer of the old house.

He fingered the beveled cherubs ingrained in the wood. The old mirror had been scarred, the glass shattered the day his mother found out about his father's affair. Her temper had gotten the better of her, and she had thrown the phone at her husband when he came into the house but missed her mark.

He could still hear his mother's shrill cry, echoing.

"You son of a bitch! What did you tell her? I wouldn't let you go? I told you to keep it away from this house."

He had been home that day, listened while she was on the phone, had seen the tears in her eyes and heard his father walk through the door minutes later. He'd witnessed the ensuing argument and leaped out of the way when the phone went sailing by him, fracturing the glass of the mirror sending it in all directions. He'd tried to stop his mother as she raced out the door, pulled at her hand without success, run down the front steps after her but could do nothing when she'd backed out of the driveway and headed towards the center of town. He had resigned himself to standing guard on the front porch, waiting for her to return. It was from that vantage point that he heard the crash, then the ambulances, their sirens blaring, the wail in the air sending ripples of fear through him. After jumping from the steps he'd started running, sensing, knowing that it was her the medical teams were racing to. With each breath he'd taken, panting hard, his lungs about to burst from his efforts, he'd prayed desperately that he was wrong. When he'd arrived at the scene, he'd recognized the car and started screaming, trying to bully his way passed the police barricade.

"Please, that's my mother. I need to see her. Please."

It'd taken two officers to restrain him. He was left staring at the wreckage for over an hour as the firemen used the jaws of life to extricate her, tears streaming down his face, wanting to tell her one more time how much he loved her. He'd watched as the EMTs gingerly placed her on the gurney. All that had been visible were the still body beneath the sheet, and the blood that seemed to be everywhere. The air was ripe with the metallic smell: her face was covered with the sticky red substance.

Pleading with the officer who was standing by him he'd begged, "Please let me go with her."

The man had put his arm around him, sadness etched on his face and thick in his voice. "No, son. They don't need any distractions. Where do you live? We'll take you home."

He'd waited until the ambulance had pulled away, the sound piercing, the pitch a deafening crescendo, before he allowed himself to be lead to the cruiser.

Not two blocks from his house, a man had run a red light, crashed into her car with so much force his mother's legs were pinned under the crumpled hood. Several vertebrae in her back were crushed.

The policeman had taken him to the address he had given them. Reid was hostile towards his father, who seemed thrown by their arrival. Witnessing his father's breakdown had hardened him to the man. He often wondered if the tears were for the woman or the mess he'd made of their lives, with his actions.

Reid was at the hospital every day, just sitting outside the ICU keeping a vigil. Internal bleeding had been a major source of worry as she hung on to life by a thin thread. She'd spent months in the hospital, longer in therapy, and had come home a changed woman. It had caused a debilitating distance between the family members, creating a huge void, which love had once filled. The fabric of the family had been ripped so badly it was unable to be repaired.

It was the beginning of the end of life as he knew it.

It changed him in the process.

Wanting to distance himself from those memories, he landed on the couch in the living room, the name ironic in that family didn't exist here. He took another sip of his wine and let his mind wander down a different trail back to Izzie...Izabella.

He let her name roll over his tongue.

He couldn't believe what she looked like now.

Her lips were even more delectable-looking than when she was in high school, when he had sampled them. The summer before he went away to college. The summer they were a couple even though it didn't mean what it implied.

Her lips were luscious, soft, soul satisfying, tasted a bit like the coconut flan her mother used to make. How they felt and tasted. He groaned and shifted position because of a rising need.

Her kisses were extraordinary but that was the extent of their physical intimacy, so the rest he had to fantasize. He had never taken it further, felt guilty for even those heart-stopping kisses. He'd kidded himself that what he was offering her was experience, giving her practice at the art. But it was his own insatiability that was never quite satisfied.

He'd promise himself that it would stop, tell himself that she knew him too well, her life was too small, his goals were too big, there was nothing about her that fit his image, and she was too closely tied to Juliana, a woman he loved too much to disappoint. But he'd remember the light touch, the invasion of velvet, and set up their next rendezvous, somewhere hidden and secluded.

That was the only summer she'd allowed him that access.

Whenever he returned to the area, he would try to cajole her into going out with him but she always refused. Either she was going out with someone or had just broken up. He'd pretended it hadn't bothered him.

There was only once he'd thought he had a chance. He'd flown home for his brother's wedding, three years into his Oakland contract. Nolan had insisted he attend all the pre-wedding activities so he'd come earlier than he'd planned. After walking through the door, he'd automatically made the turn into the family room where he caught Izabella dancing with his mother in her wheelchair to an upbeat Joe Cocker tune. He'd just stood, his bag over his shoulder, mesmerized by the ample derriere that was staring him in the face as Izzie pushed his mother around the room, first one way and then the other, both laughing. It had unhinged him. He hadn't seen his mother act that carefree in a long time and it looked as good as it always had. When the women noticed their audience, Izabella had sprung into an upright position. There was an anxious look in her eyes when she gazed at him that turned more dangerous the longer their eyes stayed focused on one another. And he couldn't force his away.

It was his mother who'd broken the connection when she said, "I've been trying to get Izabella to stay for dinner tonight. See what you can do, will you, Reid?"

And with that she wheeled herself out of the room.

His eyes had burned into hers again and hers had burned right back.

Taking a step towards her he'd said, "I'd like that. Maybe we could go out later. Catch up."

The pause seemed endless and he'd thought that maybe she'd finally agree but he'd underestimated her will power.

"*Sinto muito.* I'm sorry but I don't think that's a good idea, do you?"

"I think it's a great idea."

"So where would we go, Reid?"

"I know a very intimate spot…"

"I'm sure you do. It is a place you will never get me again."

She'd pulled her jacket out of the closet, picked up her bag from the entryway table, and with her head high, walked out the front door without a backward glance.

Her walls had become as tough to scale as his own.

At the open house her lips had shone with the palest of pink gloss, pulling him in, and he wanted to press his lips against them to see if their taste was still the same.

And for as thin as he thought she'd gotten, when she had taken off the jacket, the see-through shell told him she was more than ample where it counted for him. The curves pressed against the fabric in a way that made his body hum and his mouth watered at the thought of his lips…

Probably made her feel like Cinderella at the beginning, like the belle of the ball, before crushing the glass slipper. You never want it to fit.

Keith's words came back to him.

He had never made Izabella feel like Cinderella, not even at the beginning. Never treated her like she was the most beautiful woman in the room. He had spent his time *being* with her, not trying to woo her. He had never even offered her the shoe, never mind crushed it. Maybe that had been a mistake that he could change if…

Okay. He needed a game plan.

He felt his adrenaline pump into action.

Taking the stairs two at a time, up to the room he was occupying, his mind was racing.

This was the challenge he had been waiting for.

The hunt had always invigorated him, and he had finally found a very able adversary.

CHAPTER FIVE

After Izabella slipped into the house, the quiet unsettled her.

Her energy level was too high for silence. She needed chaos, something she could bounce off.

She called out, "Where is everybody?"

Jaco yelled in from the back garden, "We're out here."

Having a landscape designer for a brother was a nice perk. Whenever he agreed to babysit, he would inevitably bring his tools, and the small backyard of her house looked like something out of House Beautiful. He was just doing some clearing today but soon he'd plant and the flowers would start to bud. The colors wouldn't emerge for a while yet, but the spring rains would do their job so by summer there would be a riotous array of blues, oranges, yellows and purples. Sitting out here, watching Melina play was one of her favorite past times and it was something she looked forward to.

She braced herself for the leg hug she knew was coming and she wasn't disappointed.

"Mama, you're home. We missed you."

Hoover had come rushing to greet her as well, and she felt her cold nose press against her arm as she begged for some attention.

"I missed you too, *mamacita*. Have you been helping Uncle Jaco?"

"Yes, he let me dig in the garden."

It was a question she didn't need to ask. She could tell by the hand prints left on her skirt. The receding snow had left a mud pit that in no way resembled a garden.

Smiling, she noticed the addition to the patio.

"You brought the table and chairs up."

"I have to believe the weather will be getting nicer, so I thought it was time."

"Thank you."

She kissed his cheek and hugged his neck.

Younger than her by a couple of years, Jaco, as a kid, had worked every summer mowing lawns and pruning shrubs. A couple of courses at the community college gave him an understanding of horticulture which had merely buffed his very green thumb. He had made himself a reputation in the area and was busy enough through three seasons that he could pretty much take the fourth one off and enjoy his kids, although his snow plowing business this past winter had been a mint in the making.

"How's Addie and the boys?"

"Great. They dropped by for a little while. Adelaide brought lunch, which we ate inside."

"I'm sorry I was late. I actually sold the house!"

"Good job. That'll be a nice commission."

"Yes. My garage, thank you very much."

She'd purchased her small home with a lot of help. Her father had supplied the down payment, her brother the sweat equity. She never would have been able to turn the fixer-upper into a turn key without them. She'd tackled each room, one at a time and, the garage was the one thing left on her to-do list.

"Keith left you a message. Said he got Reid's signed copy and that they missed you at…" He whispered the rest, "Chucky's."

She had the good sense not to tell Leeni about that possibility just in case what had happened, happened. She didn't want to disappoint her if she had to work late.

"Then you know who bought it."

"I do. How'd that go?"

"You know him. Can't measure up."

"Are you saying he didn't like the way you look?"

Her family had always loved her just as she was and losing the weight hadn't been a conscious decision but an end result of busy and stressed. One morning she'd woken up and was pleasantly surprised with the change. It had crept up on her slowly, and her sense of pride in her appearance made the alteration a permanent one.

"Thought I was too thin."

He snapped off the gardening gloves and tossed them into the wheelbarrow.

"Then he has less sense than I thought. And we both know I didn't think he had much."

She laughed, grateful that she could, after the sizzling way Reid's smile had made her feel.

"He hasn't changed a bit."

"Still full of himself."

"His cup runneth over."

"I hope you're over him."

"I was never under him…"

Her eyes snapped up to meet Jaco's and she added, "That didn't come out the right way. Can we just drop it, please? I am older and wiser and I was never in as deep as Mama made it sound."

"I was there *querida*. I saw how sad you were that summer. You couldn't fool me. We were too tight."

They always had been.

It came from having only each other for months before the drastic move. She had been eight and Jaco five when their father left them, and within a year, their mother had packed them up and headed to a different continent, leaving their family and all they knew behind. Their first home had been in a run-down area. The school was okay but they had to learn a new language, and then when their mother moved them to a better neighborhood, they had to start all over again. They'd stuck to each other before and after their lives became a bit more stable. When their mother started getting work, it was Izabella who watched over Jaco after school, made him supper and helped him with his homework. During summers they would occasionally accompany their mother to her work and help out. It was how and when she'd met Reid.

"Okay. I might have been sad then, but this is now. He's been out of my life for years, and I don't intend to invite him back in as anything other than friends."

Although she knew being friends was outside Reid's comfort zone. He was either all in or left you out in the cold. She wasn't sure it was in her comfort zone, either, so it was best left alone.

He lifted her chin and looked deep into her eyes.

"That is good to know, my Bella. I just hope you can do that."

He collected the tools of his trade, gave her and Leeni a hug before leaving them for home.

Letting the screen door snap closed behind her as she directed Leeni inside, she mumbled under her breath "I promise he will not do that to me again."

But the ripples of pleasure he could still incite in her body couldn't be denied, nor could the sparks that flew whenever he smiled.

Well, he was a good-looking guy.

And his voice could still hold her attention. Mesmerize would be a better way to describe it.

It had a tone that sounded slightly husky and felt like undulating waves washing over her.

But that's where the lingering attraction had to end.

He was the shallowest man she had ever met.

And she had purged herself of the need to be used by him a long time ago.

After snapping on the TV, she put on the *Despicable Me* movie that Leeni could not get enough of and said, "I'm just going to change. I'll be right back."

While leaning on the corner of her bureau, she attempted to step out of the uncomfortable nylons but stumbled. In a flash of impatience, she ripped them off and flung them across the room, missing the white wicker wastebasket that sat in the corner.

Taking a deep breath to calm herself, she wondered where that had come from.

Not wanting to delve too deeply into the meaning for fear of what she'd find, she slipped off the skirt and placed it in the dry-cleaning bag that she'd have to remember to put out. A silver-grey body nudged open her bedroom door and she smiled.

"Hello girl. Had enough of the Minions?"

Stroking the fur while getting out of the rest of her clothes, she said, "Okay. Let me just throw something else on and I'll feed you."

After changing into leggings and an oversized tee, Izabella went to the kitchen to feed Hoover, who was now outside hopefully doing her business and not chewing a tree. Checking on Leeni, who was still engrossed in the movie, she started thinking about dinner. Investigating what was in the refrigerator, making a mental list of what she needed at the market tomorrow, she pulled out some eggs, leftover ham and onion out for a frittata. Before she could get the ingredients mixed and the pan heated, the doorbell rang.

She wiped her hands on her mother's apron, one of a few she'd inherited, and glanced at Leeni as she proceeded to the front door.

After lifting the middle of the shears that were pleated on the side panels, she peeked out to see who was standing on her front stoop and swore under her breath.

She was so easy to find. All you had to do was Google the white pages. Real estate made being accessible a must. But not in a million years did she expect this.

Flinging the door open, she faced him and asked, "What is it about no that you don't understand?"

He gave her a winsome smile and explained, "You said you wouldn't go out to dinner, not that you wouldn't eat with me, so I picked up some food from a little place downtown that I heard was good. I have a bottle of wine and some sweets from Tripoli and figured we could enjoy it together."

She noticed the smile on his face droop when he saw the dark-haired little girl come up behind her and grab the edge of her shirt.

She stroked the dark hair of the delicate child. She had a wide nose, shining obsidian eyes that held a tinge of blue and a small, round face.

"Who's here, Mama?"

Izabella's eyes never left Reid's face, wanting to read what was in them, when she answered, "Someone Mama used to know, a very long time ago."

His eyes had turned wary. His tongue seemed to be tied securely in a knot because he didn't utter a word.

"So, as you can see there is another mouth to feed, one much younger than you're used to so you can take your food and go home."

The door was already almost half way closed before his hand shot out to press at it, preventing Izabella from shutting it in his face. Opening it back up, she noticed he had overcome his
surprise and his smarm was back in spades.

Squatting down so he was eye level with the little girl, he asked softly, "What's your name?"

She answered quite proudly, "Melina Juliana dos Santos."

"Your grandmother's name was Juliana. I liked her very much."

"She's in heaven."

"I know. But she probably looks down and smiles on you every day."

"That's what Mama says."

When he looked back up and into her eyes there was a question.

"Your daughter?"

She nodded and he had his answer without her having to say a word.

She watched him put his skills to work, his smile charming, his eyes sparkling.

"I brought some food for your Mama. She helped me buy a house today and I wanted to thank her. Do you mind if I eat with you?"

Leeni saw the Tripoli box and reached out to take his hand. "You brought dessert, so you can."

Izabella stood thunderstruck. Not only had her daughter, usually so shy with strangers, invited Reid in but she was holding his hand. And Reid, who blew women off for nothing of consequence, had just accepted the hand of a child and was strolling into her kitchen as if he belonged there.

Throwing her hands up, she realized she couldn't fight both. Leeni knew what was in the goodie box and would make sure she stayed up until she'd shared some of the booty. Her sweet tooth was the way to her heart. She'd yet to realize that Reid didn't have one.

Following behind by several steps, she arrived to find Reid looking around the bright kitchen. Even though dusk was near, the windows and the recessed lighting collaborated in creating a light-filled space. It had been gutted several years ago, and the light maple cabinets and white glass backsplash freshened up the space and the multi-colored granite countertops gave it an updated feel. They had broken down a wall to create an openness between kitchen and dining room so it looked larger than it was.

Turning to face her, he said, "You didn't tell me you lived practically across the street from my mother."

"Didn't see the point."

"It's a cute house."

"Thanks."

"Nice floors."

The hardwood gleamed and she was surprised he noticed. Cynically, she knew that beneath the compliment there must be a complaint.

"I'm waiting for the but. Can you please get it over with?"

"It's kind of small."

The three of them didn't fit comfortably.

"We don't take up much room."

With his arms crossed, he leaned against the counter.

"When did you buy it?"

She was a bit suspicious about his line of questioning.

"Where is this going?"

"Did my mother buy her condo to live near you or was it the other way around?"

She felt her shoulders relax and answered grudgingly, "Neither. It just happened there was a house I could afford and one that had potential next to an available condo, which she was looking for. What made it all work was the fact it was an end unit so we could make it wheelchair accessible."

After pausing, as if to consider what she'd just said, he asked, "Did you sell it to her?"

She watched him with a critical squint as she gave her answer.

"She was actually my first sale."

"Good for her."

She had trouble finding the underlying meaning, but his face displayed nothing she could read.

Leeni pulled down on her tee and said, "I'm hungry."

"I'm sorry, *pequena*."

Leeni climbed up and settled herself on the booster seat in the dining room while her mother gathered things from the cabinets and set the table with napkins, silverware, plates and glasses. Reid stood and watched before sitting down across from the little girl.

"So how old are you Melina?"

She put up three fingers, having some trouble holding her little finger under her thumb.

"When's your birthday?"

Proudly she announced, "September twenty-third."

"Then you'll be four soon."

Busy unwrapping the meal with shaking fingers, opening container after container, Izabella heard her stomach gurgle at the sight of the meat and spinach pies, grape leaves, spring rolls, kibbeh, lamb chops, what smelled like cinnamon chicken and homemade pita chips.

"I'm not sure Reid brought anything you've ever had before, *pequena*, other than the hummus, so I'm not sure you'll like…"

As she scanned the contents again, she sighed.

"Well, there is lots of meat so we should be good."

"Mm," and Leeni pointed to the white pastry box.

"You have to eat something healthy before that."

Getting half out of his seat, he reached over and put a spoonful of the hummus and some pita chips on the small Grover plate in front of Melina.

"Who doesn't like this?"

He scooped some up and popped it into his mouth.

"It's so good. Wanna try it?"

"I've had it before."

She copied his movements and crunched down. Gazing up at him, she smiled.

Izabella's stomach lurched again at how easily he could get any female to eat out of his hand.

Not happy with the current situation, she pulled some chicken off the bone a bit testily before placing the shreds on the plate along with a piece of kibbeh and a spoonful of risotto.

Somewhat suspiciously, Leeni tested the food and began happily devouring everything on her plate.

The warmth of his smile registered in his voice.

"Well, at least someone enjoys eating with me."

Now that Leeni was settled, Izabella began to fill her own plate, licking her fingers after each selection.

"She's three and only doing it because she wants whatever's in that box over there."

His fork was half-way to his mouth.

"We're all motivated by something."

After picking at a piece of the spinach pie and nibbling on it, she asked, "What is yours? Motivation in being here, that is."

"I told you. I just want to catch up."

Quirking his eyebrows at her he said, "And it seems there is a lot to catch up on."

"Not anymore. You've uncovered it all."

"Who's the dad?"

"None of your business."

"Is he in your life?"

"Again, none of your business."

She took one of the grape leaves and popped half of it into her mouth.

Leeni reached for a piece, interested in what her mother was eating before she said, "I don't have a dad. Mama does. Vovo doesn't live here, so I don't see him a lot. Do you have one?"

The look was quizzical. "Vovo?"

She raised her eyes to meet his.

"Her grandfather."

Izabella handed her daughter a forkful of food before taking another bite. Wanting to change the line of questioning, she asked, already knowing the answer, "So when is your first start?"

Sitting back in his seat, looking disappointed that she wasn't as forthcoming about Leeni's dad or the person called Vovo, he swirled the wine in his glass and said, "April ninth against the Phillies."

"Away?"

She knew this, as well, but wanted to act as if she didn't give it much thought at all.

"Yeah. We start on the road. I'm third game in."

Leeni reached for another piece of the spinach pie, and Izabella gave it over, not surprised after all that Leeni liked the food. She had been exposed to many different types because she stayed with so many people during the week. But by the sly little grin she wore, Izabella thought it might just be the company and her intent to please.

With a bit of a full mouth, Leeni asked, "You play baseball?"

"I do. Do you like baseball?"

Her head nodded vigorously.

"Unca Rique plays. We go see him sometimes."

Reid looked over at Izzie, who had taken another piece of spinach pie to replace the one poached by her daughter, adding a couple more of the grape leaves and a pork chop.

After she had filled her plate, he smiled, then resumed the questioning.

"Uncle Rique? Her father's uncle?"

With a bite of pork ready on her fork, she said casually, "No. My brother," before daintily placing it into her mouth.

Apparently, Keith hadn't told him about the family Izabella had re-connected with.

His forehead was creased as if in deep thought.

"Your father's son?"

"Obviously."

His brows drew together in a pained expression.

"When did you get back in touch with him?"

Picking up a piece of pita bread and pulling off a section, she replied, "After my mother died. He contacted me and asked if he could see us, Jaco and me."

He had sat back from the table, his eyes bulging, and put his eating on hold.

"And you said yes?"

Izabella continued to eat while she talked, calmly, in direct contrast to Reid, who was sitting quite rigid in his seat.

"Yes. I said yes. Problem?"

"He abandoned you when you were just a kid."

"He left my mother. She was the one who didn't allow any communication once we moved here."

"So, you just forgot about the past?"

"We talked, I forgave him, met his family and feel good about it."

"And Jaco?"

"It took him a little bit longer but yes, Jaco, too."

"I don't understand."

She finally pushed away her plate and leaned her arms on the table in front of her, probing his eyes with her own.

"Of course, you wouldn't. You hold grudges. It's not a good way to live. I prefer to forgive. You accept nothing but perfection. I've come to understand there is no such thing."

"But he hurt you."

She gave him a steely glare and reminded him, "So have others."

She could tell by the look in his eyes he knew who she was talking about.

Placing his napkin on top of his dish, he leaned forward and asked, "You let bygones be bygones with him but won't consider doing it for me?"

"He's my family. There is love there. And I wanted Leeni to have that."

After glancing at her daughter, who was intently listening to the conversation, she stood up, ending the dialogue. Cleaning the dishes off the table and loading the dishwasher, she heard Reid pick up the box of sweets and break the string that held it closed.

In the silence that ensued, she swiveled her head to peek at the table.

Reid was chuckling at Leeni's indecision. Inspecting each one of the pastries, she'd point to one before changing her mind and pointing to another.

Turning around from her spot at the sink, hands on her hips, Izabella said, "Melina Juliana, make up your mind already. It's close to bedtime."

The little girl looked up, her eyes beseeching her for some patience.

"But Mama they all look soooo good."

Reid offered a solution.

"How about we give you a taste of all of them?"

Clapping her hands as she stood on the chair, Reid reaching out to hold her in place, she exclaimed, "Yes."

After securing her back in her booster, Reid took a knife and cut a sliver of each and placed it on her dessert plate. He took what was left of a lobster claw filled with whipped cream and ate while Izabella watched the pure joy on their faces as they savored each bite.

Reid poured more wine into Izabella's glass before refilling his own, and then raised it in a toast. "Here's to my new house."

She clinked glasses, and took a sip, wondering what lay ahead for them both.

"You're not tempted by anything?"

She was sure he meant the cream puff.

It wasn't anything in the box that tempted her. Her temptation was the man sitting opposite her, with finely sculpted muscle, round face and steely blue eyes, a bit of stubble and a heart made of clay. It was going to take all her willpower to resist what he could offer and stay vigilant against his irresistible charm.

CHAPTER SIX

Tiptoeing out of the bedroom, Izabella dragged the door half-way closed and walked the short distance to her own.

Reid had left almost an hour ago, and she'd finally gotten Leeni to sleep. It'd taken four books, three songs and a story about her grandmother, that her daughter loved hearing.

After pulling her hair back and putting it into a ponytail, she lowered herself into the rocking chair and closed her eyes.

What a day.

She was glad that it was over.

She hoped she'd put Reid's talk about a hook up to rest, because that's always what his intimate dinners implied, but she'd been thrown off by his persistence.

Knowing him, she should have just given in. Her stubborn refusal had only enflamed the fanciful need he had to bring her to heel.

Had her body spoken another language? Were the sneak peeks filled with wanting? Was there something in her eyes that made him think he'd be successful?

She hoped not. She never wanted to want something so badly again. And she had wanted him.

Maybe now that he knew about Leeni, she'd be safe from his assault. There was no way he would involve himself with a woman and child.

Josh Groban sang in the background, lulling her into a more relaxed state and she let go of her thoughts.

Just as she was beginning to feel better, her phone pinged and she picked it up hoping against hope it wasn't a customer. She was out of juice and couldn't bear to listen to a wish list that didn't meet the realities of affordability.

Sofia texted, *"You okay?"*

Placing the cell in her lap, she closed her eyes at the question.

Sofia knew the shortened version of her history with Reid.

Her friend had asked about him once. When the simple curiosity of wanting to get to know each other better had prompted questions about the past, significant others, feelings, thoughts, what they wanted in life. A few scheduled play dates right after Sofia had started nannying had afforded them the opportunity, even though the girls were too young to call them that, Leeni barely six months old. The get-togethers were primarily for them, and they reminisced about the old neighborhood, their mothers and the way life had been on another continent. It was nice connecting to someone who had a similar background. Sofia had lived in her old neighborhood in Lowell for a couple of years until her family had moved several streets over into a single-family home. Sofia was two years behind her in school, so they knew each other while growing up, but not well.

They also shared differences.

Sofia had immigrated to America with her family intact, her father the primary breadwinner both there and here. Izabella's father had left them long before the move. Her life had changed drastically when he had. No longer had she lived in a grand house, with nice clothes and good food. Her mother was left scrambling to provide the necessities. When that couldn't be done in Campinas, Brazil, Julianna had followed the advice of several of her friends and moved the small family to Massachusetts and the tight community of Brazilians in Middlesex County. Life had been difficult here as well, until her mother had gotten her legs under her and started making money as day-time or even live-in help.

Juliana and Sofia's mom, Talita Camara, had stayed close, and that closeness had lasted until her Izabella's mother's death.

Reid had come up in conversation while they were sitting out in the backyard, watching the children chase Hoover, who was just a puppy, pick dandelions and play in the sandbox her brother had assembled even though Leeni was too small to use it.

Sofia, sipping her iced tea had said nonchalantly, "Reid Jackson was at the house on Saturday. You went out with him one summer, didn't you?"

"Who told you that?"

Before the words were out of her mouth, she knew. Trying to make light of it, Izabella had waved the idea off with her hand.

"My mother, right? She nagged me for two straight months about that. I tried to tell her that we were just hanging out, but she thought Reid would push for something she didn't think I should give away."

Juliana had been very upset the summer Izabella spent time with Reid and had discussed her anxiety with anyone in the old neighborhood willing to listen, Sofia's mother not exclusively.

Mimicking the older woman, Sofia said, "She doesn't leesen to me. He is not good for her."

Izabella laughed at the exactness of the imitation.

"She was worried about what I'd do to get Reid to like me. And I suppose she had good reason. It didn't matter in the end because he never tried to get me there."

That had been insulting. She would like to have been the one to say no. She just wasn't sure she would have.

"Mr. Zamoutto's told me some stories. He talks about him a lot. It took me awhile to figure out it was the same Reid Jackson your mama had ranted about. From what I hear, he is a good baseball player, *sí*?"

"One of the premier pitchers in the league."

She had hoped the pride she felt wasn't obvious in her voice.

"When Mr. Jackson came over, he was in town, yes, they disappeared behind the study door but the conversation got pretty heated and I couldn't help but overhear it. The girls' mother is contesting the divorce and wants custody. Mr. Z said that would happen over his dead body. It wasn't pretty."

"He talks to Reid about it?"

"Yeah. They were in there for hours. There was talk, some yelling, lots of laughter. They seem to be good friends. It must be nice to have someone you trust that you can say anything to. I think women call it venting. It didn't sound as if he kept much in."

"They've been best friends since high school. But I can just imagine what Reid is telling him. His ideas on marriage are...insightful. This situation just proves his point."

"He didn't talk about it at lunch so I don't know what kind of advice he gave him. He kept the conversation centered on his team. It seemed to be just what Mr. Z needed. He's got a great smile."

Sofia sounded almost moony.

"Are you trying to tell me something?"

Sofia began to stutter.

"Oh, goodness, no. He's my boss. I can't feel like that about him. I would never put my job at risk like that."

"Is it just his smile?"

She'd meant it as a jest, but Sofia had blushed and her voice became fragile.

"I'm sorry I said something."

"Oh, Sofia. I want to be able to tell each other anything. If you have a boss crush, I'll take it to my grave."

Her friend had smiled shyly, her eyes softening.

"Okay, well, maybe a little one. And you have a little Jackson crush? He is very good-looking. And he makes lots of money, yes? I bet he'd make a pretty good catch."

"Yes, he is all those things. But he would never let himself be caught. Even though I hoped for a split second that it could be different, I realized quickly that it would never be a two-way street. Any crushing led to being crushed. Mr. Cool had an image to protect and I didn't fit into it."

The thought of that still hurt more than it should.

His kisses had been so heart-stopping, his touch so tender. She had fallen for it even though she knew it was a fatal mistake. Especially when she realized he wouldn't let a soul see her with him. It had taken a lot for her to put it behind her and then...well, she was still trying to play catch-up if truth be told.

"But now, Izabella, you are like a model. You would fit the image better than most."

"That's not what I want, Sofia. To fit some image. Let's just say I learned a valuable lesson that summer. One I'm not likely to forget. He may always be someone I care about but all we can ever be is friends."

Still looking at the phone and the text that had come from Sofia, she decided to call rather than get into a text marathon. Picking up the landline, cell reception poor in the house at times, she dialed the number and waited for her friend to pick up.

Instead of the hello she expected, Sofia asked, "So, how are you? Okay?"

This question was the result of the close connection that had grown between the two women since that first conversation. Izabella had revealed little things in their talks, about Melinda, and Reid's penchant for diversity in dating. Their lives intersected on an almost daily basis, and they'd shared a lot of confidences over the years.

It had become even more obvious with how frazzled she'd become since the trade.

Answering honestly, she said, "Seeing him at the house and putting the offer together would have been fine. But he came over for dinner. Uninvited but bearing gifts."

Sofia gasped and asked, "Really?"

"Yeah. I thought he'd do an about-face and get out as fast as his fastball, which clocks in at over ninety-miles-an-hour, the minute he saw Leeni."

"But he didn't?"

"Nope, had her eating out of the palm of his hand before we got to the table."

"I see why you can't do it."

"Do what?"

"Get him out of your life."

Rubbing the back of her neck, Izabella fought the impulse to give in to the simple statement. Denial was the river she was cruising, so she continued on course with the words, "What do you mean? He is out of my life."

"Keith has been watching a lot of sports news over the last couple of days, so I have seen a lot of the interviews with Jacks. I knew he was larger than life but he's also very charismatic when he wants to be. Patrick couldn't have been as…"

Stirrings of anger shifted the tone in her voice.

"Patrick had staying power. Or would have if things had worked out differently."

He might not have the glitz or sizzle that Reid did, but he would have been content with the ordinariness of daily living. But life had gotten so complicated while they were dating. Her mother's illness had reshaped her life. Her death caused such grief that she'd began evaluating where she was and where she was going. To compound that, her father had contacted her, revealing it was Julianna who had kept them apart. She'd had to wade through the burning anger at her mother for her duplicity, and deal with the awkwardness of meeting her other family. Patrick had been willing to wait for her, but the end had finally come when she had betrayed him and couldn't pretend that she hadn't. It meant the end of a secure life with someone who genuinely cared for her and the boredom that had become her safety valve. There had been no highs or lows, no expectations, no hopes…

Sofia asked a question she had never asked before, "There's no chance that Leeni is Patrick's daughter, is there?"

Not wanting to evade the issue, Izabella said honestly, "No. I was unfaithful and he deserved better."

"And Leeni's father was the person you were unfaithful with. You never told me who that was."

"That one-time sperm donation changed my life. For the better, but he is not a part of our lives so it doesn't really matter, does it?"

She accepted Izabella's silence and joked, "She looks so much like you I thought she didn't have one."

"Trust me, she does. I get glimpses of the inherited genes and it's not pretty."

She often worried that someone else would notice the resemblance but so far, her luck had held.

"I'm afraid Iz now that Reid's here for good and he's Keith's best friend, that I'll probably be seeing him more often than I have in the past."

"No problem. You know he can be a real charmer, lots of fun, intelligent conversation. Grin and bear it. Just don't talk too much about him and it'll be fine."

Wading into a potential undertow she offered, "Keith says he seems different now. Not as blustering, not as sure of himself."

"He seemed his old self to me. A bit egotistical, a tad arrogant."

A lot of gorgeous.

"Keith says he's older now so..."

"He'll always be a kid playing one team game or another."

"But Keith..."

"Sofia, you're making it sound as if Keith is the resident expert on all things Reid and that you've discussed this ad nauseum. Keith has been trained to put his two cents in, and it looks like you're amassing a fortune in pennies."

Laughing, she relented, "Okay. I'm done now. I'll see for myself soon enough if it's something I can take to the bank."

"Oh, Sofia."

Her laugh echoed over the air waves. Wanting to be on firmer ground Izabella asked, "What are your plans for tomorrow? I have a free day and would love to do something with the girls."

"That would be great. Why don't we bring them into town? Go to the aquarium or the children's museum? Late morning would be better for me."

"Say around eleven. I'll swing by and drive your car in. It's bigger and will fit all of us."

"Sounds good."

Clicking off, Izabella couldn't seem to stop the chords to the aching melody her heart still played. It started every time someone associated her with Reid in some way and it was

hard keeping her feelings to herself. With no one to talk to, things were buried deeper than she could handle sometimes. Maybe she should just get it out in the open. The pretense of being uninterested was wearing on her, and she wasn't even sure that Sofia bought it anymore. How could she when the mere mention of his name drove her loco?

"Come here, Hoover. I need a hug."

Padded paws crossed the short distance as the three-year-old Weimaraner bounded up and onto the dark plum coverlet.

Sitting on the edge of the four-poster bed, Izabella wrapped her arms around the softness and rested her head on Hoover's neck.

"It's been one of those days, my friend."

She waited for a sense of peace that this dog brought her at the end of a frantic day, but she felt like she was on a sugar high.

She reached for the wine she'd poured for herself before coming up, and took a slow sip.

Hoover was studying her, her green eyes questioning.

"The wine has nothing to do with seeing Reid again."

Hoover cocked her head to the side and Izabella laughed.

She had almost expected a Scooby Doo, "Huh?"

"Don't look at me like that. It's true."

The need for the drink wasn't the result of the downward spiraling curve of the adrenaline rush she'd experienced seeing Reid, nor did it have anything to do with the drain on her system from fighting off his dinner invitation. It certainly wasn't a slip in mood because of the wrenching disappointment that flushed through her when he'd said she looked like a plucked chicken.

She'd often thought that maybe if she lost some weight…

Bending low, she held Hoover's head in her hands and rubbed her head against the dog's.

She needed to let this longing go.

She would not let his opinion affect her.

She crawled under the covers and Hoover jumped off the bed, turning her head for a good-bye before she went into Leeni's room for the night.

Closing her eyes, her mind once again wandering back to this afternoon, she felt the warm rush of sensation thrumming through her, and she fell into a fitful sleep dreaming a fitful dream.

Reid paced the airport terminal while waiting for his flight to Philadelphia. The Greenies would be opening their season tomorrow in a game against the Phillies and he had to be back in his hotel room before the night was over. Management had given him until midnight to join the team and he'd graciously accepted the deadline. Being traded so late in the pre-season had set off a firestorm of activity in the last few days, wrapping up his life in Oakland and beginning a new one here. Finding a house had been imperative. The upcoming schedule was full of away games and he wanted to be settled as soon as he could. He had to be out of the condo by mid-May, when his mother returned for the summer. He still wasn't sure why he was buying and not renting. It didn't fit into his orderly routine. And he would have reverted to that if he hadn't found the house that said welcome home. No house had ever beckoned to him that way since the family home on Central Street, the house he'd grown up in.

He was glad he had booked a late flight. Otherwise he would have missed dinner with Izabella and Leeni. He took out his phone and flicked the screen, searching for the photo he'd taken of her cream-stained mouth. She was such a cute little thing, and he couldn't help smiling at the memory of her licking her fingers clean of all the gooey goodness. Next, he flicked to the picture he'd taken of Izzie. Her hair had been pulled back but her bangs spilled over her eye, leaving one midnight orb veiled. The other was visible, a greyish eyeshadow creating an exotic effect that had his mouth watering. Her neck was graceful, so feminine that he'd wanted to caress it and kiss the softness there. He had to admit her figure was stunning although he was still stung by her transformation. It didn't seem like it had changed who she was, but he knew it would change how people looked at her.

Had Leeni's father gotten to taste the perfection. She'd still been his old Izzie when she conceived Melina, but since then?

His stomach churned at the thought of someone else enjoying the beauty, both inside and out. He knew for a fact that he could have been on the receiving end of all that delectable treasure if he'd been able to see past the physical flaws. For as much as he enjoyed being with her, he could not get past the extra weight she'd carried. Or so he had told himself back then. Maybe it had been the buffer he needed to keep her at arm's length, to keep her the innocent he knew her to be.

Age had given him a new appreciation of her. She had been just as beautiful then as now.

Pinching his bottom lip, he wondered, not for the first time since leaving Izabella, who Leeni's father was.

Patrick? Someone he knew nothing about? How active had her social life been? Had she cared about the man who had given her a child. Was he still in her life? Leeni had her mother's name so the man hadn't staked a claim. There couldn't have been a commitment on either side.

Right?

He got up out of the seat, and began to pace, realizing that he didn't really care who it was, as long, as it wasn't him.

There was a plane rolling in and he stopped at the window to watch its arrival at the opposite gate.

Taking out his phone again, the desperation to know building instead of subsiding, he called Keith.

"Where are you?"

"Airport."

"Do you need something?"

"Why didn't you tell me about Melina?"

"Why would I?"

"Izabella has a daughter. Didn't you think I would be interested?"

"Not really. If you had wanted to stay current on her life you would have kept in touch."

He couldn't exactly disagree with that but now that he knew...

His voice thickened.

"Who's the father?"

There was a long pause on the other end of the line.

"I don't know."

"What do you mean?"

"I mean, I don't know. I don't think anyone does."

"Why?"

"I don't know that either. Why's it important?"

"I don't know, but it is."

Another long pause before Keith asked, "Could she be yours?"

There was a grunt before the answer.

"No. We never...went there."

Another hazy memory came drifting into his mind. A streak of lightning coursed through him as a haunting vision emerged, one that he had completely made up from need and desire. It hadn't happened, although he surmised his subconscious had wanted it to in a visceral way.

When Keith said, "Then relax," he tried to do the impossible.

Shoving his phone in his pockets as an image of some unknown man's tongue invaded the smooth center of Izabella's mouth, he saw hands feeling the curves that were more abundant than they were now and made a disgruntled sound.

His focus had to be on the upcoming game he'd be pitching. He couldn't let thoughts intrude that might unsettle him, distract him from what was important. To his career. To his life.

He shook thoughts of Izabella out of his head as the attendant announced it was time to board his flight.

CHAPTER SEVEN

Izabella peeked out the front door, scanning the area, hoping her newspaper wasn't somewhere in the front yard, where the carrier seemed intent on throwing it. Rolled up in the plastic wrap, it lay fifty feet from her steps so she sprightly scrambled out in the pouring rain, gripping the lapels of her slightly worn flannel wrapper, scooped it up and retreated to the warmth and dryness of her kitchen. Hoover had stepped out right behind her and she groaned when she had to step back out to retrieve her.

Grabbing the dog around the collar, she reprimanded soundly, "Bad girl. You know you can't go out there."

They both shook the water from their hair in the same spot, creating a puddle. Hoover wagged her cropped tail against her owner's leg, seemingly proud of her mischief. Squatting down, placing her hands on both sides of the angular face, Izabella looked right into luminous eyes.

"Now look what you've done. I swear you're more trouble than you're worth."

A sandpaper tongue swiped at her cheek and she pulled Hoover close for a hug. "I love you, too. Now let's get a towel and get this cleaned up. I need my coffee."

She toed off her crocs and yanked down the towel that always hung by the coat rack guarding her side door, swiped it across the floor to absorb the pooling liquid, then stepped to the kitchen for her morning caffeine. Taking her first tentative sip, inhaling the aroma, she let the warmth seep into her bones. She was glad they had decided to go into Boston today for some indoor activities, because it was one of those chilly and rainy pre-spring days when the sun refused to come out at all. Hopefully it would be better weather tomorrow. She had the home inspection in the morning, and standing outside in the rain while the inspector was on the roof was never fun. Afterwards, she planned on going into the office to finish up some paperwork and then out with the Seifords in late afternoon. She still wasn't sure what they were looking for. They probably didn't know themselves, so this would take some time and effort to weed out what they didn't want and find something they did. This type of customer was challenging at best, and she knew some agents who showed three houses and expected a decision. They said their time was valuable and they weren't in the business to go on a never-ending search for the perfect house. She didn't have that kind of confidence yet, although in a few years, her patience with that process might help her make the shift. On Wednesday, she was working with a relo, an out-of-state family relocating to the area, and they had to get in as many houses as the day allowed. There was another open house on Sunday for one of her new listings down the street from her, and she still had to get the listing sheet finished, keys made and lockbox on.

When she checked in with Keith to see if he was still meeting her at the Costellos's, he told her he was flying out for Reid's first game on Thursday.

She was stunned when he asked her, "Want to come with me?"

"To Philadelphia? Are you serious?"

"As a matter of fact, I am. I think Reid could use some support in the stands."

"Crackerjacks Jackson? The gods greatest gift to baseball?"

"A legend in his own mind. I know. But I'm beginning to wonder. I just thought I'd ask."

She caught the apprehension in Keith's voice but didn't want to dwell on what it meant.

"I don't even like baseball. And I'm sure he's found someone by now who makes him feel like the king of the mountain. He has been there since last night, hasn't he?"

"Didn't sound it when I talked to him this morning."

"Give him some time. It shouldn't take more than a couple more hours."

"Hey, you said he was a friend of yours. I thought he could use one."

"Use is the oh-so-correct word."

"Izzie, that's so unlike you. You're usually all warm and tender and very sympathetic."

The sarcasm didn't move her.

"Sorry but you're flying solo. Besides, I told Sofia I'd take the girls for a few hours between my appointments and showings. I think she needs a break. It's kind of hard spending time in front of the toilet barfing your brains out and taking care of a couple other kids."

Sofia had found out she was pregnant just over six weeks ago and her morning sickness was peaking. Her mother helped when she could, but she didn't drive and it was hard for her to get transportation.

"Yeah, thanks for that. I guess she needs her friends even more than Reid does."

"And she deserves them more, too."

"I won't argue with that. See you at the inspection."

"Bye, Keith."

What he didn't know was that she kept Thursday evening free just in case she got up the nerve to watch the game.

She doubted that Reid was as nervous as she was.

A small voice called out to her, and she jumped off the bar stool and headed in the direction of the stairs.

"I'm coming, *querida*."

She retrieved her three-year-old from the top of the stairs, and they made their way down one step at a time, worry filling the small girl's voice.

"I heard the rain."

"It's coming down pretty hard."

"We can still go with Junie and Holly, can't we?"

"Yes, of course. We'll park in the underground garage and stay dry."

Warm fingers continued to cling to hers as they turned the corner into the kitchen, where Izabella scooped Leeni up and onto a stool.

"What do you want for breakfast?"

"Waffles."

"Waffles it is."

Izabella opened the freezer and extracted a couple from the box and placed them in the toaster.

The ring of the phone alerted both of them.

Brushing the fine hair away from her daughter's sleep-flushed cheeks, she picked up her phone and identified the caller.

A small voice said, "If it's Auny Sofia tell her I'm wearing my new dress today."

With more brusqueness than she meant, she said, "It's not."

Taking a huge gulp of air, she swiped.

"Hello Mr. Crackerjacks."

Leeni tipped her head to the side, trying to figure out who her mother was talking to. Lifting her chin from the phone, she told her, "It's Reid, from the other night. You know, Mr. Tripoli box."

"I love Mr. Crackerjacks. Tell him I want some more."

Rolling her eyes, knowing Reid had a friend for life, she said, "What do you want?"

"Tell her I'll bring another box when I'm home."

"No. I will not. Because you won't."

"You don't sound like you're in a very good mood this morning."

"I was doing quite well until about two minutes ago."

The ding of the toaster sounded, so Izabella began to multi-task, spreading peanut butter on the waffle and putting it on the plate, pouring a glass of milk.

He waited patiently as if he knew she had other things to occupy her time.

She asked again wanting the conversation over, "What do you want?"

"Some enthusiasm would be nice. You don't sound pleased to hear from me."

"Keep talking. See if I can build up to it."

"I have most of the morning."

"It might take longer. Got a decade?"

"Izzie, I'm crushed. I need a dose of TLC and I thought of you."

She really had to stop taking care of people and get rid of the easy-touch button.

"I don't give that out for free anymore. Hope you have time to call someone who cares."

"What's your price? I bet I can meet it."

The rush of pure sensation rippled in places she didn't discuss in public when she heard the deep throaty chuckle that came at the end of that sentence.

"I wouldn't be looking for dollars and cents."

"That's not what I'm offering."

She felt something melt inside of her and knew it was a mistake to keep this line of conversation going.

"What do you want? I have things to do."

She heard a soft chuckle before his words.

"Just checking on the home inspection tomorrow."

She tightened the cover on the jar of peanut butter, placed it in the cabinet, then leaned back against the counter.

"Keith said he'd already talked to you about that."

"He did but I wanted to confirm with you as well."

"Were you this obsessed with your house on the West Coast?"

She'd never thought to ask where he lived when he was cross-country. He might not have talked to his mother, but he kept in touch with his brother, and Nolan kept Melinda up-to-date on Reid's life.

"I never bought. Only rented. It seemed too…"

"Much of a commitment?"

"I'd call it too permanent. I wasn't planning on being there forever."

Noticing that Leeni had smeared the peanut butter on her cheek, she got a napkin from the drawer and wiped it off.

"Most people sell every seven years. You could have been in your second home by now."

"Yeah, but then I would have had to go through the process of selling. Less hassle this way."

Hassle was the story of her life.

"Look I gotta go."

"Hey, I'm pitching on Thursday."

"I know."

He had already told her and it had been the topic of Greenliner Nation.

"Wish me luck?"

"You never needed that. Your arm was always your talisman."

"Yeah, but I'm getting old…er and nothing lasts a lifetime."

"There are plenty of things that last that long."

"Like what? And don't sell me on the love theory."

She was studying her daughter and knew that she couldn't say anything to him to make him understand that relationship.

Instead, she ticked off some things that might work instead.

"The sun, the moon, the planets, the Beantown barrier. Your Grandfather used to go to the games at Bogs Field, didn't he? And it's still standing. A lifetime or two."

"Okay, you have me there, but an arm is a bit different."

"I'm expecting mine to last until I breathe my last breath."

"But you won't have to throw pitches with it that reach ninety-eight miles per hour."

"I guess I just picked a better career for keeping my arm intact."

"I just went with my strengths."

"That's true, you didn't have that many. Look someone's at the door. I've gotta go."

"This early? Go see who it is. I'll wait."

"I'm a big girl and I've been taking care of myself since I was ten. Besides, I know who it is."

She could hear the gears grinding, and she held her breath, waiting for him to say something smart about big and girl. Surprised that he didn't, she rolled her eyes in an I-can't-believe-you-said-that way when he asked, "Maybe you'd like a big strong man around so he could answer the door?"

"That sounds antiquated even for you."

"I didn't say I was going to drag you into a cave."

"It's a good thing. I don't do caves. I get cold easily."

"See, you are too thin. No blood."

"I'm saying good-bye now. Good-bye."

And with that, she ended the call and turned to see her brother letting himself in. He was going to start planting today although with the downpour she wasn't sure he'd get to it.

Giving him a hug she said, "You can put this off, you know."

He poured himself some coffee and opened the refrigerator to get the creamer when he saw the Tripoli box. "Can, I?"

"Of course."

Leeni chimed in with, "Mr. Crackerjacks brought it last night for dessert."

Jaco spun around to face his sister. "He was here?"

"I know what you're going to say, but trust me, I didn't invite him."

"He just showed up on your doorstep?"

"Yup." Pointing to the top of Melina's head, she said, "I think we scared him away, so don't worry."

"I can't help it. It's in my nature to worry about you. And his intentions."

"He won't be across the street much longer and you know him, out of sight, out of mind."

"He's at Melinda's?"

His shock was easy to read.

"Until he closes on his house."

There was a tightening in his expression as if a knot had formed in his gut.

"Do you want me to talk to him?"

"Absolutely not. I can handle it, I promise."

He didn't look sure about that, but he must have wanted to give her the benefit of the doubt.

"I'll take your word for it but if the situation changes, let me know."

With that, he extracted a Napoleon with the end missing and filled his mouth with the creamy goodness. He didn't let who'd bought it diminish his pleasure.

"The rain is supposed to let up later this morning. If it's okay with you, I'll just do some paperwork until then. See how it goes."

"Can you take Hoover out before you leave? I'm going into Boston with Sofia and the girls and I'm not sure when we'll be back."

"No problem."

Her brother was sitting at the table now, taking the newspaper out of its plastic wrap, spreading it out on the flat surface. The paper she was so eager to get to.

The need to get a dose of Reid this morning from that source, had dissipated with his call.

She'd gotten more than she'd wanted.

Rushing the three-year-old into her winter jacket, she handed her her backpack, kissed her brother's cheek, and they waved as they went out to the driveway.

Reid's voice still echoed in her mind. They had picked up with the easy banter of their youth and her anger surged again that he was able to almost make her forget that this was as good as it got.

Reid took another sip of his coffee and looked out over the parking lot, watching the people arriving at the hotel. Some had baseball jerseys on and he knew they were Boston fans in to see the game. He hoped they enjoyed the play.

They were one game down, with one hundred and sixty-one to go, and yesterday's was a win. Bullard had some great stuff and they left the field with the score seven to two. Borinquen was on fire with a triple and a couple of singles, resulting in several runs that had put them ahead. They'd never looked back.

He had already gotten into the groove of their routine, which was repeat, repeat, repeat.

Up early, eat breakfast which consisted of protein and carbs, with maybe some fruit thrown in.

Then free time until after lunch, when they'd gather in the lobby of whatever hotel they were staying at and head over to the ballpark. A forty-five-minute stretch regime would get them all loose and ready. He loved shagging fly balls during batting practice. It got the legs moving and his body felt good when in motion. The atmosphere in the clubhouse was relaxed right up until twenty to thirty minutes before the game. Then some of the game faces came on. Focus was critical, and he assumed it was easier for him and the other pitchers than for an outfielder who had to stay on his toes waiting for the next hit and do that for the whole nine innings.

After the game, it was shower, eat, and eventually head back to where they'd started. But most needed some unwind time, so they'd go to a bar or play some pool. Some would look for hook-ups which was what he was famous for, but he just didn't have it in him lately. The women were there, throwing themselves at him, like they did to a lot of the other players. Some guys were married and intended on staying that way, so they headed back earlier, phoned home, read, relaxed in other ways. He had opted to stay in and play video games which was a lot more entertaining than he'd thought it would be. His lights went out as soon as his roomie returned and he woke up more refreshed than usual and ready to go.

As he stood in the lobby after eating his early-morning meal, he realized he didn't know where he was ready to go to.

Throwing himself in one of the elegant chairs, he observed the guests coming and going. Beautiful women made eye contact, and he could have pursued them if he'd felt inclined to but he wasn't in the mood to be charming this morning. It was becoming too exhausting to be on all the time, and he wanted to save his strength for the upcoming games. He fiddled with the newspaper sitting on the glass coffee table, catching up on the breaking news across the country. It took a couple of minutes to go from front to back, so he put it down and placed his head in his hands.

With the day stretching out endlessly in front of him, he struggled with what to do with all that time.

How had he filled it before?

A woman? Sleeping in late?

He had never felt at such loose ends.

He watched as some of the players, accompanied by their families, made their way across the hotel, laughing and enjoying the moment.

He wished Keith were here. They could have spent the day just mucking around like they had when Reid visited him in Oakland, right before Mariah happened.

He took out his phone, and thumbed through the pictures he'd taken of the house, wanting to get an idea of what he'd need to fill the space. With his mind racing with the possibilities of furniture selections and color choices, he was excited about the prospect of making a home in the town he'd grown up in. His thumb stopped when he noticed that Izabella had been caught in one of the frames. Peeking at him from under those thick lashes, she sparked a long-ago and dormant ember. She would look at him like that when they were younger, pretending to be busy with homework but peering up to watch him flicking the TV remote. It had made him feel uncomfortable back then, and it was doing something like that now. He thumbed his phone off and got up, finally coming up with a destination.

He'd find a mall somewhere so he could pick up some more, appropriate clothes. He'd come in from Oakland so recently, he didn't have much in the way of East Coast cool-weather stuff, so what he had packed had been mostly summer gear. Shopping was not one of his favorite things to do, and he had always counted on the various women in his life to attend to that chore. He'd go along to pay, but he didn't have to think about what would match what. He'd just try on whatever was handed to him and buy what he was told to buy.

With no one currently fitting that bill, he was on his own. He grabbed a taxi and let the driver decide the destination.

The mall was huge and he had no idea where to even begin. As he ambled from one end to the other, he pulled out his phone and found the number he wanted before hitting send.

She didn't even offer him a hello.

"We're not anywhere near done, Reid."

The voice with the slight accent sent a ripple of pleasure through him.

"I know. I just thought I'd check in."

"Don't you have anything better to do than bother me?"

"Not really. I need some new clothes, so I'm shopping, something that is not one of my favorite pastimes."

"Well, talking to you is not one of mine. If we both would rather be doing something else, why don't we get to it."

"Can I call you when I can't decide what to buy?"

"No. I am busy. I have to work for a living."

"What are you doing this afternoon?"

"Getting a new phone number."

He chuckled easily.

"Tell Leeni I haven't forgotten about her. I'll be back on the twelfth and I'll drop by with another one of her favorite boxes."

"Good-bye, Reid."

He was getting used to her cutting him off.

He almost liked it.

CHAPTER EIGHT

Izabella looked at Keith to see him burst out laughing.

"What is so funny?"

"He doesn't skip a beat."

The same couldn't be said about her heart, but she wasn't letting anyone in on that little secret.

"What is he doing? I don't hear from him for years and suddenly I can't get rid of him."

"He is what he is, Iz."

"He is a smarmer. Cross between smarmy and charmer."

"Accurate from your perspective, I would say."

"Pretty accurate from any perspective."

"I think…"

"Yes, Sofia filled me in with all the *Keith says*…He hasn't changed a whit."

"I'm not going to argue, but I disagree. He's begun doubting himself."

"Please. That word is not his vocabulary."

"Take a closer look, Izabella. I have a feeling that's why you're getting the blitz. It's his perverse way of getting what he needs, without even knowing what that is."

She studied Keith's face, looking for the truth.

But didn't dare trust it.

A few hours later, sitting at her desk, tucked inside a small cubicle, the home inspection flawless, she kicked off the high heels and rubbed her toes. Tomorrow she swore she'd wear flats whether they matched or not.

Reid had called her no less than ten times.

She had to shut her phone off during her time with the Seifords because of the incessant ring signaling an incoming call. When they had gotten back to the office, the couple not remotely interested in anything she'd shown them, she'd set up appointments for the next round of showings, almost wishing that Reid had left well enough alone and not gotten her involved with them. They were going to be a lot of work. One house was too small, one didn't have the tub Carla wanted, the closets weren't big enough, they didn't like wallpaper. They were going to have to up their price to get everything they wanted, but she wasn't sure they'd agree to it.

She reached over and fingered a pile of pink WHILE YOU WERE OUT slips that were in her tray, flipped through them, ticking off who she'd call before heading home and who could wait. Taking a deep breath, she checked the rest of the texts to see what Mr. Crackerjacks had to say that was so important.

Hey. I'm in one of the stores and I like a couple of shirts but I'm not sure they look good. Take a peek and tell me if I should buy them.

There were selfies of him in the dressing room, modeling both.

She hoped he'd bought them because the colors looked good on him, although the fit might be less than perfect. They were snug but she sat for a moment just enjoying the view, tantalized by the breadth of his shoulders, thinking what it would feel like to have her palms pressed against the rippled muscles.

When her breathing hitched, she deleted it and moved on.

Hey, I'm just leaving the mall. Bought the shirts. And a couple of other ones.
Delete.
Hi. I'm back at the hotel. Call me if you have a minute.
Delete.
I heard the home inspection went well. Keith is emailing me the purchase and sale agreement to the hotel. You should have it in your hands sometime later today. Thanks, Iz.
Delete.
Just in case you try to call me, my phone will be off. I'm going to the movies with Motts. I'll call you later.
Delete.
I just got out of the movies. It wasn't a bad way to kill an afternoon.
Delete.
Going to supper. Give me a call.
Delete.
I'm glad you didn't change your number. I just called to check.
Delete.

The last message brought a smile to her face. She wiped it off as soon as she realized what she was doing. She had never been the recipient of his beneficence although she had seen him in action. Pitching wasn't the only sport he was good at. He had a variety of other plays as well and she envied the recipients of his blatant charm. She'd overhear him describe to Keith or Josh what course of action he'd take to achieve his objective, and he'd move in for the kill, flattering and fawning, complementary and courteous, handing them flowers picked from his mother's garden, or handing out an invitation to one of his games as his date, laying it on thick so they'd fall at his feet. But within days or weeks, the finale would come and she'd hear him on the phone breaking it off, blaming them for wanting too much and for thinking it meant something it didn't.

He was the ultimate salesperson, suave, funny and smart, knowing just what image to project to the world. And he did it skillfully.

She knew his systematic approach, the steps, the words, the details, and she now knew what it felt like.

But she had also seen the real Reid, the one more engaging than charming. He was a great conversationalist, and he pulled things out of her that no one else could. Wary of most people, being the new kid in school too many times to count, she didn't share herself easily. Reid would plop down on the couch in his family room while she was doing her homework and just sit and chat about the day or what his plans were for his future. He talked about his brother, Nolan, who was the captain of the debate team, explained the rudiments of baseball, how to throw a curve and slider, where he'd like to finish out his pitching career.

Then he'd probe her life, ask what she liked in school, what she and Jaco did for fun, but he was more intrigued with her past than with her present, and he would ask her questions about it.

"What part of Brazil are you from?"

"Campinas. It's about six hours west of Rio."

"De Janeiro?"

"Si. You've heard of it?"

"Who hasn't? Parties and stuff. They have a carnival every year, don't they?"

"It's the biggest in the world."

"Did you ever get to go to one?"

She always looked around to make sure her mother wasn't in earshot before telling him anything, her voice a low whisper.

"No. Papi promised he'd take me when I turned sixteen, but that never happened."

"What happened to him? Did he die or something?"

"No. He left. He has a new family now. I don't see him anymore."

He leaned towards her, his tone hard.

"That must suck."

She noticed something like kindness seep into the next question.

"Is that why you moved here?"

She scanned the area again to make sure no one was listening.

"I guess. Mama doesn't speak of it."

Her mother had forbidden any mention of their father or their time in Brazil and she'd only found out bits and pieces of her father's current life from listening to the adult chatter that went on all around her.

There was no messy divorce because Paolo dos Santos and Juliana Escovado had never gotten married. They had loved, fought, made up, loved, and fought during the first seven years of her life, but she knew nothing else. She thought it would go on forever. Fear and loneliness had edged out happiness when her father had moved out and had completely taken over when her mother moved them to the United States. They had jumped from one place to the next, until at last there had been some stability and a lessening of grief as time went by.

"Do you think you'll ever go back?"

"To live?"

"That or visit?"

"I'd like to, but from what I hear it's a lot different now. Besides my brother is here and I won't leave him."

As if giving her his philosophy on life, he strayed from the topic. It was the closest he'd ever come to talking about the estrangement that had occurred in the family.

"Adults do some pretty dumb things. I'm sure you've noticed how much things have changed around here. Kids don't ever get a choice in what's going on in their lives. They just have to move when told and deal with it, get shut out and told to shut up."

"You are right. But someday I'd like to go see my Papi. Ask him why he left us."

"You won't get an answer. Even they don't know what they're doing half the time."

He hadn't been right about that.

She had gotten the answer she was looking for from her father. It was Paolo dos Santos who'd reached out right after her mother's death. The demons that plagued her over his abandonment hadn't been exorcised, but she'd given him the opportunity to explain his actions.

He had not let her go as easily as she'd been led to believe.

Her mother had forbidden any contact and refused any money, which he had offered in child support. Izabella had seen traces of bitterness in her mother's heart, heard the disparaging remarks made about Paolo. Izabella thought it was because he'd left them destitute.

But she had been wrong.

He hadn't betrayed his children, Julianna had.

Out of spite, Julianna had taken his children away from him without notice and had closed off any possibility of contact between father and children. Even if it meant they went without.

The revelation stung and she still had a hard time believing that her mother had done that to them. It had taken a long time to work through her anger at her mother, but with her dead, she'd decided to bury her grievances.

She'd made a couple of trips down to Brazil over the last few years, revisiting the places she'd loved as a child, accompanied by her father, his wife, Livia and their children, regaining the foothold she'd lost by the separation. It was easy to forgive amidst the backdrop of her birthplace, and for as much as she enjoyed visiting it, she knew she'd never go back. She loved her home and her friends and it was where her daughter was born. She had become a citizen when her mother applied for naturalization within five years of immigrating to the United States, and she felt like the American she had become, independent and finally free from most of the demons in her past.

It was during the second trip that Paolo had taken her to the promised Carnival. It had been exciting and enlightening, and the reconnection with her father made her feel loved and treasured.

Reid didn't have to share stories about his childhood with her. She'd known him since she was eleven years old and had seen the close bond he'd had with his mother, the hero worship of his older brother, the fractious relationship he had with his father and the carnage that had resulted when Melinda was hurt so badly.

Julianna had informed her about the accident, her animosity for Steven Jackson and his infidel ways evident in the telling. Her mother was not a forgiving person and the tension between them existed until the day Julianna died, even as she cooked his dinner and took care of his wife.

Reid's grief had been unbearable and she was moved by his sorrow. But the grief had turned to anger when his mother returned home from the rehab facility a changed woman. No longer did he issue words of love and encouragement to his mother, no longer did he beg her to let him in, to talk, laugh or love. Instead there were scathing demands that Melinda find the courage to get better.

She'd refused, unable to step out of her misery, even for her children.

When Reid gave up, he'd started bottling up his feelings until there was no outward sign that he'd been affected by the accident or its aftermath. He controlled the output of who he was as if he needed to protect himself from any kind of exposure.

She had faced something similar, a breakdown of life as she knew it.

They had each faced disruption and dissolution but they had handled it differently. She had found solace in food where he had found no solace at all.

Gathering up her things, slipping her feet back into her shoes, she slung the briefcase over her shoulder. She'd call Reid in the safety of her home where he couldn't touch her.

Reid waited, sat wondering if he dared call her again.

She hadn't answered any one of his texts and he was impatient to hear her voice. There was a savage beast within that needed soothing.

It was almost like they were back in high school, when the need to be in her presence became so overwhelming he'd search her out, grab a corner of the sofa, and talk to her like they were best friends. Always a willing participant, listening as if she cared about him, telling him bits and pieces of her life, past and present, she would make his day a little brighter with her smile. Home was an absolute horror, his mother so consumed with her disability, his father rarely there, and she had become his touchstone. She'd recognized his pain but never questioned him about it, almost absorbing it for him when they were together.

Was that what he needed?

Someone to take the doubt away?

It was asking a hell of a lot.

Irritated at his impatience, he grabbed the book he'd picked up at the mall and lay back against the headboard. Motts had gone out tonight. Although he'd invited him to go along he just wasn't up for it. Flipping to the first page of the new DeMille thriller, he became engrossed almost immediately and was startled when his phone started chiming.

Checking the ID, he smiled before answering. "I had given up hope."

"Someone's had a busy day. I didn't need such a detailed report, though."

When he heard the musical lilt to her voice, he closed his eyes and let it fill him. "Leeni in bed?"

"Yes."

"What are you doing?"

"Talking to you."

"Before you called me."

"Sewing."

"One of those things your mother taught you, right?"

He remembered one of their conversations concerning the old boys network that was alive and well in Brazil. A woman's role centered on domesticity. They cooked, they cleaned, they sewed, they took care of their men.

He had made a crack that it hadn't done her mother any good, and what he'd gotten for his effort was a withering glare.

After a pause, as if her thoughts were moving down the same lane, he said, "I think she used to make blankets."

"Quilts, Reid. They're called quilts."

"She made me one when I was a kid. I think I still have it or maybe my mother does."

He'd have to look around when he got back to the condo. He'd always loved that thing.

"She was really good at it. I just enjoy the stitching."

Julianna only made the decorative quilts for people she loved and she had loved him once. Up until that summer. Or maybe up until the time he'd became hurtful of the other people she cared about, like Melinda. He could be consciously cruel but called it honesty, and his honest appraisal of certain situations had become infuriating to Juliana, and she had stopped catering to him somewhere along the way.

Then a thought flashed across his mind.

"Make me one for my new house?"

"I don't think so. Find my mother's or go buy one. If there's nothing important you need, I'm going to go. It's late and I need my sleep."

"I'm glad you didn't say you were going to bed. It would have created too many visions in my head. Shit, I just did and the visions are breathtaking."

There was a perplexed sigh before she asked, "What is going on with you?"

Taking a minute to think about it, he said, "To be honest, I don't know. But the images I have of you in my head are taking my breath away."

"You need to know I'm not doing this with you again. There's only so many times a person can repeat their mistakes before it becomes pitiful. Besides, I never did like roller coaster rides."

"They make for some pretty intense moments."

"If that's how you want to live your life, fine. But I'd prefer quiet nights and stress-free days. Not something you can offer."

She was right, so he'd better stop there. And he would if he could just get how she looked in his fantasy to go away. Kissable lips, soft skin, breasts that made his mouth water, gorgeous legs.

He wanted to reach through the phone and taste the sweetness.

His body was pressing him on that, but there was nothing he could do until he got back and maybe steal a few kisses like he had in the old days. Although the way it sounded, she wasn't going to let him get that close.

"You going to watch me Thursday?"

"I'm not sure. Maybe if I have nothing better to do."

"I'm not feeling the love... Izabella."

The silence at the other end of the line told him he wasn't going to get what he wanted.

"I guess it's time to go. Till tomorrow."

As he clicked off, the word *porra* crossed the line.

He chuckled.

She knew she was in trouble.

CHAPTER NINE

Wednesday dawned overcast but the rain held off for most of the day. Izabella spent a good part of it with the relocation clients, and she was pleasantly surprised at how well it went. The Garbows were moving from Michigan, and they hoped to be in a house by summer so their children would be acclimated before school started. It had been a stroke of luck that she had gotten to work with them. The person on call was leaving for vacation the next day and had handed the couple off. She was the grateful recipient. She'd booked a dozen showings throughout the area, over several towns, and by some miracle, they'd found a house that suited and an offer was on the table, one she had high hopes for. Although the real estate prices were vastly different in Michigan, the clients had come out with a realistic idea of what they could afford and she had found them something in their price range, in a good school district with most of the updates they were looking for. Yeah for her. This sale would make five closings in June if all went well. In real estate, everything was a crap shoot, so she couldn't spend the money even mentally until the deals were closed and recorded.

The only one she could bank on was Reid's, bless his tiny frozen heart.

The doubt started to sink deep when Melinda called that night to check up on her and Leeni and she told Reid's mother about the sale.

"He bought it."

There was a generous pause before Melinda asked, "And he plans on going through with it?"

It was a disturbing thought but a reasonable question given who they were talking about.

"He's got a hefty deposit down, so I hope so."

"Will wonders never cease. I didn't think he'd do anything that smelled of permanence."

"Oh, *Meu Deus*, now you have me worried."

"I'm sorry Izabella. I shouldn't have said anything. He's determined to be out of my condo before I return, so I'm sure that will get him moving."

She could only hope so. She couldn't bear the thought of not having a garage this coming winter. Not when she'd convinced herself that it was a sure thing.

Biting her lip, she asked, "Why didn't you tell me he was staying at the condo?"

"I wasn't sure he'd take me up on it until he asked for the keys the day before he got back. Everything goes through Nolan, so I'm always a day behind him. Sorry. Has it been a problem?"

"Not really. He asked me if we bought our places together so we'd be near each other."

Melinda chuckled.

"Well, that was my intent."

"I have to admit it wasn't mine. The house was what I could afford, and if my father hadn't helped with the mortgage, I could never have done it, but there was a wonderful side benefit in having you so close."

Melinda had been there for her from the moment she found out she was expecting. Told her that Julianna would want her to watch out for her. And she had, filling the role discreetly but lovingly. Giving her advice when asked but keeping her counsel otherwise. She had adapted her home for an infant and then a growing toddler and had taken on role of adopted grandmother, caring for Leeni at times, when Izabella had to work. And she had been a rock during Leeni's illness. A shoulder to cry on, a helping hand when needed.

The love swelled in her heart at all this woman had done for her.

"Do you want me to pick up some groceries before you get back?"

"You are a sweet girl and I appreciate it. I'm having Honey go in the day before I get there so if Reid has left a mess, I won't have to deal with it. She can pick some things up for me on her way over. I'll be back on the fifteenth of May and I can't wait to get home."

That would be why Reid had insisted on a May seventh closing. It gave him a couple of days wiggle room.

"Leeni can't wait to see you. Do you need a ride home from the airport?"

"Nolan is picking me up and bringing Emma with him. At least I have one son who's willing to spend time with me and a granddaughter I can spoil."

Izabella squirmed in her seat and glanced around as if looking for answers.

"I still don't understand. You two were so close. I thought it was awesome when you'd go out and catch him. Pretty courageous of you, seeing he could really move the ball even back then."

"He tried his best to tone it down but on occasion they'd be more heat than I could handle. Ended up with quite a few bruises on my arm."

He'd only been twelve or thirteen back then. And she'd been a vibrant woman.

"I couldn't have continued once he got on the varsity team even if I could walk. His high speed was high speed. Even his father gave up after a while."

It was Reid who'd terminated his father as catcher. The rift had been deep and wide by then.

It was hard watching the relationship between mother and son fall apart. Melinda had needed all the support she could get back then. And encouragement. When she'd finally turned the corner, she'd realized what she had done and had mourned the loss of her son more deeply than the lost use of her legs.

Izabella had tried to get through to him in the years that followed but to no avail. He refused to discuss his mother and her handicap. Even now, after all these years, there was still a jagged edge. She thought it sad that he remembered the mother who'd given up, had crawled into herself. Mired in that memory, he couldn't open his eyes to see who she'd become.

Izabella stuck her needle in the pin cushion on her wrist when Melinda asked, "He's set to pitch tomorrow, isn't he?"

"Yes. Keith's flying out there. He says the famous Crackerjacks is a bit nervous."

"You don't say?"

"I can't conceive of anything that would put a nick in that one's self-confidence."

"He's wanted to play for this team since he was in diapers. Well, maybe a bit later than that but as far back as I can remember. And the media *is* hyping him up. It's no wonder he's a bit worried."

Minutely shaking her head, she admitted, "Ever since the open house, he's been calling me a lot."

"Ah, that would be in line with what he's feeling if Keith is right. You always were his security blanket."

She bolted forward, the quilt slipping off her legs and onto the floor.

"I was what?"

"His security blanket. He knew he was safe with you. Felt protected. Didn't have to turn the on the charm."

She laughed nervously. "I don't think so."

She leaned down to secure the quilt back on her lap.

"My dear. He might not have talked to me, but he was still my son and I could always read him. My accident changed him or should I say my bout with self-pity did. He didn't feel loved, which fed some of his insecurities. He won't let anyone see them. Except you."

"I remember a lot of wisecracks and hurtful things hurled my way."

It wasn't all she remembered but all she'd admit to.

"That was to prevent you from getting too close."

"Another successful maneuver by the mighty Jacks."

"I had always hoped—"

She quickly diverted the topic, not wanting Melinda to say it out loud. "Have you watched the games?"

"Not yet but I will most definitely be watching on Thursday."

Feeling the hurt she knew Melinda must be feeling, she said, "I'm sorry."

"For what dear?"

"I'm sorry he's such a jerk."

"That would be my fault, not yours. I never should have let my...handicap, affect my relationship with my boys. If I could go back I would but...all I can do is love him and hope one day he can forgive me."

Izabella heard a flutter in the familiar voice. Melinda cleared it and asked, "How's Leeni feeling?"

"Pretty good. She's had low-grade fevers in the last couple of weeks, which I'm worried about, but there's been no bruising, no joint pain. We see the doctor next month, so I guess I'll know more then."

"I hope you'll still let me watch her from time to time."

"I was hoping you'd say that. I don't like her being at school such long hours so I was counting on your offer. We could repeat what we did last year. With Sofia, pregnant and Addie working part-time, I'm going to be wearing out our welcome."

"That, my dear Izabella, could never happen."

"I'll call you Friday and we can compare notes."

"You'll be watching?"

"Of course not. You know I don't like baseball."

She heard the soft chuckle before she hung up.

Izabella picked up the remote and found the channel that televised the game before taking up the task at hand. Keogh was pitching tonight and they were in the fifth inning. It was of no real interest although she hoped they did well. Watching at her own peril, she was hoping to see Reid out in the bullpen. She'd never get tired of seeing the smile when he was out of the spotlight. He'd be himself out there and he'd have the guys laughing and joking around. He made friends quickly and kept them. At least the male variety. Women would come and go. He'd find an excuse and move on and there were some good excuses.

Leaning forward, she watched Ovitz at the plate. Dante was the anchor of the team, and she enjoyed the way the crowd rallied around him. If he could do some damage, the team could get their second win, which would be a good way to start the year. Sitting back after his strike out, she picked out the pins of the square she'd finished. The quilt she was working on was for Leeni's bed. It had been sitting in the upstairs closet for a couple of years, but something made her pull it out yesterday. Fingering a square that came from one of Leeni's onesies, she wondered again what Reid was trying to sell her and why.

As she wove the needle in and out joining the squares together, she began to relax into the moment, letting all thought fade away.

Reid lay on the bed, his arms under his head, using the quiet to soothe his riotous stomach. His roommate had taken off for breakfast, but he couldn't even conceive of putting food in his system this morning. Today he'd be taking the mound for the first time in a Greenliner uniform and he was nearing panic proportions. Just entering the Phillies clubhouse yesterday, his duffel over his shoulder, had given him a never-ending stream of shock waves. Becoming a member of the team had been a lifelong dream, but now that it had become an actuality, he was wondering what the hell he'd been thinking. The fans were the most knowledgeable in the world and they didn't have much patience for mediocrity; the reporters were always looking for something to criticize and complain about and he didn't want to be the fodder for the press.

Yesterday, he'd cautiously approached his locker, looking around at his new teammates, trying to determine if his initiation was complete or if they were watching him speculatively. Already put through his hazing, he still went over his full uniform with a fine-tooth comb. It had been a good thing. He had found a wad of chewing gum on the bottom of his cleats, just another example of the cumulative and frightening sense of humor that seemed to exist among the players. Jokes were played randomly on whomever seemed the most vulnerable.

He could only hope they'd leave him alone today.

As soon as he showered and shaved, dressed in suit and tie, he ambled out to the lobby to join the guys for their ride over to the stadium. He could still feel the palpitations pounding in his chest although there wasn't any physical reason for it. He'd been working with Mulligan, the new pitching coach, over the last few days and knew his pitches were there. His fastball was getting back up to speed, his curve was dipping when it should and he felt strong.

He didn't understand the tension. Usually there was anxiety, anticipation, and a rush of adrenaline, but he'd never felt this before, not even on his first professional outing. The reporters had been all over him, and although his outward persona was still in place, he just hoped he had the stuff to back up his arrogant claim that he could still knock them dead. There was some doubt, a pitcher's real enemy, and it seemed it had found a home in his gut.

Over the last year, there'd been a shift. His attitude was still there but the cockiness was gone. After a bad year, more than a few rough outings, he'd been knocked off-center. Even his luck had deserted him. It was the difference between a ball hit to a glove or a ball lobbed in a stumbling hip-hop fashion falling inches away from a diving catch. And it was as if the front office of the Athletes had known, had been watching for the signs.

The day he'd been informed of the trade, he hadn't been that surprised. There'd been a time he thought he'd spend his entire career in Oakland. The fans loved him, the press chased after him, and his stats were impeccable. Although he had fallen down the rotation totem pole, he was still considered one of their best. With no rumors or stirrings in the clubhouse or press, he'd thought he was just imagining the worst. And then the call had come. They'd wanted him gone. Due to his longevity in both the league and on the team, he'd gotten to choose whether to stay or go. Even though ownership was determined to trade him, he didn't have to agree to it. He asked himself who'd choose to stay where he wasn't respected or valued, especially in the prime of their career. Interest from the Greenliners gave him the impetus he needed to agree.

There was no more waiting. The day had come.

The national anthem had just finished, and Matt DeBartolo and Jesse Reams were doing their bit, giving the audience the background information on the pitcher who had just recently arrived from Oakland. The buildup was mind-numbing, and Izabella wondered how he could possibly meet the expectations thrust upon his shoulders.

Sitting on the couch, Leeni beside her, Hoover laying at their feet, she had a bowl of popcorn at the ready so when her nerves started getting edgy she'd have something to do with her hands.

"Come on already."

"Are you going to talk to the TV tonight?"

Izabella looked at her daughter and smiled.

"Probably. You know the man who brought you the Tripoli box?"

"Uh-huh. Mr. Crackerjacks."

She snuffled a smile at the use of that name.

"He's playing tonight."

Getting onto her knees, and leaning into her mother she asked eagerly, "He is?"

"Yes. He's the pitcher and he should be...."

Before she could finish the sentence, Reid was striding across the field from the bullpen. She pointed to the screen. "Look, there he is."

Izabella's stomach roiled and her heart lurched.

This was going to be three hours of torture. The thing she disliked about baseball was how slowly it moved. She would have to agonize over every pitch, move it mentally with her mind so it would cross the strike zone, and hold her breath with every line drive. For nine long innings, if he made it that far into the game.

Watching his warm-ups, she puzzled at his wind-up. He was off a bit. Too long in his pivot. Not enough follow-through.

"Is he the one you talk to?"

Pulling her focus from the screen and the man she was beginning to worry about, she looked at Leeni and asked, "The one I talk to? On the phone?"

"No, at the TV. You tell him to frow strikes."

"I don't."

"Uh-huh."

Tickling her daughter to hear her giggle, she said, "You're imagining things."

Oakland games weren't televised locally, so she had to buy the MLB package from her cable company. It was a rare occasion that she would see him pitch, but each and every game would find her in front of the TV. Or in the stands.

Someone had noticed.

Leeni wrestled away, stood up on the couch, balancing on the cushions as best she could. Her hands went to her hips, her chin slanted at an angle and Izabella had to stifle the laughter at the imperious sight.

The tone had gotten huffy.

"I am not. You even get mad at him when he doesn't listen to you."

Taking the small hand away from the hip, she pulled her daughter into her lap and squeezed.

"Well, that's a silly thing for me to do."

Brushing back a strand of her mother's hair that had escaped from the elastic, Leeni said, "It's not silly if you want him to win. You must like him better than Unca Rique, cause you don't yell at him."

Izabella felt a blush creep up into her cheeks. She had been so transparent that a three-year-old had figured out the truth.

Watching the game had been torture.

And she had yelled at him, inning after inning.

The only comic relief came when Leeni started to mimic her.

"Come on Mr. Crackerjacks. What are you frowing sliders for?"

Or asking questions.

"Mama, what's a slider?"

He held his own, but he was not his usual brilliant self. She had seen less and less of that brilliance as the years wore on, flashes of it here and there, but not a lot of staying power.

That was an interesting thought.

Maybe his pitching was just catching up with his philosophy on life.

Leeni had fallen asleep halfway through the game so she'd paced without constraint, jabbered at him without hesitation, yelled at the officials and waved off long fly balls.

When he was replaced in the seventh, she flopped onto the couch physically and emotionally drained.

He couldn't be accused of pitching badly. He'd had a quality start, less than three runs against him, but he left the field looking more than a little dejected.

If the guys held on to the lead, Reid might be able to put this in the win column.

They did. His Greenliner stats sat at one and zero.

The game hadn't been over for long before Melinda called. Skipping a greeting, she went right to an assessment of Reid's outing.

"Okay, that wasn't too bad."

"Yeah, it was a win but it was pure luck. His throwing was less than spectacular. That's going to be tough for him to accept."

"I agree. Like I used to tell him back in high school though, you can't be great every night."

"Did he listen?"

"Not to a word I said if you remember correctly. Of course, he was barely talking to me at that point. I should have gone to some of his games. Not let this foolish contraption keep me from them. He asked often enough his freshman year."

"Melinda, don't do this to yourself. He will never know what you were dealing with."

"No. He dealt with something entirely different. I think they call it abandonment."

"I think that's a bit extreme, don't you?"

"I think I hit the nail right on the head. Not only that, I transmitted the idea to Reid that image is important. That looks take priority over everything else and what is flawed must be shunned at all cost. Not the best legacy to leave."

Melinda had refused every one of her son's requests. He'd never seemed bothered at all by her infirmity, only by the fact that she let it debilitate her. Melinda had been too embarrassed by her immobility and her wheelchair to be out in public. She had shut both of her sons out. During his sophomore year, one of them had closed not only the door but his heart as well.

Nothing Izabella said seemed to change Melinda's perception of herself as a failed mother. Even though her life up to the moment of impact had been her children.

"He's a grown man now. It's time for him to take responsibility for his life. The past might mold us, but we have the ability to change it if we want to. Like you did."

"And you, my dear."

"Someday he'll get it."

"I hope so for his sake."

"I love you. You take care."

"I love you, too. Give Leeni a hug for me."

"I will."

As soon as the call ended, gathering her strength, she lifted Leeni up and carried her up to bed. Sitting down on the edge, she stroked the fine hair, love bubbling up and filling her.

There was so much she wished she could give her. So much she still worried about.

After she kissed her cheek, pulling the covers up and tucking her in, she'd switched on the night- light, given Hoover a pat on the head, and returned to the living room to check in on the score.

Her phone told her she had a text so she picked it up and scanned the message.

Arm still holding. Should have done better.

Knowing she shouldn't encourage him but needing to connect, she typed back.

Glad to hear about arm. Pivot off.

How?

Weak follow through.

You think?

Need more of a thrust.

Will watch video. Thanks for watching.

I don't know what you're talking about. I don't like baseball.

So, you keep saying.

Gotta go. Goodnight.

She plugged her phone in for the night and headed up to bed wanting no further communication with him. If the present resembled the past, they could have kept it going for hours.

CHAPTER TEN

He geared up for the next series, a three-game run in New York, even though he wouldn't see any pitching time there. With four days between battles, which was how he viewed a pitching duel, he had to fill the time with things that kept his mind laser sharp and his body combat ready. Jogging three to five miles a day, added to ninety minutes of weight training, would help him maintain physical prowess. It was what to do with his mind that was always the problem. Some of the guys here were into martial arts for the mental focus; some were bookworms. Since arriving in Boston, he'd taken to doing the *New York Times* crossword puzzle every night. He was also reading all he could about baseball, becoming an expert on the league stats. It was interesting stuff that was engaging and purposeful. He had almost gotten the hang of not carousing every night, surprised that the conservation of sexual energy was giving him an advantage. At this stage of his career he needed everyone he could find.

When they arrived at Citi Field, the fans waiting outside the bus greeted them enthusiastically. He'd noticed a lot of his shirts being worn by the faithful and he only wished he'd get a turn at pitching here this weekend. The tangled history between the teams went back over a century. Watching the Greenliners since he was a toddler, he'd seen the ups and downs of the club's rivalry. Lately it was only the press and the fans that perpetuated it, but the upcoming games would still pit antagonist against antagonist. They were division rivals, competitors in the race for the National League pennant and the World Series Championship.

He immediately met with the pitching coach to go over the video from his last game, analyzing his wind-up and follow-through. Reid pointed out what Izabella had noticed, and they agreed she was right. For someone who claimed not to like the sport, she was extremely good at diagnostics. Either that or she was just extremely good at pointing out his flaws.

He'd have to make adjustments to his follow-through. He was drifting a bit down the mound.

Picking up his phone, he punched in a text and sent it.

Good call. I'm drifting.

Not two seconds later there was a response.

Then get an oar.

Without any time to respond, she'd sent another message.

Don't bother me I'm busy.

He chuckled.

The day was starting out extremely well.

The end was nothing short of ridiculous.

The outing that night lasted sixteen innings, six hours and nine minutes, ending at close to two thirty in the morning when Cashman and Banco turned a double play. It was the longest game in Greenliner history but at least they came away with the win. The game would certainly have gotten coverage but the teams managed to make it a compelling reason to return to the idea that their story was rich in animosity. It had been fraught with tension and although neither team was in the running for any trophies, the rivalry had regained its traction.

———

Izabella woke up on the couch early Saturday morning. She couldn't believe the Greenliners were still playing when she'd fallen asleep sometime after midnight. So engrossed in the marathon, she'd been determined to watch until the end, but her body had decided otherwise. Massaging her shoulder, sore because of the way she'd slept, she put her attention on the television, which was still on. Clicking it to the station she knew would have the final score, she waited impatiently. It took a couple minutes before the announcers began animatedly discussing the history-making event.

"Come on already. Just tell me the score."

"Mama?"

She glanced to see Leeni just coming down the last step and extended her arms for a good- morning hug.

"You talkin' to Mr. Crackerjacks again?"

"No *querida*. I just want to know the score and they," she said pointing to the screen, "won't tell me."

Leeni sat quietly on her lap, as if as interested in the outcome as her mother. The news team finally got around to what she was waiting for.

"Yes, they won."

Leeni raised her hand to give her a high-five, then began twirling her mother's hair.

"Where am I going today?"

Looking down into the upturned eyes, Izabella smiled.

"Stephanie is picking you up from school around three and you are coming home. Mama should be here in time for dinner."

"Yeah." she said clapping her hands.

Stephanie had been a godsend. Available afternoons, weekends, and some nights she was an early childhood major at the local college and she lived in the condo complex where Melinda did and Leeni loved her.

"Can we go to Chucky Cheese?"

"That might be doable."

Maybe she'd call Sofia and see if she wanted to take Junie and Holly. Even though they had just been there, there wasn't a kid alive who didn't love the place.

As she reached for her phone, it rang.

When she picked it up, she noticed it was almost out of charge. She'd have to plug it in before

she left. A real estate agent without an available phone was like… a pitcher without a pitch. Didn't bode well for success.

Then she noticed who the call was from.

She skipped hello.

"What do you want this morning?"

"Did you see the game?"

She had to keep up with what was becoming her script, so she asked, "What game?"

"We didn't even get back to the hotel until close to four a.m."

"And you're already up?"

It wasn't even seven-thirty yet.

"Yeah. Couldn't sleep. Too much adrenaline. The one good thing about a day off is you get to catch up."

"What's on for today?"

"Some of the guys are going to hang out at a place nearby, shoot some pool. Motts asked if I wanted to join them."

"He's the catcher, right?"

"One of them. He's the guy I'm rooming with."

"Sounds like fun. Last time Leeni and I were there, we went to the Bronx Zoo."

"When?"

"Two years ago, with my dad and Livia. We went to see a couple of Rique's games."

"Who does this half-brother play for?"

"You probably don't want to know."

"Who?"

"He plays for the Syracuse Mets, but from what I hear, he's just been called up."

"New York?"

"Yeah. Ironic, isn't it?"

"What position does he play?"

"Shortstop."

"He'll be on the field tonight."

The regular Mets infielder was just placed on the disabled list.

"I know."

"Who will you root for?"

"Phone is dying. Gotta recharge. Say hi to him for me. Bye."

He did as she asked, introducing himself after he'd watched her brother hit a three-run homer that sailed over the bullpen. They were already losing, and it only

added to the carnage.

As he approached him, he admitted only to himself that the kid had a promising future

"I think I know your half-sister. She said to say hello."

"You must mean my sister, Izabella?"

He had dropped the half, which was telling.

"Yeah, I've known her for years."

"I have heard this. She is quite beautiful, wouldn't you say? With a beautiful heart."

The young ballplayer was staring into his eyes as if searching for something.

"She is. She does."

"A man's dream come true, don't you think?"

How did he know...

The conversation had turned on him and he needed to distance himself. Backing away, he moved towards the visiting team's locker room.

"I gotta go. Good luck."

"*Graci*. Same to you."

He felt Enrique's eyes on his back until he disappeared down into the dugout.

He was glad to be getting out of New York.

It was time to go home.

After slipping her shoes on, finally able to wear her sandals without the dreaded nylons, Izabella fastened the clasp of her gold-plate necklace over her two-piece white-and-black-striped skirt set. Long sleeves were still needed but she felt she could skip the coat today. The sun was peeking through already, and the forecast was for an unseasonably warm sixty-degrees.

She had to be at the office at eight-thirty this morning for her first appointment and still had to drop Leeni off at Sofia's. Since she had an appointment scheduled late in the day, Sofia offered to keep Leeni for supper so Izabella didn't have to work in shifts. Mrs. Camara, Sofia's mom, had agreed to help out, and Keith was picking the woman up before he went to work. Izabella was more than grateful.

There had been no text this morning and she was mildly disappointed. It was a way to flirt with fate without the dangerous proximity of the man and his flesh.

As she glanced up into the mirror, fragments of a face came unbidden and filled her vision.

The laughing eyes, the stubborn chin, the crooked nose that had been broken when one of his fastballs had been returned straight on while he was in high school.

It was kind of surreal to know he was home.

He had always said he'd play for this team someday.

Most thought it was a little league dream.

Some of his friends had laughed.

But she had believed him. Not once had she ever doubted he'd get his wish.

He was too good.

Watching him back then, she was mesmerized by the strength and power in his windup, his throw, the ball disappearing into the catcher's mitt in the blink of an eye.

The only thing that would tear her away would be her mother's voice announcing their departure. She'd silently pray that Mrs. Jackson would find some other chore to keep her mother busy for a little longer so she could keep her vigil.

He had been an impressive sight even then.

She knew he'd have a great future if he stayed disciplined, but she had never expected his future to come hurtling back into her present. She was beginning to like him again. And that spelled trouble with a capital T. His charm could be deadly.

She pressed her lips together to put the finishing touches on her gloss and let out a breath as the phone rang.

Her heart skipped a beat, just one gratefully, but she walked a little too fast for her own good to pick up the phone. Bracing herself for the call that would test her stamina, for a voice that could turn her to jelly, she sighed when she saw the name on the display.

Getting up as much enthusiasm as she could muster, she answered.

"Mike. Hi. When did you get back?"

"Last night. Too late to call, but early enough that I lay in bed wishing I could talk to you."

Not knowing how to answer that, knowing she couldn't answer it the way he expected her to, she asked, "Was the trip successful?"

"Yes. I think we're coming to terms and an agreement on the take-over."

"That's great. Are we still on for tomorrow?"

"We are and I have a surprise for you. Dress casually and be ready by five."

"Like jeans casual or professional casual?"

She never knew with Mike.

"Jeans."

Just what she was hoping for. She dressed for work every day, and it was nice to just get comfortable.

"How long are you in town for this time?"

"I just got a call. I have to be in Lisbon on Wednesday. I'll probably hop a plane right after we say good night. Did you sell the Costello place?"

"Yes. At the open house. It feels good."

Secure, like a warm blanket.

"That's great. You can tell me all about it tomorrow. Don't forget to bring along one of your smiles."

If he could have seen her face, he would have read consternation on it.

"I won't. See you then."

His "okay" sounded too hopeful, and she feared he was going to force an issue they had been at odds over. He was pressing for a more intimate relationship and that was not what she wanted with him. After Patrick, she'd decided to remain independent until Leeni was a bit older.

Celibate was a better word for it. She had been able to keep Mike at arm's length but she had a feeling his magnanimity was coming to an end.

They had only been going out for a couple months, if you could call it that, whenever he was in town or unoccupied with his workaholic lifestyle. It was one of the reasons she had agreed to the first date. She knew she wouldn't be in danger of falling in love with him. She'd thought it would be a night out with adult conversation, away from the routine of her life. But he was the CEO of a merger consortium, and although he spent his time flying around the globe taking companies apart and selling them off, the conversations had been a bit boring and stilted. She had tried to draw him out about the places he'd visited but it was as if he never saw the interesting aspects, only the work that drew him there.

It was time to end it, which she would do tomorrow.

She was beginning to understand that she would never have another relationship with the same colors or intensity as she'd had with Reid. That he had extinguished it before it really got started didn't change anything. He was back and the textures were still as bold and bright as they had been. Her memory hadn't exaggerated a thing and other men only paled in comparison.

His kisses had been deep and sensual, wet and wild, his tongue had invaded her mouth skillfully, and he'd taught her how to respond in kind. His touch was incredibly tender, fingers cradling her face, hands roaming over her in exploration, creating a deep ache that he refused to fill.

Attentive for days and then no call for a week. Fully present or completely absent.

A figment of her imagination or so real she could taste it.

And when he'd given in, she'd taken completely and without reservation.

"Mama is breakfast ready yet?"

Leeni came running into the kitchen, her dress on backwards, a glob of toothpaste glued to her cheek, and her shoes on the wrong feet.

Izabella smiled at her daughter and hoped like her mother before her, she had what it took to raise a child without a father. After fixing the dress and the shoes, she gently wiped the paste from her cheek and announced, "We are going to have a breakfast like Mama used to have when she was little."

Thoughts of her mother stirred something inside her and she wanted to go back to her roots. "Like Grandma Juliana made for you?"

Tying her apron on, she answered, "*Sí.*"

"When you lived in Bazil?"

Reaching into the freezer, she took out some of the cheesy rolls her father had brought her on his last visit and popped them into the microwave to defrost. She stuffed the bread as a pocket with some ham and mozzarella cheese she retrieved from the refrigerator and put them into the oven to bake. After pouring a glass of orange juice, she placed it in front of Leeni, then refilled her empty coffee mug,

Just as she was about to join her daughter at the table to describe what she was making, the doorbell rang.

Her heart skipped several beats this time because she couldn't imagine who else would be on her side porch at seven in the morning. This was crazy. It would have given him only a few hours of sleep if she estimated their return flight correctly.

"Who's here, Mama?"

"I don't know yet."

"Well, open the door."

And she did.

Leeni cried out, running to the door, "Mr. Crackerjacks. Did you bring me goodies?"

Reid looked a bit ashamed that he had forgotten his promise.

"The bakery wasn't open when I got in this morning but maybe someday this week I'll have time to get there."

"It's okay. Mama is making me the kind of breakfast she used to eat when she lived in Brazil."

His attention went from the little girl, to her mother.

Pushing the obsidian tresses off her face, she spun around without really inviting him in. With nothing to block his way, he followed her.

"What are you having?"

The kitchen was filled with the incredible aroma of baking bread, and she could almost see his mouth water.

"Juliana used to make the most delicious cheese bread stuffed with ham. My brother Nolan and I couldn't get enough of them. What are they called again?"

"Pao de queijo."

"Yeah, that's right." Sneaking a peek into the oven, he asked, "They looked just like this. Do you have enough to share?"

Leeni leaned forward, a fork and spoon in her hands.

"I'll share with you, Mr. Crackerjacks."

A quiet voice packed with a warning admonished, "You need a good breakfast. You will eat what I give you."

Bending over the oven to extract the steaming doughy goodness, she admitted, wondering if she had made extra just in case he showed up, "There are enough if you don't go back for thirds." After placing the baking sheet on top of the stove and turning the heat off, she busied herself with plates and reached in the cabinet for another coffee mug. Lifting it she asked, "Do you want some?"

"*Yes*, please. I haven't stocked up on anything yet and Melinda doesn't touch the stuff. I'll probably take thirds of that if you have it."

Her daughter's voice bubbled up, "I know someone named Melinda. She lives right over there."

Leeni was pointing to the window and what lay beyond.

Plucking the still hot rolls onto separate plates, Izabella explained, "Melinda is Reid's mother, querida."

"She is?"

Reid took a seat and nodded his answer.

Giving her daughter what she really wanted, she explained, "Reid is staying at her house until he moves into his new one."

Reid couldn't miss the excitement emanating from Leeni as she proclaimed, "She's coming back from Florida soon. I can't wait. I missed her sooo much."

Reid's head snapped up, his focus on the delicious morsel momentarily lost.

Leeni continued now that she had his attention. "When she's living there I can go stay with her when Mama is at work. We have so much fun."

He stared incredulously at the little girl before asking, "You have fun with Melinda?"

Leeni cocked her head to the side and examined Reid before asking, "Why don't you call her Mama?"

Pulling apart the roll, he popped a piece into his mouth as if to stall, then looked to Izabella for help.

Pondering what to say, not wanting to weigh Leeni down with the real answer, she went with the most plausible one for a three-year-old.

"Reid is a man now, *paquita*. He calls his mother by her first name."

The child looked up, her eyes serious in their expression. "I will always call you Mama even when I'm a hundred."

"I will like that, my love."

She reached over so she could kiss the small cheek. "Now eat your breakfast so we can get going."

Reid had gotten up, raising his mug in her direction, asking, "Can I have another cup before you go?"

"Of course. There's one more roll if you want it."

"Aren't you having any?"

"I had some yogurt and granola before you came over. I'm good."

He plucked the last cheese bread off the sheet, and it was half-gone by the time he regained his seat.

She was glad she had already eaten because she would have lost her appetite for food as soon as she saw him. Even dressed down he looked edible.

Rubbing the rim of her coffee cup, not wanting to look in his direction, she asked, "What time do you have to be at the park?"

He was dressed in sweats and a tee shirt, so she knew he still had time until he left for Boston.

"I have to leave in a couple of hours. I haven't jogged yet, probably shouldn't have eaten anything, although they were worth the side stitch I know will come."

After getting up, Izabella cleared off the table, rinsed the dishes and filled the dishwasher before taking her apron off and hanging it on the hook by the door.

She began to fiddle with her hair, and when she was done, it was plaited and off her face, except for the stubborn piece that refused to stay contained.

"You look beautiful this morning, Izabella."

She wasn't ready for the compliment and she felt a blush creep up her neck. She stammered a simple thank you before insisting, "You have to go now."

Busy stuffing her iPad, portfolio, and small black book into a satchel, she didn't notice Reid's continued appraisal. She could feel that the blush had reached her face, so she kept her head down as she slung the bag over her shoulder and headed to the door.

Leeni slid off her chair, put on her jacket, and stood beside her mother before addressing the man just getting up out of the chair.

"I wish you were going to stay living there. Then both of you could babysitted me."

"I'll make sure I visit when I can. If it's all right with your mama."

He escorted them out of the door and to the car. She could feel him watching as she got Leeni buckled in, a book resting in the small hands.

Before Izabella could slide behind the steering wheel, she heard him say, "Come to my game on Thursday."

"Thank you for the invitation but I don't think it's a good idea."

"Why not?"

"You might get the impression you've won. And you haven't."

Without giving him a chance to try and convince her, she climbed into the car.

He stepped out of her way as she eased towards the street, but he was staring at her and she fell into his eyes.

Snapping herself out of the trance, she gave him a brief wave and maneuvered out of the driveway.

CHAPTER ELEVEN

The anticipated call came just as Izabella was clearing up the breakfast dishes.

"Good morning."

His voice was a gentle swell washing over her.

She wanted to ask what he'd been doing since dawn but knew that might give away the fact she had looked for movement in the condo across the street.

"Good game yesterday."

"For Sutherland."

He was another trade in the Greenliner's pursuit of an ace.

There was a pause before he asked, "Hey, I was wondering if you've changed your mind about the game. Maybe I need to remind you it's my first one here and all."

"It's a night game. Maybe I need to remind you I have a daughter."

"Could she have a sleepover at Keith and Sofia's?"

He didn't need to know she had a date tonight and a sleepover was already in place. She couldn't make it two in a row. Nor did she know if she could sit in the stands and watch him pitch. Too public for her reactions and anxiety.

"For as much as she'd like that, no."

"You sure do have the word no down to a science."

"Been practicing since bumping into you at the open house."

"I can't ask you to have dinner with me for the next, oh, five months but maybe you can come in for lunch one day."

"I've got a very busy schedule over the next, oh, five months, so maybe not."

"I'm going to be working on ways to make the no work for me."

"Knock yourself out."

When she ended the call, she stared at the phone.

Would she outlast his siege?

Smiling to herself, she knew she would. This man had no staying power at all.

When she got to Sofia's, her friend hugged her as soon as she entered.

"I'm so glad to see you. I feel as if we haven't spent any time together lately."

"Well, you've been sick and I've been busy. We'll plan lunch someday and catch up. I'll see if Stephanie has any free time in the next week or so."

Sofia smiled down at Leeni. "The girls are upstairs getting dressed. Do you want to go join them?"

"Yes, please."

Isabella bent down and kissed her on each cheek. "I will pick you up tomorrow *querida*. You be a good girl for Sofia."

"I will Mama. I love you."

"I love you too."

And with that the little girl raced up the stairs to play with her friends, Izabella's eyes watching her the whole way up, scrutinizing every move.

An older woman strode through the archway, wiping her hands on a kitchen towel, her white hair short and curly, her eyes as warm and golden as the sun.

"Who is thees Stephanie? I can certainly manage three little girls all by myself. I don't know whether you know it or not but I raised four children."

Embracing her, Izabella said, "Mrs. Camara. It's so nice to see you. And those children turned out great. You've got my vote for babysitter."

Keith ambled in, a coffee mug in his hand.

"You going out tonight with that guy you met at the fundraiser?"

"Yeah, although I think it will be the final hurrah. He's obsessed with himself."

Blowing her bangs off her forehead she added, "I seem prone to those."

Referring to one of them, Keith said, "I got a call asking if we'd watch Leeni tomorrow tonight so you could attend a baseball game. I didn't know what to tell him."

"I already told him I wouldn't. What is it about the word no that he doesn't understand?"

Keith shrugged his shoulders, then asked, "Do you have a reason?"

She tilted her head, surprised that Keith was asking the question. With a hint of annoyance in her voice, she said, "I didn't know that was required."

He must have read the warning, because he backed off, injecting humor into his next statement.

"I thought you might want to see him, first game and all."

"Well, you thought wrong. My couch is comfortable, the drinks are free, the food is better, I don't have to miss the action because someone is stopped in front of my seat or get a beer shampoo…"

Laughing he said, "I get it."

Switching her pocketbook from one shoulder to the other she asked him, "Are you going?"

"Planning on it. My mother-in-law has graciously agreed to…stay with her grandchildren so I can take Sofia."

"I'd be more than happy to keep them at my house. I feel I'm not reciprocating at all and the scales are way out of balance."

Sofia put her mind at ease, "Leeni is no trouble at all. We love having her. Mama is staying overnight and Keith will be here, so I have all the hands I need."

Keith asked, "Where are you going tonight?"

Pushing the sleeves of her jacket up, she admitted, "I don't know. He originally told me he'd pick me up at five, but he texted and changed it to three. I almost balked but a couple of glasses of wine and a good dinner seemed too tempting to pass up. The conversation usually only goes in one direction but he did ask me about the Costello house so I guess he does listen to some of the things I say."

Throwing her purse over her shoulder, Izabella headed for the door.

"Thanks again for this. I really appreciate it."

"If you change your mind about tomorrow night, let us know. It would be fun being together."

"I don't think so. I don't need to be there to watch him, and your mother doesn't need one more added to the mix."

Kissing her on the cheek, Sofia suggested, "Have a nice night."

"I'll try."

She was staring mindlessly out the car window. Mike was absorbed by the heavy traffic and his Blue-tooth. He hadn't said much to her all the way into town, taking call after call. It was making her feel easier about the way the night would end. She didn't need a puppy dog dance but she did expect a bit of attention from the person she was with.

Her phone had pinged a couple of times, and checking to make sure it wasn't Sofia, she saw the same number come up, then tucked it back in her purse. She refused to see what Reid wanted. His texts and calls were becoming more and more frequent, and she was getting jittery with the overload of attentiveness. She wasn't going to dwell on him or his games tonight. Pushing him out of her mind, she engrossed herself in some of the worries that had cropped up over the last couple of days. Would the two sales that were up in the air fall apart or close? One had been doomed by a home inspection, and if the owners weren't willing to renegotiate the price, she had a feeling that she'd be back to square one and back out with the clients looking for a replacement. The Seifords had found a house they liked, and by the grace of some higher power it looked like the offer might move towards a Purchase and Sale Agreement.

Then Reid was there again, on the fringes of her mind.

Porra. Shit. This had to stop.

Stomping him out, she flicked her eyes out the window to the crowded off-ramp.

Sitting up in her seat, finally becoming aware of her surroundings, she gulped, glimpsing the green traffic sign and the rotary up ahead and the familiar terrain that went with it.

Holding her breath, she became more and more agitated as the car crawled closer and closer to Bogs Field. The Porsche had been swallowed up in the traffic, but her heart was racing a mile a minute as they edged their way to the magical kingdom.

As if she hadn't figured it out by now, she gasped, "Where are we going?"

Mike glanced at her for a second, and then his eyes were back on the road, hoping an opening would allow him to breeze through the bottleneck.

"To the Greenliner game. I don't go to many. I'm usually too busy or out of town. Someone offered me the tickets, so I grabbed them. Believe it or not, that new guy is pitching today."

Snapping her head in his direction, she asked nervously, "What new guy?"

"The one from the Athletes. He was supposed to pitch tomorrow, but Riley jammed his finger sometime this afternoon so Crackerjacks was moved up in rotation to tonight's game."

Her breathing had become shallow and her hands clammy.

She tried to take a quick peek at her phone. Was that why he'd been texting for the last few hours?

Stuttering, her voice much higher than normal she announced, "I'm not really in the mood for baseball tonight."

"Oh, come on Izabella. It's a beautiful night for a game and I'm interested to see if this guy is all hype or the real deal."

Apparently even people who lived in a vacuum had heard about this trade.

Trying to coax her into a more agreeable mood, he joked, "I could have made a fortune selling these tickets once that announcement was made. We could have taken a trip around the world.They're front row box. I thought for sure you'd want to inspect him."

She had already inspected him far too closely and didn't want the jolt to her system at the memory of him on the mound. Up close and personal.

She couldn't possibly sit there passively throughout the game while he did his thing.

There was just something about a guy in uniform, even if it was baseball style.

Mike didn't know any of this and she had no intention of sharing it with him.

Using the New England weather as a viable excuse for her reluctance, she put casual in her tone hoping he wouldn't see the tension in her clasped hands.

"It's too cold to be sitting outside for hours."

"I'll buy you a sweatshirt."

She all but snapped, "I already have a sweatshirt."

He seemed at a loss and all but sputtered out, "Izabella, why don't you want to do something you enjoy? Every time I've called lately you've had the game on. I thought you loved baseball."

He hadn't called all that often no matter what he thought. Maybe once a week but he was right. She would have had the game on if it was being televised, had ever since the day a certain someone was traded.

She glanced at him sideways, wondering how to tell him that it wasn't the game she loved but one of the men playing it. Reid might not have been relationship material, but that didn't mean his imprint on her heart hadn't been indelible and with his return it was becoming visible. She guessed it was time to stop vehemently denying it.

They were nearing the parking lot she usually used whenever she came into the Bog. Those trips had consisted of all Athletes games over the last ten years pitched by a certain somebody, although no one knew that little tidbit of information. Except Melinda.

Her breathing hadn't returned to normal yet, but she had to admit the thrill of seeing him was growing with each passing moment. Besides, there was no other excuse she could give Mike except the truth. And that wasn't happening.

Taking a deep breath, hoping she could contain her feelings so they didn't spill out onto the field, she pointed to the right.

"Why don't we park there. It's got good access to the highway so we'll get out pretty quickly."

Mike maneuvered the car expertly towards the lot and pulled a couple of twenty-dollar bills out of his pocket and handed them to the attendant.

He escorted Izabella across the double lane of screeching cars, they walked up the slight incline to Nickerson Street, inhaling the street smell of sausages and peanuts, watching the crowds that mingled outside the Park Street Pub, the Boston Brewhouse, the memorabilia stores, inspecting the loyalty of the fans by the shirts they wore.

She loved this ballpark.

It was full of life: smells, sights, sounds of something she grew to love because of one man and his flame-throwing arm. This was the culmination of a life-long dream for him and as she pushed through the turn style, she couldn't help but wonder what he was feeling.

—

Reid stood at the door of the bullpen.

This was it.

The culmination of every dream he'd ever dared dream.

The Beantown Barrier stood there in defiance.

Pedro had told him it was a great motivator.

Coney had told him it was a rush.

He seemed to be managing the agitation although the change in rotation had thrown him. When he'd arrived at the park, he'd been summoned into the manager's office and told he'd be throwing today, something he hadn't had time to think about or plan for.

He'd met with Motts earlier and they had chatted about the hitters and the kinds of pitches they moved well, the pitches that fooled them, what to expect, and what to throw. He knew his stuff and he was looking forward to playing catch with Motts today. He had never reached Izabella, so he wasn't sure she'd gotten the word about the switch.

He only hoped she'd be watching.

He just didn't know why it was so damn important.

The thought of her rippled into his subconscious just before he stepped out and onto the field.

To thunderous applause.

He tipped his cap, pausing for a second to scan the seats in amazement. He had expected that a homegrown boy would receive a rousing welcome, but he'd never expected this.

His eyes roamed each section until they settled back close to the dugout, where he saw a mirage amidst the screaming mass of ticket holders.

He moved forward a step, figuring the trick his mind was playing on him would end a wistful death, but as he moved closer, his mind clarified the image.

Izabella was here, standing, applauding like the rest of the fans.

The portion of her body he was scrutinizing, held him spellbound.

Her hair was down and flapping around her jean jacket in the early night breeze, her jeans clung to her long, lean legs, and her gaze locked with his for a split second.

Like a matador addressing his most ardent fan, he bent from the waist so slightly that no one would have discerned the movement before giving her his most disarming smile.

Just before he turned away, he noticed a male figure standing beside her whispering something in her ear.

Anger shot through him.

Izabella could feel Mike lean in, felt the muffled words tickle her ear.

"I told you, you looked great today."

The fact was, he hadn't. He'd been too busy to even notice, so his compliment was wasted although he didn't know it quite yet.

She was standing transfixed, as Reid's smile transformed from the disengaging one to a tight-lipped scowl. Instead of being pleased he had noticed Mike, she was close to launching an apology, but he'd already turned his back and strode purposefully to the mound.

There was a strain of frustration in Mike's tone and she gave him a half smile when he said, "I'm beginning to think I should have listened and taken you someplace else. I have a feeling if he crooked a finger you'd be out of here like a shot."

She tried to laugh off the remark that was more on target than Mike could ever guess.

"Don't be ridiculous. I've known Reid for years. He's certainly not going to crook his finger and I'm definitely not running after him."

He injected his look with apprehension.

"You've known him for years?"

"Yes. My mother was his parents' housekeeper." She offered another tidbit. "He's the one that bought the Costello's house."

The fact that he no longer felt like a hero showed in his face. "Then this is probably no big deal."

Suddenly, she was glad Mike had insisted they do this. The air wasn't too chilly, the seats were great, the atmosphere was charged with electric anticipation. And just being in Reid's presence brought a smile to her face, and today was no different, although her insides were doing cartwheels. She knew what this day meant to him and she was glad she was going to be part of it. Completely changing her tune, she quipped, "Oh, it is. I've never seen him pitch in a Greenliner uniform before."

At the end of the national anthem, she took her seat and glanced around, listened to the inside chatter about the upcoming game. There was a definite buzz, and she pushed her hair off her face, wanting nothing to distract her vision.

He was warming up when her attention shifted back to him, and she breathed a little easier when she saw how he was coming off the mound. The confident stride, the powerful stretch of his legs, the straight back all made her quiver with excitement, and her heart was in her mouth by the time the umpire called, "Play ball."

Quiet had descended and she blinked, acclimating herself to the moment. Reid was the lone warrior standing on the mound, his glove an extension of his hand, the ripples of muscle visible under his long-sleeved shirt.

She breathed in hard.

Then she shifted her attention and she watched Reid work his windup and release the first pitch.

It would be telling.

Propelling himself forward on the rubber, his leg kicked high, his extension perfect, his motion smooth. His foot came down with power right where it should have. No drifting.

Fastball. Had to be going close to a hundred-miles-an-hour.

Right down the middle.

She watched the umpire give a dramatic strike pump.

Studying his face, she relaxed some. There was attitude there. It said he couldn't be beaten. It said he was the best there was and he was going to stay in each batter's face today.

There was a cocky tilt of the head as he read the catcher's sign, an arrogant jut of the chin, a blazing spark in his eyes.

His mouth, still a thin line, was an ominous omen of things to come and he didn't disappoint.

He was magnificent.

His fastball was on target, overpowering every man he faced. His slider broke sharply. His curve was the jokester breaking down and away from the batter.

His off-speed pitches were all over the strike zone, and the batters were kept off-balance throughout the game.

He stayed ahead of the count all night. His delivery was perfection, the intensity of his focus a sight to behold.

He looked nasty, threw mean. He had a rhythm going that was throwing every adversary off. His stuff was magic and steel, and as they headed into the seventh-inning stretch they were ahead three to nothing. Reyes had hit a three-run homer and the ball had probably landed in Quincy.

The cameras panned to Reid sitting in the dugout as Reyes rounded the bases. The full screen monitor captured him, sitting off by himself, his jacket slung over his shoulder protecting the arm in the cool night air. There was no reaction on his face that would have suggested he was glad that they were now in the lead. He was in a zone and no one was going near him.

She looked around, to the fans in the outer reaches of the park who were marking their pitcher's progress with accumulating strike cards, hoots, hollers, and deafening applause. She was marking it with heartfelt pride.

Mike ventured into her thoughts with a comment she stopped before it got started. "Hey, look at the scoreboard. It looks like he has a ...."

"*Voce e estupido*? Do not say the words. Very bad luck."

Putting his hands up to ward off the scolding, he didn't say another word for the rest of the game.

Slipping off his cap, Reid wiped his forehead on his shirt sleeve before securing the hat back in place.

Two more innings to go and the anger just continued to build.

He had worried that it would dissipate too soon, decreasing the intensity so he couldn't throw as accurately or as hard. But he could still feel the blood simmering.

The meanness would last.

He had almost beaned Dan Marshall, the third baseman, for crowding his plate. He'd knocked George Martin out of the batter's box when he tried to outstare him. He was playing by the old unwritten code that said you didn't piss off the pitcher or you'd pay.

He could feel how tightly his face was locked in its cold-stone position.

He could hear the fans on their feet every time he was close to a strike-out.

He could see the red haze just beyond his peripheral view as he kicked into his windup.

The grunt from the gut.

The ball just skirting the corner.

His foot on the rubber, he waited for the ball to come back to his outstretched glove. Flicking his wrist as the catcher lobbed it back, he turned towards the outfield, his eyes narrowing, his nerves humming.

After the next pitch, marking another strikeout, he made a solitary walk back to the dugout still thinking about the woman in the front row.

Izabella had come to his game.

With someone else.

After he had issued a personal invitation that she had declined.

I am too busy.

I would have to find someone to watch Leeni.

She seemed to have tied up all those loose ends for someone else.

It was obviously a date, the way the guy was hanging on her.

He had blocked her out while he was on the mound, had to or she would have distracted him into oblivion. But during his practice throws at the beginning of each inning, he looked to where she sat and was beguiled again by her loveliness.

Then he would shake off all thoughts of her.

Or let thoughts about her with some other man create the heat he needed to get this job done.

He knew unconsciously that he was having an extraordinary outing and they would leave him in until...He couldn't think ahead. Three more outs and it would be over.

Before he took his place in the final inning, the players ran out onto the field without uttering a word. They didn't dare.

Leaning in, his gloved hand resting on his upper thigh, he read the sign.

Standing, glove up at chest level, the ball left his hand going ninety-four miles per hour.

Strike one. How could she have shown up here with someone else?

Looking over to the seats just behind the dugout, a mistake on every level, he noticed the seat next to Izabella vacant.

Relax.

As soon as he let the next ball go, he felt his shoulder open up too quickly, and he knew he had rushed the throw.

Taking a deep breath, he calmed his mind.

Put it down. He likes to go fishing.

The sinker went just where he wanted it to, and he turned to see Rodriguez scoop it up and throw the runner out at first with time to spare.

One more out.

Don't think meat. Just throw.

On his third pitch, with the count at zero and two, Espinosa connected with the ball and Reid's heart sunk. That ball was hit and he couldn't believe he had made it to this point to see it all….

Letts was running hard, his legs pumping as he gained speed and dove up at the last second, crashing into the wall to catch the ball before it landed in the bleachers.

His arms went up in victory and he met the outfielder half-way to thank him with an over enthusiastic hug.

The people were standing, the roar was obliterating all other sound.

The dancing group hug made it all the way off the field.

He had thrown to twenty-seven batters and no one had gotten a hit.

A perfect game.

The one he was playing with Izabella was not.

CHAPTER TWELVE

The game was exhilarating and her thoughts raced the whole way back to Andover. Mike knew it was over and had been severely civil until he dropped her at her front door. The only thing he'd said to her was, "I don't like being called stupid." and the good-bye had been all but nonexistent.

She couldn't even pretend to care. He was a stream of endless, useless chatter that she had no patience for. Not when she was fighting a form of the flu. It was the Crackerjack strain and it infected her system with chills, fever, and a variety of aches and pains.

The problem was there was no remedy.

After letting herself in, she was greeted enthusiastically by Hoover, who had gone far too long without a bathroom break, so she let her out back. She shrugged off her jacket and hung it on the rack before letting her back in. She wanted to celebrate with someone, get up and dance, sing, shout, rejoice, and Hoover was up to the task, so glad that she was home again. Once the dog was appeased with enough pats and hugs, Izabella texted Keith to check in on, not only her daughter but his impression of the game.

You awake?
Who could sleep? Watching replays
I was there.
Kidding?
No. Mike took me.
What a coincidence. I almost texted you but thought you might be bummed you missed his first game.
I couldn't have planned it if I'd tried. How's M?
Sweet as always.
I'll pick her up first thing.
No rush. I think we're going to need a bigger house. Know any agents I can work with?
Think I just might.
Talk to Sof tomorrow.

Will do. Night.
Night.

After climbing the stairs to her bedroom, Hoover resting quietly now that she was home, she began to undress, her nerves still churning, the stimulation caused by the game like a caffeine high. After donning a nightgown, she returned to the family room and hit the power button on the remote. She wanted to watch every replay, every nuance that she might have missed by being so consumed with the immediate action. The major networks' regular night programming was still in progress, so she quickly heated up her leftover lunch, a bowl of pinto beans with bacon and egg. She hadn't been able to eat anything at the park and was now ravenous. Her quick trip to the Brazilian bakery in Lowell this morning, for more rolls, had her craving some authentic food that she just never had the time to make, so she'd stopped for take-out. Eating the barbeque early this afternoon had filled her, and she was glad now she hadn't consumed it all.

She settled into the couch, timing the start of the news perfectly.

The first segment was about the Greenies, as she'd known it would be. It didn't matter what else was going on in the world, if there was a major story on the sports front in this town it got first billing.

The camera panned to the locker room, which was filled with celebratory shouts, and a lot of joking around. There was nothing like the camaraderie of a team. It was all for one and one for all.

Larry Rucker seemed beside himself with enthusiasm for all things Jackson.

Covering the interview, microphone in hand, he called over to the star of the night. Izabella couldn't help but notice the grin on the pitcher was all-consuming, the hair sticking up from sweat and the baseball cap, twirling the ball she assumed Letts had caught doing his dare-devil routine.

Larry had asked the proverbial question, "How did it feel to pitch a perfect game?"

With a voice that was hoarse and scratchy, Reid answered, "Great. Better than the one I pitched in my rookie year. But I couldn't have done it without help from the team. If it hadn't been for Letts, I would have lost it in the last out of the last inning."

"You thought you were pitching tomorrow. How did you feel when you were given the news it was changed to today?"

Laughing, he quipped, "Maybe Farina should shift the rotation more often. It worked for me today."

"There's been a lot of controversy around your trade. Do you feel you've put some of those reservations to rest?"

"Look, a pitcher goes out every time wanting to win. We're competitors or we wouldn't have gotten this far. I had a great game today but next time out it's a different ball game. If people who weren't glad to see me here feel better about that now, great. Do I want to help this team make it to the Series? Sure. I'll give it my best every time out, I can promise you that."

"You looked like you were in a particular zone all day. Was there anything specific that got you there?"

Izabella shivered when he smiled.

"I wish there was. Then I could bottle it."

"Great win, Jacks. Good luck with the season."

"Thanks, Larry."

Putting the empty bowl on her end table, Izabella sought the MLB channel to get another perspective of the all-pervading mood in the Greenliner organization tonight.

There had been an interview with Perry, who once again gave his opinion on the trade of the season.

Letts had slapped Reid on the back during his.

"We give it up when we have to. That wall was not going to prevent me from catching that ball, not even if I had to go through it."

Farina had confirmed that pitchers weren't great with that kind of change but Reid had proven that the best got it done no matter the circumstances.

Glancing at the clock, she confirmed it was getting late but her hunger for Reid still wasn't satisfied. She had a busy day tomorrow and she had to get some sleep. It was just a question of whether sleep would come to her.

She took the bowl to the kitchen had started running the hot water so she could soak it overnight when she heard a light tap on the side porch window.

Alarmed, she stealthily approached the glass to see who was out there. Her protectress started barking but she shushed her when she saw who it was.

"Hoover go lie down."

The dog miraculously obeyed.

With an accelerating heartbeat, she licked her lips before unlocking the door and opening it.

Moments passed as they stood just looking at each other. His eyes were steel blue, which should have told her something, but she couldn't get her brain to function. Her eyes were working over-time.

"Are you alone?"

Tilting her head as if she didn't understand the question she said, "Yes, Leeni is at Keith and Sofia's."

"That's not what I meant."

Finally seeing through the fog, the air thick with something she didn't want to define, she said, "Oh, Mike. He's not here."

There was a spark of ice in his blue eyes.

"You said there was no one special in your life."

Scowling, wondering why he thought he had a right to this line of questioning she admitted,

"There isn't. I've gone out with him, maybe four or five times. Tonight, was the last. And I don't know why I'm telling you this because my social life is none of your business."

With a twist of his mouth, he asked, "But you accepted his invitation to the game and not mine?"

Putting her hands on her hips, becoming unnerved by his closeness and annoyed at his prodding, she said, "I accepted a date on a night I did not think you were pitching. That he chose to take me to a ball game and that Riley jammed his finger making you next in line did not figure into it."

"I texted you and called, trying to let you know."

"I found that out later. I thought it rude to be going out with one man while talking to another."

What does it make you if you completely ignored one while paying the most intimate attention to another?

More than rude, she would have guessed.

She shivered and gave him a choice, "It's cold. Either come in or go away."

The beautiful spring day had turned frosty as it approached midnight.

He moved forward without warning, let the outer door hit his back, framed her face with his hands, and leaned in to kiss her, smothering the gasp that tried to escape.

It was light, his lips barely brushing against hers.

But the electric shock it sent through her detonated small quakes in other parts of her body.

With trembling fingers, she touched his cheek, and the kiss automatically deepened.

Now his lips covered hers completely and he pulled her closer. He brought his hand up, and cupped her breast, brushing the nipple with his thumb. It hardened in pleasure.

His hands began a slow exploration of her body, lazily sliding down until he cupped her derriere, the material of her gown inching its way up, almost completely exposing her. One hand travelled down her leg and back up, stroking the bare flesh as it went.

The light touches were like pinpricks of lightning and her heart was thundering in her chest.

When his fingers brushed the secret spot she'd been exclusive with, she sagged into him wanting nothing more than to be consumed. The spasms were just another brush away.

His hoarseness was back in his voice when he asked, "You said you were alone?"

Her breath caught and her senses cleared.

With all the strength she had in her, she pressed him back and away from her. "No."

His regained his footing, nestling his face back into the cleft behind her ear and his whisper was hot against her.

"I thought you said..."

Although she needed him, wanted him, she also knew it had to stop here.

"I did. But unless you can do forever, you go home."

He broke away, his hand coming up to linger on her hair, tucked it behind her ear. His eyes searched hers before he admitted in a voice so low she could barely hear him, "You know I can't do that."

"And I can't do it your way."

Throwing caution to the wind he kissed her swollen lips again and asked, "Then where does that leave us?"

Stepping back out of his embrace, the magnetic pull making it nearly impossible to do, she straightened and said firmly, "In separate beds."

He tilted his head back and groaned before saying, his voice raspy, "Izabella, this feels too good to stop here."

"*Si...* It feels good."

She closed her eyes and steadied herself, her body ready to swoon back into his arms.

Placing her hands around his face, she brought his head down and looked straight into his eyes.

"*Meu amor*, physically you are all there is. Everything a woman could want. Emotionally you are missing. I can't have one without the other."

He dropped his head, his breathing strained, his body hard and rigid. "This sucks, Izzie. What is so great about forever? Can't you just go with how it feels now?"

"I can't. Not again. I've already told you that."

Rubbing the back of his neck, he finally muttered, "Fine. If that's the way you want it."

It was in no way, shape, or form how she wanted it, but she knew that what she did want, he couldn't give her. Moving past him, she opened the door and softly said, "Goodnight, Reid."

Proceeding through the doorway, he looked back at her again and tossed her a baseball. "I'm glad you were there tonight."

Her smile drooped as she caught it, holding it close against her chest.

"Me as well."

She watched him jog across the street and enter the condo without a backward glance.

The sobs were there right below the surface, but she wasn't going to let them have their way.

Closing and locking the door, she climbed the stairs to her room, folded back the covers. The sexual tension mounted with each passing minute, and she wondered again what *was* so great about forever.

Reid entered the vestibule and headed straight for the kitchen. Removing the bottle of wine, swiping a glass off the sideboard, he poured the dark red liquid and took a long sip.

The inkiness of her eyes and her words permeated his soul.

She had called him her love.

Something that should have him running fast but instead it struck a chord at the deepest part of him.

Had he hurt her before, like Keith had suggested?

Was she just protecting herself from future pain?

The pain only he could inflict and she knew him too well to think otherwise.

His body rebelled as his brain processed what this meant.

It was on strike. No, it was on fire.

This should have been a red-letter day. He'd pitched a perfect game on his first time out as a Greenie and he should be celebrating. Instead...

After taking another long swallow, he refilled the glass and slumped into a chair at the small table.

His hands streaked through his hair and he muttered, "What the hell."

It had taken only seconds for that kiss to flame into a conflagration.

How could she have sent him away? Not demand a release from what they were feeling?

Cause she felt it, too. He was sure of it. She'd been shaking with desire. He'd felt the trembling while he stoked the fire.

He had always thought of her as a sweet confection, extra weight and all. Her kisses had always been molten fire, her touch a torch. Tonight? It had been over the top.

She had been needy once, too ready for someone to love her.

But she wasn't needy anymore.

Today she knew what she wanted.

And it was something he just couldn't give her.

CHAPTER THIRTEEN

There were no texts, no phone calls, no late-night visits over the next four days.

He had taken her at her word.

It had to mean he'd given up the chase. Permanent was not something he'd ever contemplate.

She'd be safe.

But from what?

Not need, or desire.

Maybe his absence would help temper his hold on her. It had worked when he was on the West Coast.

But now he was here, across the street…as close as a heartbeat.

Something she had to ignore.

Staying busy was the antidote.

She filled her days with showings, inspections and closings. She went out on a couple of listing appointments and with the hope that she'd get at least one of them. Jaco's neighbor in Lowell, who was moving to another part of the city, called her to handle the sale. The other had come from her canvass of the Mount Vernon neighborhood in Lawrence. Spending time on the comps of the area and making a list of staging requirements had taken time, something she wanted to fill.

Then the direction of her work took a different course.

Approached by the owner of a real estate company in Andover, who asked if she would like to become "part of their team," she was taken to lunch at Palmers, wined and dined, and offered a commission split that was more than generous and the opportunity to increase her Andover clientele. She didn't even need to think about it. The agents in that office had great reputations, the company had a national link, and the exposure for her listings would generate far more buyers than the company she was with. Agreeing to start after the bulk of her closings in May, she was penciled in for the desk on the thirteenth. Feeling elated, she drove around the town, getting to know every square inch so that she could look the part of a seasoned professional. North Andover was unfamiliar territory and she wanted to get a sense of the town and its culture. Some of her potential clients had agreed to wait until she had joined the new firm before listing. For those who were intent on selling now, she had another plan in place.

As she followed Route 28 past the downtown area, she called the person she thought might have referred her to the office management.

"Diane, I just left John..."

"Did you accept?"

"You knew? Why didn't you say anything?"

"Didn't want to put any pressure on you. When do you start?"

"Next month."

"I am so excited we'll be working together."

"Me too. I assume you're the one who suggested they talk to me."

"I am. You're too good to be working for someone else."

"Thanks. Can you have lunch someday next week? My treat."

"I'd love to. Text me with a day and time."

"How about after our closing on Thursday?"

"Perfect. Iz. You'll be sitting in the cubicle right next to mine. It'll be a lot better than just seeing you here and there."

"I can't wait. I also want to talk to you about a possible split on some listings. I have some clients who want to get their house on the market ASAP and I hoped you'd be willing to service them until I get there. I really don't want to lose them."

"Absolutely. We can talk details at lunch."

"Thanks Diane. See you Thursday."

Elation rushed through her at the thought of being with one of her good friends at one of the premier agencies in the area. With a big smile on her face, she turned left and made her way through the area, noticing the types of houses, the neighborhoods, and the for-sale signs that were scattered along the tree-lined streets.

Another way she killed the ticking of the clock was in the kitchen. She had made it her playground, a place to explore her creativity. Trying out some new recipes in a Brazilian cookbook purchased from Amazon and some Livia had sent through email, she stewed, baked and froze. If she remembered to take a meal out in the morning to defrost, she was a couple of weeks ahead in supper preparation. Desserts had to be made on an eat-as-you-cook basis. The coconut and egg yolk pudding was one of Leeni's favorites, which didn't surprise her. The dessert satisfied the little girl's sweet tooth, and she had begged for more, long after they were gone.

Thursday nights were for dancing. Taking her courage in hand almost a year ago, she had joined a class, something that made her feel good, happy. Her ex-boyfriend Carlo, who she had formed a friendship with, owned the studio with his wife, Camila, and they had welcomed her warmly. Learning the samba, a dance that was Brazilian to the core, had been amazing and she had impressed her father with her moves on his last visit. This week they had learned the tango, a Latin dance that oozed heat and emotion. A new student had created an odd number so she was paired with Carlo, whose expertise, coupled with the fact he knew her, allowed them to move together with ease. She was able to lose herself in the music and become the dance as her partner walked her to the music, improvising steps that were seductive and filled with feeling. It gave her a way to express what was in her heart, transmitting the sexual tension that constantly thrummed lately to a dance rather than a partner. Safer than giving in to the maddening fixation she had on one man's body.

The lunch with Sofia had presented itself as part and parcel of the real estate assignment of finding a new house for the Zamoutto family. Spending time in her office, going over the list of must-haves that included an in-law apartment, she set up appointments for all the available properties that could work for them. Talita had been overjoyed by their willingness to have her live with them, but she was adamant that they have their privacy. Keith had met them for the showings, and with an unlimited budget due to clients like Crackerjacks, they had found one almost immediately. They would have to do some configuring, moving their bedroom upstairs to be with the children, and assigning the current master and en suite to Talita, but it was large enough that they could all comfortably reside there. After she had sent the offer to the listing broker, the two women had kept the lunch date they had promised each other.

Seated at a table by the window in the small restaurant on Post Office Avenue, they picked at the same delicacies that Reid had delivered on his first visit to her house.

"You haven't heard a word from him?"

Sipping the lemon water, she arched her eyebrows and admitted, "It's not like it's a surprise."

"Come on, he was all over you for a while there."

Compressing her lips, she countered, "That's the Reid I know and love. Here today, gone tomorrow...but don't relax. He just might come back again someday and break your heart if you let him."

"That's crazy."

"That's Reid."

Sofia moved the fattoush around with her fork before admitting, "He came to dinner last night."

Izabella's mouth turned down.

"He did?"

Finally looking up and into Izabella's eyes she said, "Yeah. He had a free day yesterday and he invited Keith to go golfing if you can believe it. They had to search for a club that was open but eventually found one. They got back in time for Mama's pork chops and rice. He agreed to stay before we asked him."

The laugh slipped out. "He always did love my mother's food. Talita's is very similar."

Taking a bite of the falafel, Sofia said, "They're keeping him second in the rotation so he'll be pitching against the Orioles on Monday. I think we're going to that game."

The plan to go to his opener had been averted by his early start.

"He's great to watch. All thrust and power."

"Interesting word…thrust."

The smile slipped easily across her face.

"Can't help it if I connect the two."

"Are you ever going to tell me what really happened between the two of you back then?"

Playing with a lone pine nut that had escaped the kibbe, Izabella almost let the question go unanswered but decided against it. She didn't want Sofia thinking she was avoiding the topic for a reason.

"I've told you. Nothing happened in the way you mean. A few kisses, a few feels. Nothing close to what I would have liked or needed."

"I'm curious about why. Keith says…" Sofia looked up and smiled before continuing, "He seems to be a man who gets it where he can."

Taking another slow sip of water, inclining her head to one side, Izabella said, "My mother might have had something to do with it. He loved her a lot. I also think he shared too much of himself with me. I knew his history. He doesn't mix his emotional with his sexual. You either got one or the other but never both. I was just one of the lucky few who missed out on his sexual prowess."

"What happened last Tuesday? From what you told me, he seemed willing to cross the line."

She had admitted how close they'd come to a real sexual encounter. The need to talk about it had allowed her to open up with someone she trusted.

"Something he would have nixed immediately after the fact. I didn't need the rejection, although it seems that's what I got anyway."

"He seems so complicated. Keith is so easy and open. I'm not sure I could handle it."

"Who's handling it?"

She certainly wasn't. Not well anyway.

She'd just have to content herself with watching him on television.

Or maybe she'd push the envelope a bit and go to another game. He wouldn't have to know. She'd been numerous times without his knowledge.

Sofia laid her hand on her friend's and said, "I'm sorry."

"Don't be. I'm a big girl. I'll figure it out."

"You'll see him at the closing."

"I don't know. It wouldn't come as a shock if he had Keith handle it."

Her phone pinged and she glanced at it to see who was texting her.

"Excuse me I have to take this. It's about your offer."

It was good news.

The women bustled out of the eatery, arms entwined, and headed for Keith's office for a signature.

Izabella had left a large tip.

Why shouldn't the nice waitress enjoy some of the money that she was going to make from this expensive sale.

Reid had tried to stay busy.

Thoughts of the way Izabella looked, the way she'd felt hadn't left his mind yet, and it had been almost a week. Maybe he just needed to give it more time. How many days would it take to curb this obsessive need to talk to her, to see her, to taste her again or go stark raving mad? He had picked up his phone a dozen times wanting to say good morning or, better yet, goodnight.

After pulling himself away from the window the day after his game, when he had checked the house across the street for lights, activity, motion of some kind, he had stomped into the bathroom to take a cold shower before getting dressed. Reyes had drafted him to do some work at the Jimmy Fund so he had spent this morning at Dana-Farber with the short stop. It had been a heart-wrenching experience. Visiting with the sick kids, some without hair, so many tubes attached to their small bodies, faces puffy from the steroids, had been sad but rewarding. They all had such heart, fighting sometimes insurmountable odds, and he committed himself to helping them in any way he could. They were never far from his thoughts now, either.

Thursday, he had run five instead of his usual three miles but it hadn't accomplished what he'd hoped. If Keith hadn't cleared his schedule to go golfing, he didn't know what he'd do with all that free time or those images floating through his mind.

However, Keith knew him too well. And the questions started as soon as he got into the car.

"What the hell is up with you?"

"What do you mean?"

"You don't even like golf that much. Why was it so important to find a course today?"

Tapping his fingers on his knee, he said, "Needed something to do."

When Keith glanced over at him, he had a smile on his face that suggested he was finding this humorous.

"I can think of lots of things that would have kept you busy...say a month ago."

"Yeah, well I haven't found anyone or anything of interest yet."

"Are you sure?"

Reid inspected the face before asking, his voice prickly, "What are you getting at?"

"You were pretty busy texting a certain someone for weeks. What happened?"

"Yeah, well, that certain someone put the brakes on it."

"What do you mean? Aren't you just *friends?*"

The way Keith said the word made him think there was some underlying current to this line of questioning so he opted out of his usual retort and went with the truth.

"That's the thing. It's getting kind of murky."

Keith couldn't seem to get rid of the smile. He continued to prod Reid on, wanting answers to questions, answers he didn't have.

"Murky how?"

"Things are getting in the way."

"What things?"

Shoving his hand through his hair, he bit out, "She's too fucking hot."

"You noticed. The last thing I remember you saying was she was too thin."

His jaw was clenched as Izabella's image came to mind.

"She's not."

"And she's become immune to your charm?"

"I wouldn't say that exactly."

His body instantly remembered the way she gave into his kiss and pressed for more. He shifted in the seat to get more comfortable.

"But she is damned straight about what she wants."

"And it's not you?"

"Only if I promise her forever and we all know that's not going to happen."

Sitting at a red light, Keith looked over at him and smirked.

"Oh, that's right. I forgot your aversion to all that is intimate."

Reid folded his arms across his chest.

"I can do intimate very well, thank you."

"No, you can do sex really well. Intimate means connection, permanence. You don't do those things well at all."

"Whatever. It's done. She's made her decision, one that I don't agree with, but what the hell can I do about it? Force her to want it my way?"

"There's no possibility of a friendship?"

Reid's strategy usually consisted of throwing the bathwater out with whatever happened to be floating there. Being honest with his friend and himself, Reid admitted, "I'm not sure I can do that with her, either."

He hated the shit-eating grin on Keith's face when his friend asked, "How does it feel being caught between a rock and a hard place?"

Releasing the stifling straight-jacket of need, he smiled back.

"It's the hard place that's got me stumped."

Back at his window again yesterday, hiding behind the curtains so she couldn't see him, he'd watched her leave the house, Leeni right behind her. She'd had a red dress on, the kind that clung to every curve that the belt accentuated. His hands had reached out instinctively and he'd held one of them on the window pane, wanting to do so much more than just look. Her braid hung over her shoulder, and all he could think about was pulling it loose, letting her hair cascade down her back so he could run his fingers through the thick tresses.

Jumping into another cold shower to start his day, he'd decided to head into the park earlier than usual to avoid the temptation of following her. There was an eerie quiet in the locker room when he'd arrived, an hour to go before other players started trickling in. Needing something to occupy his time before activity started to buzz around him, he'd decided to watch some video of the Diamondbacks to refresh his memory for Monday's game. When Motts got in, they'd lifted weights, popped in on a tour, and signed some autographs, all while he'd done his best to avoid the alluring vision that refused to leave his mind and the debilitating situation he barely survived.

The strategies he'd used for avoidance were meaningless by Saturday.

He was in his car heading into Lawrence, the absurdity of it all baffling him.

What was happening to him?

He was doing some odd things lately.

He had even listened to his mother's message the other night congratulating him on his perfect game. She had sounded so proud that he didn't have the heart to click her off.

He heard the dog barking as he approached the house.

Izabella shushed the dog as she moved to see who was at the door, Melina close behind. She swung it open before he had the chance to knock.

When she'd seen who was walking up the drive, she began to circle the small space, wondering how to act. Blasé? Angry? Happy to see him? The last one struck her heart as the obvious but, she was not going to give him that.

Impertinent won.

With her hand on her hip, holding the door ajar, she asked, "To what do we owe this pleasure?"

"I come bearing gifts."

Leeni seemed excited to see him.

"What is it, Mr. Crackerjacks?"

"Pastries?"

There was a question in his voice that had nothing to do with what was in the bag.

"Are you not sure?"

"It's definitely pastries with fruit squares, cinnamon rolls, Danish, turnovers and muffins. I wanted to do breakfast so I stayed clear of sugar."

Izabella looked at him dubiously. Everything he'd mentioned had sugar embedded in every bite.

"I want some," Leeni stated imperiously, grasping for the box.

"Can I come in?"

Against her better judgement, she acquiesced.

"*Si, si,* come in."

He crossed the threshold and commented, "Nice shirt."

She looked down, trying to remember what she had thrown on this morning when Hoover had announced she needed to pee.

Shit.

Tossing her hair back she said defiantly, although it was a small white lie, "It would not have been my choice. Someone bought it for me."

He didn't have to know that someone was her.

With the playful give-and-take he was good at, he added, "Don't have to wear it."

Her eyes connected with his and she was out of her element, drowning in them.

Leeni had run out of patience with them and shrilled, "Mr. Crackerjacks, *the box.*"

"Okay, okay. Let's get it into the dining room and we'll see what you want."

Jumping up and down as she moved, Leeni quickly pushed a chair over to the counter, climbed up on it, and withdrew a plate from the cabinet, and then reversed the procedure so she was sitting ready and waiting as Reid maneuvered the red string off.

Hoover was sitting tall and waiting expectantly for her share, too.

Opening the magic white box, he stood aside while Leeni peered into it.

"Which one would you like?"

"That one please."

It didn't surprise Izabella that it was the gooiest one of all. Seeing that she hadn't gotten to breakfast yet, this was a welcome surprise.

She'd decided to take it easy today. With no scheduled floor time and her next appointments set for tomorrow, she wanted to spend some time with Leeni, maybe go see the new movie that was out, go to the park. Her daughter had had a low-grade fever yesterday, so she wanted to keep an eye on her and see where it might go.

She grabbed a couple more plates, and handed a knife to Reid, directing him, "I think half will be enough."

Once he'd finished with Leeni's order, she placed her own.

Holding a napkin in her hands, she said, "Fig square, please."

As soon as he'd opened the box she'd known she couldn't resist. They were one of her personal favorites.

"You're going to have something?"

The look on his face was almost comical.

"I told you I eat when I'm hungry."

There was hunger in his eyes that had nothing to do with pastries and she felt an ache low in her belly that began to burn.

Clearing his throat, he said, "Coming up."

Her eyes lingered on a certain part of his anatomy before bringing them up to meet his. Her thermostat inched up a few degrees and it continued to rise when she read desire in them.

With a pained stare, he asked, "Is this how it's going to be? I'm not sure I'm up…"

He squinted, glad he had caught himself before finishing the sentence.

The moment was broken when there was a shrill cry.

"*Noooo,* Hoover."

Hoover had taken an opportunity presented, had put her paws on the table and sideswiped Leeni's treat.

Clutching her collar, Izabella scolded, "Bad girl. Paws on the floor."

Pushing the grey body towards the family room, she commanded, "Go lie down."

She began to wipe up the crumbs, explaining, "Now you know how she got her name. She is a vacuum cleaner."

Leeni had a look of mild annoyance on her face.

"She had more than I did. Can I have the other half, please?"

Izabella agreed and placed it on her daughter's plate before taking a seat and finishing her own in just a few bites.

Reid leaned across the table and wiped away a few crumbs that had collected on the crease of her lips. He snatched his hand away. He must have felt the sparks, as strongly as she did.

The blush was creeping back up her neck, but they both ignored it.

After regaining her balance from the light touch of his fingers, she rose and collected the plates from the table.

"Thank you. That was delicious."

"My pleasure."

The awkward moments of silence stretched on until Reid said, "I hear you sold another house yesterday"

She knew he was talking about the Zamouttos' purchase and her face crinkled in a smile.

"Yes. I am so glad we found something so quickly. They want to be in before Sofia gets too uncomfortable and there's some work they have to do before they move."

"From what I hear, it's not too far from mine."

He had leaned back in his chair and seemed a bit more relaxed.

Having finished her breakfast treat, she wiped her face with the napkin supplied.

"Mama, can I watch TV?"

"First you need to get dressed and brush your teeth. Then we'll talk."

"Okay."

The little girl slipped out of her seat and paused before walking away from the table.

Izabella grasped her hand and pulled her gently towards her.

"Are you feeling okay, *querida*?"

"I think so."

Closing her eyes for the briefest of moments, she kissed her daughter's cheek and asked, "Do you want me to help you?"

"No, Mama. I'm okay."

Izabella watched her daughter, who seemed to gain some energy when she reached the steps and went up smoothly.

"What's wrong? Is she sick?"

What to tell him?

Too much, not enough?

The basics.

He watched as she shoved her hands beneath her arms, her shoulders drooping as he waited for her answer.

"She was sick when she was about two. We've been waiting to see if she's...outgrown it."

He glanced to the stairs, where Leeni had headed.

"Is there anything I can do to help?"

Exhaling shakily, relieved that he hadn't asked a more significant question, she replied, "No, but thank you."

"I hate to leave you but I have to get to the park. Early game today. Are you going to be all right?"

"*Sí.* I will be fine. You go and thank you again for breakfast."

She was thrown off-balance when he enfolded her into an embrace and her arms wound around him tightly.

She felt a brush of lips against her temple before he put her at arm's length.

"Look, I got your message loud and clear the other night. And I guess I don't blame you. I'm not what you'd call a rock to lean on. The last thing I want to do is hurt you, Izzie. I'm not sure I can do the friend thing, but I'd like to try if you're willing."

Was she willing to see but not touch? Laugh with but not love?

The choice was not a good one. It wasn't the one she wanted, not with him and she wasn't sure she could manage it, either.

She'd known from the time she was eleven years old that she wanted him in her life, and if she'd learned anything from the last few days, it was that nothing had changed. She just wasn't sure it was the prudent thing to do.

Linking her fingers behind his neck, she spoke to his eyes.

"We shall see."

Removing her hands, he kissed them before heading quickly out the side door.

"Call if you need anything."

"I will."

CHAPTER FOURTEEN

Sofia called right after Reid left, telling Izabella she'd phoned at his suggestion.

"He said you seemed upset about something. Is this about him...or Leeni?"

His insight was unexpected but welcome.

After Izabella explained what was going on, the friends chatted about what might lie ahead.

It didn't make her fear any less potent, but being able to bounce it off someone, made it better somehow.

Instituting an all-girls day, she and Leeni walked Hoover, went for a pedi, caught a movie, and still got home in time to watch most of the late-afternoon game. It was only background noise when Reid was watching from the bullpen so they contented themselves working on a puzzle, reading a couple of books before heading into the kitchen to make dinner.

That's when the texting started.

She put the phone down with Leeni's question.

"Is Mr. Crackerjacks going to come for dinner?"

"No, sweet one. He is still at the ballpark. He won't be home until after you are in bed."

"But the game is over."

"Yes, but they clean up, eat supper, hang out a bit before going home."

"Will he bring breakfast again, tomorrow?"

"He can't do that every morning, *querida.*"

"Why not?"

"Because we are not his family."

"Can we make him be?"

She looked at Leeni with sadness.

"I'm afraid not."

"Why? Melinda isn't really part of our family but we made her be."

"Melinda wanted it as much as we did."

"Mr. Crackerjacks wouldn't?"

Pausing, trying to phrase it so Reid didn't come across as the anti-family man he was, she tried to explain, "Reid likes to be on his own."

"Nobody likes to be alone, Mama."

"I didn't say alone. He doesn't like people to depend on him for anything."

"Like we shouldn't depend on him bringing us breakfast every morning. He wouldn't like that."

"Exactly, *querida*. You are a very smart girl."

"I think he likes bringing us food though, Mama."

"It's probably his subconscious wanting to fatten me up."

"Huh?"

Brushing her hand over her daughter's head, she laughed and said, "Reid wants Mama to gain weight."

It would probably be easier for him to do the friend thing if she had layers on like before. But that wasn't happening. Let him suffer.

"I think you are beautiful."

"Thank you. I think you are, as well."

"Can I help you make supper?"

"I was hoping you would."

After the supper dishes were done, Leeni in bed for the night, and Hoover was set, Izabella sat down for her nightly ritual of watching the news. Her worry had lessened a bit. Leeni seemed in good spirits, didn't seem more tired than usual, so maybe it was just a case of looking for trouble. She would be okay with that. There had been so many times that a shoe had dropped, hitting her on the head, that she couldn't help but glance up from time to time.

There was no guarantee her life would be safe and secure and no guarantee the lemons she got periodically would make great lemonade.

All she could do was to add a little sweetness to the pitcher and stir.

She would need to face what was ahead be it good or not so good.

Time would tell which way it would go.

The knock came right before the door opened. During the last sequence of texts, she told him to just let himself in. Hoover just lay there, although her head came up in greeting, as if Reid were becoming a part of the daily pattern in their lives. She had yet to take herself up to Leeni's room for the night, where she slept beside the bed.

"I'm back here."

He made his way to the family room, where she was seated on the couch, her iPad in her lap, a quilt partially covering her.

She had warded off any potential for trouble. Cotton pajama bottoms and a tee replaced the short nightgown that had gotten them both in over their heads.

Still in his suit coat and trousers, he'd lost the tie and unbuttoned his shirt so she could see the hair sprinkled on his chest. He could still affect her system fully clothed.

He sat in the chair opposite the couch, as if he too, was keeping his distance.

"Sorry, I know it's late. I didn't mean to keep you up."

"You didn't. I am just checking inventory in the Andovers. I don't think I told you but I'm moving offices. Fine Homes invited me to join them and I start there next month. I have to get a handle on the styles and prices so I'll feel more comfortable."

"That's great. I'm sure you'll do well. I might be a know-it-all but sometimes I really do know what I'm talking about. You are very good at what you do."

"Thanks for the compliment. I like working with people so I guess it shows."

"I hear you're going to Jaco's tomorrow."

"Yes, earlier in the day than I thought. I was going to hold an open house for one of my new listings but we got an offer on it within twenty-four hours."

"That's great."

"Yes. I am having one hell of a month. Three sales in Andover will get me more in a month than I usually make in half a year."

"You told me that the commission you earn from mine, goes to your garage."

"I did. You can tell everyone that you bought it for me."

He dropped his head before meeting her gaze and asked, "Would you like to take Leeni to my game Monday night? The Zamouttos are going, all four of them. I thought she might like it. They planned to come to my first one, but that didn't work out, so we thought this would be a lot more fun. The game will get over kind of late but you could grab something to eat at the park."

"You'll be pitching."

"As far as I know. I don't say yes or no automatically anymore."

He gave her a quizzical smile.

"If you come a bit early, I can show Leeni around, let her meet some of the players. She can go on a tour of the Bog."

"She'd like that."

He got up and reached into his inside pocket and took out two tickets, handing them over to her.

"Sofia is going to call you in the morning to see if you want to go in together. Your decision."

Heading to the side door, he looked back at her and slipped out without a word.

She fingered the tickets before getting up from the couch to put them someplace safe. One never knew what Hoover was going to be interested in eating, and some things were only safe in high or out-of-the-way places. After pushing the off button on the remote, she walked through the archway and stuffed her admission stubs into her pocketbook, which sat on her desk. Sitting down wearily, she felt the heavy weight of his absence. He *was* larger than life, and she didn't know what she'd do with the feelings too strong to be denied. Resting her arms on the wooden surface, she placed her head down, wanting to cry.

Damn you, Reid Jackson! Why did you have to come back?

Her life had been so orderly, so sane, so...routine.

She'd dated every once in a while, men she'd meet at fundraisers, Rotary Club, coffee shops, even one of her customers, once the sale had closed. Always safe, she'd made sure of it. But in truth, there had never been anyone who could make her feel more than Reid, or who she wanted a future with. He was the only one who could satisfy her need for smart, funny and very, very sexy, but he got his kicks from the hunt, wasted money on things that didn't matter to her, found variety the spice of life, and refused to open his heart to love. Allowing him to outwit her in a game of bait and switch, she was repeating the mistakes of her past. She had obviously learned nothing or the wisdom she should have gleaned would have put her on another path instead of strengthening the thread that bound them in some unusual way. His vanishing act would never stop, unless she was the one to stop it.

It had been like that the summer before he went away to college.

She had been astonished when he'd asked her to grab something to eat one night. She had been helping her mother with Melinda and he had stopped her before she left for the day. Her facial expression must have given away the fact that she was more than surprised."Are you joking with me?"

He'd looked insulted.

"Why would I do that? I just thought it might be nice to talk somewhere that didn't have ears."

With fidgeting hands, she'd asked, "Why?"

"Well, I'm going away soon, and I guess I'd like to get to know you better before I do."

"You already know all about me."

His cockiness was easy to read on his face. He knew she'd agree and was just waiting for her to reach the same conclusion."Come on, Izzie. A nice meal, quiet surroundings, someone waiting on you for a change."

Against her better judgement, she'd agreed.

From the day she'd first met him, there had been something about him that drew her like a moth to a flame. That's why she'd sit at the window when she could, to simply watch him with his friends. He was offering her the opportunity to be with him alone and she knew she couldn't turn it down.And the first few nights were unbelievably good. His hand on her back as he escorted her into the small restaurant in Marblehead, opening her car door when they arrived at the eatery in Newburyport, the good-night kiss after they had taken a walk along the beach in Rye, New Hampshire. That was the night that had induced the first sabbatical and she was sure it had been the kiss.It had started out chaste, light, and shallow but soon turned deep, satisfying, powerful.

He'd almost disappeared from the face of the earth for almost a week. And then there he was again, searching her out, touching her hair when no one was looking, inviting her for a ride along the Maine coastline, stopping to grab a lobster roll and French fries, sitting in one of the parking lots, kissing again until she was on fire. His fingers caressing her face, her neck, her breasts until she was ready to move to a higher place with him. And in one frenzied moment, it would come to an abrupt stop and he would drive her back to her house, banishing her again from his world. It became their routine over an eight-week period, and although she'd known it would never be a forever relationship, she'd been willing to go up in flames until it was over.

And when summer finally came to an end, he'd left her without a backward glance, not even a goodbye and she was left living in the ashes.

It had been one of the last times she'd seen him in person until her mother's funeral, when the explosive feelings were detonated once again.

She'd sworn she'd never be that easy again and yet here she was, willingly opening herself up to her need, aching for him to come back and love her.

Tired, more from her roiling emotions than lack of sleep, she locked up for the night, casting a glance at the condo across the street before dragging herself away. When Reid entered the condo, he immediately compared it to the little house across the street. Izzie's family room looked and felt comfortable, a refuge from the world. It had life and reached out in warmth to all who entered. There was a crate in the corner where Hoover made her home when she wasn't causing havoc, a brown couch and matching chair that sat against the wall with colorful but mismatched pillows all around, a coffee table that held a stack of hardcover books, a candle, a newspaper opened to the sports page, and assorted magazines. The TV was sitting on a credenza, and although it was on, it was muted so there was quiet in the air. A basket of folded laundry was sitting by the staircase as if waiting to go up. What a difference a laundry basket and dog crate made. They told a story of who lived there and what their life was comprised of.

Here, very much like his own West Coast house, there was no story. No one entering could get a sense of what the owner liked, what they did, or who they loved. He threw his keys on the kitchen counter and got his nightly glass of wine before heading upstairs. It was late and he had to be at the field early tomorrow for the Sunday game which started at one. He almost ignored his mother's closed bedroom door again, the one he'd stare at in the morning while he drank his coffee.

What was behind it?

Curiosity finally got the better of him. He needed to see if her personal space was as devoid of detail as the rest of the house.

She had been so alive once, their home filled with clutter, a messy scene of bustling activity and busy schedules. She was taxi driver, cook, teacher, catcher, play-date planner, raucous fan, devil's advocate, everything a mother could be and then none of those things. How many times had he asked her to come to his games after the accident? But she would always refuse, using the excuse that his friends would make fun of her, that she couldn't manipulate the chair on the ball grounds, that she didn't have a ride. Her embarrassment had outweighed her love, and it was something that still had the ability to cut him off at the knees.

He paused with his hand on the door knob, unsure about what he was doing, but he turned it slowly and eased it open. As he flicked on the light switch, his breath hissed, his eyes widened, and his heart almost swelled. Taking a step inside, he stopped abruptly, to take in a panoramic view, because she was everywhere. And so was her family.

His eyes went first to the quilt on the bed, one he hadn't seen before. It was made up of some of his old baseball uniforms, and he slowly made his way over to it to examine it more closely. There was a pattern to it, his little league days in the center, spiraling out to include his high school and college years. There was even an Oakland color scheme, and he wondered if she had bought one of his shirts to complete this baseball file of his life. He fingered it, knowing that Juliana hadn't made it.

He knew in an instant who had.

Izabella was here in the room with her, with them.

It seemed he couldn't get away from her lately no matter how hard he tried.

He glanced to the side.

On the nightstand was the paperweight he'd bought her one Christmas, along with a little trophy Nolan had given her for a birthday, awarding her Mother of the Year. Over her bed was a wall of pictures, her sons at various stages in life, pictures of Leeni as a baby, a toddler, and a more recent one, pictures of Izabella and her, at what looked like a picnic and at a ballgame. His immediate thought was that it was one of his, but he shook it off, not liking what it meant.

He swiveled around, already almost on overload, and walked to her bureau, which was littered with odds and ends that embellished the pages of her story. There was the mirror and brush set he and Nolan had bought for her, a clay pot he had made when he was in grammar school, a similar one of Nolan's along with his first debate award, more pictures of her and Leeni, her and Izabella, her and Emma in four-by-six-inch frames. He picked up a newspaper that was folded and worn that contained the article written about him in the *Globe* when he'd won his first Cy Young Award. His gaze was drawn to the other wall, where there were childlike pictures, both signed by the little girls who had drawn them for her. A baseball rested on a holder, and he plucked it up, turning it slightly until he saw the faded signature. He had signed it for her when he was about eight, crowing that she'd be the first to get his autograph, kissing her soundly when she showed her appreciation for the dream and the boy he was. Her smile had meant everything to him and he had come close to idolizing her. It had been a huge fall from grace when she'd shown him how human she was.

Slowly he scrutinized the room again, not wanting to miss anything.

There was a stand that held another quilt, folded and hung, and he recognized it as the one that Juliana had made for him when he was a boy. He'd need to ask his mother if he could take it to his new house, because for some reason it was important for him to reclaim it.

He squatted down to a two-tiered bookcase so he could read the spines, see what she liked to read. A lot of hardcovers, many by Nicholas Sparks and JD Robb, a few biographies of people like Steve Jobs and the Wright brothers, and a few inspirational tomes like *Living Your Unlived Life*.

The rocking chair that she'd had for years, sat in a corner, and he dropped into it, still dazed by what he'd found in here. He could feel moisture in his eyes and instead of fighting it, he gave in. His mind took him back to the days when she'd tickle him in this very chair, making him squeal in laughter, to nights when he'd had a nightmare when she'd soothe away his fears. She had been his rock for so long that he had faltered without her and was angry enough that he'd sliced her completely out of his life when she disappeared from it.

Well, she certainly hadn't cut him out of hers.

And she seemed to have found some peace, in spite of her condition.

When had she started to live again?

Was it in incremental steps, like the day he'd found Izabella dancing with her, the outings that Izabella included her in, her first granddaughter, her trips to Florida, her pride in her children's accomplishments, a burgeoning awareness of her own sense of self?

Had it happened after his father's death or had it happened before?

He hadn't paid attention, made everyone think he didn't care.

But he had cared far more than anyone realized and he let the tears wash his face.

CHAPTER FIFTEEN

Izabella was watching Leeni like a hawk. Scrutinizing each move, constantly feeling her forehead, double-checking her body for bruising. She was on high alert for potential disaster. One she did not want to relive ever again.

The call to the doctor's office had gained her an earlier appointment than the one they had, but it was still too far away for comfort. Doctors always seemed to take a less critical view of a situation than a mother, and she had to be content with what they gave her.

The receptionist had added, "If things get progressively worse, please bring her in immediately."

She hoped it didn't come to that.

Leeni was older now and at least she could describe what she was feeling and pinpoint the pain or discomfort. She said she was feeling okay, but the low-grade fever had Izabella worried and the worry wasn't going away anytime soon.

Sunday dawned overcast with a brisk breeze signaling spring was still a few weeks away. It wasn't a great day for a cook-out but the company would more than make up for it.

After making sure that Leeni was bundled up for the outdoor activities planned for the kids, she packed her daughter and Hoover in the car and set out for her brother's house. Unlike her, he had stayed in Lowell, buying the 1800s farmhouse when he married Addie. It was in a much better section of the city than the one they'd grown up in. Born with an aptitude for growing things, he was also great at renovation, and he had completely transformed the house into a realtor's dream. The house had a large barn attached to it, which was where Jaco kept all his landscaping tools and equipment. He ran his business out of it and it suited his needs as well as the house did.

Today they were celebrating her birthday something Jaco always made a big deal about. There wasn't a year that went by that he didn't throw a party for her. The Zamouttos would be there with Mrs. Camara, some of their friends from childhood and from work, and Addie's brother, sister and families were joining them as well. The huge deck was great for these kinds of gatherings, and the kids loved the half-acre yard to play in.

Tuesday, she was turning thirty.

Driving down Route 133, close to hitting a milestone in age, she thought about how their lives had changed, now both with children and responsibilities. Jaco had met Adelaide at a retail store where she had worked as a salesperson. It had taken them three years to tie the knot, but once they had, they had wasted no time in adding to the family. Julian was three and Jaiden was two and as much as he'd love having a daughter, Addie wanted a break and had even found a part-time job to get some adult conversation. Kids had a way of advancing time, and it had flown since Leeni was born. Any expectation of marriage and having more children was dimming. It was her one disappointment. With Reid back in the picture, she doubted she could date just anyone.

The siblings were both in a good place but there had been setbacks along the way.

When her mother had whisked them away from Campinas, it'd taken years to get used to American ways. Coming from the wide, grassy plains of the Brazilian Pampas, with trees, greenery, and wide-open spaces, she'd found the city to be confining and drab. Schools in her homeland let out for lunch and the children ate large meals at home, with their parents. The school day was shorter and there was always time to take a nap in the afternoon. In Lowell, the days were long, with no release at midday, a short recess, and when school let out in the afternoon, there was still work to do, the thought of a nap only a wistful memory. It didn't help that she was the brunt of jokes because of her weight and accent, and she found it difficult to make friends. Her brother had been her only source of comfort other than food. It had taken a long time to feel at home in the new environment but once she did, she knew she'd never return to her former life.

Her father had moved his family away from the crime and turmoil that had taken over her birthplace and now lived in Sousas, commuting to his job at the bank, retaining his position and his financial security. Since her father's return to her life, the feeling of well-being had returned as well, along with a more positive outlook. With her success in real estate and her new figure, she had become self-confident and discovered that she was resilient as well. It had been a long journey but one that made her feel strong and secure.

Days like today brought back the feeling of community that was part of the Brazilian culture and her brother was still the family she would always cherish. He never failed to show his love and his support.

Pulling in at the end of Jaco's long driveway, noticing that she must be one of the last to arrive, she released Hoover, unbuckled Leeni, and scooped up her contribution to the meal.

As she headed for the door, a short, stout man stood in the entryway, and the smile was wide and welcoming.

"Papi, it's so good to see you."

"You do not think we wouldn't come for your birthday? I have missed too many, my Bella."

He bent down and picked up his granddaughter before drawing Izabella into a warm hug.

Opening the screen door, he let her slip by him.

"Come in. Jaco is already lighting the grill and Livia is excited to see you."

Livia and their daughters, Felicia and Leia, were busy in the kitchen, along with Addie, creating a wonderful Brazilian meal, and the aromas drew Izabella into the homey atmosphere. After giving hugs all around, she placed her own offering, the coconut flan her mother used to make on the counter, knowing it would pale in comparison to what other foods would be on the table.

Her mother might have been a good cook but Livia was exceptional. She was a warm and kind-hearted woman who had welcomed her husband's other family into her life with open arms, and Izabella understood why her father had found such happiness with her. They had been married for over twenty years.

Junie Zamoutto had come in to claim Leeni, and the girls squealed as they hugged before running outside.

Her father picked one of the coxinhas off a tray, Livia playfully slapping his hand as he did so. He closed his eyes as he popped it in his mouth, savoring the flavor of the delectable raindrop of fried goodness stuffed with chicken and cream cheese.

As soon as he was finished, he informed Izabella, "So we saw this Reid Jackson of yours playing."

"Papi, he's not mine. He's the property of the Boston Greenliners."

"We didn't get to see him pitch, which I was sorry about, but maybe next time. I think it would be fun to go into a game together."

"I'm not sure about that. I have my loyalties to the home team and all. If Rique was on any other team, maybe.

"He seems to have a good reputation among the players. A leader, if you will."

Livia had offered her a piece of pasteis and she placed it on her tongue, the same look of contentment on her face as her father had earlier. After she had swallowed, she asked, "Where did you hear that?"

"Players talk. Enrique did speak to some that made it to the base."

"Um, not possible. Shortstops don't stand around a base."

Her father still didn't know a lot about the game and was puzzled at Enrique's choice of sport. Soccer was where his passion lay but he would get to know it because he loved his son.

He also loved his daughter. He'd told her time and again over the last few years that she was his first and she would always hold a piece of his heart.

"Okay. Reid introduced himself to Enrique. Said he knew his half-sister, which Rique corrected him on. We are family, plain and simple. No halves or have nots. I had him ask around after. I want to know what this man is made of."

Laughing openly, she said, "It's not sugar and spice."

"That's little girls, my *querida*. Puppy dog tails and snails or some such thing. Anyway, it would seem he is well thought of. A good team player. High on the ladder, which I think means he is one of the important players. Rique, he tries to teach me the what they call unwritten rules which I still don't understand. This

Reid gets a lot of first choices, like in rooms, plane seats, time with the trainer. Enrique is very low on this ladder, from what I understand."

"Someday, Papi, Rique will be very high on the ladder. He is an exceptional player. But why is this important? He and I are not dating."

"I have heard…"

Izabella looked to Jaco and made a face.

"What is that? Your brothers must look after you."

"I can look after myself. I've been doing it for a long time."

"Yes, but you got into trouble once and I don't want to see it happen again."

She could feel her temper rising. "Leeni wasn't trouble, Papi. And you should talk?"

He couldn't take offense, because she was right but she was sure he didn't like the disrespect it suggested.

"This America. It has changed you."

She leaned over and kissed his cheek, "I love you and thank you for the concern but Reid is not marriage material and I'm in it next time for keeps. Trust me on that."

"I hope you mean it, *querida*. I don't like seeing you alone. You need a man who will take care of you."

She rolled her eyes and caught her brother's smirk. Making another face at him, she decided to let her father believe what he did. He was from the old school and that would never change and it was just good having him in her life again.

It was two months after her mother's death that she had answered the call, an unfamiliar number showing on her phone, but an area code she knew by heart.

Taking a deep breath, not sure that she should even answer it, her need had overcome her fear.

Her voice was small when she'd said, "Hello," a question more than a statement.

There was a pause so long that she almost broke the connection.

"Izabella?"

"Papi?"

Her eyes had immediately filled, the voice such a cherished one from her youth, and the tears had doubled to accommodate her most recent loss.

"My Bella. I am so sorry to hear that your mother is gone. I think it is too soon for me to call you but it is so long now that I wanted to hear your voice."

She could feel a desperate hope fill her voice.

"It is?"

"Do not doubt my words, Bella. You were my first born, my heart, *querida*. Did you not know how I missed you?"

Her response had been filled with a Brazilian temper she was just beginning to embrace.

"How could I? I haven't heard from you in a very long time, Papi."

"Too long I am afraid."

"But why didn't you call before? Why now?"

There'd been a spurt of anger in the voice.

"I will not speak ill of the dead, Izabella, but your mother made it impossible for me to be with you."

She'd all but fallen into the chair in her small rented living room. The accusation had taken the legs out from under her.

"What do you mean? You left us."

She could tell he was trying to tamp down his surge of anger and insert some patience. Suddenly, he'd sounded very tired.

"I left your mother, not you and Jaco. That was never my intent."

"But she said that you had a new family and didn't need your old one."

"That is what she wished for you to think. Something in Juliana broke when I left, but I had no choice. I did not love her anymore and I could not sacrifice my life like that."

Izabella was attempting to merge these two conflicting identities: a loving mother with one who had taken away the love of their father. She couldn't quite believe it. Or she didn't want to.

"You never came to see us."

"She would not allow it."

Her mother had held her so tenderly when she cried for her father, soothing words of love and sympathy. How could she have done that if she was the cause of the estrangement?

"I still don't understand, Papi. How could she have stopped you?"

When Izabella was little, she'd thought her father could do anything, her own superhero. He was another larger-than-life man with a big personality.

"I hired someone to find you, and when I flew up to confront your mother, she had moved. I did it again and again but had no luck. I gave up, Izabella and I am sorry for that."

Was that why her mother had moved them time and time again, stopping only when Paolo had given up?

"You loved us, Papi?"

"Of course. Always and forever. I would like you to come and meet your family. They are very much interested in meeting their older sister and brother. Would you think of doing this?"

Her heart had spurted with joy. It had been something she'd always dreamed about but had no idea how to make it happen without fear of reprisal. If she had only known there wouldn't have been any.

"I would. I very much would."

She had been six months pregnant when she arrived in Sousas. Since she had not given him any warning of her condition, he'd been mildly shocked when she stepped into the terminal on debarkation.

Embracing her first, he backed her up to look at her burgeoning body.

"What have we here?"

She had cradled her belly protectively.

"I think you can guess."

"How did this happen?"

She'd given him a half-smile.

"The usual way."

His face had held a scowl instead of the return smile she hoped for.

"I have let you down again. Who is the father? I will make this right."

She'd stepped towards him, kissed his cheek.

"It is right just as it is, Papi."

"What do you mean?"

"I will not say she is a mistake, because I love her already, but she was not planned. It was a very foolish thing for me to do. A one-night stand, so there is no future with the father. You need to leave it be."

He'd wrapped his arms around her, and she'd felt safe at last.

"We have wasted far too many years, my Bella, so I will do as you ask. Come. Meet your family."

She had, and they had made her feel welcome and loved.

They still did.

Noticing that Livia and her daughters had the kitchen under control, she turned and asked her brother, "Do you need help?"

"Not really but I'd love your company."

She kissed his cheek and helped him carry the platters of meat out to the deck.

One held skewered meats set to go. There was a pork loin marinated in beer and herbs with parmesan cheese, sirloin, and tenderloin beef in slabs that would be sliced thin, some to be cooked on the grill, some cooked rotisserie style. Meat by the wheelbarrow, with lots of delicious side dishes as well: rice and beans, deep-fried polenta, shredded collard greens, golden farofa, and palm heart salad. Her father supervised the grilling, but Jaco had become an expert after years of trying to perfect the gaucho-style technique.

Stepping outside in the chill air, she watched the children and dog for a moment. Hoover was sitting peacefully, her head resting on her paws. The children were swinging and sliding on the massive gym set in the yard. Satisfied that all was well, Izabella gave her attention to her brother and father.

After they were seated around the dining room table, her father saying a few words of gratitude for the abundance, they dug in with the gusto Reid had spoken to.

Leeni, with a mouth half-full of food asked, "Vovo, when can we visit you again?"

"I would like to have all my family come for my sixtieth birthday next year. It is one to commemorate, is it not?"

Izabella laughed and said, "It's a good thing it's in November. Rique wouldn't be able to make it otherwise."

Her father wiped his mouth before agreeing. "Yes, this sport has far too many games and too long a season. I think Rique is beginning to like it here. He comes home less and less."

"He just got a place in New York, didn't he?"

He had recently called Izabella to ask her opinion on price and location and she'd given him a list of questions to ask, things to look for.

"Yes, a place of permanence. It does not sit well with me. Now three of my children are far away."

Livia had been urging him to get a place in America but he was still procrastinating a decision.

Directing her query to Izabella, she asked, "We are thinking of a summer home here. Do you have any suggestions?"

"There are a multitude of beaches on Long Island, so I'm sure you could find something. I can make a few calls to some brokers, get you started. You'd be close to Rique and about five hours from us."

"Would you please do that? I don't want to be missing everyone so much."

After the banquet was served and eaten and the kitchen cleaned, the rest of the day was spent with music and dancing, conversation and wine.

But watching the love expressed by Addie and Jaco, Paolo and Livia, Keith and Sofia made the longing for what they had all the more tangible.

Her heartbeat to that rhythm but she was dancing alone.

The feelings only intensified later that night when Reid began another text marathon.

I hear you had a real fiesta today.
Yes, it was wonderful.
You didn't happen to miss the game, did you?
I'm sorry but I did.
The party had lasted until just past dark.
That would be a good thing.
I did catch the news. You lost pretty badly.
Eighteen to seven.
Ouch.
Let's not talk about it.
So, what shall we talk about?
Keith sent me a picture of you doing the samba with your father.
What?
Yeah, he sent me a couple others. Jaco didn't invite me so Keith felt obliged to share the festivities.
That was so very underhanded of him.
He gets his kicks making me feel like I'm missing out on something.
My father was there. You would have spent the night scowling.
Keith says they're really nice people. And they love you.
Love doesn't usually play a part in your assessment of things.

Let's not talk about that either. So how old will you be on Tuesday?
Thirty. Time for the home.
You have at least a couple more good years.
One more than you.
One and a half, thanks.
Are you at your mother's yet?
Of course, I am. I don't text and drive. It's against the law.
Do you want to come over? I have a few pieces of cassava cake left.
I keep watching the video *Keith sent me* of *you dancing* the samba. *It's kind of* X-rated *so* I think I'll have to pass.
Okay. Good luck tomorrow.
I'll be looking for you.

CHAPTER SIXTEEN

Izabella spent the whole day steeped in anticipation. Barely able to keep her mind on her work, she gave it up and left early, picking Leeni up at Jaco's, where she had stayed over. Her begging to stay with her Vovo, who was only here for one night, had worked. Jaco had made the offer and Izabella had agreed reluctantly. It seemed as if her daughter was spending an inordinate amount of time at other people's houses, and she truly missed her when she wasn't around. The underlying problem was that Leeni was an only child. Loving large groups and constant activity, the little girl was happiest when there were lots of relatives around. Shy in groups of strangers, she shined brightly when she was with her family and her personality bubbled up and over.

Izabella had truly been blessed with her. Sweet, patient, and loving, Leeni had one of the kindest hearts she'd ever encountered. And brave. Her daughter had shown her true colors during her illness, and Izabella could only marvel at her spirit.

Making the turn onto Lowell Street, Izabella asked, "Did you have fun?"

Leeni clapped her hands and answered from her booster seat in the back, "Oh, yes. I love it when I can stay with Vovo and Grandma Livia. Julian and I helped Unca Jaco mow the lawn this morning."

"You got to ride on the mower?"

Leeni clasped her hands as if in prayer.

"I wish we had one of them."

She laughed at the picture in her rear-view mirror.

"Our yard is a little small for that, *paquita.*"

There was a momentary pout, then a quick smile.

"Vovo made grilled ham and cheese sandwiches for breakfast this morning and I ate three of them."

"Three? My goodness. You must have been hungry."

Closing her eyes, Izabella offered thanks to the eating gods.

"And we had guava juice and coconut milk."

"I'm getting hungry just hearing about it."

Never one to stay on a subject long, Leeni asked, "What time are we leaving with Junie to go see Mr. Crackerjacks?"

"Keith is picking us up around three."

"How long from now is that?"

"A few hours."

"Is that long?"

"Not really. Although for you, perhaps it is."

Izabella was relieved when Melina shouted happily, "Oh, can you put this song up. I love it."

With the music blaring, Leeni seat-dancing to the beat, her arms moving back and forth, they rode the rest of the way home singing along.

Dressing carefully in her skinny jeans, a white cami, her Greenliner jersey, and three-inch navy heels, her make-up as flawless as possible, her hair tumbling down, Izabella was ready to go.

But Leeni was not.

"I want to wear a Crackerjack shirt, too, Mama."

Leeni refused to wear anything she suggested, until Izabella promised they would buy a Jackson shirt for her once they got to the park.

Keith had picked them up right on the dot so the girls could tour Bog Field before the game and possibly meet some of the players. Keith excitedly showed his girls the parking lot where his grandfather used to leave his car. Nostalgia was imbedded in Keith's storytelling as he relayed memories about the games he'd gone to as a kid. As a skilled negotiator of baseball contracts, he needed to keep his natural love of the game out of his head when doing business. Tonight, he felt free of all that and was passing on the tradition to his own children as Massachusetts natives were prone to do. This was a new experience for the family, and he enjoyed Holly's incessant questions about the Bog, the team and the history. It was a rich one. There were plans to build a new stadium near the harbor, the foundation already poured but Izabella knew they couldn't erase the memories. Keith seemed to be savoring them tonight.

Reid had given them a parking pass so they could bypass all the cars lined up outside the lots close to the ballpark. They maneuvered around the cars packed into the small enclosure and handed over the keys to the valet attendant before making their way out to Park Street.

As they walked outside the historical landmark, built in 1915, and one of the oldest baseball fields in the league, Fenway being the other, Sofia held Keith's hand, listening intently. Animated, he looked like a kid enjoying the sights and sounds that assailed the fans as they approached Baseball Way. Holly insisted he buy her a Greenliner jersey when Izabella had stepped into the shop for Leeni. She put it on with pride, showing just where her loyalties lay. Junie had wanted an Ovitz shirt whether to be different than her sister or because she just loved him, no one was sure.

The scent of sausages and peppers permeated the air, vendors hawked their wares, scalpers did their business, shouts of "get your programs here" converged to create the gameday-vibe.

The flags outside the park rippled gently in the breeze, sharing pieces of the past.

Once through the turnstile and into the dark and dingy subterranean area, Izabella could smell a different kind of aroma, and they stood in one of the food court lines for beer, sodas and peanuts.

Izabella was glad for the company and felt the excitement continue to build.

After walking up the ramp, emerging from underground, Leeni's hand in hers, Izabella scanned grass that sparkled, as if dew had settled on the surface. Adjusting her eyes to the change in light, she looked onto the field and was amazed again how brilliantly green it was. Watching a game live was different than watching it on television. Here there was a melding of the senses, the noise from the fans, the crack of the bat, the smell of beer, the sideline actions of players, coaches, batboys, and umpires. It was alive and she never tired of how it felt even though she would never admit that to anyone.

Keith had texted Reid to let him know they were here, and as promised, he appeared outside the dugout and called them down to introduce them to some of the players, giving the girls a chance to get some autographs. Meeting Reyes, Ovitz, Letts, Napolitano, Bance, Borinquen, Motta and Grizzle had been as exciting to Izabella as it was to Leeni. Her other thrill was feeling Reid's hand on her lower back as he made the introductions as if she were important to him and he wanted to convey that to his teammates. She knew it didn't mean anything, but it didn't lessen the pleasure she got from that simple gesture. Or the tingles that went with it.

They went on the tour, as Reid had suggested, walking around as the guide told them the history of the park, of Gruff Cliff, the original left field hill that had become the Beantown barrier. Another highlight was touching Posy's Pole, the dividing line between a home run and foul ball, named after a former player who'd wrapped quite a few balls around it over his career. Last but not least, they were taken to the scoreboard, where three men worked it manually every game, sliding number cards in to tabulate the score, inform the fans as to who was pitching and gave a running tab of the standings, and they did it without running water, air conditioning or heat. The one piece of information that made an impression on Izabella was that every player who'd ever played here, had scrawled an autograph within the small inner sanctum of the wall. It had copied Fenway in all the time-honored traditions. This place, like Fenway, was almost mystical.

Was Reid's signature there? His first game at Bogs Field was as an Athlete, back in 2006. What had it meant to him to hold the Sharpie and sign his name? She'd have to ask him.

The girls watched every move with an attention on detail as everything was cleared from the field, once batting practice was over. They chatted amongst themselves trying to pass the time until the game started.

Leeni was the first one to notice Reid, who was stretching at the wall.

"There he is. Number twenty-three, right Mama?"

Izabella looked in the direction Leeni was pointing in, and felt the ripples flow through her as they always did.

"Is he trying to hold it up, Mama? What will happen when he stops?"

Izabella's laugh tinkled as she explained what he was doing.

"He's just stretching, *querida*. He needs to do that because he uses his legs to pitch and he has to make sure they are loose."

"I thought he pitched with his arm."

"He does but he pushes off the mound with his legs. You'll see."

"When's it going to start Mama?"

"In a little bit."

"This is better than watching on TV. Can we come all the time?"

She smoothed the hair on the little girl and explained, "No. There are far too many games during the season and it would be all we do."

"That's okay."

Holly asked Keith a similar question. "Can we come again, Daddy?"

"I think so, Hollyberry. We can get tickets any time we want them now that Jacks is here."

"And you'll take us?"

Izabella sat amused at the look Keith gave Sofia, a crinkle at the corner of her eyes.

She'd been told that Mariah had never wanted to come to the games, thought they were a waste of her time. And Keith had clocked so many hours it was easy to let it slide.

Izabella dipped her eyes when he leaned in to kiss Sofia on the lips, as if he wanted to thank her in some small way. She pretended not to notice, but she swallowed a bit of envy that was there on the edges of her heart.

She lifted her face to the sun and looked around.

The seats weren't as good as Mike's, but she had a clear view of the action, and she followed the play-by-play on her scorecard, explaining the code to Leeni as she went, something Melinda had taught her to do during their outings. Reid got twelve strikeouts, only walked two batters, and kept the opponent's score low enough to win, two to one.

When he came off the field in the eighth inning, knowing the closer would be going in and he wouldn't be back out, he looked in their direction to see Leeni waving so enthusiastically that she almost fell out of her seat. Tipping his hat, he gave her a dazzling smile.

Worry etched Izabella's forehead.

Her daughter was becoming much too attached to a man who wanted no attachments. She'd have to be careful. Her heart could take the bruising but she didn't want Leeni's to be broken. Her daughter's endless chatter on the way back to the car about the player and the game did little to allay her fears.

Once they hit Route 93 North, the girls fell asleep, and quiet descended.

Izabella, in hushed contemplation, couldn't shake thoughts of how Reid looked on the mound and wished it had been an earlier game so they could have waited around for him.

She blew her bangs off her face, emitting a small moan.

She was also becoming much too attached to the man and she didn't know what she would do next time they were alone or where that foolish act would lead her.

She didn't have long to wait to find out.

He rapped at the door a few times before she answered it.

"I texted but you didn't respond."

As she rubbed her eyes, the sleep shirt went from mid-thigh to upper thigh.

He swallowed hard.

"I guess I fell asleep."

Suddenly he wasn't sure this was a good idea. Not with her sleepy eyed and looking very dangerous. It wasn't a combination that boded well for their fragile new friendship.

"I just wanted to stop by and wish you a Happy Birthday. It's after midnight."

"Thank you. It was a great game. Leeni loved seeing you play. It held her interest more than when Rique plays. His fielding is sporadic but watching every pitch kept her busy. She insisted I buy her a Crackerjacks shirt. I don't know whether you noticed her modeling it."

He had to admit he hadn't noticed much besides the woman standing in front of him, but when the little girl had almost fallen over waving to him, she was hard to miss.

He didn't have to lie.

"I did. She looked adorable."

Izabella looked up at him. He saw a question in her eyes that he didn't know how to answer.

His eyes locked with hers, and without thought and with no direct command from his brain, his fingers reached out to touch the patch of skin revealed in the button-down nightshirt. He traced a point from her chin, down her neck to the open vee, ending at her breastbone. His body reacted to the simple gesture as if she had stripped naked and begun to move sensually to a silent samba beat. He could still see the hips swaying gracefully, her long hair moving with her, tempting him, inciting a fire that raced through his blood. He knew he had to stop now or all thought would be gone.

Pausing, waiting for her to step back, to tell him to go home, he held his breath.

When she did the unexpected and began unbuttoning the small pink buttons, the breath he'd been holding came out in a deep rush, and he let his fingers slowly follow the opening until she was completely exposed to his view.

When he pushed aside the soft silk, her eyes fluttered closed. His fingers continued their exploration with great care, moving to her sides, making his way down to her hips, caressing her bottom, his thumbs sliding along the hem of her panties. His hands began an upward climb, grazing the bare skin of her stomach, before he captured her breasts in his palms.

When her nipples came alive beneath his inspection he kissed the small nub, his tongue licking hungrily at one and then the other. She unconsciously arched back slightly, offering herself up and when she felt his lips envelop a nipple gently sucking her in, her stomach clenched. He teased each sensitive bud, flicking his tongue across them before taking one, then the other, back into his mouth and gently suckling it. Once he'd gotten a taste, his fingers never stopped their exploration.

She reached around, encircling his neck. His eyes met hers. They were dark and filled with an incandescent glow. When she leaned into him, her lips danced fire across his, taking them in her mouth, sucking gently, nipping at them with her teeth, until he was nothing more than a throbbing mass of unbridled energy.

He captured her face and he counter assaulted, his tongue thrusting deep into the recesses of her mouth, tongue matching tongue, coiling, lashing. He felt her hands go beneath his shirt and lift it up, pulling it over his head in one sweeping, fluid motion before she pressed against him again so they were skin to skin. Her nipples teased and taunted him, and she shifted her body to better reach his lips, the brushing motion against his chest starting a fire that was heading towards a firestorm that raged completely out of control.

Her groan must have given him the signal to keep moving, keep pressing, keep kissing until she wanted him as exposed as she was.

Her fingers slid to his belt and she worked it off before undoing his jeans. When her hands began massaging that part of him that wanted more, demanded more, he could wait no longer.

After sweeping her up into his arms, he strode up the stairs, knowing she should stop him, stop this but he heard her whisper, "Door on the right." Elbowing the door open, he crossed the threshold, and he knew there was no going back.

He stood at the edge of the bed, her in his arms, her mouth still clinging to his, diving deep, taking hungry possession of it. His tongue met hers stroke for stroke until their bodies demanded something more. She caressed his neck and broke contact to gaze into his eyes.

It gave him the opening he needed. Laying her gently down on the quilt, her arms bent at the elbows, her legs long and lean, he studied her, his eyes laser beams of desire.

His body reacted violently to hers, a body that was everything a man could want and as she lay there, his eyes raking over her, taking her in, he felt her eyes on him but this time there was only the discomfort of his burning need.

Craving contact with her, he shoved his pants down and kicked them off.

When he put his knee on the bed and lay beside her, he began stroking and tracing her naked skin with his palms, not wanting to miss an inch of her. He caressed her shoulders, her arms before his mouth was once again drawn to her lips and their sweet taste.

Brushing away her hair, fanning it out around her head, he straddled her, continuing to maraud her body with feather-like kisses, telling her she was beautiful in languages they both understood.

When he felt her quiver beneath him, the rush of fire swept through him, impelling him to plunder, when what he'd wanted to do was to taste the sweetness in a long and leisurely fashion, to feel her breath against his face and hear her whimpers of delight. Needing to be inside her, needing to share her center, he readied them both for their joining.

But she stopped him.

Reaching for her night stand, she took out a packet that he recognized immediately. He managed to fumble the rubber on, and then in one swift move, she rolled on to his chest, teasing it with her nipples, kissing his neck, her hands in his hair, kisses chaste on his eyes, his nose, his mouth, becoming more passionate as she made her way down his body, her hands following, roaming every inch of his exposed flesh until he was unable to contain the feelings that were ready to spill out. It was torturous ecstasy and he began to grapple with his control.

After flipping her onto her back and placing his hands under her hips, he lifted her and plunged hard and fast, the hot, wet recess of her taking him in as far as he could go. He moaned low and throaty as his throbbing member told him to stop. She had him on an edge he could come off too quickly. He interlocked their fingers and raised them over her head, putting his forehead against hers trying to pace himself but the connection was too strong, his beating pulse too erratic to stop now.

The single movement, as Izabella tried to take more of him in was his undoing, and he began to thrust and edge out, thrust and edge out until he felt her muscles contract around him, pulling him deeper and deeper. He could do nothing but let go, and he poured all of who he was into her, holding nothing back. When her spasms were no more than slight tremors, he pulled her to him and buried his head into her neck. He wanted nothing more than to hold her in his arms the whole night through, and it scared him to death.

It hadn't surprised her that she woke up alone.

Not only did he have to catch a flight out of town this morning but the total consumption of each other would make him flee fast and far. Something she'd known going in, but the need to taste him had overshadowed all other thought. With merely a touch, all her promises to herself were forgotten, and before she could think it through her fingers had been working the buttons so she could feel more, taste more, and ultimately hurt more. It was probably the perfect way for her to end his siege, for there was no way he was coming back for a re-play. His fear had been tangible, in the air between them, locked as they were in the aftermath of sheer emotion.

She smoothed the pillow where his head had lain when he had kept her tightly pressed against him and shuddered as she remembered what his touch had felt like.

She had wanted him again, one last time, but her need would have seemed a weakness, one she wasn't letting him see.

And the hope that he would take her again was now forever lost.

She breathed in deeply, part satisfaction that she had gotten to be a part of him, part a residual of sweet longing.

After getting up for the time it took her to put her nightwear back on, knowing her daughter would be up soon, she crawled back under the covers. Only minutes later Leni ran in and jumped on the bed, squealing, "Good morning, Mama."

They got only a minute of snuggle time before Hoover jumped up on the bed, letting them know she had some business to do. Izabella readied herself to resume the life she had lived before last night.

That her body was still humming was something she'd just have to learn to live with.

Kissing her daughter's temple, she said, "Up, my little one. The day has begun."

"Is Mr. Crackerjacks coming over this morning?"

She wasn't sure how she was going to tell the little girl that Reid's visits would be a thing of the past, so she put it off for now figuring it would become plain as the weeks wore on.

"Sorry *paquita*, but he is travelling this week. He flew down to Florida early this morning for a game tonight."

"When will he be back?"

"Next week."

"Can we go to another game?"

"We will talk about it later. Right now, we have to take care of Hoover."

At the sound of her name, the dog flew off the bed and scrambled downstairs to wait by the back door.

By Friday, Izabella's suspicion of her fate had been confirmed.

What they had together was too powerful, something that most people yearned for, but something Reid wanted no part of. And something she was sure she would never find again.

Describing her feelings to Sofia, leaving out a lot of the intimate details that she wanted to keep as part of herself, felt good.

So had her friend's assessment of the baseball player.

"He is an idiot."

"Yeah, but he's my idiot. Or not."

"Why in the world does he do this to himself?"

"It has a lot do with his parents, his mother, his personal issues. Ghosts from his past have him spooked and I don't think he'll ever be free of them."

"Now what?"

"Now, I take a shower and wash that man out of my hair."

Sofia sang the next verse over the phone waves.

"And send him away?"

Izabella laughed out loud.

"Don't have to. He's already gone."

"Do you and Leeni want to come for dinner tonight? Keith's out of town and my mother is cooking."

"We'd love to. It'll be good to get out of my own head. I'm also trying not to think about the appointment coming up."

"How's Leeni been?"

"The fever comes and goes."

"Is she sleeping more?"

"A bit. But it could just be the way almost-four-year-old's are when they are very busy."

"We're there for you, you know that."

"I do and it helps. I talked to Melinda last night and she said she's catching a plane home if things…" She didn't want to go there, so she switched gears. "That won't be pretty. Reid will have a fit if he has to live with his mother for even one day."

"He can stay with us if he wants. It's a bit cramped with Mama staying with us, but we could squeeze him in."

"It might be good for them to be confined to the same space. Maybe he'd start talking to her."

"Do you really see that happening after all these years?"

"No. But like you said, he's an idiot."

"But he's yours so I'll keep my insults to a minimum."

"Thanks. What time should we be there?"

"Any time this afternoon. We can hang out. You can drink wine, I can watch."

"Has the morning sickness gone away?"

"For the most part. I'm actually feeling pretty good."

"I'm glad to hear that. See you later."

After dropping Leeni off at school, she busied herself with the listing she'd gotten yesterday trying to ignore the fact that she'd probably lost him for good.

CHAPTER SEVENTEEN

Reid picked up his phone and scanned for the number he was trying hard to avoid calling. He had spent the last couple of days doing his old routine, nights in bars, hitting up women with the intention of getting laid, but it wasn't doing anything to erase the night he'd spent with Izabella. And he had yet to see any of his advances come to fruition. He just wasn't up for it, both literally and figuratively. Izabella had taken him apart piece by piece, and he wasn't sure he'd ever put himself together again.

But it could not work.

She deserved forever with someone not the *here I am today, gone tomorrow* ritual he'd perfected over the last fifteen years.

The ring of his phone gave him a start...

Clicking on, Keith on the other end, trying not to let the disappointment show, he answered, "Hey. What's up?"

"You tell me."

"Pitching tomorrow."

"I know that. What are you playing at?"

"Baseball?"

"You know what I mean. I thought you were going to be friends."

Reid flopped down on the unmade bed, his morning almost ready to start.

"Murky again."

"But you waded through all that murkiness, didn't you?"

He looked over to see Motts just coming awake, so he put his head down and mumbled into the phone.

"Look she was the one..."

"Who knocked on your door after midnight?"

"It was her birthday. I just wanted to say..."

"Reid, you can't keep doing this every ten years or so. It's not fair to her. Either be her friend or don't but don't try to have it your way. This isn't Burger King."

"I know. I'm trying to figure things out but…"

"But nothing. Give her a chance to find someone else."

He jumped up and started pacing.

"Hey, wait a minute. She could have done that in the last ten years, don't you think? My coming back has nothing to do with that."

"It has everything to do with that, you idiot."

The undertone in Keith's voice was serious and his curiosity was piqued.

Coming to a complete standstill, he asked, "What do you mean, exactly?"

"She's been in love with you since she was a teenager. Girls don't get all puppy-eyed about someone they don't care about. What you did to her that summer was almost unforgivable."

"Don't tell me that."

"What the love part or the unforgivable?"

"Either."

"I'm going to tell it like it is, friend of mine. Just like you would."

Reid watched Motts crawl out of bed and head for the bathroom, giving him the privacy he needed to continue the conversation.

Once he was alone, he hissed, "Being in love with me would be downright dumb."

"We *all* know that. Her better than most. Love is blind, as they say. Reid, you can't offer her what she deserves, can you?"

There was a hesitation that had never been there before leading to words he'd never said before.

"Probably not."

He could just see Keith's expression. *Probably not*, was almost the same thing as, *I'm not sure,* in any other person's vernacular. *I'm not sure,* meant there was a possibility.

No. There was not one ounce of a possibility.

"Have you talked to her since…?"

"No. I'm doing my best to leave her alone. Even I know I can't keep doing this."

He looked up to make sure Motts wasn't listening from the other room. The pounding water from the shower told him his roomie was occupied, so he continued, "She hasn't called me either."

That part wasn't a complete shock to his system, although there were many parts that were. Women always called him when he'd vanish, if only for some closure, although it was usually to find out what the hell had happened. Izabella would already know the why. He could even wager a guess that she had done it on purpose to get him to leave her alone.

Well, she had shown him, hadn't she?

He was back between a rock and a very hard place.

He was going to have to shimmy out soon, but where his steps would take him, once he was free, he wasn't quite sure of yet.

"Did you expect her to?"

"No, not really but…" He cleared his throat and he told his friend honestly, "It was kind of…intense."

Reid felt a tightening muscle remind him of just how powerful their coupling had been and how he had almost reached out to taste her again.

Tempering his frustration Keith asked quietly, "What do you want from her, Reid?"

"I don't know."

"A relationship?"

"No. We both know that's not an option."

Keith provoked him by barking out, "Well, you've dumped her before, so I'm sure you have it in you to do it again."

Bristling, Reid countered most vigorously, "I never dumped her. That's insulting. I left. To go to school, to play baseball. There's a difference."

He'd never rejected her. Only his feelings for her. The problem was it was never easy leaving her no matter what anybody thought. He wasn't sure, after the other night, that he could do it again. Not as long as he still felt the reverberations from the earthquake that had hit him.

Keith's temper flashed. "What are you playing at?"

Reid's flashed right back.

"I'm playing with fire. I just have to find a way to put the flame out."

"And if you can't?"

"I honestly don't know, Keith. I've never been in hell before."

"Maybe she'll smarten up and leave you there."

Not liking either alternative universe at all, but one being much more acceptable than the other he said hopefully, "Maybe she won't."

"Are you planning on seeing her again?"

"I don't know. Why don't you butt out?"

"I'm her friend. And yours. I know your antics. I don't want to see a beautiful, kind, sweet person get hurt because you're an idiot."

Reid could hear the frustration in Keith's voice and he had to agree with him. Izabella was every man's dream. And she wanted him if he was any kind of judge of sexual interaction. In love with him if Keith was right.

Why couldn't he want her as badly?

But if he examined it closely, that was really the underlying problem, because he did.

His swallowing became obsessive as anxiety flooded his system.

He wasn't just fighting off the effects of their sexual encounter but the feelings that he didn't understand or appreciate.

Reid was pacing, his fingers pinching the bridge of his nose, his body totally out of control.

Motts had come out of the bathroom, rubbing his wet hair with a towel so Reid ended the call with, "Look I gotta go. I'll catch up when I get back."

As soon as Reid was finished with the conversation Motts asked, "So what was all that about? Who's in love with you now? I swear Jacks, you could give lessons on how to love 'em and leave 'em."

Struggling to find the right words to ward off Motts' curiosity he finally answered, "No love or leave to this story. That was Keith. He was just warning me that a friend has developed deeper feelings for me than she should."

After pulling a pair of pants out of the small closet, Reid slipped them on and zipped himself in before shrugging into a shirt, beginning the ritual of buttoning it up. Motts was getting dressed as well on the other side of the room. While in motion he asked, "When are we going to meet the bevy of beauties we figured you'd already have lined up? You couldn't have gone through all the single women here on your road trips."

Reid paused, knowing there were other expectations that came with his move.Motts added with a short laugh, "You might not know this, but I drew the short straw on roommate assignment, and I figured you would have already kicked me out of the room at least once by now. You have been trawling, right?"

Not knowing how else to answer, he admitted, "Just haven't found anyone worth throwing your ass out for."

"Thanks, friend. I do appreciate it. But that does seem a bit un-Jacks-like to me. Hell, to the entire team."

Reid slid his tie through his shirt collar, and started tying it, with difficulty. He had to restart it several times before getting it right.

"I guess I'm just still acclimating. My mind is on the team and pitching."

"And we appreciate it, me especially."

"You'll be the first one I introduce the lucky girl to once I find her, and I'll get a room, so don't worry about being out in the cold."

"Good to know. And I can hardly wait."

Returning to the bathroom, Motts left Jacks standing there wondering what the hell was going on with him. Then he pulled up the video of Izabella gliding in and out of her father's arms, the sensuality of her moves causing a shortening of breath, her hair floating around her, her smile so warm it beckoned.

He thumbed the scene off.

Determined to stay out of her web, he shoved the phone into his pocket and, with Motts tagging along, joined the guys in the lobby for their trip to the Marlin's home stadium.

The image of her was just as crystal clear the next morning. It hadn't helped that he'd watched the video close to a dozen times. He'd be texting someone, Keith, the trainer, one of his old teammates and his fingers would automatically pull her up so he could see the smile that lit up her face. He should delete it so there was no more temptation but he couldn't do it. He knew he'd have to banish her from his mind and other body parts, if he was going to pitch with any semblance of skill.

The unexpected visitor walking towards him as he was coming down to breakfast was the perfect diversion.

"Nolan, what are you doing here?"

His brother would come to his games whenever the Athletes played in Boston, but it wasn't often he'd take a road trip.

"Trying to get tickets to today's game. I'd love to get a look at the new Greenie player."

"You've got them. But seriously what are you doing here?"

"Lawyers convention starts tomorrow. I thought I'd come a day early and watch you pitch."

They finally hugged each other before Reid asked, "Join me for some food?"

"Love to. What's your day look like?"

They were seated as soon as they got to the hostess podium, decided on the buffet, and headed for the line.

Taking a tray and handing one over, Reid said, "I have to be at Marlins Park around ten, but you can come with me, meet some of the guys, hang in the locker room with us."

Nolan said, a smile on his face, "I was hoping you'd offer."

Scrambled eggs and bacon made it onto the plate, along with toast, orange juice, a Danish, and pancakes with syrup.

Making their way back to their assigned seats, they got down to business.

"How are you doing?"

"Good, I think."

"You settled in?"

"As much as I can be. Did you get the money I sent?"

"Yup, it's in her account. I wish you'd let me tell her…."

"That was the agreement brother of mine. I help this way, while you get the emotional brunt of it."

After their father's death, Reid had called Nolan long distance and laid out what he planned on doing for their mother to make sure she was well taken care of. No matter what people thought, he would never be able to stop loving the woman who had loved him so well when he was younger.

"I don't consider it that. She's really self-sufficient now."

Nolan had been trying to tell him that for years but he didn't believe him.

Buttering his toast, spreading some jam on it, Reid said, "I hear she watches Izabella's daughter when she's home."

Nolan's fork stopped halfway to his mouth, his expression showing his surprise that Reid broached this subject.

"Iz tell you about that?"

Taking a bite of the eggs, as if they were having a casual conversation and his senses weren't registering high voltage from the topic, he said, "Yeah, she lives across the street, so I've seen her from time to time."

"It was fortuitous that she bought that place. She checks on Mom daily so I don't worry as much. She looks amazing, doesn't she?"

Wiping his mouth, he tried to scoff, "Another Brazilian model," but it didn't come out that way.

The needle just jumped another few notches on his emotional Righter scale when he visualized her in his arms.

His brother prodded with a stick of dynamite.

"Wouldn't that be just your type?"

His face became a composition of a scowl.

"I don't have a type."

"Sure, you do. Beautiful and thin. She fits the category. Now."

"She's Izzie. She's not a type, doesn't fit into a category."

Reid was thumbing his ear. Nolan gave him a speculative look and asked, "What does that mean exactly?"

Unable to explain it, he merely said, "I liked her fine the old way."

"I'm sure you did, bro"

"What do you mean?"

"It helped you keep her at a distance. You'd get too close, you'd remember that she didn't fit your lifestyle, you'd disappear."

"How the hell do you know how close we got?"

"I had eyes, brother of mine. I'd see you sitting and talking to her in the family room, leaning forward, listening intently. You never wasted your time in conversation with anyone else. Too busy plotting and planning how to score."

"I'm a great listener."

"That would mean you'd have to stop talking and schmoozing and I didn't see you do that with anyone else."

"That was in high school. I've matured."

Nolan was finishing off the bacon, one strip at a time.

"Don't think so. Remember I used to visit you across continent. Didn't seem anything had changed."

"Things have changed."

"I might be able to buy some of it. You weren't with a woman this morning."

"Been busy."

"With what?"

"This and that."

Nolan must have been amused. It showed on his face. He loved seeing his little brother squirm.

"So now that Izabella looks the way she does, have you amped up your schmooze?"

"She's Izzie. I wouldn't make moves on her."

Lies, lies, and more lies. But who are you really lying to?

"The weight's gone, so why not?"

Sitting up straight, becoming almost belligerent, he said, "It was never about her weight."

Wiping his fingers on the napkin, swallowing the last piece of bacon, Nolan leaned back against his chair.

"I remember a time you told her to stop stuffing her face with the flan, that maybe eating an apple would be better for her. How about the time you took her to pick up something at the drugstore and left her to walk home? Said it would be good exercise. Or the time she asked you to go to her junior prom and you said you couldn't because you had a rep to protect."

Reid closed his eyes wishing Nolan hadn't brought that particularly sleazy remark. He still couldn't believe he had said that to her but she had thrown him so off guard with the request that he had said the first thing that came into his head. A night with those full lips, intelligent conversation, a chemistry that he still couldn't understand or deal with was out of the question.

Even with the weight, Izabella could ramp up his system.

"That wasn't one of my finest moments."

"She never did go. Did you know that?"

"I know, Nolan. I'd call a redo if I could, but I can't."

"Have you ever apologized?"

He hadn't. Didn't really know what to say or how to tell her the why behind it. He couldn't lie to her and he certainly couldn't tell her the truth.

"I'm an ass sometimes. Okay? I admit it. Can we drop this? I want to enjoy your visit."

Nolan couldn't help adding, "Well, if it hadn't been the weight, I guess you would have found something."

"If anyone finds fault with Izabella, they've got a screw loose. She's one of the most real people you'll meet, chubby or thin."

"I have to agree with you there. Does that mean…"

"Not a thing, Nolan. It doesn't mean a thing."

With a heavy sigh, Nolan finished the last of his toast before saying, "I worry about you, Reid. If you don't try to figure out what makes you act this way, you'll be doomed…"

"To a life without shackles?"

Looking his brother directly in the eye, he said, "No, to one without love."

And there it came again, the waves of desire for that woman washing over him to the point where he was drowning in her smell, taste, and touch again.

Wiping his brow with his napkin, he knew he was done with breakfast and only hoped he could focus on the game and not on a certain pair of lips.

Needing to put this conversation behind him, he said, "Okay, big brother enough philosophizing. Let's go play ball."

And he had, like a pro.

The Greenliners had won seven to three, and it felt good.

All wins did, but he wanted to impress his brother just like he had when they were kids.

And Nolan was impressed. It wasn't a perfect game but it was a good one.

They had been close when they were younger and he had idolized him, followed him everywhere he'd been allowed to go.

The night of their mother's accident had brought them even closer. They had cried in each other's arms, not knowing whether she'd live or die. And they'd ostracized their father to the point that Steven had given up his family. Getting through those first weeks with her in the hospital had been harrowing, and they had become a unit of worry and anxiety and solidarity. Nolan had taken care of him, had reassured him that everything would be okay, that their mother would come home.

And she had.

Or so it had appeared, but the woman who had returned wasn't the woman she'd been before.

Shutting herself away in a prison of self-absorption, she hadn't allowed them entry.

They had dealt with the transformation differently.

Nolan had been his mother's champion and had been there for her every day, aging overnight from a teenager to a man. He'd stayed close, going to college and law school in Boston while living at home. Only when he married Terry had he moved, but not very far. His little family lived in Andover, in the west part of town, like his mother and, where he practiced divorce law, taking their father's place in the firm upon Steven's death.

They spoke often but skirted most important issues.

It didn't seem as if Nolan was going to continue to let him ignore the details of their life now that he was back home.

And he wasn't sure he wanted to run away from them anymore, either.

Exploring his mother's room had given him a new perspective of who she was today, a woman who closely resembled the one indelibly engraved in his childhood memories.

He was beginning to want to open his heart a crack and see if it was true.

CHAPTER EIGHTEEN

Before Izabella could stop her, Leeni opened the door to Reid's knock. She couldn't scold her for allowing a stranger in. The front door was open so Leeni could see who it was beyond the screen. The welcoming smile on her face was almost comical.

"Mr. Crackerjacks. I'm so glad you came to visit."

Ruffling her hair as he entered, he returned the smile, with the one that could melt ice, and wandered into the kitchen.

She was on the phone, explaining why she couldn't show a house this morning, which he must have overheard. He was waving his hands in front of her trying to get her attention.

"Can you give me a minute, please?" Then a pause. "Thank you."

She placed the phone along her leg to give them some privacy.

"What are you doing here?" she whispered hoarsely.

"I...I just came over to say hello."

"Well hello...now good-bye."

The phone was on its way back up to her ear, but he snagged her arm preventing her from doing it.

"I can stay with Leeni. I have to leave by noon but it sounds like it's just a one-shot deal."

"Are you serious?"

"I wouldn't offer if I wasn't."

Exasperated, she whispered again, "You wouldn't know what to do with her."

Looking down at Leeni, he winked and said, "I think between the two of us we'd figure it out."

Leeni started doing her happy dance.

"Oh, please, Mama. I want to stay with Mr. Crackerjacks."

Giving herself a moment to think it through, she looked from one to the other, their looks expectant.

"*Meu Deus*, I must be crazy."

Returning to her conversation she said, "It looks like I might be able to after all. Let me just call and see if a showing is even possible. I'll get right back to you."

She pulled her iPad out, and she scanned to find the house her clients were interested in and called the number of the listing office to set up the appointment.

Confirming with the clients, she hurried to the stairs.

"I've got to change. Let's see if you two really know what you're in for."

Jumping into the shower, she cursed for agreeing to this. She had just promised herself she wouldn't put Melina at risk of being hurt, and here she was offering her to Reid on a silver platter. But the sale would be a good one if it worked out, and she couldn't take the chance the buyers would call the listing agent, which would cause her to lose the sale. It happened more often than people thought.

After racing down the stairs, not sure of what she'd find, she stopped at the foot, struck spellbound by the heads leaning together, Reid reading one of the Magic Tree House books Leeni loved listening to. Her heart constricted at the sight. Leeni was tucked into his arm, her head resting against his chest, as she paid strict attention to his words. Reid had a nice reading voice, inflective and modulated. His patience surprised her. Still unsure how long he could handle it, she almost changed her mind. Then changed it back.

Leeni looked content. She'd never taken to a man so completely, not that Izabella brought them home often. There had only been one or two who got to meet her daughter. Her eyes rested on Reid, his fingers turning the page, his eyes sparkling as he told about an afternoon on the Amazon. She had never seen him so complacent with a child. Not even Keith's.

As she moved into the room, they both looked up at her.

"I shouldn't be long. The house they want to see is only five minutes away."

"Like I said, I have until noon. Take your time. Make the sale."

Leeni looked up at him and said, "Doesn't she look beautiful?"

His eyes met hers, and a deep well of longing surged through her.

"She does, Leeni. But then your mother has always been beautiful."

She backed away from the heat, moved to her desk, and grabbed the hair clip resting there.

Pinning the ebony tresses up, she plucked up her keys and iPad.

She walked over to kiss her daughter good-bye, but stopped short. Reid's presence became overwhelming the closer she got, and she had to do a boxer's move, a feint to the right, then left, until she could manage a quick swipe on the small head before telling Leeni to make good choices and rushing out of the house.

He sat thunderstruck. In not even ten minutes, Izabella had managed to shower, the still-wet tendrils framing her face, dress, the skirt a multi-colored design of swirls and jersey a vibrant green both form fitting, apply makeup, if only minimally, which made her look even more beautiful than usual. Her heels were in her hands, and he studied the way she balanced on the stair bannister to put them on. Three inches at least, which made her frame look even leaner. He could feel the saliva collect in his mouth when Leeni asked, "Doesn't she look b-e-a-u-tiful"

He couldn't help but agree, even though he'd had to pry his tongue out of the knot to do it.

Mesmerized by her fluid movements and her glowing energy, he was also captivated by the halo emanating around her head from the sun filtering through the
window.

When she had come towards them, his breath held not knowing exactly what
her intent was. Watching the staccato moves, she finally leaned down, placing the
merest touch on the top of Leeni's head before twirling away. The heat surged and
there was a magnetic pull. He'd almost raised his lips to her in offering but caught
himself just in time. The loss of the succulent kiss was an acute one and he wondered again what he was playing at.

Agreeing to watch a three-year-old was totally out of character but the slight
weight against his side felt oddly gratifying. The experience might help him gain
some ease with the children at Dana-Farber.

As soon as Izabella was out the door, Leeni said, "Read, please."

When she pointed to the book, he regained his wits and continued with the story.

They had finished a couple of chapters and it seemed that Leeni was ready for
something else when she asked, "What are we going to do now?"

Reid had no idea what to suggest. He'd never really thought about kids as people
before. When Keith's were around, he rarely even acknowledged them.

The thought disturbed him.

Looking down at the face so much like Izabella's, a bubble of emotion rose, and
he wondered again who her father was. Who had gotten to taste that sweetness
before him? Who had helped create this remarkable little girl?

Relegating that thought to the back of his mind, he asked, "What do you nor-
mally do when your mother's working?"

She scooted to her knees and told him.

"I'm at school, Auny Addie's or Auny Sofia's. I play."

Brushing the fine hair off her face, the skin so soft beneath his fingers, he asked,
"What do you play."

"Dress-up with my dollies."

He wasn't sure he was ready for tea parties so he went another route.

"I tell you what. Why don't we clean up the breakfast dishes for your mama, and
cook something for dinner? Then we can play with your dollies. How's that
sound?"

He hoped the dinner would take long enough that he wouldn't be faced with
dressing Barbie. Her curves would remind him of someone else's he'd prefer to
dress or undress.

"I like that. What can you make?"

He had learned to cook for himself over the years and he knew his way around
a kitchen.

She slipped her hand into his and pulled him up off the sofa and the sensation
was compelling. It was so small, and he felt protective of her for a split second
before the jitters set in.

He released himself from her grasp and opened the refrigerator.

"Let's see what Mama has."

She was right beside him as he took an inventory. Izabella's taste ran to healthy and organic. Yogurt, fruit, fresh vegetables, several kinds of lettuce, almond milk, and a package wrapped in brown paper. Pulling it out, he read the Whole Foods label that said roaster chicken. He could do that.

"Pull a chair over. I'm going to fill the sink with soapy water and we can get these dishes into the dishwasher."

Clapping her hands in delight, she raced over to the stool in the corner and pulled it in front of the sink.

"I love to wash dishes."

Go figure. He had gotten it right.

The time flew and before he knew it, Izabella was racing into the house.

She wore a look of bemusement, as she inspected the small kitchen.

He had one of her mother's aprons on, peeling potatoes, Leeni sitting right beside him, the aroma of sage and chicken in the air. The kitchen was spotless, all the morning dishes out of sight, the counters clean, the dining room table set for dinner. Hoover was sitting beside the table, her head down on her paws, exercising excellent control.

Reid almost laughed at her expression.

"Think I couldn't handle it?"

"I must admit, I didn't."

"We've had a great time, haven't we, Leeni?"

"Yes, Mr. Crackerjacks. Mama, we took Hoover for a walk, cleaned up the breakfast dishes, read a couple of chapters in my book, and then made chicken. Mr. Crackerjacks said we could go to as many games as we wanted. He said that he'd take me to the zoo and the children's museum, to the park…and he wants us to go furniture shopping with him on Thursday. He really needs my help."

Leeni looked up from her assigned chore of putting the cut pieces of potato into a saucepan filled with water and said, a bit dramatically, "He has a whole house to fill, you know."

Shooting sparks of obsidian flew his way. He'd gone too far with his conversations with Leeni although she understood why. The little girl was easy to talk to and so inquisitive about life.

"That sounds like a very busy schedule, *querida*. You do know that Reid is gone a lot of the time."

"Yes. But he's not leaving again until ten days. Can we go to his game in California? It's his old team and he'd like us to be there to meet his friends and see him pitch."

"That is very far away Leeni. I'm not sure we could do that."

Her bottom lip came out in a pout as she thought about it.

"We go to Brazil."

"That's to see your grandparents. Not to watch a game."

Her face must have told her it was out of the question but it didn't deter her from springing a trap.

Her small head tilted, her eyes wide, her look devious, Leeni asked, "Then can we go help him buy furniture?"

"I'll have to look at my calendar. I might be busy on Thursday."

"He said I could see his house. You sold it to him, right, Mama?"

"I did."

Reid interjected a question, "Do you think I could get into the house again? I've been making a mental list of what I need but maybe you can fill in the blanks. You know, for the windows, rugs, what will fit, what I should buy?"

He looked so earnest.

This was the kind of things friends did, so maybe they would be able to make the transition.

Besides, he had just done her a big favor by watching Leeni, so maybe she owed him.

Tentatively she asked, "When did you want to go?"

"Thursday morning before I hit the stores. I've got all day. Would you be willing to come? I have no idea what I'm doing."

"Don't you think it's time you learned?"

"Absolutely. That's why I'm not hiring an interior designer. I want the house to look lived in. I don't want a showcase."

"You're not hiring the most prestigious firm in the city? To help boost your status?"

"No."

"My tastes run simple. You might not like my suggestions."

"I think it's just what I want. But even if you just point me in the right direction, I can buy what I like, with your input. So, would you?"

With an imperious air, Leeni reminded them, "With me."

His eyes went to the pretty little girl.

"Yes, Leeni, with you."

Begrudgingly, Izabella pulled out her iPhone, checked her calendar for Thursday and found she only had one appointment in the late afternoon and it could probably be re-scheduled.

"Well?"

"As your friend, I am willing to do this."

"As your friend, I accept your willingness."

He cut the last potato and watched as Leeni dropped the chunks into the pan, before asking, "How'd the showing go?"

She couldn't help a smile from emerging.

"They put in an offer, so thank you."

"That's what friends are for."

She noticed where his gaze had landed, right on her lips, and the fire instantly burned low in her belly. She had to get him out of here now or she'd be in trouble. Eying the exit she asked, "Don't you have a game to go to?"

He glanced at the clock on the wall. Pulling himself out of the chair quickly, he untied the apron, and in two steps had reached the door.

With one last glance at the two females, he said, "I'll see you Thursday."

Over the next three days, Reid took his morning coffee in his mother's bedroom. It had become routine just like his three-mile jog. He knew it was a gross invasion of privacy, but he was beginning to crave the feeling of belonging somewhere and it satisfied the need. He'd read the morning paper sitting in the rocker, looking out across the street between articles. He'd catch glimpses of Izabella and Leeni as they left for the day, admiring the way the two of them acted with each other. There was love in every glance and touch. The need to be with them was burning in his gut.

To the extent that he found himself knocking at her door bright and early Thursday morning, an hour earlier than they'd planned.

Leeni answered, dressed in a pretty dress with black patent leather shoes and a headband in her hair. Without thought, he lifted her up and said, "Good morning, Leeni."

She placed a quick kiss on his cheek and returned with, "Hello, Mr. Crackerjacks."

"Where's your Mama?"

"She's still getting dressed." Rolling her eyes for effect, she said, "I don't know what is taking her so long."

"Well, I came much earlier than I said I would, so we'll just have to wait patiently for her to finish."

Hoover was barking at the back door so Leeni let her in and the dog greeted her with enthusiasm, checked every inch of the kitchen floor for any food that might be available before finally settling down in her crate.

Taking Reid's hand, Leeni lead him back to the family room where the TV was on.

Taking a seat next to her on the couch, he asked, "What are you watching?"

"Despicable Me."

"What are those little yellow guys called?"

"Minions. Haven't you ever seen this?"

"No, I have to admit I haven't.

"You can watch it with me whenever you want. It's one of my favorites."

He looked over to the stairs when he heard footsteps, and his breath held at the vision Izabella created. He didn't miss the frazzled expression on her face or the stress in her voice.

"You're early!"

He dipped his head, sorry now he had made the impulsive decision to arrive when he did.

"I know. I apologize. I was just hanging around waiting and I figured I'd rather wait with you guys than alone."

Her eyebrow arched at his admission. After a moment of silence, she asked, "Do you want some coffee or something?"

"If it's no trouble."

"It's already made."

He watched as she disappeared into the kitchen, his eyes not leaving the doorway until she reemerged, a coffee mug in each hand.

"No sugar with a splash of milk?"

He took it and nodded.

"Pretend I'm not here. I'll sit with Leeni and watch the movie. I've never seen it before and it's one of her favorites."

Sitting on the edge of the couch, he took a sip of the coffee and became totally absorbed in the animated movie.

"So why does he want to shrink the moon?"

"He wants to be the baddest villain."

"Why did he adopt the girls?"

"So, he could get into Vector's place and steal the shrink ray."

"That wasn't very nice. What does the shrink ray do?"

"Just watch, Mr. Crackerjacks. You'll see."

CHAPTER NINETEEN

Izabella smiled when his legs went up on the coffee table and he leaned back against the cushions to do what Leeni suggested.

It gave her time to relax a bit.

Maybe she should go back upstairs and tidy up. Her bedroom looked like a cyclone had hit it. Clothes, shoes, and accessories covered every inch. She'd had no idea how to dress for the outing. She'd started out with jeans but tugged them off. People would be assessing her because of who she was with and she didn't want to embarrass him. After flinging another skirt on the pile, she'd heard Reid's voice and couldn't believe he had arrived so early.

It'd amped up her panic.

Out of time, she'd settled on a pair of tapered navy slacks with a white-button down shirt and her blue flats with the fruity swirls, spent a few minutes in the bathroom to throw on some make-up, brush her teeth, and braid her hair.

She'd wanted to present a calm and detached demeanor but as soon as she'd came down and saw him, her nerves had begun to buzz.

He had gone for the casual look and his jeans were old and faded, with one of the shirts he had modeled for her on his shopping spree. The shade was the exact color of his eyes and it enhanced his skin tone. His arms were folded across his chest and there was a swell of muscle that was clearly defined. It made her heart skip a beat. Spinning around, she retreated to the kitchen and puttered around dumping the coffee and washing out the pot, watering the herbs that sat on her small counter, remembered to check the freezer and take something out for dinner. And watched the clock tick away the minutes, thinking.

She still couldn't believe this.

She was going to help him decorate his home. It was far too personal an undertaking and she wasn't sure she could make the kinds of suggestions he was looking for. Sure, she staged houses, knew what he'd need for furnishings, but it was his space and she didn't really want to be so invested in it.

What was worse, he was behaving as if nothing had changed between them. As if the early hours of her birthday, when they'd burned the sheets in her bed, had never happened.

She didn't understand how he could be so blasé about it all.

The visual replay was incessant, and her nerves were a jangle of electric jolts every time she thought about his kisses, his skin pressed against hers.

But then again, it hadn't been a dream come true for him or he would have initiated something years ago.

Why couldn't she close herself off as easily as he did?

She'd tried putting up walls, bolting the door, but he always found the key and opened it so easily. She hadn't been able to change that or the way he made her feel.

The only thing she could change was how far she let him in. And she wasn't sure she could change that at all.

Stepping to the threshold, the credits beginning to roll, she announced it was time to go.

Leeni got up to put on the jacket she had laid out for her.

"What did you think, Mr. Crackerjacks? Wasn't it good?"

He was sitting on the edge of the couch and considered the story. Gru was a meany turned soft and mushy by three little girls. It wouldn't have been his movie of choice but it had its merits.

He asked, his curiosity getting the better of him, "What do you like about it?"

She exhaled, slumped down, her hands clasped in her lap and said, "They got a dad."

His heart took an unexpected hit.

He glanced over to see a look of horror on Izabella's face as if Leeni's admission had gutted her.

Her eyes met his and they held.

He no longer had the impulse to tell her to fix the situation so Leeni didn't get a complex.

She felt bad enough as it was.

Where was her damn father?

He wanted to throttle him, make him sorry he'd left them both in the lurch.

Neither one of them deserved it.

Leeni came over and cupped his face. "Don't look so sad, Mr. Crackerjacks. In *Despicable Me 2,* they get a mom. I have the best one ever."

Trying to lighten the mood, he asked, "What's going to happen in *Despicable Me 3?*"

He wasn't anticipating an answer, not realizing one was already in the works.

Leeni shrugged her shoulders and said, "I don't know. It's not out yet. Maybe they'll get a brother or sister."

They were just out the door when Leeni gazed up at him and announced, "I've been asking Mama for one, but she says I have to wait. Can you give me one?"

The door Izabella was closing slammed shut.

Her expression gave her exasperation away. Her blush, her mortification.

"*Pequita*, that is not how it works."

"Well how does it work? Keith and Sofia made it happen. Holly and Junie didn't even ask."

Taking her daughter's hand, she said, "That's a talk for another day."

It took a little wrangling to get the booster seat into the back of his BMW, but they were finally able to get Leeni buckled in and on their way. Izabella had brought her iPad so the little girl could play some games on the way to the house, making her oblivious to what was going on in front.

"Thanks for thinking about a notebook and tape for the measurements. I never even thought about it."

"It's what I do. And out of the mouth of a know-it-all, I'm good at it."

His thoughts slammed into a wall of desire when he remembered just how good she was at something else.

Shifting in his seat, he put his focus back on the road. Or tried to. Her presence was a major stumbling block.

Her warm voice didn't do anything to help his balance.

"While we were on the tour of Bogs Field, the guide told us every player gets to sign the wall inside the scoreboard. I assume you did so?"

With something concrete to side track his wandering mind, he smiled and admitted, "Yeah, and it was awesome. It was my first game there as an Athlete. I had heard about the practice but didn't give it a lot of thought until they invited me to do it. I wasn't prepared for the feeling. That park means a lot to me. I've been a fan since I was Leeni's age."

"We weren't able to go in or I would have looked for your name."

"I'm going to go back and sign as a Greenie in the next few days. Maybe I can get you a pass to come with me."

It was another milestone he wanted her to mark with him. He waited for the discomfort, but it never came.

"We'll see. Maybe you should take your mother. She lived your dream right alongside you. It would mean a lot to her."

"It's not exactly wheelchair accessible."

Glancing at her profile, her brows arched in thought, he asked, "Did you take her to one of my games?"

She turned her head and peered at him as if wondering how he knew she had or if it was just a lucky guess.

"I took her to every game you pitched here."

His eyebrows shot up and his eyes widened.

"Every game?"

Leaning back in her seat, she said, "Every one."

He was flabbergasted.

"Why?"

"Why do you think?"

He didn't have time to answer her because they had arrived at the house. But he thought about it as they measured every window and discussed what he'd need for every room, Izabella taking notes as they did. He realized it was not something he could process in a day, so he let it go as they headed to the strip in Nashua that housed several big outlets.

When they got to the first store, he had a good idea of what he was looking for. They went from one store to the next, buying what he liked, going back and forth about color and style. Greys and blues were the chosen hues, and painters were scheduled to go in as soon as they closed. He found a master bedroom set that he liked with a huge ebony four-poster, the scrolled headboard large enough that it wouldn't look dwarfed against the wall, a love seat and chair for the reading area in the blues he favored. The next stop was where he found an antique desk he wanted for the library. Izabella didn't understand the purchase because he didn't really need one and thought couches and chairs would more suitable, but he disagreed. He won that one. They agreed that the sunroom was designed for summer living so he chose a floral fabric that would liven up the space. He must have looked at a dozen dining room tables before deciding on one with twelve chairs he thought ideal for dinner guests. Izabella thought it would the perfect way to separate the open space between kitchen and family room. For his man cave, he chose in a masculine style with linen sofa, leather bench, cozy armchairs, and a bronze-iron-legged coffee table. A big-screen TV would hang on one of the walls.

As they were going through a warehouse, which they hoped would be their last stop, Leeni, who had been so patient and helpful but who was winding down, cried out, "Mr. Crackerjacks, look at that bed!"

Pulling her mother towards the full-size canopy, her face alight, she went on, "I would just love this. Look, Mama, it has a cover. It is a princess bed. Can I please get this?"

Izabella's eyes widened when she saw the price.

"I'm sorry, my love, but I don't think so."

"But why not, Mama? It is so pretty."

"For one thing, it would never fit in your room. For another, I'd have to take another mortgage out on the house."

"Please."

"I cannot do that."

Reid listened to the exchange, Leeni's face scrunched in desperation and need. Izabella might not be able to buy it, but he could.

He called a salesperson over and arranged the sale.

Izabella looked panicked.

"Reid, it will not fit in her room. What are you doing?"

"I have too many bedrooms anyway. I can put it in one of them. Besides, if Keith and the girls stay over some day, I'll have someplace to put them. Keith said they love princess stories."

"But I want it. I don't want Junie and Holly sleeping in my bed."

The voice began to quiver, the frustration giving way to tears and a high-pitch wail.

Squatting down, Izabella took Leeni's hand in hers and said softly, "I do not like the way you are sounding, *querida*. This is not your bed."

"But Mr. Crackerjacks is buying it for me."

The whine was loud, and Izabella glanced around to see if there were any witnesses to the bratty scene.

Reddening, she said more firmly, "No, he is not. He is buying it for his new house."

Izabella looked up at him, demanding something.

What did she want him to do?

Had he just made a mountain of a mistake?

He got the answer from the searing look that wouldn't end.

Sitting down on the edge of the bed, he drew the little girl between his legs and tipped her chin up so they were eye to eye.

"You promised to help me today and you just did that by pointing this out. I need a little girl's room in my house and I would never have known what would have worked as a princess bed. I promise that I will have you, Junie, and Holly over one night with their daddy for a sleepover, and you will get to sleep in the bed with them. Is that all right?"

The look of disappointment was still buried deep in her eyes, but she gave him a sad smile when she said, "I like that idea. And I'm glad I helped you. I promised I would."

She leaned in and gave him a kiss on the cheek and said, remembering her manners, "Thank you Mr. Crackerjacks."

"Thank you, Leeni."

With a slow, disbelieving shake of the head, Izabella stood speechless.

Meeting her eyes, he asked, "Okay?"

"I can't believe it. She was going into meltdown. Now look at her."

He did.

She was gazing up at him with hero worship, as she held on to his hand.

By the end of the day, he had purchased everything they thought he'd initially need to live comfortably and arranged for delivery. He was leaving on an extended road trip the afternoon of the closing, so Izabella agreed to be there to arrange the furniture the way he'd wanted it. When he returned from his upcoming road trip, all he'd have to do is head there instead of across the street from where she lived.

He wasn't sure he was going to like it.

Just as Izabella climbed into bed, her phone rang.

Reaching over, she picked it up and answered.

"Thank you for today."

His voice held that baritone growl but it lacked the swagger. It made her smile.

"It was a nice day. Thank you for dinner."

"It's the least I could do after all the help you gave me."

"I really like what you bought. It matches the style of the house."

"Maybe I do know what I'm doing."

She was picking at a thread on the quilt that was coming undone.

"Yes, I think you do."

It was a pleasant surprise. He had picked pieces she might have if she'd had the money to spend on a house that grand.

"Wanna come to my game tomorrow night?"

Her heart rate spiked at his invitation, but she breathed deeply and got it back to a more regular tempo.

"I can't. But I'm coming in on Saturday."

"Why not to see me pitch?"

"My parents are in so they can see Enrique play. We planned it so we could go as a family. It's an afternoon game so Leeni can come. No one's sure how long he's going to be on the road with the team, so they want to catch as many games as they can before he's sent down again."

"That's right. I forgot he'll be playing shortstop against me."

"Don't tell him but I'll be rooting for your team tomorrow."

"Not on Saturday?"

"He *is* my brother."

"Can you and Leeni wait around and go home with me?"

The thought of that constricted her chest and she gulped in a breath.

"I think we're grabbing something to eat after the game so we can be together. Do you want to join us?"

"Not sure that's a good idea."

"They won't give you a hard time."

"I know but I'm still kind of on Juliana's side in this."

The thrill that had shot through her at his invitation faded into annoyance.

"Reid, she's not here, but my father is and I love him. There are no sides any-more."

There was a pause, as if he were thinking about it. She knew his loyalty would be with the woman, who'd taken such good care of his family.

"Why don't you and Leeni come into Boston for tomorrow night's game, stay over and I can meet you both for breakfast before you meet up with your father and his wife."

This was getting complicated and she balked.

"Oh, Reid I don't think so. That's a lot of baseball for a little girl who, for as much as she loves watching you play, doesn't do well sitting still for long."

"Can she stay at Keith and Sofia's? I'll call them and see if they want to bring the family in for another game. Leeni can come in with them and she'll only have to sit through one long, boring game without me pitching it."

She missed his attempt at humor.

"Another sleep-over. I'm not sure."

"I think it's an excellent idea. I'll get back to you in the morning."

When she went to speak, he had already cut her off.

His text arrived the next morning as she was sitting at the table reading the paper. He'd arranged everything.

The tickets would be at the box office. The hotel room was booked at the same one the Mets were staying in so it would be convenient for her to join her family for the next day's game.

We'll have the whole night.

Her heart-beat accelerated when she read the last line.

The whole night? What was he doing?

She thought she'd just be going in to see him play, not spending the night with him, assuming that's what he meant. That hadn't been part of the dialogue, not that he'd let her have a part in it.

Maybe it was just a resurgence of his smarm, a part of him she didn't like very much.

She needed to figure out what he was playing at so she could arm herself with the rules of the game. But knowing him, he'd change them as he went.

Then another thought intruded.

As legendary as his pick-ups, was his exclusivity when dating. He might spend weeks finding that certain someone but when he was involved, he was monogamous.

He stayed with someone until he didn't.

So maybe…

She slumped back in the chair.

She was exhausted from trying to analyze his motives or where she stood with him, and it didn't do anything to solve her dilemma.

Her choice was to go or not to go.

How far to let him in?

Her solar plexus tightened at the thought of being in his arms tonight so she guessed there was no choice really at all.

She packed a small bag with the necessities, still debating if she had worn the right thing. Her room was becoming a changing station with the number of outfits she tried on and discarded, all over the bed, chair, and floor.

This had to stop.

As she drove to the Zamouttos', one hand rubbing her stomach, the question came back to echo in her brain.

What did he want from her?

Was this just friendship Reid-style?

If this weekend proved to be as intimate as she expected, she knew she'd be on the receiving end of another round of delays and departures as soon as it was over.

Was she ready for that and would one more night be enough to satisfy?

Maybe she just needed to let go of the control she was trying to wield over their time together and go with the flow. Let it be what it was, which was something too delicious to be denied.

Sofia greeted her at the door and hugged her.

"So, a Greenie fan by night, a Mets fan by day?"

"It would seem that way."

Keith appeared with Junie in his arms but set her down when she saw Leeni. The girls ran off to play as soon as Leeni kissed Izabella goodbye. Keith placed his arm around the oldest one of his females.

"He sure planned this out, didn't he?"

"Life in his fast lane. I didn't expect to be spending the night."

"Are you sure you're…"

"No, I'm not. I truly don't know why I'm letting him sweep me away like this. I should have told him no, like I've been trying to do since he got back but I guess I have to mean no when I say it."

"He doesn't do no well. He would have dug in his heels until you gave in."

"I know you're right, but I should have more will-power than this."

Sofia took her hand in hers and squeezed.

"We'll call you when we're leaving. That way you can meet us at the park."

"I'm staying at the same hotel as my family. Do you just want to meet me there? Then we can go over together?"

"That might work."

"Okay."

Turning the knob of the front door, she added, "I packed Leeni's Jackson shirt, so she shouldn't give you any trouble. The girl has got a serious Crackerjacks crush going on."

"Like mother, like daughter."

She gave a slight shrug. "If it's easier for you, I'll meet you at the park and join up with them later. That way I get to hang with you guys for a while. I might need some loving kindness. Who knows if Reid will be speaking to me by then."

Keith gave her a knowing look, concern etched in his face.

"We'll call tomorrow and work it out."

Reid was back on an adrenaline high, but it wasn't the upcoming pitcher's outing that had him reeling but the thoughts of another night with Izabella. She had let him stage the scene without the usual no, although he was beginning to think the no was just a knee jerk reaction to avoid the see-saw ride they shared every few years.

He'd gotten to the field at his usual time, gone through some of his rituals, and then texted her to see what she was doing, but she hadn't gotten back to him. An hour later, he texted again with the same non-result, and he began to worry that she was going to blow him off. He hadn't really given her the time to decline his invitation. And they had never discussed the staying-over part of his plans. Maybe she was doing what Keith had suggested, but he didn't like the thought of suffering in hell alone. He wanted her company.

Texting Keith, he asked, *Izabella coming?*

Didn't you talk to her?

Not returning my texts.

She's not here, buddy. Don't know where she is.

Is Leeni there?

You sound like a man who's getting desperate.

Cut the shit. Is she there?

Yes, Reid. Leeni is here. Relax. You're finally on the other side of the coin. I kinda like it.

I kinda don't.

Deal with it. You expect others to.

Completely ignoring the jibe, he asked, *What time did she drop Leeni off?*

Reid had to wait almost fifteen minutes for Keith to get back to him. All he could do was pace the small confines around his locker.

Around four thirty.

Why isn't she answering my texts?

My crystal ball is at the shop being buffed so I can't answer that.

He gave up at Keith's attempt at humor.

Maybe she'd been driving when he'd sent the first text and couldn't respond. But certainly, not the second. Why hadn't she gotten back to him by now? She had to be in Boston. It was close to six thirty.

After throwing his phone in his duffel, he pushed himself out onto the field so he could do his stretching and get ready for the game to start. As he headed out towards the wall, he looked back to the section of seats he knew she'd be sitting in.

He exhaled in relief.

She was here, being welcomed into the exclusive wives' club.

His nerves pulsed and screamed for another reason. He had just given her a golden ticket, and he wondered how he'd be able to rescind it when the time came. For as much as he wanted another night with her, he wasn't planning anything permanent.

She had to know that, right?

CHAPTER TWENTY

When she gave her ticket to the usher, unsure where she'd be sitting, she was disconcerted when the man in green snapped to attention. Her stomach gave away her anxiety. It was churning again. The seat assigned was in the Greenie section and as she made her way along the aisle, she got some speculative looks from the other women there.

Sitting here were the players' wives, girlfriends and family.

What the hell was he doing?

As she took her seat, she was glad she'd gone with a more upscale version of casual. Her black fitted pants were matched with a feminine white cotton lace blouse. Over her arm, she carried a black-and-white-check jacket that she hoped would be warm enough. Her black ankle boots were new, something she'd broken down and bought this afternoon even though they were more expensive than her taste usually ran. Indulging herself had never felt so good. She'd anticipated the prospect of meeting some of the women but never thought she'd be sitting amongst them. It was way outside Reid's comfort zone.

Dressing to impress wasn't in hers.

The thought that she had made her cringe.

If she was playing charades, she had to rethink her game options.

The pretty blonde woman sitting next to her introduced herself.

"Hi. I'm Millie Boxberger. Who are you here with?"

"Um, Reid Jackson."

"You must be Izabella. I'm Nancy Motts. My husband catches him."

There was a gleam in her eye that Izabella didn't understand.

"Yes, Hello. Izabella dos Santos."

She shook the woman's hand. The devilish smile on the woman's face was making her stomach queasy.

What had Reid said about her?

Another blonde, who Izabella didn't recognize, introduced herself. "Hi, I'm Janine Swindell. You're dating Jacks? We have so been waiting for this. I was beginning to think his reputation was all hype."

It was a reasonable question. She was occupying a seat in the VIP section.

"Goodness no. We've been friends for many years."

"Oh. We keep waiting to meet a girlfriend or two."

There was a tinge of disappointment in the voice.

Leslie Bullard, one of the pitchers' wives, seemed excited when she said, "We're so glad he's here. He makes a big difference in the rotation. That perfect game he threw had me on pins and needles."

An easy smile came over Izabella's face.

"Me, as well. It's like I pitch the game right along with him, tell him what to throw, where to put it. It's hard leaving it in the hands of the catcher."

She gave Nancy a shy smile. Nancy gave her a knowing look.

Schuyler Keogh agreed. "I know what you mean. Whenever Ollie is on the mound it's nerve- racking whether he's pitching well or not."

Several of the wives drew her in and she felt welcome, laughing before the start of the game at some of the stories and shared history. It was a tight group, and she wished she could find a home here but knew the pumpkin would replace the seat somewhere around midnight.

With the first pitch, she withdrew from the conversation and put her focus on the man she came to see.

He looked like the old Jacks, in control and command of the ball. Motts was becoming his catcher of choice. They had found a rhythm that was hard to beat.

Izabella leaned toward the field and pointed towards shortstop.

"That is my brother, Enrique."

Nancy asked, "Your brother? He's been giving the team a hard time. Swings like a natural."

Michele Napolitano laughed. "My sister thinks he's dope. I believe that's a good thing. Maybe you can get her his autograph?"

"I'm sure I can. I'll be here tomorrow with my family to see him play."

"So tomorrow you'll be rooting for the opposing side?"

"Yes and no. The Greenliners have become my team of choice. That might change when my brother moves up, but for now...I'm a fan."

"Because of Jacks?"

"I guess you can say that. It is more fun when you have someone to root for, yes?"

"Does Jacks know?"

"About Rique? Yes."

"Let's see what he gives him."

Izabella was sure it wasn't what Rique wanted. It was youth vs. experience and experience won hands down. He struck out on three pitches, like many of his teammates had, but one of the few hits of the night was Rique's single in the fifth inning.

Relaxing a bit, the score five to one in the Greenies' favor by the bottom of the seventh, she lent her attention back to the wives. Conversation centered around their fundraiser.

Leslie glanced over and asked, "We'd love you to be a part of it. It's a fashion show and you'd look amazing on the runway. Would you be willing?"

Not really knowing what to say, the night's adventure a potential for exile to a faraway no-Reid's land, she offered back, "I'm not really family. I will have to talk to Reid about it. He might have a girlfriend by then and it would be awkward."

Not wanting to let Izabella escape that easily Leslie added, "We also hold the Strike Out Hunger campaign in July. Fans receive autographed pictures of the players for a ten-dollar donation. We could always use some help. It's been awhile since we've had a former Cy Young recipient on the team, so his signature will be highly sought after. We were hoping he'd have a girlfriend to spark interest. People always like to dish about us, meet the women who got the ballplayer."

Shifting in her seat, Izabella reiterated, "But like I said, I am not his girlfriend."

She wasn't sure anyone would get this ballplayer.

Nancy Motta piped up, "Well, you're something girl. Motts tells me that you're the only one Jacks talks about."

Izabella knew Motts was Reid's roommate, but she couldn't quite wrap her brain around that statement.

"Jason tells me he sticks close to the hotel while they're on the road. Doesn't sound like the Jacks we anticipated."

Leslie looked at Izabella while weighing her words. "It's not what we expected when he was traded. There were some pretty wild stories."

"Yes. I have heard them."

What else could she say? She wasn't going to share his history. That was his story to tell, not hers, but it unhinged her knowing that he had not invited anyone to a game before. His penchant for a woman a month was legendary. Well, if she was this month's flavor, she'd be terminated soon. Then the group would get to meet a bevy of beauties over the course of the season. There were only a few days left until her expiration date. Maybe he was just making the most of it. But the intense pleasure at hearing he didn't go out nights bubbled up, and she allowed it to float through her system.

After the game, the women milled around, knowing it would be some time before their husbands and boyfriends joined them. The press, ever present, was holding interviews with the players, Reid always the first one tapped when he was on the mound. Izabella watched on the screen in the underground tunnel, just outside the wives' waiting room, as engrossed in him as when he'd been on the field.

"Great game, Jacks."

"Thanks. The guys really rallied behind me. Today was the kind of team effort a pitcher hopes for."

"Your fastball was right on target. I don't think anyone hit it."

"Oh, someone did. Dos Santos is already an asset to the team. Give him a couple more years and he'll be irreplaceable."

Izabella smiled at the tribute to her brother. There was respect in Reid's tone, something she hadn't expected.

She stood on the outside looking in as the men began to emerge from the locker room. There was kissing, hugging, joking shared by the couples and Izabella's nerves started to jangle.

She hadn't thought about this part of the night.

How should she greet him?

With a congratulatory hug? A chaste kiss on the cheek?

How would he respond to the connections she had already formed to the people around them? Would he realize what he'd done? Her exile might start sooner than she'd expected.

Her mouth was dry, and as she continued to wait, she began to think he had changed his mind and was staying put until everyone was gone, including her. She wished she'd gone back to the hotel to wait for him there. It would be far less humiliating for him to abandon her in private than in front of all these witnesses.

As she was just about to turn tail and run, he came out, zoomed right in on her, and smiled that heart-melting smile. She returned it tentatively and waited for a cue.

In that instant, she knew that she could not live her life this way, always walking on eggshells, wondering how he'd respond to her presence. This would be the last time she'd go out on this very brittle limb. For one last time, she'd take what she could get and be done.

When Reid exited the locker room, he didn't even need to search for her. Something inside told him right where she'd be, and he ambled slowly over to where she was. She looked beautiful, fresh and feminine, and he could do nothing but help himself to a light brush of his lips over hers, his hand around her neck, holding her in place.

The vibrations began their hum and his blood began to race.

He regretted taking his time, but he'd made the mistake of mentioning to Motts that Izabella was here, it hadn't taken long for the entire locker room to be in on his secret.

When he'd first arrived in Boston, the guys had been open about his reputation and past exploits, ribbing him about his flavor-of-the-month routine. Tonight, expectancy hung in the air that his long-standing pattern had begun, and the jokes about Izabella had pissed him off. The locker room talk had never bothered him before, so he didn't know how to respond without giving the guys the impression that this was for real. Which of course, it wasn't. It was just a friendship with some impressive benefits. One he'd love to maintain no matter who came in and out of her life. As hard as it was for him, he kept his mouth shut, hoping he'd be the last one to leave and avoid the speculation he'd already seen growing in his teammates' eyes.

Until her face came unbidden and the need to see her, to touch her overcame his need to outlast the inquiring minds. She was more beautiful than the image that had nettled his heart.

"Are you ready?"

Motts' question interrupted the hum.

"Some of us are going to McGreevy's. Want to come?"

Reid didn't want to share her company with anyone.

"Not tonight, Motts."

Nancy took Izabella's arm and started walking away and said, "I like this girl and you are coming with us."

Motts said under his breath, "They've already talked amongst themselves, and it seems like she's made the grade, but from what they've heard about you, they figure she won't be around very long. They are definitely taking advantage."

When Reid gave him a sharp stare, Motts looked sheepishly at him and confessed, "You already knew your reputation preceded you. And the girls have been waiting a whole month to meet the first of your beauties. And just so you know, they already hit her up to model at the fashion show."

Reid's gaze bounced from one wife to the next. The fashion show was in September, over three months away. Who knew who he'd be with by then. His skin was prickling when he whispered, "What did she say?"

Continuing the dialogue in undertones, he said, "That you were only friends, you might have a girlfriend by then, and it would be awkward. That kiss you gave her, though, said something else entirely."

Motts gave him a jab to the ribs.

Reid silently commended her for being honest, and the bristling started to dissipate, despite Motts' assessment of the kiss.

"I've known Izabella for more than half my life. We'll always have a connection."

"Is this the friend who has deeper feelings for you than she should?"

Upset with himself for letting that tidbit out, he avoided the question, hoping it would go away on its own.

Other words were out of his mouth before he could stop them, and they were directed to Jason's wife. "If she wants to be in the fashion show, she certainly can be."

Leslie gave a small whoop.

"I'm keeping you to that, Jacks. No matter who you are dating by then."

Mott's lead the way to a couple of tables in the back of McGreevy's.

"They always save these for us on game nights. We're what you call regulars."

Reid positioned Izabella between him and his catcher, with Nancy, the Bellasario's, the Bullard's and the Keogh's filling the seats. The second string, the Swindell's Carros', Pimental's and Garcis' were seated at the table to their left.

The waitress came over, and they ordered numerous appetizers. While they waited for their hunger to be appeased, they sat and talked about the game, families, the upcoming road trip.

Reid had his chair pushed back out of the circle, his leg crossed over his knee with one arm draped over Izabella's chair, his fingers stroking her shoulder. It took all his will power to sit as part of the group and not whisk her out of here.

Nancy asked, "So what do you do for a living, Izabella?"

"I am in real estate."

"Really? We've been looking for a house for a couple of months now and haven't found anything yet. Now that Motts is here for a couple of years, we decided we liked the area enough to buy. I don't like renting. I like roots."

"Where did you move from?"

"Cincinnati. We just sold the house so we have money in hand and we're ready to go."

"Where are you looking?"

"Winchester. I love the vibe."

"It's one of the best suburbs of Boston."

"Yeah, schools are supposed to be great. It's a priority."

Motts put his hand on his wife's and said, "Enough shop talk, girls. You don't like it when we talk baseball. Ditto."

Janine Swindell asked across the tables, "You say the two of you are friends but that kiss said something else, Jacks. What is it? Friends with benefits?"

Reid fumed. He'd heard about Janine. No one seemed to like her and now he knew why. She had a penchant for gossip, and he was pissed that she and her husband had tagged along.

The chilly tone in Reid's voice all but placed her out in the cold.

"I'd say that's between me and Izabella. Wouldn't you?"

Not one to be denied, Janine turned the conversation back to Izabella, and asked, "Just killing time until you find your Prince Charming? You are looking, aren't you?"

Reid noticed Izabella's fingers clasp more tightly in her lap. He didn't like this question either.

Thought it was way out of line and a lot intrusive. And he didn't want to know if Izabella was looking for someone to marry.

As if pissed off by her question, Nancy, who'd been studying them, asked, "Does a person actually go looking for Prince Charming? I thought it was something that just kind of happened."

Talking over the group surrounding her, Janine went on. "She's with Jacks. If they're friends she knows what the requirements are for an invite to a game and that she won't find her white knight with him."

Reid almost smiled as that Brazilian temper he thought might be below the surface flared. "Can't two friends just go out to enjoy each other's company?"

Janine looked from one to the other.

"Not with the way you two look. Sexy times sexy equals bed."

Reid was now glaring at Janine, who must have realized she'd crossed a line. She tried her best to get back across it.

"Sorry. Too inquisitive by half and the two margaritas didn't help. No inhibitions when I'm curious. You two are just ridiculously attractive together."

He stiffened. Izabella glanced at him as he did. Probably to cover their scent, she said in a quiet tone, "I'll get married someday. It just hasn't happened yet. Jacks, on the other hand, will always be Jacks."

Never hearing Izabella refer to him as Jacks, he was discomforted with the tinny way it sounded to his ears. He took one of her hands and linked her fingers with his own, needing to ground himself. That she hadn't already gotten married was just pure luck on his part. She'd had the opportunities but for some reason had decided against it.

But for how long?

Until someone came into her life who swept her off her feet and could commit to a future? The implication caused a wave of anxiety that knocked him completely off guard. It would mean an end to their friendship, something he couldn't even contemplate. Not yet. Not today. Certainly not tonight.

Brushing his fingers against the palm of her hand helped restore his equilibrium. The panicked haze was clearing, and he waded back into the conversation, which had settled on baseball, a safer subject. Or so he thought.

Janine, curiosity rearing its ugly head again, asked, "Did you happen to see the blog that's resurfaced with you and that blonde?"

He had been caught on video at a sorority party, a girl straddling his lap, her legs dangling over his, the kiss deep and wet. It was a lesson learned and a mistake he never repeated.

"No, can't say I have. In my defense, I was twenty-three, single, had just won the Cy, was feeling my oats. Hopefully, I've become a bit more discreet since then."

His hand had tightened on the one in his lap and he pulled it to rest on his chest.

Victor Bellasario added, "It's the way of the world now. Don't know who's recording what. It's caused a whole lot of problems in some baseball marriages."

Nancy countered, "Serves the guy right for being so stupid."

Reid knew who they were talking about. A married player on the team was outed when a video on YouTube emerged. Flaunting his animal prowess had caused major repercussions and ultimately a huge divorce settlement.

The guy had been a fool.

There was an unwritten rule among the players that a warning was issued before a wife's arrival so those still playing the field outside the bonds of matrimony got a heads-up to keep their affairs out of sight. That rule was sacrosanct. If a player was discreet, his wife never found out about his infidelities. If he wasn't, it was his own damn fault if he got caught.

There was an unwritten rule for wives as well. Keep the secrets. It made it hard to trust their spouses, and other wives, and caused moral dilemmas that most of them didn't want to confront.

Their server brought over several dishes, including spinach and artichoke dip, marinated chicken tenders and wings, flatbread, and nachos, and spread them out between the tables.

Reaching for a tender, Schuyler Keogh asked, "Where are you going to be living, Jacks?"

After taking a swig of his beer, he answered, "Andover. Hometown as most of you know."

Reid hadn't made any move to share in the bounty, but he asked Izabella if she wanted any and she shook her head. She was on her second glass of wine, and he thought she might want something else in her stomach, so he grabbed a plate and put a couple of chicken tenders on it, placing it in front of her.

Nancy, transferring a pile of nachos to her small saucer, asked, "Have you moved in yet?"

While he was serving Izabella, he noticed Janine excuse herself to go to the ladies room, and he smiled when no one offered to go with her. It made him feel better about the couples at the table. From what Motts had told him, it was an exclusive group that was committed to keeping their lives out of the public and intact.

"The closing's next Thursday."

"Do you have stuff coming from Oakland?"

"No. I was renting a furnished place. All I took with me were my clothes and some personal stuff."

"Does that mean you're here to stay?"

"I sure hope so."

Jason Bullard slapped him on the back. "I hope so, too. It makes my job easier."

He felt Nancy's stare before she stated, "We heard you had an attitude. Left that behind?"

The hesitation was brief.

"It would seem so. I love being here so I'll watch my p's and q's."

Victor signaled the waitress over, ready to order their third round of drinks, when Jacks stood up, gently pulling Izabella up to join him, still holding her hands. Extracting some bills with his free one, he placed them on the table and said, "Thanks for the company but I think we'll get going."

Izabella said to the room at large, but Jason, in particular "Good luck tomorrow."

Reid joked, "I thought you were going to route for the other team."

"I think whichever way it goes, I'll win, no?"

Maneuvering around the tables, he led her out, his hand still linked with hers.

At the bar, Reid stopped and pulled out a few hundred-dollar bills. "I'm buying the next round for the two tables back there."

"I'll make sure they get them, Mr. Jackson."

As he turned to rejoin Izabella he heard a strident voice call out to him, "Well, if it isn't Crackerjacks."

Turning, he recognized a woman he had been involved with one night during a three-day series last year. He had left without calling and never answered any of her texts. The time hadn't been memorable, a diversion at best, but the voice he'd remember on his deathbed.

"Regina. How are you doing?"

"Getting by. I'd say let me buy you a drink but you'd probably be gone before it arrived."

"I'm actually with someone, so I guess you'll just have to buy for someone else tonight."

"Of course, you are."

Peering around him, she caught sight of Izabella, standing quietly to his right.

"Word of advice, he's a user. Don't get your hopes up."

Taking Izabella by the waist, rolling his lips into a straight line, he led her out to the parking lot, got her settled, got behind the wheel and leaned over for the kiss he'd been waiting for all night, a deeper, more in-depth offering than the one earlier. His hands worked her hair off her face.

He whispered, "I'm sorry about that."

Her words were said softly, as if she didn't want to hear them herself.

"Why? She didn't tell me anything I don't already know. There's nothing exclusive between us. I know the rules. You can be with anyone you want, as can I. If you'd rather be with her tonight, I can find my way back to the hotel."

Sliding his hand behind her neck and pulling her towards him so they were eye to eye he said,

"It is exclusive between us right now so you better not be with anyone else. And you are the one I want to be with tonight."

And to prove it, he kissed her again, his lips plying hers with skill and feeling. When his tongue entered her mouth, she welcomed it, meeting it thrust for thrust until he couldn't take any more.

His breath came out in a hiss of steam and heat.

"We'd better leave. I'm a bit too old for the back seat and I can't guarantee I won't take you here and now."

He breathed into her ear, "You are mine Izabella. Only mine."

His hand never strayed from her thigh, caressing it as they made the short journey to the hotel.

They hadn't even gotten the hotel door closed when Reid's hands were on her, quickly stripping her of her clothes and her doubt.

Emboldened by the way he was making her feel, she gave herself up to him completely. The touches lingered, the kisses smoldered, the tension mounted, until they could stand it no more and let the flames consume them. And unlike other nights, their bodies joined again and again, the heat never being entirely extinguished. As she lay beside him, inhaling his scent, feeling the hairs on his arm around her waist, his fingers warm to the touch, she put it all to memory.

When she woke, she glanced at the clock rather than the other side of the bed. She knew he was gone, his body heat no longer emanating to her. The night had been nothing short of magic and this was only another dimension of the illusion. Devastated that he could not feel what she did, her eyes began to burn with unshed tears, but she refused to wallow in her misery. She had expected nothing less than total desertion.

Throwing the sheet off, sliding out of bed, her body sore but well-used, she padded to her suitcase and pulled out her bathing suit. She needed something to soothe and calm her, and the thought of cool water on her skin was just the balm. It might also help wash away the hurt of his abandonment. Retrieving her scattered clothes that lay across the carpet, Reid's already plucked from the floor and gone from the scene, she was unsure she could stay in this room another night, without him. Slipping into the bathing suit and flip-flops she'd brought in case Melina wanted some water play, she picked up the room key and headed for the elevator. She passed a lot of ballplayers on the way down. One could tell who they were just from the attitude, the way they walked, held themselves.

She'd have to check to see what room her father was in when she got back, agree to a meeting time and place once Melina arrived.

So engrossed in her thoughts, feelings, and destination, she missed her brother's short wave as he escorted a beautiful girl down to the lobby.

The pool room was all but empty, it being very early in the morning, so she dropped her cover on one of the chaise lounges and dove in. The water was warm, and it felt good against her skin, and with each stroke, she regained the strength she'd need to face the day.

Reid was whistling when he opened the door, stopped when he noticed the empty bed. He was surprised that she was already up this early after the night they had spent doing everything but sleeping. When he called to her, there was no answer. He dropped the coffees on the bedside table and spun on his heel searching the small space.

Where could she have gone?

Her suitcase was still there on the floor, so he knew she was here somewhere but the silence coming from the bathroom told him she had abandoned the room. The hotel was huge, but he promised himself he'd find her if he had to scour every square inch. He hadn't meant to be gone so long, but he'd bumped into some of the Mets players on their way to breakfast and had taken the time to chat. Not pitching today meant he could interact and not hold back.

Exiting the elevator, he saw Rique and hurried his steps to catch up with him.

"Hey, have you seen your sister?"

"I did. She looked very sad."

That was impossible. He knew he had satisfied her completely. He felt like crowing.

"Where is she?"

"It looked like she was on her way to the pool."

"Thanks."

Rique caught his arm. "You do not dare to hurt my sister again. You may be bigger but I will win that fight."

"I care about your sister. I wouldn't consciously do that."

He had to assume it was Jaco who had told him some of their history, a history that neither one of them seemed to be learning from.

"You have a reputation, no? You are playing with fire there, and it will be my sister who gets burned."

He couldn't say anything to refute Rique's assertion about playing with fire. There was so much heat between them it scorched everything they touched. He wasn't sure Rique had it right, though, about who'd get burned. He was beginning to think it might be him.

As soon as Izabella's brother released his arm, he raced back to the banks of elevators, read the hotel grid to find the floor he needed, and punched the button, his fingers tapping a quick beat against his leg.

Stepping off, he saw her through the glass, graceful strokes from one end of the pool to the other, and he stood mesmerized. She was beauty in motion, slow, sleek, and silky. Unable to tear his eyes away, he watched, transfixed, as she finally pulled herself up the steps, her body shimmering, almost completely revealed in a barely there bikini that gave everyone a strong indication of what was beneath. And his breath was trapped in his lungs.

Her bottom was round and the suit looked more like a thong until her fingers pulled it back in place, covering the most obvious curves. The front panel was a tiger print, attached to the back by mere strings on either side, and it lay just above her pubic bone, the abundance of visible flesh breath taking. The top fit her perfect-size breasts like a glove, and his fingers itched to undo the crisscross back strings to uncover the orbs that lay underneath.

He was as hard as he'd been last night before their midnight marathon, something she seemed to invoke just by being in the same room.

The thought of bolting this morning had been a strong one, but when he'd looked back for one more glance of her, the pull to stay was far stronger. He needed time to think it through, what it would mean, whether he could do it, but when he'd been consumed with getting back to her before she awoke, he'd had his answer.

When he'd found the room empty, he had panicked.

Looking at her now, the panic resurfaced.

A man was walking over to her, a predatory look in his eye, one he knew from use, and he recognized him as one of the Mets. Reynolds reached out his fingers and touched the tips of Izabella's wet hair, too close to her breasts in Reid's estimation, and he waited for Izabella to step back. When she didn't and the fingers seemed to be brushing the side of one of them, he felt something surge through him.

Keeping his tone as neutral as possible, he called, "Hey, Iz."

She turned towards his voice, the pale look of shock clearly visible.

"I thought you had gone," she said in almost a whisper.

He was beside her, his arm around the petal-soft skin of her waist in two strides. He refused to let her see how much he needed his hand on her. He said easily, "Yeah, to get coffee. Thought you might want some."

Facing the man who was now his rival in more ways than one, he simply said, "Jamie, I think you'd better find someone less engaged."

"Sorry, Jacks. Didn't realize. You shouldn't let this one out without an escort."

It seemed everyone knew his tactics. *This one* implied a string of them.

"Seems you're right. She's got a mind of her own. Go for coffee, she goes for a swim."

"Next time tire her out."

Picking up her towel from the chair and wrapping it around her, gently pushing her hair off her face, he whispered, looking into her eyes, "I thought I had."

Taking her by the hand, he led her back to the room, where he made another attempt at doing just that.

When they woke, they had breakfast in bed, made small talk, made love, his hand never far from some part of her, until he had to shower, dress, and leave for the ballpark. Kissing her again with as much passion and depth as when they'd started, he realized the ardor hadn't diminished at all. The searing look he gave her before closing the door behind him spoke volumes.

Pausing outside the room, his hand still on the knob, he hesitated.

The thought struck him right in the solar plexus that he did not want to leave her.

He had booked himself a room down the hall but had never even stepped foot in it. It was his safety valve, the one always in place for times like this. For the first time ever, he hadn't used it. He had wanted to stay by her side, even when the fear of the profound connection they shared was bone deep.

He didn't know what any of this meant, and he wasn't sure how long it would last, but he knew he needed to stay with it until the freaking fire was out. If his hands weren't on her, he felt adrift. If he didn't hear her voice, he felt alone.

He reinforced the thought that they weren't dating, that it was just a passing phase, that it couldn't last a lifetime, but his heart just wasn't buying it. Being with someone else was something he couldn't even contemplate, and the thought of her with someone else set his teeth on edge. When that Mets player had been within an arm's reach of her, a green monster had rebelled. He'd had to work at keeping his jealousy from rearing its head.

Jealous.

Him.

It had never happened before, and he didn't like the way it sat heavy on his shoulders.

He didn't know what to do with the burden, or the fact that he was even acknowledging that it existed.

What was he going to do about it?

He just didn't know.

When the word *forever* flashed in his head, he thought of Bogs Field, being a Greenie player, the Beantown Barrier, his brother...and beneath it all was Izabella's face, her smile, her heart, and he didn't like the fact that she was so closely attached to that word. He was going to take some time and space over the next couple of days to find his way to a solution they could both live with.

CHAPTER TWENTY-ONE

Izabella watched him go. She'd never felt so well loved.

And yes, that was the feeling.

Love.

Reid had made her feel that he was here with her completely.

His touches had been tender. He had taken her with gentleness and care and then, as if the demons from hell were at his heels, with urgency and power. They had spent what little time they slept entwined together. And he had stayed all night and into the morning, something she thought he'd never do. She would have bet money he had a room somewhere in the hotel, his safety net in the event it didn't feel right or he needed his space.

She didn't know what she was going to do now.

It felt right being in his arms, such a natural extension of her feelings, and she wasn't sure she could end it. Taking it day by day, seeing where it would go, might be her only option. She knew she should walk away before he did. Keep her dignity, her pride intact. The outcome could only be affected by his willingness to change, to accept the inevitable and what they had together. All she could do was what her heart and mind dictated. If he walked away, she'd just have to manage it the best way she knew how. And if the past was any indication, she knew that day would come.

She also had to take care of Leeni's heart. The little girl was crazy about him. An invitation into their lives had already been extended, so what did she tell her daughter when the vanishing act occurred?

As if thoughts of her daughter conjured her up, the phone sang.

"Good morning. Someone here wants to say hello."

Keith must have handed the phone off, because next she heard Leeni's voice whispering, "Hi, Mama. I'm coming soon. I missed you."

"I missed you as well, *querida*."

"I have my shirt on."

"That's good. I'm glad I packed it."

"Will we see Mr. Crackerjacks today?"

"Only in the bullpen, my love. He pitched last night. Today you go to see Uncle Rique."

"Do I have to root for his team?"

"We will be with Vovo, so I think you might have to."

"Then I don't want to go."

Her personal brand of stubbornness was revealing itself and Izabella sighed. Lack of sleep and the inability to be decisive was going to make her less than patient, and it sounded like patience was the order of the day.

Forcing tolerance, she asked, "You don't want to hurt Uncle Rique's feelings, do you?"

"No."

"And seeing that Mr. Crackerjacks isn't pitching today, you won't be rooting against him."

"I guess."

"So, maybe you can root for your uncle when he's up at bat?"

"I could do that."

"Good. Can I talk to either Sofia or Keith, please?"

"Yes, Mama."

Waiting on the line, hearing voices in the background, she was relieved when Keith finally came back.

"Has she been like this since I dropped her off?"

"No. She woke up a bit cranky."

There was a pause before he admitted, "She had a nosebleed about an hour ago."

A freight train of terror hit the tracks and was barreling into the unknown.

"I'm so sorry. Was it a bad one?"

"Izabella, don't apologize. It took a bit of time to get it to stop but she seems okay."

"*Meu Deus*, I left her and I shouldn't have."

"You went out and enjoyed yourself for a night. There's nothing wrong with that. You did enjoy yourself, didn't you?"

"Too much. Now I'm afraid. He's confusing me again and I don't know which way to turn."

"I'm sorry, Iz. If it's any consolation, he called this morning from the field to see when we would be in. He sounded a bit...off."

"What do you mean?"

She noticed the pause, as if he was trying to figure out what to give away and what to keep.

"He told me that he stayed the night and most of the morning. I can tell it has him rattled."

The disturbing situation of Leeni's nosebleed cleared up any confusion she had over Reid Jackson. She didn't have the energy for his useless self-protective instincts and she said as much to Keith. Her energy needed to go elsewhere if her intuition proved correct.

The symptoms were explicit and clear, no intuition needed.

Self-recrimination set in and the roots had taken hold.

"Leeni's my number one priority right now. I won't have the time or the toler-ance to play his game. No more eggshells. I need to have my feet firmly on the ground."

"I think that's a good strategy. Let him stew in his own juices for a while. He won't like it."

"This is not a strategy, Keith. I am not out to catch him. I can't help how I feel, I can't stop loving him, but he just dropped on my list of priorities."

It was the first time she'd acknowledged that she loved him. She guessed it was way past time.

Keith hadn't missed her declaration.

"As Sofia has pointed out on more than one occasion, he is an idiot."

"I think maybe that phrase refers to me. I keep repeating the same mistake, over and over. Maybe this will put out the fire."

Why should he change if she was so willing to run into his arms at the merest inflection of his finger? There might possibly be something much more important to deal with in the days ahead, and that was where she would put her focus. It would no longer be on a man who wouldn't even attempt to break down his wall.

"I get it, Iz. I just hope he does."

"That is not my problem anymore."

"It never was."

She could hear noise in the background and Keith say, "I'll be right with you."

His voice was back in her direction.

"Troops are getting restless. We're leaving now so we should be there in about an hour."

"Thanks Keith. I'll be in front, waiting."

Melina seemed exuberant when the game started. Full of energy, she watched the hitting practice, pointing Reid out to Paolo and Livia. Giving her uncle equal time, she enthusiastically waved to him while he was warming up on the field. She seemed happy to be with family and sat on her VoVo's lap during the first few innings. As Izabella studied her daughter, her throat constricted, and her concerns grew heavier than she could bear. Leeni was still so pale, and from what she'd been told, she had skipped breakfast.

Waves of anxiety washed over her.

She couldn't do this again. It had taken everything out of her, and it had taken almost a year for her to get back to what most considered a normal life. She had never celebrated the end of the treatment. There had been no relief when the days of driving to Boston were over, no easing up of the hopelessness, only the worry that it would return, and they'd have to start all over. And here it was. The day she'd feared had arrived. She was sure of it.

It was so easy for her to slip back in time and feel the ache of seeing her daughter so drained and exhausted from the painful treatments. Leeni was older now and would understand more, would know what she was facing. When the little girl crawled into her lap and fell asleep, a wave of pure panic overcame her, and all she could do was hold on tightly, letting her love surround and protect her.Reid attempted to stay away from any conversation about last night or Izabella, but he wasn't successful. The guys were still ribbing him about his choice of date, in that she was the Brazilian beauty of this Boston sports team. He ignored them by arranging things in his locker, a useless activity, but it kept his hands and mind busy and off a particularly beautiful woman.

He couldn't believe the fascination was still so strong, that he could feel their connection growing instead of diminishing each time they were together. She had become an obsession in his blood and it still raged inside. In fact, it had gotten harder to stay away from her.

His strategy hadn't worked at all, and now he was left with no backup plan and a lot of sexual frustration.

Ha.

After all those times he had taken her, he was still as hard as a rock, still needed to feel her under him, taking him into her hot, sweet center...

Cursing under his breath, he took his glove and headed out, needing to run and release some of the pent-up energy that still incessantly pulsed through his system.

Motts watched him stomp away and said to his back, "Who woulda thought you'd sink so deep."

Reid noticed when Izabella, holding a sleeping child, left with Jaco. Until then, he had split his attention between the two families. The Zamouttos were having a great time, the girls animated, part of every wave that wound around the stadium, and the dos Santos' huddled together, as if discussing something other than baseball. Their looks were somber, even when Rique hit a homerun into the grandstands. He thought about texting Izabella but he was forcing himself to keep his distance for the time being. It was important for him to discern what part of the attraction was physical and what part was emotional, or if heaven forbid they were merged into one. And what he'd do if they were.

With as much discipline as he had in him, he kept his promise and didn't contact Izabella over the rest of the weekend. But by Monday he had run out of will power and had given up his attempts to stay away from her. Reaching out to pull her close every waking morning only to find the space beside him empty was taking a toll he'd never had to pay before. Each day they were apart he was losing a part of himself he hadn't even known existed. He had almost resigned himself to wanting those shackles he'd sworn he'd never wear. With Izabella, they didn't feel binding.

Dressed for his morning jog, he let himself out the front door, gearing up to pay a short visit before he headed down Beacon Street. What he found was an empty drive-way. It was barely light out and he wondered where she could have gone so early.

He wished now he had contacted her last night when he'd gotten home from the ballpark, and his unease at her absence gnawed at his gut. He hoped everything was all right. Hopeful that pounding the pavement for five miles would eventually lead to a clear mind, he realized that nothing was going to extricate her from his life except his own idiocy and he just better figure out what to do with it.

He texted her as soon as he returned to the condo.

I need to see you. We need to talk.

He kept checking his phone, but after an hour, after he'd showered, shaved, and dressed, she still hadn't responded.

He texted again before leaving for Boston.

CHAPTER TWENTY-TWO

Reid had visited a couple of rooms at Dana-Farber already, the kids in the cancer unit, always so happy to see him. Numerous doctors and nurses had gone out of their way to introduce themselves, congratulating him on his perfect game, wishing him the best. He had met numerous other caregivers who seemed to genuinely care about the children here and he felt diminished by the little he could do to improve their lives. Bringing in autographed balls and photos didn't seem like much but the smiles he received when he'd hand them out brought him a little satisfaction.

One of the nurses stepped out from behind the counter and pulled him aside.

"Reid, we just admitted a little girl. Would you mind going in and sitting with her? Her mother is downstairs waiting to talk to the doctor to go over the blood-work. She was wearing a Jackson shirt when she came in so we thought she might like to meet you."

"Sure. What room?"

Girls were the hardest to talk to. He didn't know what to say, quite how to reach them, but then he smiled and remembered he had just watched *Despicable Me*. Maybe that might be a good ice breaker.

"Room1335. Down that hall and third door on the right."

Reid combed his hair back with his hands. He was still a bit on edge and hoped the movie line worked. Not that it mattered. He'd have to come up with something. Letting his aversion to hospitals and sick kids prevent him from entering this room would be the coward's way out, and these kids deserved better. He was taking a small step forward and refused to turn tail and run.

Hesitating outside the door, he gave a little knock and peeked inside.

She was lying on her side, her small head on the pillow looking pale and drawn, but the smile she gave him when he entered, hurt his heart.

"Mr. Crackerjacks. What are you doing here?"

His heart froze and then began to pound without mercy. His hands trembled and his voice lost the power of speech.

He barely croaked out her name.

"Leeni?"

She gave the briefest of nods, and her eyes slipped closed, the exhaustion clearly visible on her face.

Walking slowly over to her bedside, he gently sat at the edge and brushed the hair off her face. She was warm to the touch and fear the likes of which he'd never experienced, coursed through him.

Licking her lips, she asked, "Did you come to visit me?"

Taking her small hand in his own large one, he said simply, "Yes, I did."

"Did you bring me anything to eat?"

Trying to get his brain to work through the haze he said, "I didn't know whether you could have anything."

"They pretty much let me eat what I want. But I'm not very hungry. You would have wasted your money."

"I could never waste my money on you. Before I come next time, I'll check in and see if there's something you want."

Her body curled into a ball.

"I don't feel so well."

He began to stroke the fingers he held.

"I can see that."

"Will you stay with me for a little while? I'm kinda scared."

"Of course, I will."

What could he say? How could he reassure her? There's no reason to be afraid? She was lying in a bed at the Dana-Farber Center which could not mean anything other than what it implied.

"I don't want to hurt again, Mr. Crackerjacks."

Again?

"Were you sick like this before, Leeni?"

She nodded feebly.

"When I was little."

When she was little? She was still little. Why hadn't Izabella told him?

Because you weren't around back then, imbecile, wouldn't have done her any good if you had been. Never once did you call in all the time you were in Oakland.

The thought thundered in his brain. How had he let her go so easily?

What had it been like for her to live through this nightmare?

He had met some of the parents of the children admitted here, the ones who stayed by their kid's bedside twenty-four-seven, experienced the tears, witnessed the looks of anger and helplessness. It was agony for him on the outside. He couldn't quite capture what it must be like for those close to the illness. In one second, he had come in from the outer perimeter and knew exactly what they were feeling.

Nursing your child through something like this? He cringed when he thought about the drama he'd brought to Izabella's doorstep.

A weak voice caught his attention.

"I'm sorry but I want to go to sleep now. Is that okay?"

"Of course. There's nothing for you to be sorry for. You rest. I'll stay right here until your mama comes back."

Although his immediate impulse was to go searching for Izabella and see if she needed anything, a shoulder to cry on, an arm to lean on, he sat, stroking the fine hair on Leeni's small head, impatient to find out more and see how Izabella was holding up.

Eyelids fluttered up to look at him, maybe to make sure he was still there, maybe to find something she needed in his presence.

His heart went from hurt to cracked when she said, "Mama's scared, too, Mr. Crackerjacks. You tell her not to be okay? We'll get through this."

Placing a kiss on her temple, he assured her that he would.

She clung to his hand, shifted her body closer to his, and he gently lay down beside her and cradled her in his arms.

She was so small and vulnerable and she felt light as a feather, resting her head on his chest. As he stroked her back, pictures of her came into his head, playing out like a video. The first time he met her, leading him into their kitchen so he could eat with them, watching that movie and holding an almost adult-like discussion on the merits of a good father, walking Hoover while she talked at him a mile a minute about her friends, her school, her family, the smile that could make his day, so like her mother's, grabbing chunks of his hair when she wanted his attention, her kisses on his cheek. He brought her even closer to his healthy body, wanting to impart some of his strength into her frail one.

A nurse stuck her head in to check on how they were doing, and he gave her a thumbs-up, not wanting to move for fear she'd awaken.

He looked around the hospital room, taking in all the special equipment they would need for her care. After visiting other rooms, other children, he had some idea of what she'd be hooked to soon, certain it would be more than the IV that was already pumping liquid from a bag into her system. He knew very little about the disease itself other than it was potentially fatal and that people had to go through a rigorous regimen of toxins injected into their bodies. He glanced down at the sleeping form, quaking at the thought she would be one of them. Had already been one of them.

A thought slammed into his head and he asked himself, did her father know?

He couldn't conceive that someone would not want to know his child was going through this. Be there for them. He must be a real shit if Izabella hadn't even contacted him when she was diagnosed before.

Did she even know who he was? Or where he was?

She'd said he'd been a one-night stand but that was so out of character for Izabella. Had she really slept with some stranger?

Unbuttoning his shirt, the warmth of Leeni's body infusing his own, he refused to picture Izzie with anyone other than him.

His musings were brought to an abrupt halt when he heard an irate voice ask, "What are you doing here?"

Jaco had come into the room, his tone filled with an anger that Reid still didn't understand.

"She asked me to stay with her until her mother got back."

"How did you know about this?"

"I visit the sick kids when I can. I came in this morning and found her here."

He was trying to extricate himself from the tangle of sheets without waking her. She clung to him even in her sleep. Would Jaco notice or refuse to see?

"We've got this covered. You can leave now."

He wasn't sure if he should stay or go but decided this wasn't the time or the place for a confrontation.

He bent down and told Leeni that her uncle was here and that he had to go, kissed her head, and tiptoed out the door, his eyes not leaving Jaco's as he did so.

Striding to the nurse's station, he asked gruffly, "Where's Leeni's mother?"

"Melina's a patient of Dr. Cutler. Ms. dos Santos will probably be talking to him by now."

"Where is that?"

"Downstairs in the Pediatric Oncology Department."

Pointedly he asked, "What's the diagnosis?"

"We're not sure yet. Her medical chart hasn't come up yet. But from what I understand, she's had a relapse: leukemia."

His heart shrunk when he heard that word. Just another word for cancer. It was such a big word for such a little girl.

"What will happen now?"

"That's up to the doctors and Ms. dos Santos. Dr. Cutler will set a goal for her, write up a protocol, and then they'll begin treatment. Sometimes a relapse calls for a different option than the first go-round."

"Will she get chemotherapy? Radiation?"

"I don't know that, either, Mr. Jackson. Like I said, we don't have her chart yet. Are you asking out of curiosity or is it something more?"

"I know this little girl. Her mother is a...friend."

Such a small word for such an enormous feeling. He wished he knew what to call her...

Still stunned, Reid walked distractedly towards the bank of elevators and, once he exited, stopped every ten feet to get directions. His mind wasn't holding information very well.

This was not something that would be cured with just some medicine, and he winced at how cavalier he had sounded during his conversation with Keith this morning. His friend had told him Leeni was sick but he didn't realize...

Why hadn't Keith told him the severity of the situation?

If he'd known...

Don't blame this one on Keith, asshole. If you had just picked up the damn phone over the weekend, maybe she would have told you. You saw them leave the game early. All you had to do was ask what was wrong. But no, you had to take care of your bleeding heart.

Closing his eyes, he battled for control, castigating himself for his selfishness.

He had taken the weekend to think, to find a way to extricate himself from the hook that had him by the....by the what? Balls? Heart?

He knew very well that Izabella hadn't set out to hook him, and she hadn't become the stone that was dragging him down. She had called him only once since he'd been traded, and it was in response to his succession of texts. She had put no pressure on him, had said no numerous times to his invitations, had only reacted to his advances, had never issued one of her own. Knew him too well to depend on him when the chips were down.

This hook was self-inflicted, his own demanding need causing him to seek her out, before the bone-deep fear had him backing away. He was the sinker, weighing her down with his unfailing need to take care of himself.

He was dealing with an age-old problem and it was his. Keith had been right.

She was dealing with *real* fear.

He needed her like breath but never once considered how she might need him. Didn't want her to. He never once gave a thought to what was on her plate, his own selfish agenda taking priority over everything else.

And it had to stop.

Fear sucked, but he was in too deep now to turn and walk away.

At another station, he stopped to inquire about Dr. Cutler, and it seemed as if he had found what he was looking for.

With no thought to hospital protocol, he knocked and entered the small space where the doctor sat holding Izabella's hand, but all he noticed were the tears streaking down her face.

When she glanced up to see him standing there, she swiped at them. The doctor firmly told him he had to leave, that it was a private consultation and he did not belong there.

Before the doctor could escort him out, Reid explained, "We're…" he glanced at Izabella before continuing, still knowing the word didn't adequately describe what they were. "Friends, Dr. Cutler and when I found out Leeni had been admitted, I wanted to see what I could do to help."

Izabella, almost as pale and drawn as her daughter, asked weakly, "How did you find out?"

"I've started coming in periodically to see the kids. The nurses asked me to go sit with a new patient until her mother got back. It was Leeni."

Her eyes met his with a fierceness he hadn't seen before.

"The only thing you can do for me now is something you won't do."

"I'll do anything. What is it?"

"Pick your mother up at the airport and bring her here."

He was staring at the pained expression on her face, and all the issues he had with Melinda evaporated into thin air. This was something he could do for her. And would.

"What airlines and what time?"

Her relief was visible and he felt his chest puff out as if he was doing something of consequence.

"JetBlue. Ten thirty. She'll have her wheelchair."

"I'll carry her if she doesn't."

Her expression softened, the tears still glistening, when she thanked him.

Her eyes held his for the briefest of seconds before she cast them down towards the floor. His arms ached to hold her. He wanted to tell her it was going to be all right but he had no idea what the implications of this meant or what the ramifications were. Feeling helpless, he just stood there, until the doctor excused him from the room and closed the door in his face.

He placed his hands against the barrier separating him from Izabella and bent his head to rest between them. He could not believe this was happening. That she would be shouldering something so onerous. Alone.

He'd heard how well she had taken care of her mother, all but giving up her own life to make sure that Juliana was surrounded by love and well-being. He had been a continent away, and although he had called Nolan from time to time to get an update on her condition, he hadn't given it any significance. His life had not been altered one bit. He'd still played and partied and lived in the spotlight, all the while coming undone, although he hadn't realized it until looking back now in hindsight. Juliana's sickness hadn't made any imprint on his life, but her death certainly had. It was the reason he had flown home. The reality of it had hit him square in the chest, especially after seeing the grief on Izabella's face, studying the body in the casket that looked so unlike the woman he had known as a child, and he'd needed to drink away the fact that his life was getting away from him and death just sat on the doorstep, waiting. It had been a sobering moment and the last few years had been conflicted with what he wanted and what he needed. They weren't necessarily the same anymore.

For Izabella to have to nurse her daughter through the same disease had to be terrifying. And to do it again... He knew she would give everything she had to it. It was just her way.

There was little he could do for her here. He wouldn't be involved in any of the decisions, would not be consulted on treatments and it was probably for the best. He wouldn't have had any answers, proving just how clueless he was about this and the effects it had on people's lives. It was an area that he hadn't been interested in exploring. Until today.

He stood, looking around him, confused with his surroundings, not remembering from which way he'd come. Moving slowly towards the nurses' station, he asked, "How do I get back to the parking lot?"

With no alternative, not wanting to depend on his non-functioning brain cells, he asked her to jot the directions down. He made his way through the maze of hallways and hurried out of the hospital. As soon as his car was headed in the direction of Logan Airport, he turned his Blue tooth on. He needed to let Farina know he might be late and why. He didn't exactly ask for permission but explained the situation, letting him know how important it was. There had been only a brief discussion before his manager had clicked off. Reid had heard surprise and a bit of gratitude in the manager's voice, something he could blame on his attitude and reputation. Those days were long gone. He had felt nothing but great since getting back here, affiliated with the team, his buddies, his friends...his friend. He began to wonder and seriously consider the possibility it was Izabella who had improved the quality of his life. He was a different person when he was with her, when he was thinking about her, when he was...

He shook his head. Too overwhelming to think about right now.

Izabella was relieved that the doctor had closed Reid out. Now that her fears had been confirmed she couldn't deal with him right now. Leeni was in relapse. Her blood work had proven what Izabella had known in her heart. The white count was not as high as they feared so things didn't look dire, but the fact that it was recurring was the problem. The physical findings corroborated the diagnosis. Her spleen was enlarged; there was joint pain, fatigue, and a loss of appetite. Izabella tried to take it all in but knew she would ask a hundred questions as they moved forward. At least she was already somewhat proficient in the medical terminology and understood a large part of what Dr. Cutler was saying, but it didn't make it easier for her to cope. The emotional stress was excruciating, and she wasn't sure how she'd release it so she could better help her daughter. If she had learned anything from the last time, it was the importance of appearing calm and positive. She had also learned that even when something seemed insurmountable, it could be endured if taken one day at a time.

When the consult was finished, the doctor stood and engulfed Izabella in a tight embrace. She was crying again and he did his best to soothe away the terror.

"We've beaten it before Izabella. We'll do the same this time. You know the odds are extremely good."

"I do. And I know you will take very good care of her. I just don't want to see her go through this again."

"Her original team is intact, and you know them personally. It should make it easier for you to trust them."

She nodded. It was one of the reasons Leeni couldn't be at a better facility than this one. It was world renowned.

"She's a resilient little girl, with a heart as strong as a lion."

"I know, but she is still my baby."

When she got back to Leeni's room to find her sleeping, Jaco sitting in the chair beside her bed, his head leaning back, his eyes closed, she gently woke him up.

He quickly offered her the seat and went to stand by the window, his arms crossed against his chest.

Izabella went over to where he was standing and gave his arm a squeeze.

"You can go home now if you want."

His voice was gruff, and she got the impression he was choking on unshed tears.

"Nope. You've got me for the day at least. I'm not leaving you alone."

Crossing her arms, she took in the parking lot and the people moving around free from the oppression of this room and all it meant.

"Melinda should be here soon. There's not much we can do. They'll be coming to take her for a chest X-ray in a bit. The spinal tap is later this afternoon."

"Yeah, so what's in a bit, like in two hours? That's the one thing that used to drive me crazy. Someone will be right down means we wait half a day."

The nurses had already been in to get Leeni settled, taken her vitals, prepped her for what was to come. There was more than enough space for all of them to be here. It was one of the things she was grateful for. Because of the risk of infection, most of the children got private rooms. They wouldn't be cramped and fighting for territory amidst the machines and staff.

Rubbing at the cold chill that had seeped into her bones she steeled herself for what was to come until she heard a voice that was parched and raw.

"Mama, where's Mr. Crackerjacks?"

She noticed the scowl take over her brother's face at Leeni's heartfelt question. She sat on the edge of the bed and brushed at her daughter's forehead. Still warm.

"He went to pick up Melinda, *querida*. Then he has his game."

"Will he come back to visit me?"

Jaco was ready to tell Leeni that she didn't have a prayer at seeing him again, but Izabella stopped him cold with just a look.

Taking her daughter's hand in her own she said, "When he can, I'm sure."

Although she wasn't. Didn't know what kind of stamina he'd have for this.

"Can he bring me a poster for my wall? Then he'll be with me all the time."

There was a grunt that she ignored, too dismayed by Leeni's request and the reason for it.

The small voice asked, "I can decorate my room, like last time, can't I?"

She had hoped the memories had faded a bit. It seemed they hadn't.

"I'm sure you can. I'll text him if he doesn't come by for a visit."

"When? Can he bring it tomorrow?"

Izabella hadn't taken the time this morning to gather Leeni's favorite things to bring with them, although she'd have to get to it soon so her daughter could feel more at home. She had wished so fervently that it was all a mistake, didn't want to accept that Leeni might be admitted at once, so she had put that off. Jaco had picked up Hoover and brought her to his house before he came in so she didn't have to worry about getting home to take her out, feed her, although she might need to hold her furry friend just for the sensation of feeling loved. Poor Hoover. She didn't like change and she would probably pace until they went to take her home, a bundle of nervous energy. Trying to work through some of her own, she said, "Let's make a list of things you want from home."

"Okay."

Izabella rummaged in her purse for a paper and pen and sat back down to take the order.

"Your quilt?"

"Yes, please. And our picture."

She knew exactly which one Leeni meant. Her father had taken it while they were in Brazil, visiting. They were smiling into the camera, and Leeni had claimed it as her own.

"My scarf for when I get bald, the lion that Vovo gave me, some books, please, so that you can read to me. Can you get some of those score cards so when we watch Mr. Crackerjacks pitch we can keep track of his strikes?"

Just then the nurse came to take Leeni for her first test. This one wouldn't cause any pain, so Izabella let her go easily.

Sofia knocked on the door as they were getting the gurney ready for travel.

"Hello, Auny Sofia. I'm sick again."

"I heard little one. That's why I am here. I brought you some flowers. I thought they'd make the room smell nice."

"Thank you."

Sofia gave Izabella a warm embrace before they stepped outside the room, Izabella holding tightly to her hand. Melinda would be here soon, and she'd have another one to hold. There were never enough.

Once inside the terminal, Reid found his mother's arrival gate and waited. As always, the handicapped disembarked first, so it wasn't long before she came rolling over to him.

She looked surprised to see him even though he'd texted that he'd be the one picking her up.

Breaking into his thoughts, she said, "Thank you for coming. I told Izabella I'd just take a taxi but she wouldn't hear of it. Jaco was going to have to come and I didn't want her alone right now. It was serendipitous that you were even there."

Serendipitous? That was a word his mother would have used when he was a boy. There had been such a long time she hadn't said anything at all. He hadn't let her. But the formality in her voice spoke to their estrangement.

Without a word, he took the handles of the chair and pushed her towards the baggage claim.

They moved in an uncomfortable silence until Melinda broke into it.

"It's good to see you, Reid. I'm sorry that you'll have to share space with me until Thursday. I'm sure Izabella would let me stay at her house if it's a problem."

He hadn't gotten to the realization that he and Melinda would be sharing her condo until she mentioned it. He waited for the annoyance to appear but it somehow bypassed him. Letting what she said compute, he asked, "How could you do that? It's not handicap accessible."

"You learn to make do. I can sleep on the couch. Besides, I'll probably be at the hospital more than at home."

Uncertainty hovered for a moment before evaporating.

"Then I guess we can make it work for a few days."

He didn't see her eyes close when he uttered those words. He only heard her answer.

"That's good. It was something I was worried about."

"I think we have enough worry on our plates right now, so dump that one."

As they approached the claim area, he asked what her bags looked like before parking her by a column and locking her chair.

"There are two and they're purple. I wanted to make sure whoever retrieved them for me didn't have to second-guess. Poor Nolan used to have to check every piece before he found mine. I decided to make his life easier with the bright color. You won't be able to miss them."

Pinching the bridge of his nose, guilt and regret moving through with all he had laid on his brother's shoulders, he was glad he had taken this one for the team.

As they waited for the conveyor belt to start moving to serve up her luggage he asked, "I was sitting with Leeni when Jaco got there. He's got some serious issues with me. Do you know why?"

Her hands were sitting primly in her lap, her head immobile. With thinned lips she said, "I don't think you need me to answer that."

He let the silence build until they heard the churn of the machine and the buzz signaling the suitcases would be right out.

"Izabella's a big girl. One who can take care of herself."

"She is that and she can. But no one likes to see their loved ones hurt. And now...well he's just trying to protect her from *something*. There's little he can do about the leukemia."

He didn't miss the word uttered out loud, but he couldn't dwell on it without it eating a hole in his gut, so he addressed the first issue.

"I'm not going to hurt her. We're just..."

"Friends. Yes, I know. You've been saying that for close to twenty years. We both know the truth of it, though, don't we?"

"I don't know what you're talking about."

She put her hands on the wheels, unlocked the chair and quickly turned around to face him causing him to step back out of her way.

"You know exactly what I'm talking about. You accused me of giving up on life and you were right. I did. Until several people made me realize what I was missing. Whether you realize it or not, my boy, you're doing exactly the same thing."

His fingers threaded their way through his hair before they landed on his hips.

"I am so not having this discussion."

She reached out and grabbed his hand but kept her voice in a subdued tone so others wouldn't be privy to this very personal discussion.

"Reid, I taught you how to exclude the people who loved you. I showed you how to close your heart. But you are a grown man now, a very successful one, I might add, one I am proud of, but you are missing out on the best part of life. It's time for you to grow up, grow as a person. You are stunted and will be in this same place next year, ten years from now, unless you do something to change it. Izabella will always be more than a friend. It's time you admitted it."

He looked into her eyes, the eyes he saw in his mirror every morning, and saw the disappointment in them. He also saw the love that had been missing for so long.

This was a topic he was struggling with all on his own and he didn't need his mother's opinion of where he was and what he was doing...or not doing.

"Look, Ma, I'm going to be late if I don't get you to the hospital. Can we have this talk some other time?"

She was watching his expression, her eyes boring into him. Then she let them go.

"I'm sorry. I forgot you had a game tonight. My mind's been on other things."

In short, clipped steps, he excused his way through the crowd surrounding the carousel and watched until the bags came into sight, then hefted them off.

Once he returned to her side, he looked at the chair and the bags before asking, "What do we do with these?"

"You carry them. I wheel myself out."

He should have known, but he'd never given a thought to transportation issues surrounding his mother's condition.

As he continually checked on her progress with backward glances, she followed him easily to the parking spot.

"See how that works?"

She was making fun of him and he couldn't blame her. Instead of getting defensive, he gave in with an awkward smile.

After helping her into the front seat and then stowing the bags and chair in the trunk, he got behind the wheel, headed towards the exit, paid the attendant, pulled out of the garage, and got right down to what he needed to know.

"From what I understand, Leeni's had a relapse. Can you give me some background?"

His mother chose her words carefully.

"She was diagnosed with leukemia when she was just over two years old. She had stopped eating, was sleeping a lot, and would just cry all the time, saying the only word she knew which, was *ow*. Her doctor, thank goodness, took immediate steps, ordered blood work and referred her to Dana-Farber when her white cell count was off the charts. She was rushed in immediately and they began treatment within a week, but the hospitalization did a number on Izabella. She met parents with children who didn't make it, and although Leeni's prognosis was good, she couldn't stop thinking about the children who didn't beat it. Needless to say, she was a wreck, as was I. It's hard watching the people you love suffer like that. It wasn't just the treatment but watching Izabella grapple with what her child was going through. Your children can be your greatest joy but also your most constant source of agony. I needed to be there for her as she had been there for me."

"You two were always as thick as thieves."

Pressing her fingers to her lips, she said, "She helped me learn to laugh again. And she gave me a beautiful child to love. It was as if I had a second chance to get it right. When Emma came along I was more than ready to be part of her life."

It had taken Nolan and Terry years to get pregnant so when Emma had finally arrived she was truly welcomed.

There was a slight frown on his face.

She boldly went on, "You've always loved her, you know."

That statement should have stunned him. It didn't, which didn't help his frame of mind.

"No, Ma. You are mistaken there. I care about her, but love…"

He was still struggling with that term but he had to admit it came far closer to what he felt than friendship.

"The word too strong?"

He took a large gulp, flicked his fingers through his hair as she went on.

"You wanted something with her you were afraid to want. You'd get close and then take off like a bat out of hell. I tried to get inside your head but it was cluttered with so much fear I couldn't see anything clearly."

He glanced out the window at the buildings that told him they'd soon be at their destination.

"It seems like I'm still doing it."

"Only with her. Did you ever wonder why no woman ever met your standards? Why there was always a flaw you couldn't contend with? Did you ever do this dance with anyone but Izabella?"

Silently he acknowledged that he'd hadn't. Usually when he was done, he was done. Izabella kept drawing him back with a siren song she didn't even know she sang.

When they arrived at the hospital, Reid pulled into the front entrance parking lot.

Placing her hand on her son's arm, she said, "Izabella is going to be going through a very emotional time. She's afraid that if the last treatment didn't work, maybe the next one won't either, that there won't be a donor if they want to go the stem cell route, that Leeni might die. Do you understand the gravity of this?"

He nodded his head solemnly.

"If you can be there for her, she could use your...friendship. If you can't, then get all out. She is in a battle and will need all her wits about her. Things will be unpleasant. There'll be nausea and vomiting, diarrhea, fatigue, sores, skin problems, catheters, IV drips, doctor's appointments, all side effects of her treatment. Leeni will most likely lose her hair, get thin, be cranky. Izabella will need reminders to eat, to sleep, to breathe. These are the things you will need to confront if you stay. They aren't pretty."

He couldn't bring himself to commit to watch that little girl suffer, and he wasn't going to make promises he couldn't keep.

"I want to be there Ma but..."

He noticed his mother holding something back, something she seemed to want to share, but before he could ask her what it might be, she had opened the car door and asked him to help her out.

As he brought the wheelchair to her side of the car, he asked, "You're going to be there for her?"

As he helped her into the seat, she answered him.

"I am as will Jaco, Addie and Sofia. Her father will be flying back and forth from Brazil. She will have her family. We will take care of her if you find you can't carry something this heavy."

When they got off the elevator, his mother took control of the chair away from him, using her arms to spin the wheels toward Leeni's room. He watched from a distance as she became part of the small group that included Izabella, Jaco, Addie, and Sofia who were waiting outside room 1335. The two women in his life hugged, both crying openly for the future of the little girl he assumed was beyond the door.

Backing away from the scene, he made his escape to the playing field. He could not help but leave a piece of his fragmented heart behind with them.

CHAPTER TWENTY-THREE

Farina had approached him when he'd arrived, barely ten minutes later than usual.

"How'd it go?"

"I don't know yet. I dropped my mother off at the hospital and came here. There's nothing I can do now. I'll catch up after the game."

"Tough break."

"Yeah, she's so little."

"I have a friend who went through this with their ten-year-old. It's never easy."

"No, I imagine it isn't."

He didn't need to imagine. He knew. It had all but kicked him in the balls.

"Keep me in the loop."

"I will. And thanks."

Farina patted his shoulder and walked away.

Reid had thought long and hard about what his mother had said, and his roiling stomach told him how anxious he was about what was to come. Watching Izabella's wretchedness, so clearly visible on her face, right before his mother joined them had broken his heart, yet what could he offer her? He was soon going to be gone for two weeks, and his season would see him on the road as much as at home. He had games most every night, and the wear and tear over the course of the next few months and beyond, if they were lucky, would empty his own cup. The baseball season was a grind. What would he have left to give her? He had always just taken what was presented and moved on, never willing to give much to anyone. It's the way he'd built his life and it's the way he had liked it. But he was already feeling a hole within him widening, a space Izabella had occupied over the last few weeks, one he couldn't fill on his own. She fit perfectly there and the thought of that missing piece lay heavy on him.

He had already used up his 1001 ways of running by drinking, dating, dodging. He couldn't even commit to dinner never mind to a stretch that included so many things that could affect his heart. Was he willing to take that risk? That was the ultimate question that needed an answer. Maybe he'd just have to wake up every day and see where it led him.

After Keogh's loss, one he hadn't really participated in, physically, mentally, or emotionally he called his brother to let him know their mother was in.

"I know. I'm picking her up at the hospital in a little while. She'll be heading right back in tomorrow but wants to get home to pack some clothes for Izabella, some of Leeni's things to perk up the room."

"If it helps I can pick her up and take her home, bring her back in, in the morning. I won't be leaving here for another hour or so but then I'm available."

"That would really help, Reid. Emma's not feeling well and Terry didn't get much sleep last night."

"No problem, bro. Should I let her know?"

"I'll call and get back to you."

"Okay. I'll sit tight."

She was waiting in the lobby when he got there and looked as tired and drained as Leeni had earlier.

"Thanks for this, Reid. It helped a lot."

"Well, we're in the same city and have the same destination. It seemed a no-brainer."

Looking back before exiting the door, the elevators inviting, he had hoped to get a peek into Leeni's room before taking off, and he wondered if they had diverted him on purpose. Maybe Izabella didn't want him here. She hadn't answered any one of his several texts.

He'd try again when he got home to see if she needed anything.

There was a niggling feeling at the edges of his heart hoping it would be him.

He'd parked in a handicap spot, his mother's card hanging from his dashboard mirror. He didn't think it was cheating if she was riding with him. The closer he got, the better she'd be able to maneuver. Once she was settled in the car and they were on Storrow Drive heading home, he asked what he'd been dying to find out all day. The loop had closed him out.

"How are they?"

His mother sighed deeply before answering.

"Leeni had a chest X-ray and spinal tap today. The bone aspiration is set for tomorrow."

"Okay. What does all that mean?"

"The spinal tap is to determine if there are leukemia cells in the fluid that flows around the brain and spinal column. The cells in the bone marrow tell them what kind of leukemia they're dealing with."

"Were there cellsin the fluid?"

"No, thank goodness. It looks like it's not as progressive as we originally thought."

"What type did she have last time? And wouldn't it be the same?"

"Her diagnosis is acute lymphoblastic leukemia or ALL, and it's not a before and after, it's continuous. She hadn't finished her maintenance although she was getting close to being done. That's why this is so debilitating. We thought we were in safer territory. It has a good prognosis, and she had a really good response to the chemotherapy before. Her white blood count is hovering in the median range, but because she's out of remission, chances are they will have to plan a more aggressive form of treatment. Dr. Cutler thinks that stem cell transplantation might be the best course of action if they can find a matching donor. But this is all speculation at this point. They need the results of the other tests to even begin to think about how to attack it."

"And Izabella?"

"About ready to fall apart."

He remembered the tears, the abject look on her face and the need to comfort her was inching its way toward maddening.

"How long will Leeni be in the hospital?"

"Depends. Could be weeks, maybe a month before she can go home. But the treatments continue on an outpatient basis, with some overnight stays periodically."

"What will Izabella do? Can she still work?"

"She'll work out of her house and I will be there to manage Leeni's care with Honey's help, when she has to go out. It's how it worked before and it worked well. My catheter skills are rusty but I'm sure I'll get my sea legs back soon enough."

Honey was her aide, taking care of her during the week, and she'd been with her for years.

"What do you mean?"

"The doctors will implant a tube under the skin where they will feed the chemo drugs, transfusions, IV fluids so they don't need to keep pricking her and it needs to be flushed daily to prevent infection. I was a pro and it all became second nature. I hope it's like riding a bike."

His mother had taken life by the balls again and he'd missed every one of her steps. The guilt was slithering there beneath his skin.

"How can you do that in Izabella's house?"

"It's not great, but it's doable I'll sleep on the sofa; Leeni will have a bed in Izabella's office."

Tapping his fingers on the steering wheel as they sped toward home, he took a deep breath and said, "Look, I've been thinking. I don't know whether she'd agree or not, but what if I made my house wheelchair accessible, converted two of the downstairs rooms into bedrooms, one for you and one for Leeni. Izabella could work out of my house and I could help when I'm around. Which won't be much for the next couple of weeks. I can make the call tomorrow, get a contractor in there to build a ramp, whatever it requires. The furniture is being delivered on Thursday, so we can set up everything to meet the necessary accommodations."

He'd also have to find someone else to be there for delivery. Izabella had other more important things to do now.

When he glanced over to see why she hadn't responded, pure shock was on her face.

She didn't say whether it was due to the thinking part of the equation, or the asking.

"It's very generous of you."

His fingers tapped in staccato beat.

"I've got the means and the space. It seems like a good idea. It'll put you all under one roof with the tools you need to make it more than doable."

"I'll talk to her about it in the morning. Are you sure? That's a big change in your orderly life."

"When I moved, I had hoped to shake things up."

He glanced over to her and gave her a lopsided grin.

"I never expected a blender shake, though."

She placed her arm on his, a bit more serious than he'd wanted.

"It will be that, Reid. If you find it too much, you can stay at the condo. You'll have your own space there."

There was a bit of relief at his mother's suggestion, his own personal trapdoor.

Pausing, not sure he should bring up the other thing he'd been obsessing about, he pushed himself to ask, "What about her father? Doesn't he have a right to know?"

Rolling her neck, massaging her shoulders, she said, "Tough subject. I broached it before but she was adamant that he not be told. She said he would be of no value."

"Do you know who he is?"

"I have my suspicions. But nothing concrete."

"She said it was a one-night stand."

She looked at him critically. "Does that sound like Izabella to you?"

He shook his head. "No. So it doesn't make sense to me."

"Me, neither."

"Leeni is a beautiful little girl. Who wouldn't want to be part of her life?"

"Someone commitment-phobic?"

Her head was slanted in his direction and her look was piercing. He squirmed but reassured her, "It's not me. Couldn't be. Not back then."

"I thought...I must be mistaken."

His tone expressed his incredulity.

"You thought it was me?"

"Yes, Reid. I did. I knew it wasn't Patrick. Izabella broke up with him soon after her mother's death, and he hadn't been around much before Juliana passed. He didn't even come to the cemetery at Izabella's request. You two were together the night of Juliana's funeral. Who else could it be?"

Shadowed images appeared, but they were nothing in comparison to the vivid memories of her taking him in, sleeping in his arms, and he broke into a cold sweat.

"That's not something I would have forgotten, trust me. Besides, a one-night stand implies stranger and I'm no stranger."

"Then I guess I don't know who it is."

The look she gave Reid was a sad one.

He could tell she was disappointed.

His heart wobbled, suggesting he might be too, if he were honest enough to admit it.

As soon as they entered the condo, he flicked on the lights, caught Melinda yawning.

She was already wheeling herself towards her room.

"I hope you don't mind. I'm exhausted."

Looking back, she thanked him once again before disappearing behind her door.

He was glad they had arrived at an amicable understanding. He'd readily agreed to help her gather some things from across the street to take into the hospital tomorrow, before he went to the park.

It had taken longer than he'd wanted but she finally got back to him. Never once did he let the phone out of his hand, even to go the bathroom and his heart almost leaped out of his chest when he heard the ring.

"How are you?"

"Trying to assimilate. She's sleeping."

He could see Leeni clearly, her head resting on the uncomfortable pillow, wrapped in layers of sheets, the IV dripping from a stand by her bed. He wished he could visualize Izabella as clearly, but all he saw in his mind was her naked and laying in the crook of his arm. His breath stuttered.

"Did you suspect anything? Or did this come out of the blue?"

"Maybe. Deep down. Refused to accept it."

He heard the muffled sniffle with that admission.

"I can understand why."

There was a long, pregnant pause, a half sob, a strained voice.

"Reid, I can't do this right now."

His chest heaved in panic.

"Do what?"

"Whatever it is you're doing."

He didn't know how to answer that because he didn't know what he was doing. He had stepped into a quagmire that was sucking him under, a morass he'd never been willing to wade in before. He was stuck in place and it was driving him crazy.

The truth was, "I want to be there for you and Leeni."

"What happens when you decide you don't?"

Or can't?

"I can understand your concern but…"

His fumbled the phone, and he hit end call before he finished the sentence.

"Shit."

His fingers were a bit shaky and he wasn't hitting the contact number with any accuracy.

He was in unchartered territory.

She was the magnetic force pulling him along.

When the call connected again, she asked, "But?"

"I need to be part of this. Please don't shut me out."

The nagging feeling of loneliness was back again, the hole an aching void.

"Why? You've always got one foot out the door."

Unable to say the words that really mattered, he gave her a lukewarm version of the truth.

"Because I care about you."

More than she knew and more than he'd admit.

"Let's talk in a couple of days. I'm not good company right now and my head's about to implode."

"I don't need good company. You don't have to entertain me, Iz."

"You never handled tears well and I've been crying buckets."

"I'll bring a pail."

Frustration, exhaustion and terror, a lethal combination were evident in the way she choked out, "Reid, stop. I can't afford to have my heart broken in two places."

Those words stopped him cold. And then the remembered warmth wrapped him in courage.

One part of him wanted in, the other was screaming for out, but he could tell it was losing velocity and volume. His fear of losing her was overcoming the fear of being there.

Not wanting to take all the blame for their situation, he put some of it on her.

"You are doing what you accused me of."

"What is that?"

"Running away from what you're feeling."

Her voice rose with the intensity of her anger.

"I never ran away from my feelings. I spent far too much time protecting myself from the door you'd always slam in my face."

"I'm not doing that now."

"Now? You've done it at least twice since you got back."

He couldn't refute what she was saying, but he had to ask, "You must have figured out by now I can't seem to stay away."

There was a delay and then her response, the exhaustion evident in her defeated tone.

"I'm not the all-knowing Oz."

Fragments of a conversation they'd had when he was a sophomore or junior in high school whizzed through his brain. She had asked him if he had an answer for everything and he'd told her that in fact he did. He was smarter, better, quicker, more athletic, more handsome, more talented than most. That he was the all-knowing Oz. It was a smart-ass remark that she had apparently tucked away. And he winced.

He'd been such a fool.

Maybe he still was. Her daughter was lying in a hospital bed right next to her and he was making it all about him.

"I'm not very all-knowing at the moment either."

She must have gotten tired of this inane conversation because she clicked off. He didn't hear another word from her for the rest of the night.

CHAPTER TWENTY-FOUR

Izabella didn't sleep well. Not only was she still a wreck over Leeni but her last conversation with Reid had been unsettling.

He sounded sincere, as if he wanted to be a contributing partner in this, but she was still unsure about his end game, so she didn't know whether to trust him or not.

Had he really opened a door between them or was it the swinging style that could go either way based on mood or fear factor?

Her energy had to go into Leeni's care, not to this mish mash of emotion, not to a constant analysis of Reid's agenda, so after the last call she had put her phone away. Tempted to believe him, she wanted to share her feelings about Leeni, her fears, her hopes, her worries, but that compulsion could lead her into a world of sorry. He might have the capacity for sympathy, but he had proven he didn't have the aptitude for commitment, and this would take everything he had. Envisioning his strong arms around her, she let herself linger in the image that was so clear in her mind. Closing her eyes, she allowed the feeling of safety and protection to surround her before staring into the face of reality, knowing the feeling would be only one-dimensional. Any dependency on her part would lead to claustrophobia on his, and it would prove too much for him. She needed love and caring, sheltering from the storm that had hit her with the force of a hurricane, but she wouldn't get it from him. It wasn't that he didn't want to offer her those things. He couldn't. He just didn't have it in him. Without any communication from him while he was in Oakland, she'd been able to forget about him on some level. Stability had become standard issue but nowthe road had gotten bumpy again and the ride he was offering went straight down and around treacherous curves.

Seems we only put off the inevitable, Reid. At least I did.

When they were together it was like being home for her. Yet home to him was something impermeable, temporary, and impersonal. Fences and walls had been built to protect him from anything that smacked of love, and she was just too tired to climb them anymore.

Better to give the deep well of emotion time to dry up, like it had when he'd been far away.

She was determined to put him out of her thoughts and for the next twenty-four hours she was almost able to manage it.

Reid was standing by the wheelchair in Izabella's driveway, his hands on his hips. He'd just pushed it across the street, over the mess of stones, cracked asphalt and other debris and the last time he'd stumbled with it, wondered why he hadn't driven them over in his car.

"Here, let me carry you. I'll be the hands and legs, you be the brain."

He picked his mother up in his arms, held her while she opened the door, and then set her down upstairs in Izabella's room.

"There is no way you can take care of Leeni here!"

"I know it's not optimal but we will make do if we have to. We did before."

"And Nolan would not have been able to do what we just did."

"I know that, too."

Satisfied that she understood they did need him for something, he asked, "Now what does she want us to bring?"

"Comfortable clothes. Jeans, tees, yoga pants, sneakers, flip-flops."

"Okay, where are they?"

"You'll have to go through the drawers and find them."

"I have to go through her drawers?"

"Too personal?"

Yes, an inner voice screamed but he wasn't going to admit it so instead he put it on Izabella again.

"She wouldn't like it."

"Reid, do you really think she's giving this any thought right now?"

No. She had far too many other things filling her mind.

Rubbing his hands together, wiping his fingers on his mouth, he inched towards Izabella's dresser and began his expedition through her personal belongings.

He found tee shirts and leggings, his mother telling him what matched what, and he handed the selections over, Melinda stuffing them in a carry-all she had brought from the condo.

The socks went in next, and then he opened a drawer that held Izabella's nightgowns. Sitting on top was the one he had found her in on her birthday, the pink buttons almost staring him down. Quickly shutting it, he looked over his shoulder and asked, "Does she need them?"

It was as if he had just touched a hot potato and had charred his fingers.

He noticed Melinda compress her lips, as she tried not to laugh.

"No. She'll sleep in her clothes. She's too modest for that."

Modest? He didn't think so. A predatory move flashed through his brain. A strip tease dance?

Where did that come from? Pieces of a dream invading his days now as well as his nights.

Forcefully banishing the picture, he proceeded to the next drawer. The contents had him right back where he'd been, not a minute before. It fueled the fire that had started burning with that gray and pink number. Bras and panties were neatly folded in the top drawer and he handled them with caution.

Sitting back on his haunches, wiping his brow, he lifted himself and went to the closet, where he found jeans, sneakers and flip-flops. They also made their way into the carry all which was beginning to bulge.

"Just her toothbrush, brush, deodorant, skin lotion, now. Izabella will probably be willing to leave for a few hours after all the tests are done, so we just have to get her clothed until then. I think we have enough. She can grab her make-up, work clothes and anything we forgot, when she comes back. Sofia is going to pick up the incidentals that Izzie will need like coffee creamer, snacks, and water. Now Leeni."

He had an easier time in there. Pajamas were all she'd need for now, more comfortable than the hospital johnnies provided even if they were colorful and kid friendly.

Melinda, with Izabella's list in hand, began pointing out what was on the short list of necessities: her lion, picture, quilt, pillow, doll, coloring books and crayons, playing cards, and books.

"Oh, and Leeni asked for one of your posters."

It brought him up quick and he faced his mother, asking, "Which one?"

"There's a choice?"

He dipped his head down and admitted, "I know it's a bit over the top."

"Well, they'll do anything to make money. Do you get a percentage?"

"Yeah. A small one."

"Good. As to which one, I'll leave that to your discretion. And sign the thing, will you? It'll give her status."

"They have a bobble head doll that I can…"

"You have a bobble head lookalike?"

"Yes, ma'am."

"Get me one too, will you? Then when I ask you a question that deserves a yes, I'll hit the thing and get what I want."

He smiled at her then. A real, just-like-he-used-to-when-he-was-young-smile.

"Reid, she wants the poster so you'll be with her all the time. Can you handle that?"

The words of a book his mother read to him when he was little came into his head and he put the words to a railroad beat.

"I think I can, I think I can, I think I can…"

"Said the little engine that could."

Izabella had spent too many hours rehashing the last conversation with Reid, had steeled herself to push him out of her thoughts but when he followed Melinda into the room on Tuesday morning, her breath hitched, and her resolution evaporated into thin air.

He was in suit and tie, all ready for his day at the park. The color was taupe green, white shirt, Jerry Garcia paisley tie setting off his eyes, the jacket emphasizing his shoulders and his build. You couldn't get a package much better than him. She hoped he was too engrossed in what he was doing, to notice the way her eyes consumed him.

He had her satchel, a quilt thrown carelessly over his arm, and the bag with Leeni's sundries. Pulling her attention off the man who took her breath away, she noticed Leeni's face. Color had infused her cheeks and her eyes lit up.

And Izabella's fear reared its ugly head.

"Mr. Crackerjacks, I'm so glad you're here."

Izabella knew he couldn't give Leeni the attention she craved with a heavy load resting in his arms. Taking it piecemeal, she put the quilt on the hospital bed, the pillow under her daughter's head, and the bags that held the only semblance of home they'd have for a while by the window. When his hands were free, he extracted a white box with red string from the bottom of the wheelchair, and said, "Ta-da."

Izabella slapped him with her words. "She doesn't have an appetite, Reid."

His smile faded to nothing when he said, "I know. But I promised."

The blush gave away her embarrassment for cutting him down like that. Twisting her fingers, she said, "I'm sorry."

"Don't. I told you I didn't need entertainment. I don't need you to placate me, either. I don't know a lot about this yet, but I spent the night online reading all I could find so I'm willing to learn. Have some patience, okay?"

She took a step back, his eyes dark and penetrating.

He sat on the edge of the bed and took small hands into his own, gentling his voice. "So how are you feeling this morning?"

"Not a lot better."

"My mother told me you want a poster. I'll get it to you as soon as I can. Maybe I can lend you one of my pitcher's gloves. You can hold it on my pitching nights. Root me on from here."

"Yes, please."

"I better find a way to get it to you for tomorrow's night game. I need some luck. We're playing a good team."

"You'll win, Mr. Crackerjacks. You always do."

His eyes sought out her mother and he admitted sadly, "Not always, Leeni.

Izabella turned her back to him, inspecting the bag to see what they'd brought for her, but heard Melinda's response.

"You can't win if you don't play."

What was being said between the lines?

Was this about her?

She snuck a peek at the three-some, taking in the way Reid was staring at his mother. She could tell he was digesting it.

Then his attention was back on Leeni.

"I've got to get going and I'm not sure I'll get back before I leave for Oakland on Thursday. Would you let me take a picture of you so I'll have a good luck charm against my old team mates?"

Izabella turned around then, the earnest expression on his face suggesting he cared.

This was a side of him she hadn't seen in a long time.

Leeni tucked her chin into her chest and said, "I don't look so great."

He tapped her nose with one of his fingers and said, "You look beautiful to me."

She grabbed his finger and held on to it as she said, "Wait until I have no hair."

"I don't know. I think the bald look is becoming a trend. I even thought about shaving my head in unity."

"Oh, no Mr. Crackerjacks." She reached forward slowly and grabbed a handful. "I like how you look in it."

Izabella heard his breath hitch before he went on.

"No bald head for me, then?"

"Nope."

He touched the fine, silky hair and said, "I get it. You want to be the only one who looks cool."

"No, silly. I would keep mine if I could."

"Do you mind if Mama and Melinda are in the shot with you? Then I have three of my favorite women all in one place."

His mother asked carefully, "Can I have a copy of that, Reid?"

"Absolutely, Mom. I'll email you a copy."

Patting Reid's face Leeni said incredulously, "Mr. Crackerjacks, you just called Melinda, Mom."

"You made me see the error of my ways, Leeni. I think my mother would like me to call her that until she's a hundred, too."

Izabella heard the depth of emotion in his mother's voice when she answered, "She would."

She caught a glimpse of mother and son as they used to be. And couldn't help but smile.

Reid seemed flustered, as if he'd seen it, too.

"Okay. Gather round the sick bed, ladies."

Melinda pushed herself as close to the bed as she could and Izabella scrunched down between them, giving the best impression of a smile that she could for the camera.

It slipped as he slipped out the door.

Standing by the window as the nurses got Leeni ready for her bone marrow aspiration, squeezing her eyes shut as she heard her daughter's whimpers, both knowing what immediately lay ahead, she felt Melinda's presence beside her. Melinda clasped her hand.

She looked down at the woman in the wheelchair and gave a brave smile before returning her gaze to the parking lot. Reid was walking toward his car, his gait measured, his hand pushing through his hair, her hands fidgeting, wanting to reach out, call him back, tell him she needed him but all she could do was watch him walk away. She hadn't expected him to turn and look back up as if trying to find their window, his keys in his hands. But he did. When his search proved a fruitless one, he got in his car and pulled out, looking up once more before heading for the exit.

Emptiness filled her, an ache so strong she winced.

Coming back to herself, she heard the nurses talking to Leeni.

Jim was whispering words of support to the little girl, "We're going to put you to sleep and when you wake up it will be all over. No pain, Leeni. None at all."

"Really?"

Since her last stint in the hospital, the doctors had finally figured out sedation was the best way to alleviate suffering during the procedure. If Izabella had known it was an option she would have advocated for it back then, but she hadn't. Relief flooded through her and she closed her eyes in silent gratitude. Pulling out the jelly-like marrow with the syringe was the most painful part of the entire process. It had been her biggest worry and her daughter's biggest fear.

Jim was tucking her sheets under the mattress as he assured, "I promise. It might ache a bit when it's over but you won't feel that big, bad needle. And while we're there we'll put your port in."

Gillian, the other nurse, held her hand. "Jim and I will be there with you the whole time. We'll make sure the doctor gets it right."

"Okay. But I'm still scared."

Jim nodded. "And I can understand why. But you can trust me to tell you the truth, always."

Izabella quickly made her way to the bedside. "I'll be here when you wake up, querida. As will Melinda."

"Mama, I love you."

"And I you."

She gave her a kiss before she was wheeled out of the room, and then let the tears fall again once the door had closed.

When the results came back, the doctor wrote the protocol, set the treatment schedule and Izabella braced herself for the siege ahead.

By Wednesday, Izabella had already perfected the morning ritual that she'd adapted during their last hospital stay. Showering and changing were behind her, and she was just beginning to get Leeni ready for her day. There had been no further texts since she'd cut off communication with her baseball player, and she was relieved but also disappointed that he hadn't taken care of

Leeni's request.

It shouldn't have surprised her but she'd thought…

There was a knock at the door.

Straightening, she called out, "Come in."

Dante Ovitz walked through the door, a smile on his face. They had met him the night they went to Reid's game with the Zamoutto's, although even without a formal introduction they both knew exactly who he was.

The little girl's eyes lit up when she said, "Hello, Big Vitz."

"Hi, Leeni. Someone asked me to drop these off this morning. I think they are for you."

He covered the distance from the door to the bed in two strides. He was the type of man who filled a room with his presence.

"Mr. Crackerjacks remembered. Look, Mama, a glove just like he said."

She tried it on but her hand was too tiny to make it fit, so she hugged it to her chest instead.

Izabella pulled her long hair back with one hand and held it ponytail style while watching the interplay, her stance a restless one.

Dante handed over the next gift.

"And the poster, which he signed."

It was rolled up like a scroll with an elastic around it. Melina waved it like a magic wand as she asked, "Can we put it up now, Mama?"

Letting her hair go, refitting the stray behind her ear, she reasoned, "In a bit *querida*. We have a visitor."

Mr. Ovitz wasn't done playing the Santa routine.

"The team got together and signed one of Jack's shirts. You can hang that up with the poster or…"

"No. I want to wear it. Today, please."

They were starting her treatment later this morning but Leeni didn't know that yet.

"I tell you what, we'll save it for Reid's game tonight. You can wear it while you're watching it."

The small lip came out in a pout but she nodded her head at her mother. The look changed immediately when Dante placed a stack of something on the girl's tray.

"And a bunch of programs so you can keep track of all his strikes."

A heart-breaking smile emerged.

Izabella gave a small gasp. It was something they'd forgotten to ask him for and yet here they were. He must have remembered Leeni showing him the scorecard they had completed. His thoughtfulness was making her dizzy.

"And one last thing. He wants you to guess how many strikeouts he'll get tonight. He thinks seven. If you get closer to the actual number, he'll bring you something from the sports gallery."

Izabella couldn't help but ask, "Is there anything left she doesn't have?"

Dante looked at her good-naturedly and said, "He's already got it picked out."

A smile warmed her eyes and it reached out to the big man whom everyone in Boston loved. She gave him her thanks and said, "I'm impressed with the delivery service."

"I was coming in this morning anyway and I was looking forward to seeing you both. Jacks would have come himself but he had to take care of some paper-work for the house closing tomorrow. We're leaving earlier than he thought and he had to sign over power of attorney to Zamoutto."

"Oh, my God. I'm supposed to be at the house Thursday for the furniture delivery."

"Not to worry. His brother Nolan, is taking their mother over. She's agreed to get everything in place."

She looked to Melinda, who'd arrived nearly an hour ago to hold her hand during the procedure. A slight nod told her she'd agreed to the task. Then intrigue set in. It was the only word to describe her feelings. The famous first baseman knew an awful lot about Reid's plans. And the information had come from someone who didn't share much of anything.

"Well, I have some other kids to see, so I'm going to get going. You take care of yourself, Leeni. I'll visit again when I can."

"Tell Mr. Crackerjacks I'll be watching him in Oakland. I know he'll beat them."

"I will and we'll make sure he gets that win."

Taking Izabella's hand in his large one, he said, "It was very nice seeing you again but I wish it was under different circumstances."

"Thank you so much for coming in. And please, thank Reid."

"Will do. You might want to tell him yourself, though. I know he'd love to hear from you. Besides, he'll need Leeni's estimate before the game."

And with no further ado, he left the room.

After Leeni was wheeled out to receive her first dose of the new chemo combination, Melinda introduced Reid's suggestion about living arrangements.

"I know this isn't the best time to broach this subject but I want to discuss it while we're alone. I know what Leeni's reaction will be and I don't want it to put pressure on you."

Izabella was sitting on the ledge in front of the window, gazing distractedly out into the parking lot, still marveling at Reid's largesse.

"What subject and why would Leeni pressure a decision?"

Laying her needlepoint sampler aside, Melinda took a deep breath and plunged ahead.

"Reid made a proposal yesterday that I think we should consider. Can you keep an open mind?"

Crossing her arms over her chest, Izabella gave Melinda her attention, skeptical that it would be a productive one.

"What did he propose?"

"He wants us to use his house during Melina's recuperation."

Izabella looked at her aghast, the panic registering at full velocity.

Melinda held up her hand before she could say anything.

"Please hear me out."

With a slight nod of her head, Izabella gave her permission to proceed, her eyes still wary.

"He's willing to get someone in to make it wheelchair accessible, make two rooms downstairs bedrooms for Leeni and me so that I can take care of her while you're working. Honey will take on the household duties there and Claire will be available as needed. I think it's a good idea and will make it easier on all of us. You know what a hassle it was last time with going back and forth between your house and mine. This will put us all on the first floor under one roof."

Izabella's mouth was open, her arms tight around her waist.

"You've got to be kidding? You don't really think he's up for all of this, do you? Does he know it could be months before she's on maintenance? A year?"

"He's away a lot, Iz, and I told him he could always stay at my condo if things get too oppressive."

Rubbing her hands over her face, the exhaustion so deep it hurt, Izabella couldn't get her brain to work this one out.

Melinda added, "I know it's hitting below the belt, his words not mine, but Leeni will get to use the bedroom set she picked out."

That *was* below the belt. Leeni would like nothing better than to be in Mr. Crackerjacks house, sleeping in her princess bed. It might make her recuperation go more smoothly which really made this decision an easy one from that perspective but from her own? Dangerous.

She was dealing with his absence only because she had so many other things filling her head. And pure grit.

There was a void, a deep one, especially at night, but she was staying vigilant.

Then her mind hit a snag.

"Where would I sleep?"

"He's asked Sofia to buy a bedroom set for one of the rooms upstairs. He's run out of rooms on the first floor. She's agreed to if you agree to the proposition."

Uneasiness flowed through her and it gained momentum as she considered it.

She hadn't seen this coming, on any level.

He had obviously thought this out, thought about their comfort and his mother's and Leeni's needs. It was so out of character that she didn't know how it would ever succeed.

She looked to Melinda for guidance.

"You really think this is a good idea?"

"I do."

"Do I have to decide right away? It will be weeks before we leave here."

"With the furniture being delivered this week, it would be smart to put everything in place now so we don't have to reinvent the wheel. And it gives him time to get someone in to make the adjustments."

"He's willing to have a ramp put up at his house?"

"You have to remember, Izabella, he was never embarrassed by my chair. I was."

"I can't think. I don't know. It's such a…"

"Commitment? I know."

"There has to be a catch."

"There doesn't seem to be."

Before any decision could be made Leeni, was wheeled into the room looking peaked but alert.

CHAPTER TWENTY-FIVE

Leeni called him the next day to congratulate him on his win and gave him the strike-out estimate for his next outing. She'd set the number at fifteen, and he knew his arm would never take the beating over the long haul. Needing another way to stay connected, he asked Keith to purchase a Beanie the Bog Monster stuffed animal, the Greenie mascot, and FedEx it out to him. He'd come up with the idea when one of the trainers told him about his kid's school project. The class had a cardboard figure of someone called Flat Stanley that went on the road with any parent who travelled. They'd take a picture with it in whatever city they were in, then take it back home. The parent got to be involved while away and the kids got to learn about the country.

It not only might save his arm but it would give him an opportunity to interact with Leeni in a fun way. She loved the idea, so when Beanie arrived on Monday, just in time for his series against the Athletes, he took pictures with some of his old teammates at the stadium, at Jack London Square, and the Oakland Zoo. He'd introduced Beanie to Stumper, the Oakland Mascot, and when he'd emailed the pictures to his mother, who printed them out, Leeni called to say it was her favorite.

She was throwing up non-stop, from what he'd been told, but she always had a smile in her voice when talking to him.

"I love this, Mr. Crackerjacks, but I miss you. When will you be home?"

How could he not fall in love with this child?

There had always been a limit on what he could feel. She was raising his bar.

Over the next seven days of the road trip Beanie was a very busy monster and was caught on film with Reid on top of the Space Needle and at Waterfront Park.

"Mama's put the pictures up all over my room. I can see you everywhere I look."

He hoped they told the story of where he was and what he was doing so she felt like he was with her.

The latest had been of him and Beanie on the mound at Safeco Field with the caption, "The little monster nagged me until I gave in. He wanted to know what it felt like to pitch from the rubber."

She had called him and left a message.

"Will you let me stand on the rubber with you when I'm better, Mr. Cracker-jacks? I want to see how it feels, too."

His heart was taking a beating.

There was nothing he could do to make this easier for her.

And yet from what his mother told him, he was helping take her mind off her illness. She studied pictures of him every night, slept with her iPad tucked in her arms.

Soon she'd have the princess bed to think about. They hadn't told her yet, but Izabella had given in and they would soon be living in his house.

He'd know soon enough if he could deal with it.

He was on his way home, sitting at the back of the plane, the guys partying around him, but he couldn't even hear the noise. Totally lost in his thoughts, he contemplated what he'd do when they landed.

His new house was ready for occupancy and he'd be heading there for his first night. The problem was, he wasn't looking forward to it. He knew it would feel empty. It was much too big for one person and he rubbed his temple wondering what he'd been thinking when he bought it. Maybe he should have opted for a condo, maybe where his mother lived, putting him near family, something that was becoming important to him again. It would also have put him near a certain house on Beacon Street, where he felt a certain coziness in the surroundings whenever he visited. Within a few weeks, they would all be staying with him, and he'd hoped they'd bring life into the wasteland he'd created for himself.

He still couldn't quite believe that Izabella had agreed with the arrangement, although he thought that dangling the princess bed in front of her might have tilted the scales a bit. Leeni loved that canopy and he was glad she was going to get to sleep in it. Once they were there, maybe the gnawing loneliness would abate or maybe he'd drive home his inability to share personal space with anyone. It was an experiment of sorts. He just didn't know how destructive or curative it might be. Watching Leeni's recovery might be too much for a heart unaccustomed to pain, one unused to taking a beating.

The last two weeks had been rough. The only thing that had kept him sane was the interaction he had with Leeni. He had somehow managed to get those fifteen strikeouts against the Athletes, which had guaranteed the win against his former team, but with how sore his arm was the next day, he'd been glad he'd introduced her to Beanie. The stuffed animal had been a lifesaver, quite literally, and what he hadn't expected was the fun he'd have introducing the green monster to all the sights he'd missed in Oakland. He'd lived there over ten years and had never set foot in Jack London Square. Motts had taken a picture of him and Beanie standing under the arch at the entrance, which he emailed immediately, wanting to get the Beanie thing going as soon as he could. Then they had walked around, Sutherland and Bellasario tagging along, the weather a true measure of California's claim to sun and warmth, before eating at Boscanova, which had unbelievable views of the yacht harbor and great food. He wished he could take Izabella here. She would have loved the menu. Meat, meat, and more meat.

Being in Oakland again should have meant more to him than it did, like coming home. He'd lived there for over a decade but had never put down roots, never felt as if he belonged there. He'd had a house, friends, a job that he loved, but it had been so easy to keep his heart sealed off from any kind of feeling that he'd done exactly that. It was the escape hatch he had used so long ago to keep the demons at bay. As he refused to make intimate connections, life here had been devoid of meaning.

It was the day he'd touch down at Logan Airport that had given him the true sense of coming home, memories flooding through him, people and places crowding his mind. It was where his true friends were, most of whom he'd had in school, Keith specifically, and they had picked up right where they left off. His brother Nolan, had become more than his older brother and they were beginning to bridge the divide over some of their past issues.

Over the course of the last month, finally returning from his self-imposed exile, he was learning who his mother was, the woman she'd finally become after years of withdrawal. He liked her again, and the love he'd felt for her as a boy was steaming open the seal he'd used to shut her out.

Leeni had been a real eye opener. Such unconditional love emanated from that child that it filled him with a courage and strength he hadn't known he had.

And Izabella.

He was a better person when he was with her.

And he missed them all.

Izabella had been tightlipped and refused to answer any of his texts from the road, but his nightly calls to his mother had kept him up to date on Leeni's treatment. The effort it was taking to stay involved was enormous, the twists and turns coming too fast and furious for any sense of equilibrium. But it seemed he was ready to be brave.

They had started Leeni on a brutal regime of chemo. Because she had relapsed while on maintenance, they were aggressively treating the disease, and it had been hard on the small body and Izabella's psyche. Leeni had hit most of the points his mother had listed for him like vomiting, hair loss, and pain in her extremities. The nausea was being kept at a minimum through some other medication. Thankfully she was sleeping a lot and they were managing the pain as best they could.

Paolo had been there for a few days and had been a solid presence, offering support and love.

Melinda had told him that Izabella left periodically to work, show houses, and wrap up the last of her closings before she jumped ship and joined the other firm. Diane, the agent who was waiting for her at the new office, told her she would cover whatever Izabella had to miss or reschedule. He was grateful she had a friend who was helping her in a time of need.

Most of her time, as he knew it would be, was dedicated to Melina. His mother admitted to him that it was beginning to show. They had done another aspiration and the blasts were down, so the chemo was doing its job but it had robbed Leeni of most of her hair, and the steroid medications had resulted in puffiness and fluid retention. He knew about steroids and what they could do to the body. The league had a ban on them for a reason.

He could just imagine what the little girl was going through and he couldn't wait to see her.

Izabella made her way back to the hospital just as it was getting dark. The tears had mostly stopped now. Driving her father to the airport had been hard. He had made himself indispensable while Melinda put the finishing touches on Reid's house, held her while she wept, sat at Leeni's bedside while she attended closings, wrapped up some paperwork at her old office, and put in a day at her new office to get acclimated. She had already acquired prospective clients and showed some properties. Her heart wasn't really in it, but she had to keep her finances in order so she could afford the health care package she had put into place when Leeni was a baby. It was a good thing she had or she would have been so far in debt already she'd never see the light of day.

The time out in the real world was good for her, and she was looking forward to the day that Leeni would be allowed to go home. They could sit outside on the patio and get some sun. Reid had a wonderful backyard and it would be one of the perks of living there for a while. Melinda was pressing for her to take some time for herself, a sabbatical from the cancer, go for coffee with Sofia, or on a shopping spree, her treat. The raw vulnerability was still so deep that she wasn't able to take her up on it yet. Maybe after the induction or the second phase of the treatments. Right now, the preeminent course of action was to take care of Leeni. Nothing else mattered and she could not be coerced to take a break for useless activity.

There would be time for all of that soon enough.

Over the last couple of days, she'd become a little more at ease with the idea of living at Reid's. Unwilling to speak to him about it, or anything she was feeling, she'd kept her distance. He had stopped texting within the first few days of his road trip, probably because she had ignored the texts and never responded. She just couldn't trust herself not to need him.

He had surprised her by keeping up with the protocol through his mother and had stayed connected to Leeni through Beanie and his escapades.

She had hoped total abstinence would make her life easier but she had been wrong. She missed him, the good him that made her laugh, spontaneously texted her with tidbits about his day, made her body sing.

How was she going to survive living with him?

Avoiding him wouldn't be possible. He'd be there in the flesh each morning when he joined them for coffee or breakfast. She'd spend endless hours in bed, listening for his footfalls, signaling he was home after his game, and then his wind-down routine in the room next to hers. Just the thought of it set her heart to beating erratically.

How would she deal with being in such close, proximity to someone she didn't trust?

Of course, all this concern could be meaningless. He could very easily opt out of their lives and disappear to his mother's. Or he could pick out another woman to dote on.

Opening her window, she breathed in the warm air.

Had he found someone to take her place in his bed?

The thought of it seared her brain and caused a sob to rise.

If he had, how could she pretend that it didn't matter, like in the old days when she had hidden her feelings so well?

There was no hiding them anymore. The love bubbled just beneath the surface, still pounding in her blood, persistent, rowdy, nudging her. All he had to do was appear and it'd surge upwards and out, spewing the white-hot lava that melted everything on contact.

But if he had moved on…?

Knowing these thoughts were useless and she was powerless over what course he took, she turned on her iPod and let Joe Cocker do his best to get her out of this melancholy mood.

When she returned to the hospital, she expressed her gratitude to Jaco, said her good-byes, and closed the door against the world. This room had become her cocoon, insulating her from what was to come. The doctors, nurses, and aides took care of things that she would be doing soon enough. Food was served, medication dispensed, temperature taken, vomit cleaned, sterilization maintained. She would soon be in charge of all of it.

Did a cocoon ever die on the branch, unable to make the leap from caterpillar to butterfly?

She was sure it did.

The upcoming months would tell her which way it would go for her. If only she didn't feel so all alone.

Reid crept stealthily down the corridor, feeling like a stalker as he peered around the corner to make sure the coast was clear. He slipped by the front desk, the hallway eerily quiet, hoping he'd make it to room 1335 before someone caught him. Once he'd reached the door, he glanced to his left and right, pushed the lever down and squeezed through the narrow opening.

Izabella was standing by the window, dressed in her Jackson shirt with yoga pants, which were a bit loose rather than form fitting as they had been. No one was reminding her to eat…or she was ignoring them.

The light over the bed cast a ghostly glow that made her look more like an apparition than a woman. When she noticed his presence, there was a look of devastation etched deeply on her face. For a few seconds she merely stared at him and then stepped forward. His hope surged, giving him the impetus to move closer and when they met, he slowly wrapped his arms around her. Shivers ran down his arms when she welcomed his embrace.

They held each other close, breathing each other in, just being in the moment.

Without letting go she whispered, "Great game today."

His breath tickled her ear when he asked, "You watched?"

"I have no choice. Leeni refuses to take off the shirt you gave her and insists the game be on whether she's sleeping or not."

He looked down at her face and into her eyes.

"Are you sleeping?"

Shaking her head, she said simply, "Not really."

"You need to keep up your strength."

"I know. But as soon as I lie down I think of all that could happen if…" She didn't finish the sentence but rested her head against his chest.

His hand went to her hair and he brushed it with his fingers, holding it where it lay. His sweet spot was sighing in relief at the feel of her in his arms, something that it had screamed for while he'd been away. He knew there would be no seduction tonight, no skin to skin that his body craved but he could offer something perhaps more important to her well-being.

"I brought you something."

Lifting her head to look at him, she asked, "What?"

He retrieved something from his jeans pocket and held it up for her to see. It was a very small red pail.

"When I saw this in the gift shop at the airport, I couldn't resist. I know it's not very big but we can empty it a lot."

The laugh tinkled out and she quickly stifled the sound with her hand.

"Thank you. I needed that."

"The pail?"

"No, the laugh."

"You need a couple of other things as much. Come here."

He placed the gift on the bed tray, took her hand, and led her to the sofa that sat against the wall. It was available for parents to rest and sleep. Kicking off his shoes, he sat down and slid to his side and gently pulled her spoon fashion against him, his arm never leaving her stomach.

"Try to sleep. I'm tired, too. Maybe we can both get some shut-eye."

She gave in to the fatigue and drifted off, gripping his arm as if her life depended on it.

The pressure of her grasp grounded him against her and when he heard her soft murmurs, he knew he'd be staying the night. It wouldn't include sleep, not with her pressed against him, but there was a feeling of wholeness that was almost more enticing than the sexual pleasure he had known with her.

He felt himself relax and he did the unexpected.

He rose to consciousness when he heard Melinda's greeting. "Well, good morning, Leeni."

Ruthie, one of the nurses, had pushed open the door, and Melinda wheeled in, her cheerful greeting hushed by the little girl on the bed.

"Mama and Crackerjacks are sleeping."

He felt Izabella stir, and then stretch.

The sun was streaming in through the big window and she sat up abruptly, when Melinda chuckled, "Will wonders never cease."

He heard her ask, "What time is it?"

"Almost nine. Did you sleep well?"

She looked at him as he moved his arm in and out trying to get rid of the pins and needles.

The expression on her face was one of embarrassment. "I'm sorry."

"For what?"

"Your arm…"

"It's fine. Just a bit numb. It'll pass." When he realized who had just come in he asked, "Mom, what are you doing here?"

"I've been so busy with your house, I've been derelict in my duties here and decided to come in early and play catch-up."

The nurse had finished up with her daily tasks and informed them, "Leeni's breakfast should be right up."

He noticed a sly smile on her face as she left the room.

He'd swung his legs over the side of the couch as soon as Izabella had gotten up. He noticed Leeni was wearing one of the baseball hats he'd asked Nancy Motta to bring over on one of her visits. He thought it might be a change from the small but colorful scarfs his mother told him she was wearing to cover her balding head.

He gave Leeni one of his shit-eating grins and said, "Good morning, sunshine. Seems you've been decorating."

He looked around the room to see it had transformed from the empty sterile one he had seen not so long ago to one with life and color. Most of the additions were of a Reid Jackson nature and he felt humbled. The bobble-head doll sat on Leeni's tray, a couple of score cards were laying on the bed with her as were a coloring book and crayons and she was wearing the shirt the team had signed. His mother had told him she rarely took it off. He smiled at how big it was and decided to pick up a kids' version and have his teammates duplicate their efforts.

Cards and flowers were everywhere. A picture of Ovitz was hanging on her wall right beside his own.

Leeni corrected him on the decorator status. "That was Mama. Did you bring me this?"

It was the red pail. Izabella leaned over and snatched it out of her hand.

"Nope. That's mine. I think you have enough Crackerjack gifts to last a lifetime."

He noticed her cheeks blush red, an expression of contrition on her face as she grabbed it away, tucked it within her fist. She was probably an afterthought, everyone attending to the little girl to lift Leeni's spirits. The pail seemed to lift Izabella's and he was glad he'd found it.

As if it just hit him, he looked at his mother and asked, "How did you get here? Claire?"

Fluffing up Leeni's pillows, Melinda admitted, "No, she had a doctor's appointment. I took a taxi. He was a very nice man who helped lug my chair in and out and got me through the handicap door here."

Reid whistled. "That must have cost you a pretty penny."

"You can afford it."

He stood up in his stocking feet and shoved his hand in his pocket. "How much?"

"I don't want any more of your money. I took care of it."

He looked at her quizzically. "More of my money?"

"You give me more than enough."

Standing stock-still, dismayed by the pronouncement, he glanced over to Izabella, who was looking at Melinda for a clue as to what she was talking about.

His mother asked, "I don't have an S on my forehead, do I?"

"An S?"

"I can't say the word. It's a bad one according to the little word police over there. S-T-U-P-I-D I'm not."

"Nolan…"

"Didn't say a word. He makes a good living but couldn't afford to give me what I get every month. And your father's estate was less than…Well let's just say I know where he stood financially, and even his life insurance wasn't up to date. So that leaves you. Why anyone thought I'd believe it came from the estate is beyond me."

"How long…"

"Have I known? The first month I had an unbelievable amount of money at my disposal."

"You didn't say anything."

"I would have loved to say thank you, but I wasn't supposed to know and you weren't taking my calls. And if you weren't making the kind of money you are I wouldn't have allowed it. I don't spend very much of it, so you'll just get it back when I die."

He winced at the thought of that.

Both hands were in his pockets now and he didn't know what to say. He thought he'd been able to pull the wool over her eyes but her vision had been infrared.

He admitted, "I was shocked when Nolan told me about the will."

He hadn't stuck around for the reading but took the first flight out he could find after the burial. It was only later when Nolan had given him the update on his father's finances, that he had learned there was nothing there but debt. Nothing for his mother to live on, nothing to help her maintain her independence.

"Then you were the only one."

His hands came out of his pockets and sat on his hips.

"You knew he had nothing?"

"I did."

Wheeling herself away from Leeni's bed, she came to a stop in front of him.

"I think you're old enough now to know the truth."

She paused before going on.

"He didn't sell the house on Central St. because of my accident. At least not in the way you thought. He sold it because he couldn't afford it anymore. My hospital bills were outrageous. It nearly killed him to do it. He loved to act the big shot, show everyone how well he did, how much he made, but he had very expensive tastes and they didn't run to me. That's why we moved to Main Street. It was smaller, less expensive. It was his well-appointed condo that nearly wiped us out. But I didn't care about that either."

He felt a sucker punch to his gut.

"Why didn't you ever tell me?"

"You were too young for that kind of news, then, well, we weren't speaking, remember."

"But I blamed you."

He crouched down to see sadness fill her eyes.

"I know. I didn't have the energy to deal with your grief or your anger. I was too busy dealing with my own, I'm still sorry to say. I wanted to die for a long time and in a way, I guess I did. I'm extremely glad now that I didn't."

"So am I, Mom. Always was."

She patted his face, cupped his cheek.

"I know that. I'm just glad it's out in the open now."

Wanting to understand, needing the answers to some old questions he said, "I heard him tell you how sorry he was. I thought he was sincere. Was I wrong? What did I miss?"

She waved her hands in dramatic effect.

"Whenever he had an audience he became Laurence Olivier. His acting skills were so underrated. They had no effect on me because I knew the truth. He was contrite in a way but it was usually because he didn't have the money to pay for something, like Nolan's trip to Italy and your league fees, cleats, gloves. And I continually told him to go toh-e-l-l. but to find the money on the way"

Looking him in the eye, she admitted, "The affairs started when you and Nolan were boys. They didn't end with my accident any more than the spending did. Everyone loved him. So gracious, so long-suffering, so penitent. That's what he wanted the world to see."

Reid was confused and his eyes conveyed the fact. His brain was trying to sort it out.

"I don't know what to say. I thought it was a first and only time, resulting in a total mess."

"I was long-suffering myself in those days. I stuck around because of you boys. If I had gotten a divorce, his spending would have meant you went without. I could never have earned enough to keep you in Andover, in your schools, near your friends. After the accident, I had no chance of getting a job, so the subject of divorce was muted forever. I stayed. He didn't."

He clasped her hand in his.

"I'm so sorry Mom."

"Water long gone under the bridge. But I can finally say thank you, Reid. You have taken wonderful care of me. And I love you."

He half rose, placing his hands on the arms of her chair. "It was the least I could do and I love you, too."

Mother and son hugged. Something they hadn't done in almost twelve years. Not even when Steven Jackson had died had Reid comforted her. He'd kept his distance.Melinda's eyes were shimmering with tears when Izabella said, lifting up the little red pail, "Could you use this?"

They all laughed at the absurdity of it all.

CHAPTER TWENTY-SIX

Izabella was sitting on the edge of Leeni's bed, completely thrown by the story, unaware that Steven Jackson wasn't what he'd appeared, at least financially. That Reid had given his mother money for support was mind boggling. She had thought he had completely cut her out of his life but that was far from the truth. He had given her the capacity to hire people to take care of her, drive her around, and spend the winter months in Florida.

After the major revelation, Melinda all but kicked them out of the room, telling them to go grab some breakfast and not come back for a couple of hours.

Izabella was against the idea, not having showered or changed since yesterday but Melinda wasn't taking no for an answer.

"Who will you meet who will care?"

"I'll be with Reid and everyone will talk."

Reid gave her a wolfish smile. "I like the idea of having breakfast with you. You look beautiful and the shirt will only impress upon those you meet your good taste in ballplayers."

"It'll actually give the impression that I'm a groupie who's just spent the night with the object of her affection, which I am not."

He took several steps over to where she stood, tucked her hair behind her ear, placed his nose against hers, and said mischievously, "We did just spend the night together."

She moved away and gave him a look that could have melted ice. "I'll be advertising something that will be misconstrued!"

"Let lascivious minds think what they want. What do we care?"

"We care."

"We shouldn't."

"That's easy for you to say. I'll be the one they're judging as...as…"

"Are you kidding? They won't even notice me, never mind figure out who I am."

Melinda was brooking no argument.

"Will the two of you stop? Just go."

"But Leeni…"

"Will be fine. We'll take care of each other, right, Leeni?"

"I feel good this morning, Mama. Go ahead. You're here *all* the time. I can manage without you two for a little while."

Izabella knew this was a good day and she selfishly wanted to enjoy it. Another dose of chemo would be coming soon and then the cycle would start all over again.

But she had no choice because Melinda all but shooed them out.

"He got you to sleep, maybe he can get you to eat. So, go."

Leeni asked, her eyes shining like burning candles, her hands in prayer form, "Can you please bring me back something gooey?"

Without checking in with her, Reid heartily agreed.

"Of course. I'm the connoisseur of goo."

Flopping back on the bed, Leeni almost cackled.

"I know, Mr. Crackerjacks, that's why I asked. Mama would bring me back a fruit smoothie."

"You need your vitamins, *querida*. Goo doesn't have any."

"Yeah, but it sure tastes good."

Leeni licked her lips in anticipation, as if impatient for them to go and get back. He took her hand and led her out, linked his with hers as they walked.

The morning had dawned chilly, but Izabella could feel the sun's struggle to come out from behind the clouds. The silence between them was not a strained one but one that left them to their own thoughts concerning the recent admissions.

Martin's was about a fifteen-minute walk from the hospital, and they strolled from block to block listening to the buzz of morning traffic, carbon monoxide thick in the air, waiting at crosswalks so they could make the mad dash before crazy Boston drivers went whizzing by, dodging other pedestrians racing to reach somewhere important, viewing the city with myopic tendencies taking a short-sighted view of what was immediately around them.

Izabella felt an awakening take place as she joined in the hustle and bustle of the unfolding new day. Melinda had been right. She had needed this.

So zoned, she walked right past the coffee shop until she felt a snag on her hand and the words, "Here it is."

Giving him a shy smile at her preoccupation, she stepped back towards him.

Opening the door, he escorted her in, his hand on her back. He'd been wrong about the appreciative glances. He was Crackerjacks, recognized wherever he went, and this was no exception. Nods and smiles accompanied them as they were led to their table. Some wished him good luck, others congratulated him on his past wins and there were autograph seekers but for the most part they were left alone.

Picking up the menu and opening it up, Reid began to read out their options.

"What do you feel like?"

"You won't like my answer."

"I'll order for you then."

"No. Just some yogurt, please."

"Izabella, you insist that Leeni eat even when her appetite is lacking, don't you?"

"Yes, but that is because she needs to replenish what the drugs steal from her."

"You don't think the stress is doing exactly the same thing to your body as the chemo does to hers?"

"I suppose."

"So, protein, carbs, vitamins would mean eggs and bacon, a side of sausage, wheat toast and some fruit. I think you can manage that. I know you love your meat."

"It's a cultural hazard, I'm afraid."

The waitress came over and asked if they wanted coffee and both answered emphatically yes, so she poured the steaming brew out of the carafe into the mugs sitting on the table. Dropping little tubs of creamer in front of them, she said she'd be right back to take their order.

Lifting the sugar shaker, Izabella dropped the equivalent of a teaspoon into the liquid before peeling the tops off the creamers and adding it to the mix. Taking a sip and closing her eyes as the caffeine jolted in, she apologized.

"I'm sorry you didn't get much sleep last night."

His cup was already almost empty and he signaled for another before he answered.

"I'm glad you did. I can always catch a nap later, day off and all. I've got some things to take care of but they won't take me all day."

"You'll finally be moving into the new house."

"I will although I'm going to talk to my mother and see if she wants me to stick around for the week so I can drive her in every morning. Even I can't afford to let her take a taxi in every day. It'd make it easier if we were in one place. I've got the jogging route down pat and we can keep an eye on your house. Then I'm off again."

She hadn't expected him to delay moving in.

"I thought you'd be excited."

"A month ago, I probably would have already been out. Now, I feel like I'm getting to know Melinda again. She's almost the mother I remember. She's pretty cool."

"I've always known that."

"Even when she was absent?"

"Even then."

Unfolding the utensils from the napkin, he admitted, "You apparently saw things that I didn't."

When the waitress had taken their order, they went back to the silence that seemed to fall comfortably around them.

Reid broke into it with a question, "Do you want me to pick up another crate for Hoover so there'll be one at my house?"

He smiled at her stunned expression.

"Hoover's invited?"

"She sleeps with Leeni doesn't she?"

"Yes, but a dog?"

"I think it will be good for her to have her friend with her."

"You are really stepping in it...my friend."

The word *friend* just hung there in the air and Reid's fingers traced Izabella's knuckles.

"We might as well throw everything into the mix. If I'm churned up a bit, I'll survive."

"I'm glad you have a fall back plan. You really don't know what you're getting into."

"I have no clue, seeing that I have quite willingly kept away from these kind of wentanglements. It'll be enlightening to see what I'm made of." He admitted, "The result of this test could be a shattering illusion of who I could be given the right circumstances."

"Snails and puppy dog tails."

"What?"

"It's that kid's rhyme about what little boys are made of."

"Are you saying I'm a little boy?"

Giving her a look of chagrin was the only indication he disputed her estimation of him.

When the food arrived, they continued to talk amidst bites. He was watching every forkful she placed in her mouth, and before he was done, she had eaten most of what was on her plate.

Pushing his plate away, his napkin sitting on top, he exclaimed, "What a good girl!"

"That's me. Sugar and spice and all things nice."

Taking her hand across the table, he kissed the palm in agreement.

"What do you say we get some pastries to take back to the nurses. I hear it's a way to say a small thank you for what they do."

"That would be thoughtful and I can't believe you thought of it before I did."

"Well, I was thinking of the gooey surprise for Leeni and it expanded from there."

She just shook her head and smiled.

With the boxes safely packed in a bag, the they exited the shop and began the walk back to the hospital. Izabella tucked her hand into the crook of his arm, and he felt a sense of belonging that was becoming too familiar.

He was being a true friend. Last night there had been no push for something intimate. Instead he had been there for her and given her what she needed: sleep.

Today, with his easy companionship, he had gotten her talking, so the food didn't lodge in her throat. He was donating his house for Leeni's recuperation and allowing Hoover to be with her family. What she was going to do with all these gifts, she didn't know. Rip the wrapping with flourish or look for the return date.

Just as they got to the entrance of the building, Reid said in a solemn tone, "I'm calling in a designer today. I didn't want to, but we need drapes or blinds for the bedrooms or we will all be up at the crack of dawn. There's so many gaps I figured someone could help me fill them. I was hoping you would help with it but things have changed a bit. Any suggestions?"

"You know what you like. And you did a great job with the furniture. Just stick to your guns and don't let her talk you into something you don't want."

"How do you know it's a her?"

"I don't. Just assumed. Everyone in the company will be fighting to do your house. My guess is that a woman will win that battle."

"Maybe I'll call them back and insist on a guy."

"Why?"

"Don't need the aggravation."

"I didn't say they were going to fall all over you."

She laughed good-naturedly as they got off the elevator.

"It's good to know that your arrogance is still in place."

The old Reid was becoming unrecognizable. It was good to know some things wouldn't change.

"Hey. I resent that. I'm not arrogant justconfident."

"Overly."

"Just the right amount."

As soon as they pushed through the door, Leeni jumped to her knees on the bed and reached for the magical box.

Reid held it back for a moment and said, "You get first pick and then we're giving the rest to the nurses. I think they'd like some gooey treats, too."

Melinda wheeled over to the bed to see the offerings, rubbing her hands at the sight of all the sugary goodness.

"No way, Jose. We keep a few in here for us. Right, Leeni?"

"Absolutely."

With a mouth full of whipped cream, Leeni mumbled her thanks, the smile on her face priceless.

Reid walked her down to the nurse's station where she dropped off only one of the boxes. Melinda, it seemed, had just as much of a sweet tooth as Leeni. She watched him as he got on the elevator, the kiss good-bye a clear sign that he'd be back.

Reid drove straight to Keith's office to pick up his keys to the house.

It was a bustling practice, and Reid heard multiple phone lines ringing, people conferencing in the hallway, and his head swiveled from side to side watching aides scurrying back and forth between offices.

The meat of Keith's business was not sports representation but contractual law, an area he was considered an expert. Most businesses contained contracts of some kind, so it was a significant area of jurisprudence. From what his friend and agent had told him, he'd just hired two more attorneys to help him reduce the number of hours he was in the office, on the road, or in court. Once a workaholic, he had begun to streamline his life, taking more time at home with his growing family. Reid had never seen him happier.

Keith ushered him into his private sanctum, closing the door behind them to give them privacy.

"I'm sorry I don't have more time. As you can see, it's a bit crazy around here today. Maybe you can come for dinner soon."

"Tonight?"

Sitting back in his swivel chair, Keith placed his hands on his chest as he smiled.

"Free day?"

"Yeah and I spent last night and this morning at the hospital. I can't be running back there every night."

Keith's eyebrows knit together.

"I thought it would have been the other way around. It's a surprise. Maybe light has dawned on your marble head."

Looking down at the floor, Reid admitted, "A lot has changed since I got back, bud. I don't have the same knack for attitude as I did. And I'd like to apologize for the insults. Sofia is a beautiful woman."

With a lift of his eyebrows, Keith said, "Apology accepted."

Reid got out of the chair and moved to the bookcase filled with law reviews and court cases. He fingered the old bindings, his back to his friend.

"You've probably heard that I'm going to have staying guests for a while."

"I did."

"I'm a little nervous about it. I haven't put myself in this kind of a position in a long time, and I'm not sure I'm cut out for it."

Turning back to face Keith, he crossed his arms at his chest and breathed.

Keith was staring at him as if he couldn't believe he was admitting it.

"I have a feeling you'll do fine. It might get hairy from time to time but most of life does. Just remember that part. When you're dead, nothing can touch you. When you're alive, almost everything should."

He was beginning to think he'd been dead inside for a long time. The prickly feelings were just pins and needles warning him that he was coming back.

"I might need a friend to see me through this. You up for the job?"

"I've always been there for you. You just didn't notice."

"Yeah I did and appreciated it although I probably never mentioned it. High time I said thank you."

Keith sat back in his chair, studying him.

"I'll call home and let them know you'll be joining us. I won't be getting back there until about seven. Late night tonight so I can get out early tomorrow for your game. Holly has become an obsessed Greenliner fan and now wants to join a little league team."

"You go, Hollyberry."

"Reid, she's six."

"They start that young. Do you need tickets?"

"I bought them while you were on the road."

Reid admonished, "Why did you do that? You have an in, ya know. I'll give you a name you can call whenever you want them. They'll always be available."

"You don't give them out anymore?"

"Just to good friends and family. I've been warned about inviting strange women to sit in the holy wives club now that they've met Izzie."

Pausing, Keith steepled his fingers under his chin.

"Your swagger is gone. I thought it was doubt."

"The doubt disappeared the night I pitched the no-hitter. The attitude? I guess I don't need it anymore."

"I hope the attitude's back in time for our next round of negotiations."

Sitting back in his seat Reid said, "I don't think it matters much. I'll take whatever they want to pay me to stay here."

"You didn't just say that and I didn't hear it. Now get out of here. My client's waiting and his time is valuable."

He left, a broad smile on his face. He was thinking about the females in his life and wondering what they were doing.

Izabella sat back, pleased that they'd brought the crème-filled doughnut back for Leeni. She'd all but inhaled it. It might not be healthy but at least she seemed to be able to taste it. Nothing affected her sweet tooth or the cravings to satisfy it. The steroids had helped increase her appetite, although vomiting limited the calories that stayed ingested. It was the diminished sense of taste that dulled Leeni's desire to eat. The food they sent up from the kitchen was picked at. It was bland and, although nutritionally sound, did nothing to stave off hunger. Her daughter loved to munch on the foods Talita sent through Sofia, and although the woman did her best to send in an abundance of the Brazilian cuisine Leeni was used to, she couldn't keep up. When Paolo had been here he'd driven all over the city intent on finding spicy dishes that would satisfy, and he'd found great Mexican and Italian eateries that would satiate both taste and hunger issues. Leeni had developed a voracious appetite for chicken enchiladas and sopas. She had woken up a few nights screaming with hunger, and Izabella had had to quickly heat up some leftovers for her to chow down on. Now that Paolo was gone, it was left to Izabella to forage the neighborhood for things that would appease Leeni's constantly growling hunger. Leave it to Reid to have found something to put a smile on her face.

Picking up the journal she kept, she jotted down the pastries consumed so that she could return and replenish their supply. Lack of sleep made her memory hazy, and if she didn't write things down, she'd forget to remember.

May 18
Slept a few hours. Went for breakfast and ate. Fueled up now and ready for the day. It's a nice change. Brought M back some gooey delights from Martin's and will go back for more this week. She's in good spirits and might try for an excursion later on for supper. Found an Asian fusion place close by, and if M's up for it, we might give it a try.
Half-way through first phase of treatment and M's doing so much better than expected. Relieved. Seems when R is here, the day is a good one.

As she wrote, she listened to the animation in Melinda's voice as she read one of Leeni's favorite stories. It was the book *Grandma and Me* that Melinda had bought the last time Leeni was in the hospital and the little girl never got tired of hearing it.

Melinda was a wonderful grandmother, and Izabella only wished that Leeni could truly call her Grams like Emma did. She'd never imagined how embedded in their lives Melinda would become and how much help she'd be. From the first breath Leeni had taken, Melinda had been there. Accepting the job of birth coach, she was the second person on earth to hold the tiny infant. Maybe the bond between them had started there.

"We've never been to the beach, Melinda. Can we go someday?"

Izabella looked up from her writing to see what Melinda's response would be. The question hadn't come out of thin air. It was the basis of the story they were reading.

"I don't know, my love. I don't do so well in the sand with my chair."

Leeni was lying on her stomach, her legs crossed in the air.

"Maybe Mr. Crackerjacks could figure something out. Like maybe he could carry you or something."

"We'd have to ask and get him on a free day. You know he can't be with us a lot because of his games."

Scooting into a sitting position, criss-cross-applesauce style, Leeni demanded, "Mama look at his schedule and see when his next free day is."

"Melina Julianna, I think you forgot the magic word and I don't think this is such a good idea. We can't be asking Reid to carry Melinda around for your benefit. It's not fair to either of them."

"We won't know unless we ask him. Can you text him please?"

"I'm not going to do that, *querida.*"

"I want to go to the beach with Melinda like she's my grandmother."

In a small voice, Melinda explained, "That's not all grandmothers do, Leeni. We could write our own book about going to the aquarium or the children's museum or better yet, *Grandmother and Me at the Ball Game.*"

Leeni clapped her hands in delight.

"Yes, that would be awesome."

A more serious expression came over her face when she said, "But I can't call you Melinda if we do that. I'd have to call you Grams, like Emma does."

"I would like that just fine."

A stampede of fear raced through Izabella's brain.

"Reid wouldn't like…"

Sitting straight in her chair, ready for a fight, Melinda said quite firmly, "It doesn't matter what Reid wants. This is between me and Leeni. And if I want her to call me Grams, that's my decision. He'll just have to deal."

CHAPTER TWENTY-SEVEN

Reid drove up the long driveway and sat in the car. It was a grand house and it was his. He had never owned anything, not outright like this, and it felt strange to know that he'd signed on for fifteen years. The grounds were still in good shape, but he was hoping Jaco would return his calls and agree to take this on. He figured he'd keep it in the family, but the unanswered messages were making him think he'd have to look elsewhere. There had to be a way to reconcile their differences. They had never been close, too many years in between, but Jaco had been a constant in his household for a long time. There were afternoons that he'd let him hang out with him and his buddies, let him play in some of their scrimmages, helped him with some of the chores Juliana would give him to keep him busy. There had been friendship of sorts that he realized had fizzled because of his own inability to connect on more than a shallow level. Maybe it had blown up outright because of his interest in his sister and what it had led to. Another one of those connections he'd let lapse over time, although for the life of him, he didn't know why. The ease he felt with her was refreshing. Izabella wasn't impressed with his celebrity so there was no need to suspect she had ulterior motives in being with him, and the sizzle between them was a different kind of tension than he was used to. It was real, on every dimension and more than skin deep. In truth, he did know why he had stopped all communication. What he felt with her was far too real for his senses. Maybe Jaco just read between the lines and didn't like the story. Trust was the underlying issue. If he didn't trust himself with Izabella's heart, how could Jaco?

He'd just have to get some other contact numbers for a landscaping crew, set up some appointments, because he had a feeling Jaco was not going to change his mind.

He'd met with Beth Bryant, an interior decorator from a local firm in the area, and had gone over what he was looking for. She was meeting him here tomorrow so she could see the space and begin collating ideas. He hoped she'd adhere to his list without adding to it. Too many times, people tried to take advantage, figuring he had the cash.

Finally, ready, he made his way up the walkway and through the front door. Standing with his back against it, surveying the interior, taking in the airy feel, he remembered why he'd loved it. It was welcoming and had a hominess he hadn't felt since his family had moved from Central Street. Even as big as that house was, his mother had made it feel as if the family within its walls came first and it was just a comfortable backdrop to their lives. Kids were always in and out, his and Nolan's friends always welcome, with doors slamming, music blaring, shouts and laughter.

That was missing here and the quiet was deafening.

He dropped his keys on the table sitting against the wall in the vestibule and meandered through the rooms, checking on what Melinda had done to make the necessary accommodations for his soon-to-be-guests. She had done an excellent job arranging the furniture and it looked like she had brought reinforcements with her. Claire must have taken her shopping and done some of the heavy work, because the beds were made with comforters he hadn't bought and the canopy on Leeni's bed had a beautiful pink covering, with white stars. It was truly a princess's room. The living room was arranged like he'd mapped out, and the dining room was perfect for entertaining. He could envision the people gathered here, eating, talking, laughing and the picture of Izabella across the table from him skittishly shot through his mind. Instead of banishing it, he let it linger. Throwing him completely off guard was the fact the he relished the scene, letting it play out with animation and dialogue, and he felt her radiance permeating the space. He spun around quickly and departed the scene before it became too real. This was only temporary, and he needed to keep reminding himself of that fact or he'd suffocate.

Slowly he mounted the stairs and turned into the room made up for Izabella. Sofia had chosen a dark mahogany wood, and the delicate posts of the bed were more feminine than he would have chosen, but it would suit very well. The comforter was lime, white, and aqua making a bolder statement with color and vibrancy. He liked it and he could picture her here, sleeping, working at the desk he'd bought that could not be placed in the library quite yet.

Although there were several other bedrooms to choose from, they had set up her room right next door to his. He swallowed hard, knowing having her this close would be a temptation he'd have to live with. It wasn't what he'd bargained for.

In two steps, he was standing on the threshold of his room.

The master was stately yet his mother had softened it a bit with ice blues and browns. He had never given her credit for creating a warm home. Of course, he had never thought to. He hadn't even known there was an art to it, until now.

Stripping off his shirt and pants, he crawled under the covers to try and grab a quick nap before heading to the Zamouttos. Everything on his list had been checked off. The only thing left to do was assemble Hoover's crate, which he'd do before leaving.

Putting his arms under his head, he stared at the ceiling, wishing they were all already here, wondering when the buzz of the saw would start churning in his stomach. But all he felt was the sizzle of sexual tension that hit him at thoughts of

Izabella. And something deeper that he was still refusing to define.

Sitting in the large room filled with toys, Izabella watched Leeni play dolls with another little girl who resided down the hall from them. It was a more cheerful place to be, and she made sure Leeni got to spend as much time here as her condition allowed. It brought a sense of normalcy to their lives, something that was a rare commodity here at the hospital.

As Izabella watched, her mind wandered, conscious of the fact that the days when Reid was with them, even for a short period of time, were much better than the days he wasn't. She marveled at the way he made her daughter feel connected through Beanie's journey, how he never failed to visit when he was in town.

Leeni's tests were encouraging. The last bone marrow aspiration showed the white cell count almost normal, but they knew those pesky cells could be hiding anywhere. The protocol no longer included a stem cell transplant, and they were talking about releasing her within the next several days. They would be returning every week for her consolidation phase, but she'd be able to rest in comfortable surroundings, and all Leeni talked about lately was her princess bed.

The light had been bright in her eyes since the day they told her.

Her enthusiasm boundless.

"I get to sleep in my bed all by myself?"

This was one of the touchy aspects of the move. Leeni just might get used to the house and all it offered. Izabella knew getting her back home might be a big problem and she needed her to understand this was only temporary.

She'd tried to explain, "It is not your…"

Reid had taken Izabella's hand and stopped her.

"For as long as you're living in my house, you will be."

"How long will that be? More than a week?"

Reid knew the consolidation phase lasted much longer than the first part of treatment, and when he'd talked to her about the duration of the stay, they decided jointly to keep the end date open.

"More than a week for sure."

"Until I'm all better?"

"That could take a long time *querida*. We will have to move home at some point. Let's just be grateful that Reid has allowed us to be there for now. Okay?"

"Okay."

"And don't forget that Melinda will be there as well."

"Grams."

Izabella was glad he wasn't wincing at the term anymore, and he'd actually admitted out loud that Melinda was in fact her Grams for the amount of time and effort she'd put into this relationship and Leeni loved her like one.

"Grams," he corrected.

After she had asked for the fourth or fifth time since he'd left when they'd be going there, Izabella had gotten out a small calendar book from her bag and showed her again, promising to mark off the days until she was released from the hospital.

But the little girl seemed in too much of a hurry to get back to a normal life.

When Dr. Cutler arrived the next day on his morning rounds, Leeni asked him a question she'd already answered. Could she go to Reid's game on Saturday?

His answer was the same as hers, although he went on to explain it would be a while before she could be in that kind of crowd. She hadn't dared.

"But Mr. Crackerjacks is pitching. I want to see him."

"We'll get you some popcorn, some juice and you can watch it on TV."

With all the force and power of a three-year-old, a tantrum swept through the room like a hurricane with gale force. Water gushing, voice exploding, arms flailing, Leeni threw everything she had into the attack, and everyone in the room stilled just to bear witness to her fury.

It rarely happened, but Izabella wasn't surprised it erupted due to a certain ball player and her daughter's inability to be with him.

"I'm sick of this room. I want to go home. I want to go to the ballgame. I want to be not sick anymore." Her volume escalated as she screamed, "I want my Mr. Crackerjacks."

They all understood the complaints.

Leeni became irascible so infrequently that they judged themselves lucky that the tantrums were few and far between.

Thankfully, Reid came in just as she was pitching the fit. He'd met with the interior designer earlier that morning and was just dropping in before heading to the ballpark.

"Hey, what's this?"

"I want to go home. I want to see you pitch and they won't let me."

With her sobbing against his clean white oxford shirt, he patted her back, oblivious to the tear stains now covering the front of him.

"That's because they want you to not be sick."

Emotions completely out of control, her hero doing nothing to change the outcome, she threw herself into her pillow.

Reid asked, "Can I sit here?"

It was a small patch of mattress but he had learned that jostling her could cause pain so he stuck to just a sliver of seat.

He barely heard her yes through the convulsion of tears.

"I'll be here tomorrow morning when you wake up and maybe we can go down and grab some breakfast before I leave. Anyone can go to a game and see me pitch. There aren't too many fans who get to eat with me."

Throwing herself into his arms, moaning into his shoulder, she said, "I love you Mr. Crackerjacks."

Holding her head in the palm of his hand, he pressed her gently to him. "I love you, too Leeni."

Izabella gasped at what had come out of his mouth, and tried to grasp what had happened.

This was the second time in the last couple of weeks that Reid had said those three little words. Words she had never heard out of his lips since almost a year after his mother's accident. He had said them a lot during those first six months, but they were never reciprocated so he had given up, thinking his mother wasn't capable of loving him anymore.

But here he was, totally preoccupied with the little patient, his gentleness still a surprise, expressing his love in ways she hadn't expected.

He had been true to his word and had learned as much as he could about what she was going through. He'd read everything he could find, talked to parents and patients, doctors and nurses. He had asked pertinent questions when she'd explained the protocol and all it involved. He had evolved from a bystander to an insider, had become one of the best friends she'd ever had, brought laughter into the room and stories about the games and the people he played with and against. He was still striking out numbers that were becoming legendary. She wanted to fling herself in his arms like Leeni and announce her love for him as well, but she still felt the distance between them. He had been nothing but a gentleman when he was holding her at night. There had been no kisses, no touches, no intimacy unless you could call laying in someone's arms the essence of all those things. She missed the physical part of their bond but knew he was giving so much already it might be all he had in him to give. She couldn't be greedy. He had given them a part of himself she hadn't thought possible.

Leeni calmed down in his arms, his hand stroking her back, her small, bald scalp, and it struck her how her daughter responded to a male touch.

Was it Reid's alone?

Leeni had asked about her father on occasion and then just accepted there was none in her life. Was she looking for Reid to fit the role?

That might be a huge mistake, although she was beginning to believe Reid in fact loved the little girl and would see her through this. The aftermath might be bloody but now was really all that mattered in Leeni's recovery.

As she studied them together, she seriously considered, for the first time ever, introducing Leeni to the man who had contributed to her existence.

Maybe he did have a right to know.

The reverberation could be cataclysmic, changing the dynamics of their lives, the routine they had come to cling to. It might alter the plans for the upcoming move and make it more difficult to find a comfort zone they could all exist in. Deciding there had been enough change in their lives at this point, she kept her silence and only hoped she was doing the right thing.

As he comforted Melina, he couldn't help but take Izabella in. She took his breath away and her taste in clothes was killing him. This dress was short, the color of pink-hued pearls, flared skirt, cap sleeves, high heels. She was leaving for a couple of hours to show some houses later in the day. Melinda had told him about the clients when he'd talked to her.

Izabella's job was tough, made even more difficult due to the circumstances. At the mercy of her phone at all hours of the day, she was a mediator, counselor, teacher, and from some of her stories, he'd qualify her as saint. He could never deal with the clients who created the kind of drama they did. He'd tell them all to go to hell. He wouldn't keep them long that way. His honesty would send them right into someone else's office. She was able to maintain her cool and guide them where they needed to go. Gutsy and strong. But when she was here, she was a mother, nurse, advocate. Gentle, caring and knowledgeable.

So many hats and she wore them all with aplomb, changing them as needed with not even a ripple during transition. Well, maybe a ripple here and there but steady as a rock for the most part.

She amazed him.

There was depth and complexity.

So, unlike him.

He had none of that.

One-way Jacks.

Feeling the soft skin of Leeni's hand in his, he felt a shift, as if the barrier he had placed on the other side of the road had opened, creating a space that could accommodate give-and-take. He liked the feeling. It had gotten far too boring being on the road all by himself. In a moment's clarity, he knew that all the restlessness had been nothing more than stagnation. His mother had been right. He had not grown as a person but had kept everything carefully controlled, circling the bowl of life, never diving in. Safety had been his first priority. He'd bubble-wrapped his heart so no one touched it.

Feeling the small hand squeeze his, he knew someone had finally been able to pop those air pockets and was peeling the protective coating away, layer by layer.

CHAPTER TWENTY-EIGHT

Jaco's scowl mirrored his words.

"I thought you'd be gone by now."

Bending down to kiss Leeni's temple, Reid said neutrally, "Just leaving."

Izabella couldn't take it anymore. These two men were the most important in her life and she didn't like that Jaco still held the past against Reid.

"Jaco, what is the problem?"

Leeni's small voice echoed, "Yeah, Unca Jaco. What is the problem?"

Reid crossed his arms over his chest and waited.

Faced with a question Jaco didn't want to answer here, he merely said, "I can't let the past go. And I don't think a leopard can change his spots."

Reid found that ironic. Had Jaco forgotten about his reaction to their father when he'd asked to see them?

Izabella put his own thought out there. "You've let it go before, under more conflicted circumstances."

Jaco dropped his eyes. "This is different."

"You don't think Reid has proven he's in this?"

"For today, maybe. What happens tomorrow?"

Izabella's eyes glistened, her lips turned down before she said softly, "There is always the possibility, my brother, that there is no tomorrow."

Jaco's eyes burned into hers, understanding exactly what she was saying, and the air whooshed out of him like a balloon with the knot cut.

Reid then went eye-to-eye with Jaco, and all that was between them passed away, the smoke cleared, the air became less toxic.

Reid was the first to take a step further toward conciliation.

"Jaco, I would appreciate it if you would agree to the job I offered. It would put you at the house a couple of times a week and with me gone so much, it would make me feel better if you were on-site."

"Putting it that way, I agree. I would have been there for them anyway, but this does make it easier."

Izabella's shoulders relaxed and her jaw unclenched.

Maybe there could be a truce after all.

Then Jaco added, "I have the right to reassess, once they are gone."

Reid handled the slight with ease.

"Yes, of course."

"Then we have an agreement. I will draw up the estimate tonight and email it to you."

"No need. I'll sign a contract if you want, but you are the best there is and I will accept whatever terms you find agreeable."

Reid held out his hand.

She waited to see if it Jaco would meet it.

She was surprised when he did.

The men shook a bit too firmly before Reid walked out the door.

Jaco turned to her as she was gathering her things, a pillowcase full of laundry, her briefcase, a finished novel she wanted to replace, and whispered so Leeni didn't overhear, "I don't like the fact that you will be living with him. It just doesn't sit well."

Looking over to the bed to see Leeni playing a game on the iPad, making sure she was occupied and not listening, she answered, "I know. But it will make it so much easier than last time."

"Does he know what he's in for?"

"I think so. There hasn't been a part of this he's missed, from being targeted with vomit to knowing how to sit on the bed and comfort her. He's read everything there is to read, and from what I understand from the nurses, he had become one of the most empathetic of volunteers. He's living this, Jaco, not watching from the sidelines."

"The sidelines would be acceptable. It's his running off the field that I have issues with."

"You see them together. They are good."

"For today."

"And yesterday. Who knows what tomorrow will bring. If he's gone, well, I can look back and say he played a big part in her healing."

"And you, *querida?* How are you?"

"If my baby is getting better, I'll be fine."

He knew her too well, and his look suggested he didn't believe her.

"For you, I will behave. I will be cordial and agreeable. But my verdict is still out for now. I can't help it."

Izabella reached for him and they embraced, holding it for longer than usual. She kissed his cheek, gave Leeni a hug good-bye, gathered her belongings, and slipped out of the room.

Relieved that the stalemate between Jaco and Reid seemed remedied for now, Izabella drove up Route 93 feeling good. Making mental lists of what still needed to be done for their move, she was heading home to finish packing. She had decided to take a week's worth of clothes at a time. She was close enough to her closet that she didn't need to fill her temporary one. She was worried that she might need some distance from the confines of Reid's personality and his personal space, and it would give her an excuse to return to the safety of her own calm world.

Once she had completed her tasks, she was heading into the office for a few hours.

Work was going well and she had made some friends, acquired some clients, and had even managed to sell two houses in the time spent outside the hospital walls.

One of the couples had been almost impossible to please. It had taken twenty-three showings in the precious few hours she had available before they got to the one they were willing to put an offer on. It was amazing how much people wanted and how little they were willing to spend for it, and for as much as she tried to stay true to their wish lists, it seemed they ended up buying something completely different, exactly what had happened with the McMillan's. It was the twenty-third listing, a contemporary rather than traditional, mid-century rather than historic, on a large lot rather than the small one they wanted because of a distaste for yard work, in the south part of town rather than downtown, that had won their hearts. What they had gotten was the open concept, stainless steel appliances, soaking tub, and walk-in closet that had been high on their priorities. She had only shown it for lack of anything else available in their price range, but she had hit the jackpot and the closing was early fall. She was exhausted that night, and it was one of the few she'd found sleep enclosed in Reid's embrace.

Attending three closings last week had put some much-needed cash into her account. Making deposits into her hospital account was critical. The balances left after the insurance companies had paid what they felt was their fair share were hefty. It helped that Leeni was making good progress and would be going home, leaving the hospital sooner than they'd anticipated. It meant a week less of bills, running around, trying to do it all. Her hospital stays weren't exactly free. She had to pay for parking, food, her own amenities, gas for her trips home and back, and for whatever Leeni needed, like the hats and scarfs she'd asked for. Her favorite was still the Greenliner baseball cap Reid had sent in with Nancy Motta, who was visiting quite regularly. They were becoming good friends and she hoped the bond would outlast Reid's propensity for change. She would miss her, if she stepped out of her life. Wanting to contribute while at Reid's, she'd planned on grocery shopping and cooking to repay a small amount of his kindness.

Maybe she'd be able to catch up on her sleep and be less zombie, more human. It was taking a toll.

After pulling into her driveway, she sat a moment trying to acclimate herself, her mental lists now a blur, her mind completely blank.

Hefting the car door open, she slipped her shoes off and hobbled over rocks and pebbles as she crossed the street before knocking on the slider, opening it, and letting herself in.

"Where are you?"

Her voice echoed out into the rest of the condo.

"I'm in here, love."

Izabella moved easily through the rooms until she came to Melinda's bedroom, where she found the older woman packing a suitcase, her chair moving smoothly from bureau to case.

Izabella leaned against the doorway.

"How did lunch go yesterday?"

"Very well. Thank you for asking. Can you believe I was on a date? At least that's what Jim called it."

"I think it's way past time. And good for him for asking. I really like him."

Jim was one of Leeni's nurses, taking care of the young girl for the second time in her life. He'd surprised Melinda by asking her out and Melinda had surprised her by accepting.

"I like him, too, but it scares me to death. At least the physical aspect of it. I haven't been exactly active in the last, oh, twenty years. And now, not being able to move. It will be a challenge, that's for sure."

Izabella thought it might be too much information for her but knew Melinda needed to talk, so she offered, "It kind of comes naturally, I think."

"Well, he's asked me out for dinner this weekend. He's driving up from Stoneham, where he lives, and picking me up to take me to some place in Tyngsboro. He told me to dress up. I have no idea what to wear."

"I can help you with that. We can go shopping in Boston. I'll ask Reid if he plans on spending some time with Leeni this week and if he does, we can hit some stores."

"Thank you. I'd appreciate it."

Plopping herself down in the rocking chair, Izabella sat silently for a moment before admitting, "I think I'm getting cold feet."

"Understandable."

"This can't work."

"Why not?"

"It's his *home*, Melinda. It's where he'd go to get away from the world, where there is no one depending on him, where he doesn't have to talk if he doesn't want to. We are taking that away from him."

"He offered, Izabella. Remember that."

Her voice was moving up an octave becoming almost shrill. It sounded tinny in her ear when she said, "Why? I don't understand the why. I don't know what's happening."

It had been such a slow but steady progress of connection that she thought her heart might be anticipating something she knew could never be. How many times had he told her he could never do forever? Yet those words had lost their meaning with all that he'd done for them since Leeni's illness, and even before that when they'd spent searing nights in each other's arms.

Melinda slid back to the bureau, taking a pile of capris from the drawer. Placing them on the already growing heap, she said, "Hopefully he is waking up."

"I can't count on hope. I'm moving Leeni into a potentially dangerous situation. Her heart will break if he moves out or if his feelings change toward her."

"Yes, I believe that's true. But his heart needs some softening, and I can't think of anyone better suited to that job than Leeni."

"It doesn't need softening, Melinda, it needs hardening. He was always way too sensitive. Hurt too easily. That's been the problem."

"Point taken. He's done a good job of balancing it over the last few weeks. I can't believe he came up with the Beanie thing. That was a stroke of genius."

Izabella smiled for the first time since arriving.

"He was afraid his arm would fall off. He had to think of something. Isn't there a saying that necessity is the mother of invention?"

Melinda returned the smile, then began looking around.

"He spent some time in this room before I got home."

Izabella leaned forward out of curiosity.

"Really? How do you know?"

"Honey found a coffee mug in here and one of his suit coats was on the back of the chair."

Izabella had never seen a light on, and she had compulsively looked over at the condo when she knew Reid was in residence.

Izabella took a seat at the edge of the rocker.

"What do you think it means?"

"That he has a need to be where life is. It certainly wasn't in the rest of the place. I made sure Honey removed everything that smacked of family before he arrived. Here, there are all kinds of reminders of who we were and how we felt about each other. For him to choose to be in this room means something."

"You don't feel violated?"

"God, no. He's my son. I love him the same way you love Leeni. You're just doing a better job of dealing with crisis than I did."

"It's not my crisis."

"True. I would have never given up if it had been Reid in that car instead of me. It still haunts me that he was on the scene when they removed me. I could hear his screams, still hear them sometimes. It was horrible."

"He was suffering for a long time."

"Yes, and then it seemed he didn't suffer at all. Closed himself off tighter than a drum. I have high hopes that he's pushing at the wall to get out. His connection with you and Leeni seems to be giving him the strength to do it."

Izabella pressed the chair back with her toe and she started to rock back and forth.

"There is no connection between us."

"Oh, my girl. That cord is so strong it scares him to death. He will never be able to break free of it. I guess he could die trying."

Izabella knew about his fear. She could taste and smell it whenever they were entwined. And then there was her own brand, on the opposite ends of that spectrum.

Folding her hands in her lap, Melinda said, "I will understand if you can't move forward with this particular accommodation, but I truly believe it will be the best thing for all of us, him included."

"I don't think I'd have the heart to tell Leeni no princess bed."

"That would be one battle I wouldn't wage."

"So, I guess we move forward. Reid gave me a key this morning. He said we could start moving things in anytime we want."

"Should we take over the first batch today?"

"I guess. It still feels so strange."

"Why don't you go across the street, pack up some of Melina's things so she'll feel more at home."

And that's what she did.

Entering Reid's vestibule, a box in hand, Izabella marveled at the changes already in place. Soft tones painted the walls. The furniture filled the space beautifully and Reid's personal sense of style was telling. It was simpler than she'd thought it would be but it was elegant. The dining room table was massive which was why he'd chosen it. He'd said he wanted to have people for dinner, parties with the team in attendance, friends like Keith, and family gatherings. He had even talked about having Christmas here with all the winter trappings, celebrating the season like his mother had. In a flash, she saw herself beside him, touching his arm, kissing him, while family and friends enjoyed good food and drink.

Turning on her heel, she all but ran away from a scene that was far too real for where their relationship stood. She would never find a place here and she needed to resign herself to that. As she wandered toward the back, where the first-floor bedrooms were located, she passed through the family room, the fireplace the focal point with the couches and chairs framed around it. She could see herself wedged into a corner of the plush fabric, the light on beside her as she read or quilted. It screamed comfort and hominess.

Picking up her pace, she moved on to Leeni's room.

It hit her that this was to be his library.

The bookcases were empty, the princess bed sat majestically against a wall, a white matching bureau sat against another, sheer curtains hung from the windows and blinds would be hung at the beginning of next week.

And she panicked all over again and sat on the bed with a plop, the box falling at her feet.

"He had to change everything."

Melinda had caught up, a box of her own sitting on her lap.

"You knew that."

"On some level, yes. But to see how far it is from his vision? He was so excited about the desk, the books he'd buy to fill the shelves, the love seat where he wanted to curl up with a novel, a fire blazing."

He would have none of that now.

"Too hot for a fire right now anyway. Besides, when would he have time for that during the season?"

"But it's his *house*, Melinda."

"One he offered you. Be grateful and don't think. Come see my room."

Slowly rising from the bed, Izabella followed Melinda into what would have been his man cave. No trace of the linen couch, the masculine feel of the space. Where had he put it? Upstairs?

In storage.

Izabella's tone was almost a wail.

"This was supposed to be his room."

"He has a whole house. He didn't need a room. What was he going to do in here anyway? Sit by himself and vegetate? This is much better use of the space."

Izabella's hands pressed at her stomach, the sheer magnitude of what he'd given up hitting her in the solar plexus.

He had sacrificed his house and his life for them.

What did it all mean?

Was it just for Leeni?

Her breath held, her heart hitched with wild hope yet pessimistic caution.

It was crazy to believe this had anything to do with her.

It was crazy to ignore the warning bell in her ear.

But she was so crazy in love with him, especially now seeing all he had done for them, that her heart refused to believe what her mind was begging her to remember.

The game was a good one. They'd won five to three but it went into extra innings which meant he'd be getting to the hospital later than he'd hoped. He wasn't going home nights any more. He wanted to make sure Izabella was sleeping, or at least resting, and she seemed to do that when he was there. And he didn't leave upon arising, either, but hung around with them most mornings, reading to or playing cards with Leeni, coaxing Izabella to eat and getting her out for walks around the courtyard, taking her to lunch and bringing back food and gooey treats for the patient before leaving for the park where he'd shower and change. He always made sure to thank the nurses, bring them sweets and stop to chat. They were taking such good care of Leeni he wanted them to know it was appreciated.

When he arrived after his game that night, he was barely through the door when he heard the sounds of Leeni having a very bad night. The anti-nausea medicine hadn't done its job. Izabella and one of the nurses were working double duty, one handling the "bucket," as they had begun to call it, and the other stroking the little girl's back, offering words of encouragement and comfort.

"What happened?"

Turning her head toward him, her eyes bloodshot, her cheeks flushed, Izabella answered him.

"She woke up hungry but I guess the smell of the enchiladas didn't sit well with her stomach. I should have stuck with the soup."

Leeni gagged but looked up at the newcomer and said, "I didn't want soup."

Having been part of the worker bees and knowing the routine, he went over to the shelves and pulled out a new nightgown for Leeni to change into when she was done. Holding it in his hands, he sat on the couch and waited patiently.

"Sometimes you need to listen to your mama."

Izabella was a blur in motion, but her words dropped like a stone.

"Stubborn to the core."

He smiled, and asked, "Who are we talking about? You or Leeni?"

"Not tonight, Reid."

He hadn't noticed the purple smudges under her eyes until she gave him one of her scathing looks. She wasn't sleeping as well as he'd thought, even in his arms. It was having an effect on her mood, so he lightened up.

The nurse was washing Melina's mouth out with water and lemon juice to remove the sour taste. Careful of the sores that had been generated by the chemo, she admitted, "We gave her a new medication which we hoped would work better with the combo. It apparently didn't sit well, so don't blame yourself, Izabella."

Wiping her forehead with her arm, some of her covered in the sickly matter, she disappeared into the bathroom and exited with a warm towel, which she placed on Leeni's stomach.

The nurse's job done for the moment, she said "I think the worst is over. I'll check in again soon. Let's see how she fares for the rest of the night."

Once she was gone, Reid got up and went over to rub Izabella's back while she sat rubbing Leeni's stomach.

Quietly he suggested, "Why don't you go take a shower. I'll change her and then read her a story. Maybe she'll fall asleep."

"That would feel good. Thanks."

He had wanted to kiss her, let her know she wasn't alone, but Leeni grasped his hand as he moved closer to her bed and he occupied himself with her wardrobe change.

After collecting some fresh clothes, Izabella went out into the hallway, heading for the shower and Reid did as he'd promised. Within minutes the little girl was sleeping soundly.

His head dropped into his hands. He didn't know how Izabella coped with this day and night. Watching Leeni retch, her fragile body shaking with the tremors, always made him feel so helpless, unable to personally change the routine, the outcome. It was one of the reasons he stayed so detached from life. If you didn't let anything in, nothing could touch you. His mother's accident had started that ball rolling. He'd felt helpless then, too. But where his mother had given up, Leeni was a warrior in every sense of the word, fighting, laughing, crying, picking the adults up when they were down, and it made him want to feel everything with her.

He got up carefully, and wandered over to the windowsill, where cards of all shapes and sizes lined the area. A basket of flowers with Greenliner balloons stood among them, and he read the note attached. It was from the front office and he gave a silent prayer of gratitude. He knew some of his teammates had stopped by, bringing the little girl all kinds of goodies. Hers was probably the most popular room on the floor. It should have made him nervous but it just strengthened the connection he felt with the team. As he started to read some of the cards to see who had sent them, he was surprised to find so many from people he didn't know. Co-workers he assumed, and friends. The thought of her having a full life before he'd arrived on the scene had not crossed his mind, and yet here was evidence that there were many people who cared about her. He stopped short when he came to the one from Carlo. His heart quickened until he noticed it was signed by Carlo and Camila, telling Izabella they missed her at the studio and their thoughts were with her. She had even stayed friends with a former lover. He couldn't recall the

number of women he'd dated, never mind remember their names or stay connected. He hadn't stayed in touch with her while he was gone, something he didn't
understand and regretted now.

When Izabella returned to the room, dressed in a pair of pajama bottoms and a
tee, rubbing her hair with a towel, he could only stare. Devoid of makeup and
tailored clothes, she was still breathtaking. This was the ordinary he had wanted no
part of, yet with her, it was extraordinary. Goals were simple: healthy children, getting through the day with at least one laugh, working at something you loved. It
was what he had fought so hard against. He was learning you couldn't be part of
anything if you weren't willing to step into the fray, get your heart kicked, feel love,
share the down times.

"You got a card from Carlo. I didn't know you still saw him."

"I joined a dance class about a year ago. He and his wife own the studio and I
like to dance. In fact, that's how I met him."

He wasn't sure he wanted to hear the story, but he wasn't letting a little green
monster cloud his curiosity.

"How? At a dance class?"

"No. This was many years ago, the fall you left for college."

A month after their summer together.

"I heard you dated him."

"I was living in Lowell back then and many of my friends would go to the clubs.
He was there and we danced."

"Is that all you did?"

The samba was back in his consciousness. Provocative and very sexy.

"I don't think you get to ask me questions like that."

His hands were in his pockets, his eyes watching her comb out her hair with her
fingers.

"As you told everyone, we were never a couple. Friends. Yes? What I did while
you were away was my business."

"Who do you dance with now, in class?"

"Different partners."

"What kind of dances?"

"All kinds. Samba, tango, waltz, cha-cha, salsa. It's not about the partner, *querido*,
it's about the dance."

He didn't believe that.

Every one of them meant she was being held by other men and he didn't like
the thought at all.

She glided gracefully over to where he stood, removed his hands from his pockets, and put one on her waist, the other in her hand.

"The tango is very expressive. You go with the feel, not any prescribed steps.
And you hold each other tightly, chest to chest. Like this."

When she looked up into his eyes there was heat. Knowing they would have to
extinguish it for tonight, Leeni sleeping not two feet away, he was relieved when
she stepped back. When she whispered, "Maybe it is about the partner as well," he
was on the verge of kissing her, his lips aching to feel hers. As he reached out to

pull her back against him, they heard a raw voice ask, "Mama, can I have some water please?"

The spell was broken and all he could do was keep the embers from sizzling into life.

If he had known it would be the last time she'd let him hold her, feel her body pressed to his, he wouldn't have let her go.

CHAPTER TWENTY-NINE

When he arrived at the hospital room after his game, Izabella was asleep in the chair, not waiting for him as was usually the case. He stood by the window looking out into the night and stayed there until she addressed him.

The tone was courteous, the meaning clear.

"You don't have to be here, you know?"

He turned to see her fully awake and wondered how long she'd been watching him.

Rubbing his eyes, he said, "I guess it's become habit."

Getting up, she transferred the blanket that had covered her to the makeshift bed. Aligning it as if to finish the night there, not even looking at him, she reminded him, "One you can break, I'm sure."

He was tired and his brain refused to compute what she was saying.

"Why...What is going on?"

Finally looking up at him, her tone cold she said, "Nothing. We're good here. I'm sure you have another life you can go back to."

Taking a step closer, he said, "This is my life right now."

Her eyes and words admonished, "No. This is *my* life right now. Tomorrow. Next week. Next year."

She was implying something he refused to admit.

Yes, it was her life, her daughter, her worry for as long as it took for Leeni to get well but he had become so immersed in it now it had become his as well. For today, anyway. Tomorrow was still the thing that was tripping him up.

"What are you trying to say?"

"Only that you don't have to do this Reid. We will be fine. I would cancel our plans to move into your house if it wasn't for the damn princess bed. Leeni would not have it and now I'm stuck. I'm sorry about that."

"There's nothing to be sorry about. I want you there. I've told you often enough."

"Yes, you have. And I think I've thanked you."

His hands were on his hips. He could feel his face getting hot.

"More than enough."

They were swiping at each other now and both were feeling the pin pricks piercing their skin.

"Would you please leave. We don't need you here. I'd like to spend the morning with her myself."

Folding her arms, she waited for him to vacate the room. When he made no move to comply, she added, "Now would be good."

He just stood there, his face blank, his eyes vacant.

"Why don't I stay until the morning. Then if you still want me to go, I will."

"And let Leeni beg for you to stay? No thank you."

"Why are you pushing me away?"

"Pushing you away? You already have a foot out the door. I want you to leave. It's quite simple."

Her eyes were darkly dangerous, and they compelled him to back out of the room and be on his way.

He stood on the other side of the door, his hands clammy, his blood pounding in his head. Not understanding any of it, feeling the withdrawal as absolute, he could do nothing but head home.

But on the way back to Andover, his thoughts raced. There could only be one reason she was giving him the cold shoulder. He was being frozen out because of the damn conversation he'd had with her about the house.

They had made their usual breakfast run this morning, and everything had been fine between them. More than fine. Wanting to be alone with her, without the hustle and bustle of the hospital routine, their time a bit constrained, they'd opted for a quick stop at Dunkins, the sun peeking out from the clouds, May finally unfolding into a spring-like month. The egg sandwiches were eaten without fanfare and the conversation flowed like it always did.

They had talked about Beanie and his next trip.

"I can't believe how much of the world I've ignored in the last decade. I would never have thought to see the Stockyards District. It's supposed to be a step back in time. I hope Beanie enjoys the trip back to the Wild West."

"People are going to start wondering what you and Beanie have going."

"Hey, let `em talk."

The smiles had been playful, the touches incendiary.

Then he'd made the mistake of bringing up her tentativeness about the move.

"My mother told me you're upset the house isn't what I'd envisioned."

Rubbing the tips of his fingers with hers, she admitted. "You're so private and here we are invading your space. I can't take it lightly."

"And I appreciate that. You are one of the few who know that about me. It's not a big deal, Izabella. We're dealing with something much more important right now, and I want you to feel at home there."

"But you've done so much to alter its appearance. Like the ramps you installed."

"Good idea to open up the room with a French door to the ramp outside, wasn't it? This way my mother can enjoy the out-of-doors with ease."

"But that was going to be your room."

Tweaking her nose, he smiled and said, "This move isn't just all about you. My mother will always be welcome in my home, and now there'll be no reason she can't come and visit. Maybe I'll just dress the library a little differently when Leeni's no longer sleeping there. Make that my room instead."

Like an idiot, he'd ambled into hostile territory by reminding her, "Things will be back where they should be at some point. Remember, it's only temporary."

Her fingers had stilled before she began to extricate them but he held on tight.

"Thank you for clearing that up for me. I must have forgotten that small detail."

Her voice was shaky, but there was an icy chill in the air, and in that moment, everything had changed.

When he went to kiss her good-bye before leaving for the Bogs, she'd stiffened in his arms, offering him only her cheek.

When he'd arrived tonight, he found her sleeping in the chair and it had gone downhill from there.

The emptiness of what his life would be if she wasn't in it hit him when he entered his house. He hadn't spent a night here since he'd bought it, preferring to be with those he was coming to think of as his family.

He woke up, disoriented but his first thought was about Leeni, so he reached for his phone.

How was her night?

No response.

Did you get the picture of Beanie at the Bog? I completely forgot to take one there."

No response.

Is everything all right with Leeni?"

No response.

He was becoming unnerved. There was a growing sense of panic that something dire had happened and that's the reason she wasn't answering.

Please get back to me.

No response.

He finally called the nurses' station and asked how Leeni was doing, relieved to hear that she had passed the night well and seemed to be over the after-effects of her most recent treatment.

He'd been a bundle of roiling emotion up until the moment he was assured that Leeni was fine, but the knowledge didn't settle him.

Why wasn't Izabella answering him?

This was about Leeni, not them. She had to know he'd want to keep tabs on her.

Through his restless night, he'd almost convinced himself her physical retreat was for the best. She had left him, for all intents and purposes. He should be relieved. He could move on now and start doing what he was good at. Then thoughts of her wrapped in his arms, his heat-seeking missile exploding on contact made him realize that was all a bunch of bullshit.

Who was he fucking kidding?

He had never felt such an intimate connection before, and it scared him to death. Made him feel as if he were choking, strangled in the grip of her, what? Her love?

Yeah, right. She's gone so you're feeling strangled. Makes so much sense, Jacks.

His thinking was so muddled he couldn't see anything straight.

He might as well just admit he was in deep shit.

But way out in the cold.

The transformation from where they had been to how they were now was going to drive him crazy if he let it. Would she continue to confide in him or would he have to question the nurses on everything regarding Leeni's condition? Would they even tell him if Izabella instructed them otherwise? He wasn't family; he wasn't blood. He had no rights when it came to Leeni, and he wanted to slam his fist into something. He needed that little girl. Her face would light up when he walked into the room, making him feel like he belonged to someone.

And Izabella. He'd miss their conversations, the touch of skin to skin even if only holding her hand while they walked.

There had always been a door between them. He should know, he'd erected it to be thick and foolproof, but the one she'd put up overnight was steel-plated and indestructible, and he needed to figure out a way to open it back up. He didn't have the instruction manual on how to break down walls. She was the expert because she had gotten his to come tumbling down. No matter how he'd tried to reassemble them, he had failed miserably, and he was getting ready to accept the inevitable.

How could he not?

Her first smile of the morning breathed life into his day. Her texts kept him informed and included. Waking up beside her had become an essential ingredient to his happiness.

About to leave for over a week, he was on edge. He didn't like being away from them, didn't like the anxiety he felt when gearing up for it.

He just wasn't all the way there yet.

Couldn't seem to jump that last hurdle without his breath seizing on him.

But he also couldn't let her get so far away that he couldn't bridge the distance when he was ready.

After he'd showered and changed, the debate raged in his head as he made the drive into Bogs Field. He forced his mind to focus on the game ahead. They were playing the Padres and he began a roster check. What kind of pitches did Trout like? Pujolis? Frustration with the process kept building as the picture of Heaney, the pitcher, gave way to a vision of Izabella in that damn bathing suit and all that glistening skin. He was exhausting himself with the effort to keep blocking her out.

Once he was in the locker room, an hour before the game, the restless energy began to get to him.

He had to pitch today and he had to be in game mode. Any outside distractions could completely obliterate his regimen, and this was one major distraction.

He almost barked out loud.

In the past, when one of his teammates was struggling with some family issue, a fight with his spouse, a sick kid, he'd been condescending and arrogant. Belittling their will power, even their wife, he'd had no sympathy for any breakdown in focus, thought it was the sign of a loser.

He was overly confident that he would never give anyone that kind of access to his mental stamina. But he was learning it wasn't something you allowed in, it was something that infiltrated the mind in subversive ways.

Somehow Izabella had snuck into his head and was playing havoc with it.

Cursing her and himself, he swore it was not going to fly.

Throwing his towel into the bin, he made his way into the video room with heavy feet, wanting to occupy his mind with something baseball related. With a flick of the switch, one of his most recent games came up on screen, and he glowered as his thoughts strayed randomly from the analysis to worry over Leeni before Izabella forcibly made her way through the door he was furiously rebuilding.

Vigorously rubbing his hands over his face, he realized this was an effort in futility and had no idea how restore his mental acuity now that she refused to budge from his head.

It appeared that not only had his walls been breached but his inner fortress had been invaded.

Motts noticed the clenched jaw, the gritted teeth, the wheels whirring while he was dressing for the game.

"Hey, Jacks. What's up?"

Unable to talk about this strange turn of events, Jacks tried to brush it all off. Gathering his glove and hat he shrugged. "Nothing. I'm good."

The tension in his voice said something completely different.

"You don't seem yourself. Everything okay with Leeni?"

Thoughts of the little girl relaxed him a bit and he smiled as he said, "Yeah, she's good. Doing better than the doctors thought she would."

"Izabella?"

He instantly became rigid, and his gruff reply told both where the problem lay.

"Why would she have anything to do with my mood?"

His catcher stood his ground. "You tell me."

"There's nothing to tell."

Motts threw the ball he was holding in his glove up and let it drop back in place, an evil smile making his face look demonic.

"Okay then. Let's get `em."

He didn't miss the smile or what it meant.

Thoughts of Izabella only festered more.

He never did get his focus back and he lost his first game of the season three to six.

As they watched his game, Leeni was talking to Reid like Izabella used to. Izabella was so intent on the piss-poor way he was pitching, she barely noticed. She was pacing the confines of the room, wondering what was eating at him. His strategy was non-existent, his mechanics looked rusty, his control was missing, and the pitches were all over the place. Motts went out to the mound a few times in the first two innings and the manager took the ball away in the fourth. Leaving the mound, he vibrated with uncontrolled fury, and his long, clipped strides made it evident he was pissed.

She'd never seen him play this badly.

He had once told her nothing ever got to him; that his focus was one hundred percent on every game he pitched.

And she wondered what had muddled the control of the once-unflappable ace.

Melinda, who had stayed to watch the game, was as upset as she was.

"What the h…heck is wrong with him this afternoon?"

"I don't know."

Melinda glanced up, her forehead creased.

"Are you sure? Where was he this morning? He didn't come in before the game? What happened between you two?"

"Nothing. Nothing happened. Nothing ever happens. He doesn't have it in him, remember? Everything is temporary. We are temporary."

Melinda wheeled herself over to where she stood, "I think you're wrong."

"No, Melinda. I'm not. He reminded me himself. He shouldn't have needed to."

He sat in his car, the sun casting a haze in the distance.

Should he just go to the park, board the bus to the airport, and be done with this? Give it up?

He didn't want to leave for his road trip with this hostility between them. It was affecting him in ways he'd never known possible.

Worry about Leeni would always be there, just under the surface of his daily life but she was doing better than the doctors had dreamed. Her white cell count was normal, and they were hopeful that the next phase would be as successful. The relapse still made the future unpredictable. If it had happened once, it could happen again, something he didn't like thinking about. But there were experts working on it, a whole team of professionals that would monitor her progress, be there to make changes if they were necessary.

Starting the engine, he let the car determine his destination, and it took him to the place he wanted to be. He needed to say good-bye, to see her face, with the hope that absence had alleviated the problem somehow. Picking up his pace, he hurried his steps down the hallway and through the open door to Leeni's room.

His mother all but assaulted him when he entered.

"What the h… happened to you last night?"

Last night his loss had dropped them another half game out of first. If they kept losing this way, they'd never have a shot at the pennant.

Distracted from his intention, he said weakly, "Sorry about that. Off night."

"If it wasn't for you, I'd have stopped watching them ages ago. The team is setting a record in errors per game. There's nothing worse than watching a bad team play night after night."

"Except being part of it."

The anger wasn't as huge as it might have been once. It was all part of a cycle and they were just in the downswing. And he had more important things consuming his mind.

He looked over to the other woman in the room.

He knew immediately he'd be on the receiving end of her silent treatment.

She hadn't even turned away from the window when he'd entered. Her arms were folded against her chest, her focus on something out on the horizon. Even when she was here, she was someplace faraway.

He used to love being on the road. New places, new people, something always going on, him at the center of it. But now, he didn't like leaving, didn't like being away from her for so long with only a phone and an iPad to keep them connected.

Her silent treatment was much worse because now he wouldn't even have that.

He'd never cared about the women he'd left before, never missed the interaction, the sexual contact.

He missed everything about Izabella but she was nowhere to be found.

His home was filled with her essence, but it still echoed the emptiness of what his life had become. Life existed here in this room with these people and he needed it surrounding him.

His fingers itched to touch her, his lips ached to feel hers beneath them, his arousal was quick and hard, and it only got worse the further away she pushed him. His recurring dream had been merciless.

"Hi, Mr. Crackerjacks."

Dragging his attention off Izabella, he put it where it might do some good. Leaning down to kiss the patient, he asked, "How was her night?"

With no response from Izabella, his mother filled the silence and announced she'd had a good one.

Leeni said sadly, "You're leaving today, aren't you?"

"I am. Beanie's going to Minnesota."

"What's there?"

"Other than a ballpark, I have no idea."

"You'll find someplace, right?"

"That's been half the fun. I ask the guys on the other team where the best tourist spots are, and I haven't been given bad advice yet. What did you have for supper?"

"We went to the Waverly Place. Mama wanted me to eat well before the last round of chemo."

The last round in the first phase. They all knew there'd be more to come.

"I hear they have very good food. Did Mama eat?"

"I try to make sure she does, just like I promised."

Izabella spun around and asked with a poisonous tone, "You put that on her shoulders?"

With a cracking voice and shrugging shoulders, he said, "Someone has to coax you."

"Not her. Don't you ever make her promise something like that again."

"Mama, he just wants to make sure you keep up your strength."

"Word for word?"

"Look, I'm sorry. You need to eat and I won't be around as much as I'd like to be."

"I'm beginning to think you are around too much. Maybe it's time for you to go."

Leeni wouldn't hear of it.

"Mama, he's going to be gone for sooo long. I want him to stay."

Pulling the chair up next to her bed, Reid leaned toward the little girl, taking her hand in his, and said, "How about if I read you a story? Then I'll head out. We're boarding the plane in a few hours and I have to get there earlier than usual."

He didn't but couldn't think of another excuse to give for his leave taking.

Leeni was wearing a cotton skull cap, the rim turned up to fit her small head, and she touched his heart again. He didn't want to leave her but her mother wanted him gone, and he would abide by her wishes. For now. Until he could say what she needed to hear easily and without hesitation, he was doomed to a very dark place.

Leeni gave it one more try, a small whine in her voice. "Please stay."

"For a story. Which one?"

Rifling through the books sitting on her bed, she pulled out the one she wanted. "*The Knight and the Dragon,* please."

It was probably the longest one here. He got the sense she was wheedling for more time. He was more than happy to give it to her.

He could see Izabella in his peripheral vision, standing by the window as he told the tale, her back to him as had become her custom, overnight. Concentrating on the story, he attempted to block her out but it was impossible. Her scent floated out to him, her indefatigable spirit enfolded him in her magic and he felt himself almost ready to fall at her feet.

When he had turned the last page, bending over the bed, he gave Leeni a kiss.

"Beanie will send you a picture as soon as he can. Okay? I love you, sweet baby girl."

"I love you, too Mr. Crackerjacks. I'll miss you."

Dragging himself slowly from the sitting position, he looked at his mother and said wearily, "Well, I guess I'll get going."

With a puzzled look, she asked, "Why aren't you staying?"

Not wanting to get into the nitty gritty, he said, "I want to watch the video from last night. See what happened."

Although he knew exactly what had happened. Izabella had put a curse on his super pitching powers from this very room.

Leaning forward, her elbows resting on the arms of her wheelchair, Melinda said, "I don't like that you'll be gone so long. You're the only one who can get her to do what she's supposed to."

She was nodding to the woman with her back to them.

"I'm not sure I have the touch anymore, Mom."

Melinda's eyes narrowed. The tone was harsh when she demanded, "Izabella, what's going on?"

Rubbing her eyes, the burning sensation from unshed tears back again, Izabella turned to look at Melinda. Did his mother notice the purple smudges?

He had his answer, when she asked, "Why haven't you been sleeping?"

Izabella said simply, "I'll catch up."

"No wonder Reid asked Leeni to watch you."

"That's not her job."

The voice was testy, the sentiment straightforward.

"Well, you're not willing to take on the assignment."

"Could you both please just leave me alone? I'm fine."

He noticed the rigidity of her shoulders as if she was forcing herself to stay upright, and knew he'd better leave soon.

She needed some privacy, at least from him.

"Mom, I gotta go."

He leaned down to kiss her forehead before glancing at the woman at the window.

His mother was not going to let this go and said, "I'm coming down with you. I want to get an iced tea."

While his mother was getting her pocketbook, he spoke to Izabella's back.

"If there is anything else you need at the house, just let me know. I'll make sure it's handled."

He barely caught the imperceptible nod.

Leeni's request followed them out the door.

"Cream-filled doughnut, please."

His mother was wheeling herself towards the elevator.

As soon as the door swooshed closed, she pressed him. "What the hell happened?"

"I told you, just an off night."

"I don't mean about that game. Why did you tell her it was temporary?"

He stopped short and threw his hands up into the air.

"What do you want from me?"

The pressure was becoming unbearable.

Her silence was cutting and she maintained it all the way down to the lobby.

As soon as he brought her her tea, he slid onto the opposite stool.

Picking up right where they left off, she whispered in a hostile tone, "So *is* this...arrangement only temporary?"

Backpedaling was habit and the habit seemed addictive, so without giving any thought at all to what he really felt, he went with familiarity.

"I thought we were all on the same page with that."

"So once Leeni's well, you'll be their crackerjack mover?"

Something huge grabbed him by the heart and squeezed.

Somewhat dishonestly, he admitted, "I hadn't thought that far ahead."

He was looking more and more at his future, but it still raged with tempests he didn't know how to control. The only way he could keep moving forward was to take it one day at a time. One step at a time. He just couldn't make it all the way out on the limb yet.

But his mother hit on a truth he couldn't quite see for his own forest.

"It seems someone did."

The familiar rallied again.

"She's ignoring me now for something we both agreed to."

"Distancing I think would be a better term."

"She sure is doing a great job. I think she just crossed the border into Cleveland."

"Don't be such an ass."

Looking instantly contrite, he said more moderately, "She should have talked to me about what she's feeling, not slammed the door in my face."

"And say what? You haven't promised her a thing. You haven't made a commitment. You've just asked her to take a ride on your merry-go-round. Well, I think she just got off. And I don't blame her."

His eyes dipped. "I thought everything was progressing pretty well."

Every time he'd felt an overwhelming urge to run he'd taken deep breaths and let the feeling work its way through his system. It was working better than he'd expected. His heart was getting braver.

"Pretty well? Is this what you call progress? From what I've heard, this is exactly how you operate. You bestow your magnanimous self on others on a rental basis. Temporarily give them all you've got and then what? Return the merchandise once it doesn't meet your needs anymore?"

"My needs have nothing to do with this. This is about what they need. And I hope you're not referring to Izabella as merchandise."

"Of course, I'm not. But my dear boy, you are what they need. But you don't like that burden, do you?"

Chewing on his lip, he braced for the heaviness of that dependency to weigh him down. There was a slight droop to his shoulders but none of the overwhelming tonnage he'd expected. Without giving him the time to think about it, his mother went on.

"All of this generosity is meaningless if you can't give them what they deserve and put your heart into it."

Totally frustrated now with his own inability to open himself up to what Izabella could give him, he asked again, "What do you want from me, Ma?"

Melinda calmed herself down with a deep breath.

"Reid, that woman deserves someone who values her. If you can't do that, then you need to stop this experimentation in relationship building. Someone who sees her gifts will come along one day and treasure her. And they won't move at a snail's pace. I hope you are not around to see it. But then again, those odds are good, aren't they?"

With that said, she sat back and stared out the side window.

After a few seconds of silence, she murmured, "Have a good trip, Reid. And no more games like last night, okay?"

He knew he was being dismissed, so he got up to leave.

She snagged his hand and pulled him down so she could kiss his cheek.

He walked away unable to promise there wouldn't be a repeat of last night's fiasco. Not as long as he was in limbo about where he stood with a woman who pretty much owned his soul.

As he drove down Storrow Drive, he couldn't help hearing his mother's words, over and over again. And the thought of Izabella with someone else was an anchor around his neck and his mother was right. He needed to remove it and move on or drown in her love. He had to *do* something and this road trip would give him the time and space to figure out exactly what that was.

And he wondered nervously how many times he was going to make that promise to himself.

CHAPTER THIRTY

Wednesday morning found Leeni with lingering after effects of the chemo. A celebration had been planned by the nursing staff, but the goodies had to be wrapped to go. Jaco had taken the morning off to help cart out the rest of Melina's things from her room, something they had been packing up over the course of the last couple of days. Izabella was happy he wasn't wasting another work day. Once he got them unpacked, he'd be spending the day tending to Reid's yard, thereby killing two birds with one stone. The few remaining boxes were placed in the trunk, and they set off for Reid's house where Melinda and Sofia were waiting for them. Jaco was driving, Izabella in the back holding the receptacle she'd get out to empty every few miles.

Reid had left for Minnesota without another word, but Leeni had received snapshots, one of Beanie at County Stadium and one at the Mill City Museum, pictures they added to the growing pile. Leeni loved Sofia's idea of creating a scrapbook, and Sofia had stopped in at a craft store to pick one up. It would be there when they got to their temporary quarters, and would give Leeni something to do over the next week while waiting for Reid's return. It was all she talked about. That and sleeping in her princess bed.

Once settled, they found a rhythm that seemed to work. Melinda was in her element taking care of the patient, and she was ready to go each morning as soon as Claire had helped her bathe and dress. Izabella had picked up her work schedule and was back to her regular routine. Things were going well financially due to the increase in commission checks, and she was more relaxed than she'd been since Leeni was admitted to the hospital. Over the last couple of days, she'd gotten her appetite back and had started sleeping again. It was so good to be out of the hospital and in a real bed, one that was so comfortable she couldn't help but doze soundly for a few hours at a time. Able to create comfort food in the kitchen and watching Leeni eat with gusto, she found her way back to the table and enjoyed eating again. What hadn't improved was her anxiety level. Without Reid around, she was free to just be and not constantly have to protect herself but his home-coming would change all that. It held more than a hint of foreboding.

They'd all live here, in the same house, temporarily.

Until it was time for them to go.

She had pulled herself back, taken her heart off the chopping block, but he had already done his job and it was in pieces.

What she had glimpsed as possible was not what it seemed.

She was relieved there wasn't a dull moment while Reid was gone.

Visitors came every day to see Leeni and to see how she was coping.

Carlo and Camila were by, Nolan and Terry, Jaco and Addie. Her father flew in for a couple of days, mystified at his daughter's reluctance to talk about Reid and all he'd done for her. He had finally accepted that maybe Reid wasn't the selfish man he'd initially thought but she refused to talk about him.

Leslie and Millie called and asked if they could drive up. They were so sweet and caring, bringing take-out, flowers and talk about Reid's game that week, something she could have done without. But she played the hostess, the long-standing friend whom Reid was helping in her hour of need. Nancy had dropped in a couple of times and for as much as she enjoyed that budding friendship she was relieved when she left.

The pretending was the hardest.

The only one she could really talk to about what this was doing to her was Sofia who was there every other day bringing a shoulder to cry on, which she used with-out mercy. The tears weren't drying up. With every sentiment expressed about Reid's unselfish act came not only grief, but guilt as well.

"I'm pitiful."

She rubbed the tissue across her nose and reached for another.

"No, you're just extremely tired and stressed."

"No. I'm a pitiful excuse for a human being."

"Izabella. How can you say that? You are doing an exceptional job with Leeni. She is getting stronger every day."

"Why can't I just be grateful for what he's doing? Why am I putting such strings on it? He never wanted to be tied down and I've got us in knots."

"You thought…"

"But why? He has never given me reason to think…"

Waves of pleasure washed over her and she knew exactly why she'd thought, hoped, wished for it to be more than he'd proposed.

Closing her eyes, she breathed him in and shut him back out.

He'd gone thirteen days without hearing her voice.

That wasn't exactly true. He listened to her voice on his voice mail over and over, watched the video of her and her father every night before climbing into bed. But he hadn't had any kind of conversation with her since he'd left.

His mother was texting him, he was talking to Leeni, but Izabella had yet to reach out. And he'd been too afraid to call for fear she wouldn't talk to him.

It would tell him nothing had changed.

His last couple of outings had been decent. He'd wanted to win them for Leeni, who had gone back to their original deal and was texting him strike-out estimates. He thought maybe his mother had talked to her about arms and anatomy, because she was keeping them within human limits. He was more than happy to comply. It was helping him stay focused.

His next duel was tomorrow in Philadelphia, the first of a three-game series.

And then he'd be going home.

What would he find?

Did she want him to stay away? Should he go to his mother's, live there until…?

He needed to know, so he took his phone out and hit her number.

And waited.

Would she answer his call?

Her hello washed over him. It was good to hear her voice but it lacked warmth and caring.

"How are things going?"

"Very well, thank you. And with you?"

His hand formed a fist by his side, his lips puckered in annoyance.

Civility was not what he wanted from her.

But she wouldn't know that. He'd told her the opposite or had given mixed messages.

If the situation were reversed, he would have told her to go to hell.

He hoped she wouldn't.

He had to find a way back into her good graces, if not her heart.

Forcing enthusiasm where fear niggled deep, he said, "So Beanie and I grabbed breakfast at this little family place this morning. He pigged out on all kinds of meat. I think you would have liked it."

She shared a piece of forward progress.

"Leeni can finally eat meat again without that metallic taste. It's making it easier to feed her."

The response fanned the flame of hope and it burned in his belly.

"That's great. She apparently has the same cultural affinity as her mama."

Silence echoed over the line and stretched until Reid broke it, the hope turning to dust.

"How's the routine going?"

"It's going well. Thank you again for doing this."

This must have been the hundredth time she'd thanked him. How much gratitude could a person take? He had given up telling her it was no big deal, that he was glad to do it and went with a more subdued, "You're welcome."

The quiet was making him itchy. Her indifference and detachment signified something he refused to accept. The dynamics had changed between them. She had severed the link that had chained them together and had set him free. Scrambling to put the link back in place, he kept the conversation going.

"Sold any houses?"

"I'm close. There's an offer in but we're still negotiating."

"Where?"

"North Andover."

"How are the clients?"

"They're good. Look, I've got to go. Lots to do around here."

Izabella, where are you? I miss you.

"Are you going to watch my game tonight?"

"When would Leeni miss one of your games?"

That's not what he'd asked.

Are you going to watch it?

Will you notice if I'm drifting? How many strikeouts I get?

Do you care if I win or lose?

"Iz…"

"All right then. I'll see you in five days."

She clicked off without even a good-bye.

When the line went dead, so did all pretense of wanting a solitary life.

This thing with Izabella was far from meaningless…or temporary.

Did he want her in his life wasn't the question anymore.

It wasn't the important piece at all.

Could he find his way back into her heart had become his primary concern.

What would he do if he couldn't?

That thought all but tore him to pieces because it would be his own damn fault.

He wanted to punch something. And that didn't bode well for the batters facing him that night.

They were in Leeni's room, watching him pitch, the twenty-five-inch TV on the wall giving them all a fantastic view of the playing field. Melinda had made popcorn. Leeni was in jammies, sitting cross-legged on the bed, her eyes shining every time he threw the ball for a strike.

He had amassed a seven and one record since donning the uniform, and tonight he was as impressive as ever.

Melinda commented, "Looks like he's about as pissed as a person can get."

"Grams!"

"Oops, sorry. My bad. He sure does look angry."

Izabella had to agree with the assessment but didn't know where it was coming from. This was a completely different pitcher than last time out. His control was perfect, his pitches were placed right where he wanted them, his stride was confident. Maybe he'd finally relaxed knowing she'd accepted the temporary nature of their arrangement. She'd given him what he wanted, hadn't she? Backed off, pried her dependent fingers from his shoulders.

When he'd called earlier, she had almost let it go to voice mail, but she had a desperate need to hear his voice.

She'd known it was a mistake as soon as he'd asked how things were going.

His deep baritone had caressed her; his intent to keep the conversation going had teased her.

But she knew the score. Reid three, Izabella zero.

She was determined to win this battle with her heart, keep him at a safe distance, keep him from getting his hands on it again.

She'd let him go so the temporary nature of their commitment wouldn't weigh him down.

So why the anger?

Critically, she continued to watch his performance.

He was throwing hard, inside, close to the chest, and there had been at least half a dozen players who'd jumped out of his way.

Motts had gone out to the mound at least a couple of times to cool him down, and it worked for the first few pitches afterwards, but then he was back, growling and grunting and in everyone's face.

When he came out in the eighth inning, the Phillies fans were on their feet, ecstatic. He had let very few hits through, and the hope was their team could play catch-up once he was out of the game, but that wasn't meant to be. Red Sox won five to nothing.

They were all counting down the days until Reid returned home, Izabella fighting the nerve-rattling battle as the X's on the calendar had almost reached the date starred. The distance between them was coming to an end. There was one looming problem. She still hadn't worked him out of her heart.

CHAPTER THIRTY-ONE

He padded down the stairs, the quiet telling him something he didn't want to know. Life hadn't consumed the place as he'd hoped, and he was still feeling the emptiness only Izabella could fill. Hoover was the only one to greet him, and he gave her head the scruffing she was looking for before she headed for her crate. Not surprised that that he found himself alone, he did wonder where Izabella was. And what she was doing.

Had she gone for coffee with that friend his mother told him about? The one Izabella seemed to be keeping secret. Had she moved on?

Grabbing a mug out of the cabinet, he poured himself a cup of coffee and opened the refrigerator to see if there was any milk. Used to limited pickings, he wasn't prepared for the abundance confronting him. It was stocked with all the things he'd seen at Izabella's, fruit, yogurt, milk, creamer. The bins were stuffed with cold cuts, cheese, vegetables, and there was a packet wrapped in brown paper that he lifted out. A roast beef awaited the oven and he wondered if he'd be invited to sit at the table with them. After pouring his splash of milk into the mug, he closed the door and began inspecting the kitchen. There were bagels from Perfecto's in a paper bag, still warm, and as he picked it up to see what his choices were, he heard the front door open. Taking a breath, he moved towards the opening. The breath held when Izabella walked into view. Apparently dressed for work, she wore a pencil skirt in the color of tangerines, a sleeveless blouse a soft shade of ivory, and heels to match, her hair cascading down her back.

His mouth went dry.

Her phone in hand, she looked almost startled to see him standing there.

He asked the first thing that came into his brain.

"No reception?"

Pursing her lips as if deciding whether to speak to him or not, she gave him a one-word answer. "No."

Andover homes seemed to be a no-call zone for most carriers.

After taking a sip of coffee, he asked, "Where is everyone?"

"Jim came up and took Melinda and Leeni to breakfast. They should be back soon."

"Going to work?"

"Yes, for a few hours."

"Will you be back before I leave?"

She cleared her throat before saying, "Probably not."

She began walking to the stairs, but he stopped her with the words, "Izabella, I can't do this."

She came to a complete standstill, and then whipped around to face him.

Squeezing her eyes closed against how good he looked, his stomach hair beckoning her to search for buried treasure, she tried hard to stop the longing. He was all but flaunting his body, teasing her the way he always had. *Look at me but don't get too close.* Here one minute, gone the next.

She should be sighing in relief that he planned to leave but she wasn't. She was more than angry at his inability to stick with this, potentially breaking Leeni's heart.

Her hands on her hips, she jutted her chin out, and with controlled fury, spit out, "You said you'd try. You haven't even been back a day. It's not acceptable."

Casting his eyes downward, he said in a monotone voice, "I thought I could give you this but it looks like I was wrong."

She took a step forward, her temper rising with each word uttered.

"How many times did you tell me this wouldn't be a problem? How many times did I ask? I knew you would be over your head with this, this...invasion. Your whole house is upside down. This is your home. If anyone moves out it will be us."

His eyes snapped up, blazing, and he charged, "You'll do no such thing. This is what's best for Leeni."

Changing her retreat into a charge, she got within a foot of him before continuing.

"What's best for Leeni?"

She was in his face, her arms akimbo.

"You are what's best for her. Haven't you figured that out yet? She's done better than anyone thought possible. Because of you. If you leave, she won't have her Mr. Crackerjacks. It won't make any difference where we are."

With a shake of his head he insisted, "Her recovery is because of her doctors and her own...her own..."

Tilting her head, she didn't wait for him to finish his sentence. It seemed he didn't know what he was looking for.

"Heart? Funny how you just can't say the word."

He straightened his posture, his hand on the counter and gritted out, "I can say it. I was going to say indomitable spirit but it sounded...cheesy."

Her eyes bored into him and she scoffed. "Can't say it, don't have one. Not one that works and I can't have her with you anymore."

His eyes squinted at her and he warned, "I have one. She's in it."

As much as she wanted to, she couldn't argue with that. She saw, felt the love between them and she truly believed it had helped in Leeni's healing. Was that a temporary aberration as well?

"For how long? Until she counts on you for something? Becomes a little too dependent, begins to rely on your love? Then what?"

Sliding his arms across his chest, his chin out, his jaw clenched he told her, "I'll be there for her. Trust me."

There was a falling sensation, and she found herself in an abyss of grief so deep that she couldn't quite breathe right. He had found his way back to his mother and had taken Leeni under his wing, so his inability to love only had to do with her.

Taking a step toward her, he said more softly, "Don't do anything you'll regret. Keep whatever problems you have with me out of it."

Agitation was making it impossible to stay still. She paced the confines of the kitchen, where he stood, looking so good it was making her shake. She might be debilitated by the thought that he couldn't love her, but she was also ashamed of the easy way he could get her to fall at his feet. She wanted to snap that finger he crooked at her in three places on his left hand so he couldn't pitch anymore. She wanted to scratch those beautiful blue eyes right out of his head. She wanted to feel his heat and douse him in icy water.

He took another step closer and said, "Think about this, Izabella. My mother's here and it makes it easier than being at your house."

She spun to face him, her eyes slits, anger emanating in waves.

"It's all I have been doing since we moved in. This was never going to be permanent, anyway, as you so willingly reminded me. Whether we leave now or in three months, won't matter. The outcome will be the same."

Wringing her hands, her body in constant motion, she all but cried out, "But how do I get her to leave now? She's got her Mr. Crackerjacks here and her princess bed, she's got Beanie, gooey snacks, she's got everything she needs with you. Maybe I'll just move out. My expiration date is up, anyway."

He asked, confusion thick in his voice, "Your expiration date? What are you talking about?"

All her extremities were shaking now, her fingernails digging into the flesh of her palms to keep them still.

"Your time limit for a woman is what? A month? My thirty days are up so I guess it's just time for you to move on. But this is your house. It's up to me to move out."

His mouth slackened, his eyes widened.

"Thirty days, Izabella? I think we've had more time than that, haven't we? More like ten years. Longer?"

She laughed even as the tears threatened to choke her. "Maybe I was just being recycled."

He shook his head and said, "Don't be ridiculous."

His condescending attitude was her undoing. Her fiery temper rose up in defiance.

Her voice was a loaded weapon and she used her words skillfully.

"Ridiculous is thinking that I ever mattered to you. That is the pinnacle of lunacy, is it not?"

He tried to reach for her but she shook him off and she ended up cornered between the wall of cabinets.

As he stepped closer, his voice rose in volume.

"Of course, you mattered. You've always mattered."

Before he could say anything else that might weaken her resolve she asked, her face afflicted with contempt, "Why did you do all of this?"

The silence hung heavy in the air until he said quietly, "For you."

Her fury surged at how obtuse he could be at times. She wished she lived in his reality. It was probably a beautiful world with no cares or woes. He always made sure he kept his life nice and clean, no attachments, no ties.

She all but shrieked, "Do you really expect me to believe that?"

Without thought she brought her fists up and began to pummel his chest and choked out, "You did this for *you*. It was always about you, what you wanted, what you needed, what you could give, what you couldn't. I'm here, Izzie. Oops, no I'm not. Too much feeling, gotta go. And I fell for it every... single... time. But not anymore. Not anymore."

Her arms fell to her sides, her breath became jerky. Appalled by what she had just done, she grabbed her keys and headed for the front door, her legs wobbly beneath her.

"I've got to get out of here."

He reached out to snag her arm but she evaded the move and ran out of the house. She could hear his footsteps close behind her.

When she pulled at the car door handle, he jerked her to him, more aggressively than she'd expected.

"I'm not letting you go anywhere. I have the strength this time around and I'm using it."

Jim's Honda pulled into the drive-way just as Reid took possession of her arm.

Melinda's expression reminded her why Reid was handling her escape the way he was.

Rolling down her window, Melinda called out, "I don't know what's going on, but he tried to stop me once, too. I wish I had listened to him."

As soon as Leeni leaned out her window, asking, "Mama, what's wrong? Where are you going?" the fight went out of her. With no other outlet for her distress, she began to sob, leaning her head on her arms on the door of her car.

Reid glanced back at his mother; whose brow was arched in question. He put his head down, rubbing his temples as he wondered how to proceed.

His mother flicked her fingers in Izabella's direction, and she turned toward Jim and said something before he reversed out of the driveway, leaving them alone.

Leeni's cries as she called for her mama were piercing his heart, but he had to set some things straight. He swore to himself he'd make it up to her.

Working to get himself back under control, he said more softly, "You're right. It has always been about me. What I needed. When I needed it. I thought I could just breeze in and out of your life with no accountability, no repercussions. And it always felt so good, Izzie, I let the feelings carry us away. I couldn't seem to stop reaching out for you."

He let his fingers trail down her spine, needing to have the feel of her beneath them. "I can't do that to you anymore."

He felt her wince beneath his fingertips, heard her ragged breath.

"I can't allow it anymore. It hurts, too much, *mi amour*. Please, let me go. I will be careful."

Gently he stroked the back of her head, her hair a silky skein in his hand.

"I can't do that, Izzie. You had a right to be angry and I think what you did back there was way past time. But I can't let you go."

"I don't understand."

He cupped her shoulders and he gently turned her around to face him.

"I hear you went out for coffee while I was gone. Could you tell me what it means?"

"It means I'm trying to put this to rest. You agree that this is an impossible situation. Your need to move out just proves it."

He gawked at her, not fully understanding. Didn't he just tell her…

"You think I'm moving out because I want you out of my life?"

He could barely hear her when she choked out, "Well, aren't you? Isn't that what you just said?"

Placing his hands more gently on her arms, he tried to lift her face so she would look at him, but she refused, still unable to look into his eyes.

He wanted to kiss her tears away, but he knew he had to settle what was between them first.

Brushing her hair back, his voice strained, he said, "Izabella I'm leaving because I want you *in* my life. You're the one who's left. You're so far away I don't know what to do anymore. Do you know what my life has become since you stopped talking to me?"

She finally let him lift her chin so he could look in those beautiful dark eyes that seemed so often filled with tears he'd caused in some way, and he rubbed some of the moisture away.

"When my mother told me, you'd met someone for coffee, my first inclination was to fly home and beat the shit out of the guy. Of course, that wouldn't have solved anything except to prove what a complete jerk I can be."

Linking his hand in hers, he brought it up to kiss her knuckles.

"Do you know what it's been like for me being unable to hold or touch you?"

Izabella gave a long, shaky sigh, as if she knew exactly what it was like.

"Before I left, you closed me out of your beautiful heart, although you should have done it way before now. If I'd known how cold it would be when you did, we might have gotten to this point long ago. I was a fool not to take the step that would have ended the freeze but I couldn't."

"This is my fault. You've told me all along…."

His finger rested on her lips to still her from saying more.

"From the first day you sashayed out our front door, you've pulled me in. I just didn't know what to do with the feelings. That summer I gave in to the need to be with you, but when I left for school, I couldn't even say good-bye because it would have hurt too much. You were a lifeline that I couldn't afford to stay attached to, but my heart has always rested in your hands."

He dipped his head to kiss her temple and he closed his eyes at the feel of her skin against his lips.

"When you closed yourself away, not talking to me, not letting me touch you, lay down with you, the only time of day I could wrap my arms around you, hell, you wouldn't even look at me, I began to understand what my life would be without you. Last night when I came home, I wanted to see your smile, to know you were glad I was back. I wanted you in my arms, feeling you around me. But that's not all I wanted. I can't stay under this roof with you shutting me out, withholding who you are, not having you in my bed."

She looked up at him now, her eyes still shimmering with tears, her hiccups small ones.

"There is a wall between us, Izabella, that I can't live with anymore."

Her lips trembled. Her words were shaky.

"There's always been a wall."

"But now it's wood and plaster. The other one you blew to bits."

Her eyes grew wide, still filled with tears that had yet to fall.

"What are you saying?"

Cupping her face with his hands, he explained, "I'm saying that if I continue to stay here while you ignore me, pretend I don't exist, in the room right next to mine, I will go stark raving mad. It won't bode well for the batters who face me. You might have noticed I was a bit aggressive last game?"

She never would have guessed that she had that kind of influence on him. But she needed clarity, so she asked, "So you want to sleep together again?"

He nuzzled her neck and said, "I definitely do not want to sleep."

"You want to have sex again."

Brushing her lips with his thumb, a habit he could not break, he whispered in a hoarse voice, "Such an ordinary word for what we have together, don't you think?"

"Are you saying it's more than that?"

"What do you want me to say, Izabella? That I love you, and want forever?"

Her head dipped again, her teeth digging into her bottom lip to hold the tears at bay.

Tipping her chin up again so she could see the sincerity in his expression, he said, "But I do love you, Izabella, and I'm beginning to think that forever is possible."

Her eyes lost their glaze and became piercing. He could feel her love all the way to his soul, so he didn't really need the words but she gave them to him anyway.

"I have loved you for so long."

It was her turn now to touch him, and her hands found their way to his chest, so solid and steady.

He gave her one of his heart-melting smiles.

"I have loved you for longer. It just took me much more time to face and accept it. What can I say?"

"You're not...?"

Unable to take his hands off her, the need to touch her more important than breathing, he answered while stroking her arm. "Afraid? Out of my mind with fear. But the thought of living my life shut out of yours was a terror I've never known before."

Sliding her arms around his neck, she moved a step closer and asked, "So what do we do now?"

Once her hands were touching him, he felt plugged back into his life force, his heart thumping in his chest, air moving in and out of his lungs as it was supposed to. Leaning his head down to kiss her lips, once, twice, deeper each time, he let her know he wanted more.

"We can't do what I'd like to."

He slid his hand under her blouse, his fingers intruding on her delicate skin, tingling at her softness, and his thumb strayed just over her breast, the material covering it too much a barrier, and he wanted it gone. He could only groan in frustration. "This is something we'll have to save for later. But I promise you it will be worth the wait. Can you come inside with me? I have something to show you."

She let him take her hand, and he led her back into the house, the sun shining brighter than it had just moments ago.

Pulling her gently into the kitchen and over to the island, he reached into the inside pocket of his suit coat that he had hung carelessly from the barstool last night when he'd come in and withdrew a little box.

Brushing his lips lightly against hers, he said, "I had some time to kill in Texas so I just wandered around the city, saw this store. I wasn't really sure what I was doing. One step just followed the next, and before I knew it, I'd walked out with this. Right now, I think it's one of the smartest decisions I've ever made." He opened the velvet square case, revealing his purchase, bent down on one knee and asked, "Will you marry me, Izabella?"

As if she doubted this was real, she asked, "What do you want me to say?"

He got up off his knee and he kissed her deeply and soundly.

In her ear, he breathed, "I'm hoping you'll say yes. I can't live my life without you."

Once they were facing each other again, she gazed into his eyes. They held his deep abiding love, with no hesitation at all.

She didn't reach for the ring, she reached for him, resting her lips against his, feeding on him with a hunger he reciprocated.

"Yes. yes, I will marry you."

Fumbling the box onto the counter, he wrapped his arms around her, engulfing him in her scent, her warmth, her delectable curves, all those things that he had missed so much in her absence. She moved in closer as if her need was as great as his and he gave in to her demands for contact, her hands pressing firmly against his back, her head in the crook of his neck where she was spreading butterfly kisses that were driving him wild.

This was pure bliss and all the fear still lurking had nowhere to go but out.

"Mama?"

They both turned to see Leeni standing in the open doorway, looking so small and afraid.

The tears in her eyes sucker-punched him. She had been so brave through her treatment, rarely crying or complaining, and seeing her so upset with him was agony. She stood so still and pale, her fingers pressed together when she asked, "Mr. Crackerjacks? Mama, are we leaving?"

Not wanting to pull out of the embrace, he had no choice. He squatted down and held out his arms.

Leeni rushed forward and he swung her up and into them.

Her tears exploded into his neck and she sobbed, "I've missed you soooo much. Please don't make us go."

Even if he had not worked things out with Izabella, he could not have left this child. She meant too much to him and he didn't have it in him to hurt her like that.

Holding her head in his large hand, he reassured her, "I've missed you too. Don't look so sad. No one's going anywhere."

Grabbing a chunk of his hair, she said, "Did you make up with Mama? You were kissing her."

"I was. Is that okay with you?"

"Oh, yes."

"I just asked your Mama to live with me forever and ever. Would that be okay with you?"

With a pouty mouth and a hand on his cheek she asked, "Where would I live?"

"With us, you silly."

The pout disappeared and her eyes lit up, the tears on her cheeks glistening.

"Here, with my princess bed?"

"Where else does a princess sleep?"

Kicking at him to get down, she went racing back through the still-open doorway as Melinda and Jim were about to enter the house.

"Grams, Grams, I'm going to live here forever."

Melinda wheeled the chair over the ramp quickly, Leeni climbing up into her lap and she glided over the threshold.

"What did I miss?"

Reid pulled Izabella closer, the hope shining in his mother's eyes making him feel like hero.

It was at direct odds with what he really was.

An idiot for not seeing this love and accepting it sooner.

Reid reached back and reclaimed the box, opened it, and removed the sparkler. It was a huge diamond with an outer rim of over a dozen smaller ones.

"We're engaged. That ought to make you happy."

Giving Leeni a huge hug, the smile on her face telling him exactly how she felt, Melinda also offered the words, "It does."

Turning to Izabella, he said, "I'm not sure if it'll fit. I just guessed at the size."

Taking her hand in his, he slipped the ring on and was more than surprised when it fit perfectly.

Melinda pushed her way forward.

"Let me see that. I need to see the evidence."

She got it when Izabella displayed the sparkling diamonds.

All Melinda could say was "Whoa."

Reid nuzzled Izabella's neck and asked in low tones, "Do you like it? Is it too much? I spent an hour trying to decide. This one is worthy of you."

Bringing her hand up to his neck she whispered, "Whatever you bought me would have been perfect, *meu amour.*"

There it was again. Those words that had both scared him and called him home. Today the word enfolded him in everything he'd been looking for and had only found through her. He kissed her in response.

It was a long and lingering one.

With his mind on other things, he almost missed Leeni's question, but Izabella heard it and became rigid in his arms.

"Does this make you my daddy now?"

After giving Izabella a squeeze, he scooped Leeni up and into his arms and said, "I guess it does."

While squeezing his neck so hard he couldn't breathe, she squealed in delight.

Izabella couldn't miss Melinda's penetrating gaze.

Chewing on her nail, she realized someone hadn't been fooled by the bold lie concerning Leeni's paternity.

One of the Jacksons knew the truth.

It wouldn't be long before the rest of her family knew as well. She just didn't know how she was going to tell one man in particular.

CHAPTER THIRTY-TWO

Bolting straight up into a sitting position, Reid scrubbed his face before shoving his fingers through his hair.

Izabella rolled to face him, "What is it?"

"That dream. I thought for sure I'd never have it again. I don't get it."

"What dream?"

"The one with you in it that is extremely X-rated. I figured I wouldn't need it anymore. Thought my subconscious was telling me something I refused to listen to. I've listened, so now what's it trying to tell me?"

She pulled herself up to sit beside him.

"What happens in this dream?"

Threading his fingers through his hair, he got a rhythm to his breathing back and just sat for a moment before describing it.

"We've been drinking, at your apartment." He looked at her and clarified, "The one in Lowell."

She nodded and let him go on.

"Well, music is playing in the background, something with a very suggestive beat, maybe Brazilian?"

He looked at her again for confirmation although he didn't know why. It was his dream, so how would she know?

"You started moving to the beat, slowly, arms in graceful motion, hips swaying, and your hands began to mold themselves to your body. I was sitting on your couch, a tumbler of scotch in my hand, my tongue I think hanging out of my mouth. Then you started doing a strip-tease routine. The real deal, Iz. I almost choked on the liquid I'd gulped down when you began to bump and grind. First you unbuttoned the sweater, one button at a time, and flung it across the room. Shimmying to the music, you attempted to unzip your dress, but you were having a hard time, so you took my hand and helped me stand up. I was pretty unsteady but so fricking turned on I forced myself to stand still and comply as you presented me with your back, your hips gyrating, your derriere slowly moving up and down against…"

He was clammy so he wiped his brow before giving her more.

"When you got your clothes off, your bra landing on top of the sweater, in all your thong-clad glory, a very tiny black thong I might add, you began to pull me toward you with the ends of my tie, which you loosened and then you kissed me, a kiss the likes of which I'd never experienced before. It was wet, your tongue velvet and wildly erotic. After slipping the tie over my head you began to undo the buttons on my shirt, your hands molding themselves to my chest, stroking, burning me up. My brain mustn't have been working, because at no time did I put my hands on you. I was a nerve ending ready to explode and just gave in to the sensation until you took my hands and put them on your bottom, the one still swaying to that ratcheted-up beat. My fingers finally got the message and I began to caress you in return. As my hands made it up your body, I was feeding a fire. Then your fingers dipped inside my pants and I almost came out of my skin. I was so ready I took you right there on the floor, the sex like nothing I'd ever experienced before, or since…except with you. It's during our second round, when you…start licking…do things to me… that I wake up so hard I don't know what to do with myself."

He lifted the sheet up to show her exactly what he was talking about.

"Izabella, we just spent half the night making love. This shouldn't be happening."

There was a smile hiding behind a sober expression.

"How long have you been having this…dream?"

"A few years. Maybe since I returned to Oakland after your mother's funeral. I figured it was just something I wished had happened the night of her funeral."

He scrutinized her face.

The shy smile told him something he didn't think possible.

"A strip tease, Izabella?"

Sitting up primly, she tried to explain, "It wasn't me. It was Jameson."

"You are telling me I forgot we made love?" Shaking his head emphatically he added, "Not possible."

"But you didn't forget, *querido*. You remembered it quite well."

Lifting the sheet to peer at him, she added, "I somewhat like the effect. Did this happen often?"

Too often for comfort and in too many compromising situations. It had made quite a few women think it was their allure. It's when he'd usually disappear in the early-morning hours and escape to the room he'd reserved.

Slapping her hand away, he said, "More and more often as time went by. Why didn't you say something?"

"What did you want me to say?"

"I don't know. Hey, idiot, don't you remember the night we spent together? It was pretty spectacular."

"I never thought you felt the same way about it as I did."

The stunned expression still on his face, he asked, "You did tell me I looked good enough to eat, didn't you?"

"I did, right before I…"

"Shh. My body can't take anymore."

She kissed his cheek, and settled back against the pillows, an open smile playing across her face, unable to believe he had remembered that night in such a dramatic way.

"I remember waking up on your couch. And I had this incredible feeling of contentment for the first few minutes. Then I moved my head and the hammering started. I guess that pounded out all other thought."

"I was mortified by what I had done. I thought I might have expressed my feelings a bit too clearly for your comfort level. Your dead weight made it hard for me to get you dressed, so I just did the best I could before leaving. I was so afraid you'd remember and laugh at me behind my back."

He looked at her, his eyes shining in apology, pulling her close to his heart, wondering again at how much of an idiot he was.

"I'm sorry for so many reasons and on so many levels. I would never have laughed at you. You are my life, Izabella. I just refused to admit it."

The apology was for the time he'd missed feeling so alive and chained to the rapture of her kiss.

"They say a man uses his dick for a brain. My brain was working overtime trying to get my attention. I felt the earth move with that dream."

She was stroking his chest, her head on his shoulder.

"I'm glad. The earth shifted right off its axis in mine."

"Oh, Izabella. I promise that from this day forward you have the real me. Heart, body, and soul."

"And you me."

A frenzy had begun as Reid gave the play-by-play of that night. He crushed her to him, the need to be part of her driving him on unmercifully, but he stopped abruptly. When he rolled on top of her, his arms extended so their bodies were close but not touching, his eyes penetrated hers.

With a ragged breath he asked, "Was I your one-night stand?"

He was swimming in the inky depths waiting for her answer. It took a long time for the short word to emerge.

"*Sí.*"

"Then Melina is…"

"Your daughter."

The magnitude of that almost stopped his breathing. That beautiful, courageous little girl was part of him.

He didn't understand how he'd gotten so lucky.

"Weren't you on birth control? You were dating Patrick back then, right?"

"I was too busy to see the doctor for pills so we used different kinds of protection."

Placing his forehead gently on hers he asked, "Stop, please. I don't want that picture in my head."

That he could have felt like this years ago if he hadn't been such a moron was maddening.

"I was privy to many girls you *dated* over the years."

"None of them was you."

His mother hadn't really needed to point that out. He had been getting to it for years all on his own.

He rested his forehead on hers, trying to control the short, shallow breaths, the maddening thought pummeling his brain.

"Izabella, if things had worked out differently...before...I might never have known her."

That thought almost broke his heart.

"I'm sorry but I just didn't think..."

He rolled onto his back, his arm over his face.

"You didn't think I could handle it. You told my mother back then that Melina's father would have been of no value."

She raised her body to lean on her elbow, one of her hands bringing his face toward her so she could look deeply into his eyes.

"The truth is I was afraid to tell you. I didn't want you to think I had manipulated that night to get pregnant, to tie you down."

She fiddled with his hair, and her eyes darkened as she continued.

"It's just...I needed to feel you inside me just once. You had brought me to the brink so many times that I just needed to know if it would be as good as I'd thought. So, I got drunk, hoping I could overcome my inhibitions about my weight and your maddening habit of bringing everything to a halt before we got there. I let the music and Jameson help me seduce you."

He pulled her down so she could fit in the crook of his shoulder, his hand grazing the skin on her thigh.

"You don't know the willpower it took for me to leave you a virgin. You were so young back then. I took a lot of cold showers. I wish now I had been your first."

"I'm not sure I would have survived your leaving."

He pulled her closer, angled his head down to kiss her.

"I'm not sure I could have left."

"I should have told you when Melina got sick. You did have a right to know then. I just didn't know how. I'm sorry, *querido*."

"No. This is all my fault. If I hadn't been such an asshole back then, it would have been easy to tell me. I don't know who the hell I've been since my mother's accident but I sure don't like him."

Needing to feel her in some way, understand what she had seen in him, he linked his hand with hers and asked, "How could you have loved me?"

"Because our hearts don't get to pick and choose. When you weren't playing your games, you were wonderful. And you sure are good at sex."

His fingers began stroking her breast.

"Sex is overrated. Now making love, that's a whole different ball game."

Before they arose for the day, he wanted to express how he felt inside, but there was one more barrier in the way.

"Are we going to tell her?"

"That is up to you. She already loves you like a father, so nothing would change."

"Everything would change, Izabella. Knowing she has my name, my protection, my devotion would be important, I would think. It was for you."

"Then we will tell her."

"Will she hate me?"

"Why would she do that?"

"I haven't been the greatest father in the world."

Until recently, he wouldn't have known how to be. His own was less than model.

"She will remember Beanie, watching you pitch, you reading to her, sleeping in her princess bed. These are beautiful memories, are they not?"

"What will we tell her? Why didn't I know about her?"

"The truth, as far as we're able. She has gone through much for her age, and I think she will just be delighted she has her father with her now."

"She'll be Melina Juliana Jackson?"

"I would like very much for her to keep dos Santos, as well."

His lips touched hers in a brief kiss, a smile playing on his face.

"That's an awfully long name, Izabella."

"It is but she will always be a part of me and her name should reflect that."

As if he had just uncovered another piece of a very complex puzzle he said, "Melina is Melinda without the *d*."

"It is."

"Did you do that on purpose?"

"That was my intent, yes, but I liked the name Melina very much."

"She was named for both her grandmothers?"

"Yes."

"Thank you."

He kissed her long and deep, and she returned the ardor match strike for match strike.

When they finally arose for the morning, they told Melina and Melinda the truth, something they'd both already known in their hearts.

EPILOGUE

Reid couldn't believe how many had accepted their invitation.

There were over four hundred people at the wedding.

Ballplayers from each coast, family, friends, doctors and nurses, members of the press gathered to witness his marriage to Izabella Graciela dos Santos.

It was the event of the winter.

They'd waited until Melina was well enough to attend, be part of a crowd, and enjoy the ceremonies, setting the date in January, after the season had ended and before spring training began.

As they stood at the makeshift altar, Nolan kept asking him, "Are you good?"

There was more than one person who thought he still might bolt.

What they didn't know, because it was next to impossible to express what he felt for Izabella, was that she had healed him. Her love had given him the will to open his heart, and Melina had shown him the definition of courage. Half-way through the second phase of her treatment, she was still responding better than expected. Izabella thought it was his presence in her life that had given her another dimension of love and support. His daughter had done the same for him.

"I'm great, Nolan. Don't worry."

He watched as the line of bridesmaids walked single file toward them, Melina in front, dropping rose petals as she came down the aisle, smiling at him broadly, and he felt his nerves quiver. Not because of any fear but because he was anxious now to get this done, make them his. When Sofia finally came into view, he leaned to his side so he could see what was beyond her.

When Izabella appeared at the back of the church, her fingers peeking out from the crook of her father's arm, his breath stopped.

She was exquisite.

She had talked to him about the gown before she bought it, telling him it wasn't a typical wedding dress. She wanted to make sure her choice would not embarrass him.

"There are two things that are important to me, *querido*. Marrying you and dancing. I want to have fun, so I will not wear something that confines me. Will you be all right with that?"

"Izabella, there are two things that are important to me. That you show up and say I do. Other than that, I'm open to anything."

She had kissed him deeply in thanks.

And as he gazed at her loveliness, he didn't know what she'd been afraid of.

The gown was loose, the beaded, long-sleeved sheath hitting just above her knee. It covered a long, sheer train, which silhouetted her beautifully sculptured legs. Her shoes had three-inch sparkled heels, her hair was knotted with some flowers and was simple but ethereal.

He was unable to take his gaze off her. His eyes met hers and he knew he would always be home there.

As the priest intoned the words of the service, all he could do was stare at the beauty beside him, thanking his lucky stars he had finally given up the fight. When it came time for the vows, he was ready, repeating them clearly, articulating to everyone present that he was in it until death did they part.

The kiss that sealed the marriage was long, and deep and satisfying for everyone present.

Never in his life had he thought this would happen, that he would have a meaning to his life other than throwing a ball, a heart so open he could take the good with the bad, promise forever, and mean to make it work, have his family around him and find it filled his soul.

The ceremony and reception were held in Boston on the Long Wharf, the waterfront views breathtaking. They had looked at many venues, most closer to home, but this one had touched both with the natural beauty of the harbor. Usually booked two years in advance, they were astounded that there had been a cancellation for a date that worked. Izabella had joked that it was due to the celebrity of Mr. Crackerjacks.

And he had to admit the staff had been enthusiastic when they'd walked in, so maybe she was right. For some reason, Greenliner nation loved the idea that their home-grown son was finally settling down, although there were bets out there as to how long it would last. Reid had assured her that he'd be the winner on that one. He was one of the few who'd taken forever.

He stood beside her after the wedding, the harbor as the backdrop, as the photographer took photos of the blended family. There was no more strife between them, although Jaco and Enrique had taken him aside at the first opportunity to tell him they'd be watching. If there was any sadness in their sister's eyes, he would answer to both of them.

"I get it. But you don't have to worry. I can promise you that."

He himself couldn't go a day without one of her smiles.

Leeni had mentioned again the desire for a brother or sister and they were already working on that one. He'd love nothing better than to give her everything her heart desired.

He hoped Melina's brothers, if she had them, would take care of her as well as

Izabella's had. If only girls came their way, there was always him to contend with. And he'd protect his daughters with his life.

After the tinkling of fork on glass throughout the meal, their kisses getting deeper and deeper as the night wore on, after the cake was cut, it was time for dancing.

Izabella had detached the sheer train, leaving only the beaded shift now that her number one priority had been satisfied and she was ready to enjoy the day.

She had picked out a song by Faith Hill for their first dance that expressed what they felt for each other perfectly, and they breathed each other in.

Lifting his mother out of her chair, Reid carried her around the dance floor for a shortened version of "In My Life", twirling her around, and she cried while he held her. He was happy she had brought a date and that the relationship with Jim was beginning to really blossom, and that she had found someone who treasured her. She deserved that and so much more.

After his dance with his daughter, there wasn't a dry eye in the place. Her little arms hugged him around the neck, and his muscular arms held her firmly against his chest, keeping her safe and warm just like the words of the song dictated. He had chosen "You'll be in my Heart", with lyrics that expressed his deep and abiding love for the small but strong little girl, with the promise to be there for her always. Everyone in the room, knowing of Melina's struggle, gulped back the tears.

Next, to the surprise of everyone, he took Izabella's hand and the mic to center stage.

"I hope you don't mind another exclusive dance for me and my...wife... but I wanted to show Izabella some moves I learned recently. Bear with me, please."

Carlo got up from his seat and whistled.

Izabella questioned her husband with her eyes, but he ignored it and asked the DJ to start the music.

Taking her into his arms, tight against his chest, arms extended straight out, the music swelled around them, and he took the first step in a tango. More powerfully than expertly, he walked her around the dance floor in a sultry sweep of tangled limbs.

When they were done, he pressed her close and kissed her.

"You're not the only one who took lessons."

"Carlo?"

"He helped but it was Camila who got her toes squashed too many times to count. I just couldn't get it at first but you were right. It is about the dance. The problem is it would never work for me with another partner."

Kissing him lightly she agreed.

"It won't for me anymore, either."

Paolo ran out to the floor and congratulated him. Jaco pounded him on the back. "I can't believe you did this for my sister. The leopard has indeed changed his spots."

Rique told him he was impressed but would show him exactly how a dancer moved later, when he got his sister to do the merengue.

Catcalls rang out and Motts asked, "Hey, should we give *Dancing with the Stars* a call?"

Taking Izabella over to the table where some of his teammates sat, he said emphatically, "Don't you dare. I couldn't do that with anyone other than Izabella."

Motts had become one of his best friends on the team and had been smug in his knowingness. His catcher had figured out before he had that his days were numbered and when told about the engagement, said, "It's about fuckin' time. I wasn't sure you'd last the season with that in-your-face attitude."

The baseball wives got a full commitment for the upcoming fund raisers and had high expectations for the donations this year. Izabella, depending on Melina's health, would support both Strike Out Hunger and the fashion show. With a devotion to the cause, he'd signed both of them up for the Boston Pan Am, him as rider, Izzie as one of the chairmen of the donation fund. It directly supported the Dana-Farber Center, a place that would always be front and center in their lives.

As he surveyed the crowd, the connections he'd built up over the years, the ones he took for granted, he smiled. He was looking forward to the upcoming season. His trade had been one of the best decisions he'd ever made, a close fourth to Izabella, Melina, and his mother. He'd had a stellar year, compiling over twenty wins and he'd won the hearts of the Greenliner faithful. He had become the top ace of the team, led the league in strikeouts, thanks in no small part to Melina and her guestimates, had an ERA of less than .086, was one of the hardest-working volunteers at the hospital and one of the largest contributors to their cause. He was at the pinnacle of his career and it didn't look like he was slowing down any.

The world at large had started calling him the flame thrower.

What they didn't know was that Izabella was the heat and the fire behind every one of his moves.

ABOUT FAITH

Faith O'Shea is a contemporary romance writer who has worn many hats during her life. She feels that her time in real estate, banking, retail, teaching, all ages, including adults, children, elementary school-age and driver's ed, has allowed her to learn about the human condition. An observer of life and voracious reader, she has finally given herself permission to develop her own characters that come alive on the page.

Faith resides in Massachusetts with her husband Jeff, two dogs, and one cat. Her children and grandchildren live close by. She graduated with a liberal arts degree, majoring in English and History before pursuing a Master's in Education from Merrimack College. In her spare time, she reads, walks her dog, cooks and visits her five male grandchildren.

Faith loves hearing from her readers. Connect with her on her www.faithoshea.com, like her on Facebook at FaithOsheaNovels, and follow her on Twitter at Faith_OShea.

Books by Faith O'Shea

The Greenliner Series
Thrown for a Curve
League of Her Own

The Scalera Family Series
Cold Sweat
Edge of Forever
Thin Blue Line
Coming Home to You
Finding Joy

Fire and Ice Series
Consumed by Fire
Skoli on Ice
Heart on Fire
Heart of Ice
Tendril of Ice
Rekindling the Fire

LEAGUE OF HER OWN

Geneticist Fiona Barrows was working below her pay grade as a dog walker, but she was only doing it until she could find a more appropriate job. It was taking more time than she'd anticipated but she'd come to appreciate the downtime as a respite after years of study, test tubes and analysis. Little did she know that the job would become more about handling the ball player who'd come to stay, than merely walking the Weim in the rain. The Brazilian was insufferable and arrogant, and more challenging than her doctoral thesis.

Enrique dos Santos had recently been traded to the Greenliners, one of Boston's hometown teams. Known for his partying skills and his attitude, he'd been warned to change his behavior if he wanted to play ball, so he'd committed himself to changing his ways. Thinking the only way to do that was to settle down, he'd penciled in a trip to Brazil to search for a bride. He expected Fifi to keep him on the straight and narrow while he attended the mandatory two-weeks of practice under the infield coach.

What he didn't expect was to find a woman so wrong for him, so right.

Excerpt from League of Her Own

Fiona Barrows sloshed along, trying to keep herself from falling flat on her face. She wasn't wearing the right shoes or the right coat, but she'd left Hoover too long without a break and she hadn't dared waste any time getting her out, not even to change. Her shoes were probably already ruined anyway. She'd never intended to leave the dog so long, but she'd underestimated the stop-and-go traffic in and out of the city and the interview had lasted much longer than she'd anticipated. In her defense, the sun had been peeking through the clouds when she left early this morning and as she sat answering those hypothetical questions potential employers always seemed to ask about situations she'd never faced before, she'd given no thought to what was going on outside the ivy-covered walls. When she stepped outside the building, she'd gasped as the pelting rain assaulted her face.

Nothing had changed since she got back, and now, even her brain was soggy.

She fought the dog for control as Hoover strained against her leash just as a Maserati came whizzing by, splashing her in the process. She sucked in her breath as the cold spray covered in in grime, her face now dripping remnants of the puddle that had to be six inches deep.

She looked up and yelled, "Asshole," but it fell on deaf ears, the driver no longer insight.

She swiped at her eyes, drew a hand down over her cheeks, inwardly seething.

This had not been one of her better days. She shivered, as the raw wind just beneath the surface of the sleet reared its head, wanting the comfort of warm and dry. She snapped the leash, commanding a change of direction for home. Whether Hoover sensed her distress or had gotten her fill of wet and cold, she did as instructed, but not two-feet later, found just the right spot to squat and got down to business. Fiona had forgotten all about Izabella's warning that she take a poop bag and paper towels whenever they went out, and now she was stuck. After looking around guiltily, knowing she was going to leave the steaming pile right where it was, she slunk down the street, rounded the corner and headed up the long driveway.

She swore under her breath when she saw the offending vehicle sitting in front of the garage.

Who the hell had come calling? A friend of Reid's? Izabella's? Whoever it was, he obviously didn't know they were not in residence.

Halfway up the winding drive, she noticed the man get out of his car, and race to the side door, phone to his ear. There was a moment when she felt triumphant. He'd be standing outside until she got there and would have to be almost as wet as she was. But when the door opened and he slipped in, a shiver of fear raced through her.

Who was he and what did he want?

She approached the door with caution and tried the knob. It swung open easily and she stepped inside. And didn't move.

"Hello. Who's here?"

Her voice cracked, her nerves quivered as she strained to keep Hoover from advancing.

Seconds later, a man came from out to the kitchen, a towel in his hand that he was rubbing against his scalp.

Hoover had started to dance, which told her the dog knew the man. When she snapped off the leash, the dog went barreling over and was caught in an affectionate hug. Large manicured hands stroked the animal, and he allowed for some kisses.

When he looked up at her, her heart slammed against her chest. The man was gorgeous. Scruffy dark hair, black eyes, and a straight nose and those lips…held a mocking smile.

"And who are you? One of Hoover's friends? Do you know you are dripping all over the floor?"

He had an accent, which only made him even more stunning.

She was fumbling, her brain singed from heat, her tongue tied in knots.

He chuckled at her ineptitude.

"Have you forgotten your name?"

"Yes. No. Izabella and Reid hired me to housesit and walk Hoover while they're away. My name is Fiona."

"Ah, the dog walker. I think I'll call you Fifi. It suits you. How did you get so wet?"

Irritation at his arrogance spiked.

"Some asshole went flying around the corner and—"

"Ah. That would be me, is that correct?"

She gave him a steely glare. When he chuckled, her eyes narrowed and her irritation with him went up a notch.

"Izabella didn't mention anything about a houseguest."

"That's because she didn't know I was coming. I told her I was going to stick around in New York for a couple more weeks, say my goodbyes, wait until she got back so she could help me find a rental. But when the coach called summoning me here for some practice, I hopped into the car as soon as I'd packed my most essential items and drove southeast. Being early will give me a chance to get to know the city."

He was standing now in all his hunky gorgeousness. She tilted her head to take another look, one minus the lust that had taken possession of her body. There was something familiar about him and it hit her.

"Are you her brother?"

"I am. Enrique Paolo Goulart dos Santos. As of a week ago, a Greenliner. Now that we've been formally introduced, why don't you get out of those wet things. I assume you have dry ones if you're staying here. Then you can start dinner. I'm famished."

Her jaw dropped. Was he kidding? He might look good, but the term *asshole* came to mind again.

"I wasn't hired to be your maid, cook, or bottle washer. I'll let Izabella know you're here and then go home. The house doesn't need two sitters."

"*Foi mal.* Sorry. My bad. I just figured you'd be eating yourself and you could cook for two."

"I don't cook. Never learned, never will."

That wasn't exactly true but let him think it was her own decision not to excel at that art rather than tell him how abysmal she was in that part of the house.

"How will you find a husband?"

Who was this guy? Had he time traveled forward from the nineteenth century?

"Not looking for one of those. Don't need one, don't want one."

That wasn't exactly true, but she was putting it off into the unseeable future. She had too many other things to settle first.

He'd crossed his arms over his chest and looked down at her smugly.

"If this is your life, you might rethink that. A man could support you and then you won't have to walk dogs for a living."

She all but stuttered out, "That's what I mean. Without one, I can do what the hell I please."

And with that she waddled across the mudroom with as much dignity as she could muster, stopping only to take off the shoes that were squishing before heading up the stairs. Her bedroom was the last one down the hall and she went directly into the attached bathroom. And stopped dead in her tracks.

She was a mess. Her curly hair was a mop on her head, her eye make-up was now a liquid trail down her cheek, and her clothes were wrinkled and damp. She didn't own many suits and she wasn't sure this one could be salvaged, the wool now smelling like wet dog.

The day had turned out less than promising, and now she had to contend with the man downstairs.

After stripping down, dropping everything in a heap on the floor, she turned on the shower and stepped in. The hot water felt good, her body still bone-chilled from the walk and the drenching.

She lathered her hair, and rinsed it, scrubbed herself clean of grime and grit and felt almost human once she was dressed in her jeans and sweater. It was her hair that would take time to put in some semblance of order. She yanked and pulled, working at the knots, but the tight curls refused to behave. She sighed, put the brush down and gave up the fight. She'd never be one of those beautiful people who caused heads to turn. She'd been given brains instead of looks and had been satisfied with that most of her life. Today she almost wished she'd been in a different line.

www.ingramcontent.com/pod-product-compliance
Lightning Source LLC
Chambersburg PA
CBHW061952170626
46813CB00006B/2611